Sadie didn't say anything.

The only sound was the swish of the windshield wipers as he drove through the falling snow. He saw that he was headed for Helena. He knew he was waiting to hear from Crawford and simply driving to stay one step ahead of the men after them.

It didn't matter what town they reached as long as it had an airport, where he planned to put Sadie on a plane home. It had been a mistake calling her and getting her up here. He'd selfishly wanted her with him, he could admit now. He hadn't really needed her. He'd been right about one thing, though...it had been their last game. He'd almost gotten her killed for nothing.

"You know that I have to finish this."

Sadie said nothing for a few moments. "What exactly is this?"

"I thought I was just coming back here to pay off Grandville and free Keira from the debt and her no-account husband. Now I'm not sure what this is. All I know is I never should have gotten you involved."

B.J. Daniels is a *New York Times* and *USA TODAY* bestselling author. She wrote her first book after a career as an award-winning newspaper journalist and author of thirty-seven published short stories. She lives in Montana with her husband, Parker, and three springer spaniels. When not writing, she quilts, boats and plays tennis. Contact her at bjdaniels.com, on Facebook or on Twitter @bjdanielsauthor.

Visit the Author Profile page
at Harlequin.com for more titles.

B.J.

DANIELS

DEAD MAN'S HAND & DELIVERANCE AT CARDWELL RANCH

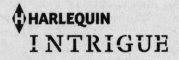

HARLEQUIN

INTRIGUE

HARLEQUIN®
INTRIGUE®

Recycling programs
for this product may
not exist in your area.

ISBN-13: 978-1-335-08134-6

Dead Man's Hand & Deliverance at Cardwell Ranch

Copyright © 2023 by Harlequin Enterprises ULC

Dead Man's Hand
Copyright © 2023 by Barbara Heinlein

Deliverance at Cardwell Ranch
Copyright © 2014 by Barbara Heinlein

For questions and comments about the quality of this book,
please contact us at CustomerService@Harlequin.com.

Harlequin Enterprises ULC
22 Adelaide St. West, 41st Floor
Toronto, Ontario M5H 4E3, Canada
www.Harlequin.com

Printed in U.S.A.

CONTENTS

DEAD MAN'S HAND

This book is dedicated to my father,
Harry Burton Johnson, who fed me lobster at
fancy restaurants when things were going well—
and free peanuts at a bar when they weren't.
He taught me many of life's lessons
and I'm sure that's why I'm a writer today.
I had so much fun writing these characters
because they were all close to my heart.

DEAD MAN'S HAND: A slang term used in poker
for a two pair of black aces and black eights.
The story goes that lawman and gambler
"Wild Bill" Hickok was shot while holding the
dead man's hand, which is why it's considered
an unlucky two pair in poker today.

Chapter 1

DJ Diamond shoved back his Stetson before glancing from the cards in his hand to the three men and one woman sitting around the table. After hours of poker, he felt as if he knew all of them better than their mothers did.

Except for the woman. She had a better poker face than any of the men. Also, she played her cards close to the vest—or in her case, the red halter top she wore. The top had the initials *AL* monogramed on it. Not her initials. He'd bet she picked up the garment at a garage sale. Her blond hair was long, pulled back into a ponytail that made her look like jailbait. All of it was at odds with her sharp honey-brown eyes and her skill at the game. All part of her act to throw grown men off their game.

It was working. The men had trouble keeping their

eyes off her as she leaned forward to ante up—forcing their gazes away from the huge pot of money in the center of the table.

DJ could feel the tension in the room around him, but he was as cool as a cucumber—as his uncle Charley used to say. He was aware of everything, though—including the exact amount of money in the pot as one of the men folded, but the other two stayed in, matching his bet, confident he was bluffing.

With luck, he'd be walking out with all the money—and the sexy young woman—before the night was over. And the night was almost over.

But right now, everyone was waiting on him.

He glanced down at his last five hundred dollars in chips for a moment, then picked them up and tossed them into the pile of money. "I'm going to have to sweeten the pot." Across the table, he saw the woman who called herself Tina shoot him a disbelieving look. He grinned and shrugged. "You want to see what I've got. It will cost you."

Sadie Montclair mumbled, "Arrogant fool," under her breath. She knew the Montana cowboy was planning on taking this pot and when he did all hell was going to break loose. She'd been reading the table since she sat down. The big doughy former football star next to her had a possible three queens. The guy in the expensive suit on the other side of her had to have had two pair, maybe even ace high. Luckily, the appliance salesman with the bad rug had folded. She'd marked him as the wild card of the group even before he'd started sweating profusely after losing so much money tonight.

She sighed as she looked at her jack-high straight

with regret and tossed in her five Cs. Placing her cards facedown on the table, she leaned back, stretching, all eyes on her heaving chest.

"Let's see what you've got," the suit said, tossing his five hundred onto the pile of money and drawing the men's gazes again to the pot.

Sadie gave the arrogant fool across from her a shrug as she reached for the gun in her shoulder bag hanging off her chair. Her hand closed around the grip. She brought it out fast as the cowboy said, "Read 'em and weep," and fanned out his cards. An ace-high straight.

"You cheating bastard!" she yelled, kicking her chair back as she jumped to her feet. "Is it just him or were you all in on it?" she screamed as she waved the gun around.

The men were on their feet the moment they saw the gun in the hands of an angry woman, their chairs crashing to the floor behind them.

"You think you can cheat me, cowboy?" she yelled at him, wiping away his grin as she pulled the trigger.

The first report was deafening in the small dark room. Out of the corner of her eye, she saw the men scrambling for the door, the appliance salesman the slowest of the group. She fired twice more, putting three slugs into the arrogant fool cowboy's chest.

He fell backward, his chair crashing to the floor. She heard the others all rush out, the door slamming behind them before she stuffed the money into her shoulder bag, tossing the weapon in after it, and looked under the table. The Montana cowboy was lying sprawled on the floor, his Stetson beside him. "Arrogant fool."

Chapter 2

"I heard that," DJ Diamond said from the floor, and groaned. "Damn, Sadie. That hurt."

"That was pure arrogance to raise the bet again," she said. "You were just showing off. You can't keep pushing your luck—and mine."

He rose slowly, grimacing in pain as he tried to catch his breath. "Arrogant is shooting me three times. One wasn't good enough?"

"Three just felt right tonight," she said, cocking her hip as she watched him remove his shirt, then his body armor with the three slugs embedded in it.

"You must really hate me," he said, and grinned through his pain.

With his shirt off, it was hard not to admire the broad shoulders, the tapered waist or the vee of dark hair on the tanned chest that disappeared into his button-up jeans.

"What do you think?" he asked, raking a hand through his thick dark hair.

For a moment, she thought he was asking about the way he looked. She blinked, realizing he was asking about their take tonight. "Not bad."

He laughed. "Come on, we made a haul. Maybe I pushed it a little, but it worked out. Don't forget the cards."

She had forgotten them, which would have been a mistake. If one of the gamblers realized they'd been had, he might come back here and find the marked deck. She scooped up the cards and added them to her shoulder bag. "I'm hungry."

DJ shook his head as the shirt and body armor went into the satchel he'd brought with him. He pulled a fresh shirt out and put it on. "You're always hungry."

"I'm so hungry I could eat steak and lobster."

"That might be a problem dressed the way you are," he said as he settled his Stetson on that head of thick dark hair, then stepped to her and reached for the end of one thin strap that kept her halter top up.

She caught his hand. "You didn't get *that* lucky tonight." It was an old joke between partners whose relationship was strictly business. But more and more, she felt an undercurrent between them, one she suspected went both ways. Yet she never knew with DJ.

He chuckled, giving her that Diamond grin that apparently worked on women everywhere. "I do know a good barbecue place and I know how you feel about ribs." He grimaced as he touched his own ribs.

"Don't you think we should get rid of the loot first?"

"Couldn't I at least count it before we hand it over?" He flashed his baby blues.

"You don't need to count it and neither do I. We both know the take. You're stalling."

"Can you blame me? We should get hazardous pay for this."

"We should get into a new line of work," she said, knowing that he never would. He was a born poker player with larceny in his blood. "One of these days... In the meantime, let's get out of here. That one player made me nervous."

"There's always one who makes you nervous," he said as he put an arm around her and steered her toward the alternate exit door.

"The one that's going to get us both killed one day," she said under her breath.

His cell phone rang. He removed his arm from Sadie's shoulder to step away and take the call. "What's wrong, Keira?" She was sobbing, begging him to help her. He stepped farther away, never mixing business with family. "You have to stop crying so I can understand you."

She let out a cry and suddenly the voice on the phone was male. "I'll tell you what's wrong, Diamond. Your sister owes me money. A lot of money. Otherwise, we're going to have to sell her parts to the highest bidder."

"One of your girlfriends?" Sadie asked as he caught up to her at her SUV in a parking garage blocks away from where they'd held the poker game. She'd left him to his phone call. Now, though, she noticed that his face was pinched, blue eyes flinty; his usual charm had vanished. Her first thought was that one of his women had called him to say she was pregnant. Then again it could be some angry husband threatening to kick his adorable ass. "You all right?"

"It's just something I need to take care of," he said, his voice tight. "Back in Montana. I'll be gone for a few days."

She went on alert. "You need help?"

"No, but thanks. Don't worry, I'll be back."

"Keep in touch," she said, and opened her car door. She saw him looking at her shoulder bag and shook her head. "You can't."

Nodding, he gave a shrug. "No, I can't. We had a deal. Don't worry, I'm sticking to it." He glanced around but she'd already made sure that the dark street was empty. As usual she wouldn't take the same route when she left, she would watch closely for a tail, she would take the usual precautions until tonight's take was locked up safe and secure.

Climbing behind the wheel, she closed the car door, but hesitated. She powered down the window. "DJ?" She'd noticed a tell she never saw at the poker table. He wasn't just nervous, he seemed…scared. "DJ, if—"

"I'm good. You take care."

"You, too," she said as she watched him walk, head down, toward his pickup parked even farther away. All her instincts told her he was in trouble. She reminded herself that he wasn't her responsibility. Theirs was a business partnership and nothing more. As long as they both stuck to the deal…

DJ slid behind the wheel of his pickup and rubbed a hand over his face. He'd tried to protect Keira from this life. He'd watched over her since the first time she'd shown up at the ranch—skinny, scraped up, hungry and scared. He suspected he'd probably arrived at the hard-scrabble, rundown ranch in the same shape.

It wasn't much of a ranch, small by any standards. The only thing they raised was dust as criminals came and went. The place was straight out of an old Western movie set, a hideout where some came to recover from gunshot wounds. Others to cool their heels from the law. The ranch had been a dumping ground for lost souls. As the way of the ranch, no one asked questions. DJ and Keira had just been taken in like all the others, fed and clothed and conditioned to never know what to expect next.

Charley Diamond had been a small man with a hearty laugh and kind eyes. He was also a crook but with a code of the West. He helped those needing help—people like him down on their luck who always knew they had a place to recover. But he also took from the richer and pocketed the take.

When DJ had asked about his parents, Charley would rub the back of his neck and look up as if thinking. "Sorry, kid, I have no idea. You just arrived one day looking hungry and lost. Can't say who dropped you off. Doesn't matter. You're here now and I'm darned glad to have you. I could teach you a few things to help you survive for when you leave here."

DJ figured he'd been dropped off at the ranch just as Charley had said. He wondered, though, if his parents had promised to come back for him—and just hadn't. He also wondered if Charley knew more than he had told him. Not that worse things couldn't have happened to him—and to Keira. They both helped out around the ranch, earning their keep and becoming the only family either of them knew of—other than the man they called Uncle Charley.

When his uncle had fallen on hard times and lost the ranch, DJ was sixteen. Lucky for him, Charley had taught him the grift. Keira, who was six years younger, was too young for the road. She'd gone into foster care.

The next two years DJ spent staying one step ahead of the law and tough guys who wanted to kill him and his uncle. A born poker player, it didn't take DJ long though before he went out on his own way—eventually going legit since he found that he could make plenty of money without cheating.

He always kept in touch with Keira, made sure she had what she needed, and once she finished high school, paid for her college education and her wedding. Uncle Charley had given her away, even though like DJ, he didn't care for her choice of a husband. Luca Cross lacked ambition, while Keira wanted it all.

DJ suspected that Keira might be the reason her husband had gotten involved with gamblers and loan sharks. Now they were using her to collect what was owed. The same way DJ had ended up where he was now—owing the wrong people for all the wrong reasons.

He started the truck. Tonight he'd made thousands of dollars. But it was money he couldn't touch. He tried to look at it as work—the same way Sadie did. Some nights, though, he'd enjoyed it more than he should have. He felt only a little guilty since the men who'd gotten fleeced tonight had all been handpicked by a man they either owed or had crossed. The boss was a man who always collected debts—one way or another.

Even though Uncle Charley was dead, DJ, now twenty-nine, was still paying off his uncle's last debts. It was the way it worked in this world. Some inherited wealth, others inherited debt. A man paid that debt.

Shifting into gear, DJ headed to his apartment to pack for the first flight he could get to Bozeman, Montana. From there Keira would pick him up. He had no idea what he would find when he got there, but that was nothing new. He'd spent his childhood expecting the worst.

Chapter 3

On her fiancé's ranch outside of Lonesome, Montana, Ansley Brookshire felt as if she couldn't breathe. Time was running out. Her longed-for Christmas wedding was days away. She was about to marry the man of her dreams. Just the thought stole her breath and made her heart pound with both excitement and anxiety.

It was all perfect except for one thing. Recently, she'd found out not only that she'd been adopted—but also that she had a twin brother. Now that she knew, she couldn't imagine getting married without him at the wedding. She had this image of him giving her away. Her heart ached for the two of them to be united and brought into the family that she'd only recently discovered.

Unfortunately, she had no idea where he was, even who he was. Like her, he'd been sold or given away right after birth by a woman who'd told their biological mother that they both had died. Ansley's adoptive mother had only wanted a baby girl and swore that she never even knew there had been another baby.

No one knew what had happened to her twin brother, since the woman who'd sold the babies was now dead. Ansley's fear was that like her, her twin might not even know he'd been adopted. She just hoped he'd gone to a good family and had a better childhood than hers. While she'd lived on an estate, never been deprived of anything money could buy, she'd been lonely and wished desperately for a family. All her childhood, she'd seen more of her nannies and the household staff than her parents.

When Ansley had learned that she was adopted, she'd gone in search of her biological mother. It had been like taking a stick to a hornet's nest. But she'd found her birth mother and the happy ending she'd hoped for. She wanted the same for her brother. Unfortunately, all leads had gone cold.

Her only hope was that the PIs at Colt Brothers Investigation would find him before it was too late. One of those PIs was her fiancé, Buck Crawford, who'd been working tirelessly for weeks searching for her missing twin. All they had to go on was the tiny bracelet his birth mother said she'd had made for him with the initials DJ on it for Del Junior. They couldn't even be sure that he'd ever gotten the bracelet.

"Maybe we should postpone the wedding," Buck had said, but she hadn't had the heart to do that. They both wanted to be married soon. She told herself she was being too sentimental. A Christmas wedding was her dream and Buck was everything she'd ever wanted in a husband.

"No," she'd told him. "We're getting married. Anyway, I still have hope that we'll find DJ before the wedding."

Now the wedding was looming and still no leads on her twin.

"Ansley?" a female voice called. "Or should I call you DelRae?"

She hadn't heard a vehicle in the deep snow, but now she heard the front door close. Footfalls headed her way. She had to smile, wondering at twenty-nine years old if she would ever answer to the name her birth mother had given her. Or if she should even bother trying.

"In here," she called back to Bella Colt, a sister-in-law. Along with finding her birth mother, she'd also found her biological father's family—the Colt brothers of Colt Brothers Investigation and their wives. She now had four half brothers, Tommy, Davy, James and Willie, and their wives, Bella, Carla, Lori and Ellie. She'd instantly felt a part of the family.

On top of that, she'd also fallen in love with the brothers' best friend, Buck Crawford, a fellow PI at the agency.

Bella came into the living room where Ansley had been wrapping Christmas presents. "What in the world! Did you buy out all the stores in Missoula?"

She shook her head sheepishly. "I've never had a family to buy for before. My adoptive mother bought her own Christmas presents for me to wrap. My adoptive father had his secretary pick up something for each of us. He usually also had the secretary return anything Maribelle or I got for him, saying he didn't need anything. So shopping for all of you has been so much fun.

Don't tell anyone, but I started shopping even before Thanksgiving. I couldn't wait."

"You really are too much." Bella hugged her awkwardly around the baby. James's wife Lori had given birth to two identical baby boys a few months ago.

Ansley motioned her friend into the kitchen. "Coffee?"

"I shouldn't." Bella lumbered in, both hands over her protruding stomach. "Water tastes so…watery," she groaned.

"Eggnog?"

"Don't tempt me," her friend said, and held her side for a moment. "They've been kicking like crazy. I suspect they've got my and Tommy's worst traits," she said with a laugh as she took a chair and the glass of eggnog. "It would be just like them to decide to be born in the middle of your wedding." All four Colt wives were her bridesmaids, with their husbands the groomsmen.

A silence fell between them as Ansley poured herself a cup of coffee and joined Bella at the table.

"Are you sure you don't want to wait?" Bella asked. "Even if Buck manages to find him, he'll be a complete stranger. Do you really want a stranger standing up with you at your wedding?"

Ansley laughed. "He won't be a stranger. I know him—that is, I feel like I do. He's my *twin*. He won't be a stranger."

Bella looked skeptical but let it go. "What if Buck doesn't find him before the wedding?"

"Then we go ahead anyway," she said, knowing how disappointed she would be.

"You could just postpone it," Bella suggested.

It wasn't like she hadn't thought about postponing

the wedding. "Wait for how long, though? What if DJ's never found? Buck and I can't wait. We love each other. We want to get married." She sighed. "But at the same time, how can I start my life not knowing where my twin is, how he is or even if he's still alive? I've always felt as if there was a missing piece of me. Then I found you and the Colt brothers and Buck."

"And still something was missing," Bella said.

She nodded. "Once I found out that I had a twin who my mother called DJ for Del Junior, I knew I had to find him." She swallowed the lump in her throat. "Even if he can't be found by the wedding, we will find him. Buck won't stop looking for him."

"Neither will the Colt brothers. They were shocked to find they had a half sister. Imagine their reaction to meeting a half brother. If he is anything like you, we are going to love him. We'll love him anyway," she said with a laugh and took a sip of her eggnog. "So, is it going to be Ansley or DelRae? Or are you going to answer to both?"

"I have no sentimental ties to the Ansley name or the Brookshire name. I love DelRae, I'm just not sure I'll ever remember to answer to it."

"I can understand that you might want to ditch your first name and last with both Maribelle and Harrison Brookshire headed for prison. But you also can't erase your past," Bella said. "You know my father almost went to prison at one point." She shook her head. "A long story for another time," she said, awkwardly getting to her feet. "I have some last-minute Christmas shopping to do, but I wanted to check on you."

She rose to show her out. She couldn't believe how close she'd gotten to her new family and in record time.

She hoped the same would be true for her twin when he was found.

At the door, Bella turned to take her hand and squeeze it. "Don't give up hope. There's still time."

All she could do was nod and smile her thanks even as she felt sick with worry that time was running out. Worse, the news might not be good. Her twin might not have survived. Or he might want nothing to do with her and the rest of the family.

Buck Crawford disconnected and leaned back, feeling more positive than he had in weeks. "I think I might have found a lead," he said, leaving his office to walk out into the main reception area of Colt Brothers Investigation.

James looked up from his father's old desk expectantly. The brothers had all done their best to find Ansley's twin brother before hitting a brick wall and being forced to move on to other clients. Buck was determined to continue looking for the missing twin right up until the wedding.

"It's an old friend of Judy Ramsey's who moved away after her house burned down." Buck remembered the vacant lot next to Judy's house. "Luella Lindley lived there and knew Judy during the time frame when Ansley and her brother were born. I'm hoping she's going to be able to help."

"For Ansley's sake, I hope so." He smiled. "Yours, too, since I know how badly you want to marry my sister. But what if you don't find him? Would you postpone the wedding?"

Buck shook his head. "I hope not, but Ansley has

her heart set on her twin giving her away. Not that I blame her. I can't imagine what it's like to find out you have a twin brother you never knew existed. I'd want to find him, too."

"Let's hope she gets her happy ending. I just worry. Ansley lucked out. Even though the Brookshires weren't the family she'd hoped for, she had what most people would consider a good life. Then she got all of us." He grinned. "But it could have turned out a lot worse for her brother."

Admittedly, Buck worried about that as well. Ansley needed a happy ending and that meant finding her twin. Hopefully before the wedding. He didn't want to think about postponing the wedding. He wanted Ansley for his wife now. The waiting was killing him. He was anxious to start their lives together.

But until Del Jr. was found, dead or alive, he knew Ansley would be heartbroken. That was something Buck couldn't stand. He'd do anything to make her happy.

Buck couldn't help but think about all that Ansley had gone through to find her birth mother. It had been dangerous. People had died, others had gone to prison. Both Buck and Ansley were lucky to be alive. He really hoped that wouldn't be the case finding her twin.

"Let's hope Luella Lindley has the answers we need," he told James. "I'm driving down to Casper, Wyoming, to talk to her in person. Don't mention this to Ansley. I don't want to get her hopes up."

Buck knew it was more than that. He didn't want to give her bad news with their wedding and first Christmas together just over a week away.

* * *

"Can you turn that off?" DJ asked after he and Keira were headed north away from the busiest airport in the state, Yellowstone International just outside of Bozeman, Montana. He wanted to put all this progress in the rearview mirror as they headed toward the mountains.

She reached over and turned off the radio and the Christmas music. DJ realized he'd lost track of not just weeks, but months. How could it already be this close to Christmas? It wasn't as if he celebrated the holiday. He had no warm and fuzzy family holiday memories. In fact, he was always glad once the season was over— not that it wasn't a good time financially for him and Sadie. The kind of people they dealt with were more reckless with their money this time of year, some out of Christmas cheer, most out of greed or desperation.

"Tell me what's going on," he said once they were on the open highway.

Keira's hands gripped the wheel seemingly tighter, her eyes galvanized on the road ahead as she chewed nervously at her lower lip. "I don't want you to get mad." Too late for that. "It was a mistake. He didn't know."

DJ swore. Of course Luca knew. No one gambled without knowing they might lose—and they might lose big if they didn't stop. "How much?"

"Seventy-five large originally," she said without looking at him. "I didn't know that he'd borrowed more to keep up with the interest payments."

He never lost his temper. It was bad for business. But right now…

"I wouldn't have called you, but…"

But there was no one else.

She concentrated on the road.

He chose his words carefully, determined not to take his frustration and anger out on her. "When you're involved with these kinds of people you don't go to another one and borrow more. That's a good way to end up in a ditch dead. Or in your case sold to the highest bidder. Who are these men your husband got involved with?"

"Do you remember Titus Grandville? He's an investment banker in the same building as his father's bank."

Is that what he was calling himself? "Crooks wear suits, too, baby sister," he said, and turned to stare out at the passing countryside while he tamped down his anger and tried to concentrate on the beauty. It had been so long since he'd been back here. He'd forgotten how breathtaking the snowcapped mountains were. The pines were so dark green against the cobalt blue of the big sky. He felt an old childhood ache for a place that he'd once thought of as paradise.

"Who's his muscle?" he finally asked.

She mugged a distasteful face. "Butch Lamar. He's the one you talked to on the phone. He's new in town. Hangs out on the Turner Ranch. He's friends with Rafe Westfall, the son of one of the men who used to live out at our old ranch." She shot him a look. "They're serious, DJ. The first time Luca couldn't pay, they beat him up real bad. This last time…"

"He still alive?" DJ asked, hoping so for selfish reasons.

"Barely. He's hiding out. That's why they grabbed me."

"Did you know?" he had to ask. Her silence said it all. He swore and turned on her. "You grew up with this. How could you let him?"

"*I didn't let him*. He thought he was—"

"Smarter, right?" DJ cursed under his breath. "And he thought he was going to surprise you, make you happy. How do I know this is the last time he's going to have to be bailed out?" He saw her jaw tighten.

"I'm divorcing him. I'm done. He's on his own after this."

He studied her, trying to decide if she was telling the truth or just saying what he wanted to hear. He made a living reading people, but his little sister was a mystery to him because he loved her so much. "Does he know that?"

"Yes. He says he was trying to make money to save our marriage."

"Bull," DJ snapped.

She swung her head in his direction. "Don't you think I know that?" She quickly turned back to her driving as the SUV swerved. "It's not the first time. We had to sell everything last time."

He found himself grinding his teeth and had to look out the side window again. In his line of work, temper was a real weakness and one he couldn't afford. But this wasn't business. This was personal.

Ahead, he saw the turnoff to Whitehall. "Take this exit. We'll get a couple of rooms here and go into Butte in the morning." What he didn't say was that he wasn't ready to go back. Not yet. The city brought back too many memories.

"By the way, where is Luca hiding out?" He asked it casually, but Keira knew him too well.

"I don't want you to do anything to him."

He waited, counting off the seconds until she finally

spoke as if she knew he'd find out even if she refused to tell him.

"Lonesome. It's a small town up by—"

"I know where it is," DJ said. "Why'd he choose it?"

She didn't answer right away. "He's staying at Uncle Charley's cabin up there."

Charley had a cabin? This was news. He thought that his uncle had lost everything back when he lost the ranch. And why outside of Lonesome, one of only a few small Montana towns that he noticed his uncle had avoided? When asked, Charley had been surprised that he'd noticed. "Some towns aren't worth the trouble." But he'd looked at him strangely, as if he wanted to say more but had changed his mind.

DJ had guessed that Charley had unfinished business in Lonesome. Those last few years of his uncle's life, he hadn't seen much of him. When he did see him, he worried that Charley was in more trouble than he could dig himself out of. As it turned out, that was true.

Charley always had his secrets. Now he knew that his uncle had a cabin that he'd somehow managed to keep—and Keira knew about it.

He glanced over at her, wondering what other secrets they'd both kept from him.

Chapter 4

Leaving Keira in Whitehall, DJ rented an SUV and drove to Butte alone. He found the investment banker's office on the top floor of the Grandville Building. He'd checked it out online last night as he prepared for this. A four-story brick edifice from the late eighteen hundreds that housed the Grandville Bank started by Titus's great-grandfather. The bank was still on the ground floor with two upper floors converted into condos and the top floor office space.

He found Titus Grandville in his corner office overlooking the historical section of downtown Butte. "Nice digs," DJ said as the banker motioned for him to take one of the leather club chairs. He declined and approached the man in the large office chair behind the massive desk.

Like all the Grandvilles, Titus was short and squat

with a cowlick at the crown of his brown hair. While dressed like a respectable investment banker, he still looked like the thug he was.

"Let me understand the problem here," DJ said quietly, calmly. "You came after my sister to threaten her over debts run up by the deadbeat husband she is divorcing. Is that right?"

Titus narrowed dark eyes that were a little too close together. He dropped his hand below the desk. To buzz for security if needed? Or reach for a weapon? "I hope we can settle this like respectable gentlemen."

DJ laughed. "We'd have to be respectable gentlemen." He lowered his voice. "You need to leave Keira alone. What is it going to take?"

The banker smiled and leaned back in his large office chair, steepling his fingers on his round middle. Apparently, mentioning money made Titus less nervous. "Someone has to pay what's owed."

Grandville was enjoying this a little too much. He remembered him as a kid. To say there was bad blood between them was putting it mildly. Titus had always lorded it over him. Not that everyone in Butte hadn't known that Titus was a Grandville. Who knew what DJ was?

Just the sight of his smug face was enough to make him want to leap over the massive desk and take the man by the throat. But it wouldn't solve the problem. DJ had known the moment he heard Keira crying on the phone that he was going to have to come up here and pay them off. The very idea stuck in his craw because of his dislike for the Grandvilles.

"Settle for twenty-five."

Titus shook his head. "Seventy-five with interest on the loan adding up every day—"

"Fifty thousand and I don't throw you out that big window behind you," DJ said.

"Diamond, you have always been a loose cannon." Titus tsked. "All right. For old time's sake, seventy-five and no more interest as long as this is handled quickly. By the end of the week."

"And you never go near my sister again."

The banker nodded, but DJ didn't feel as if this was settled. "Do I need to say it? You never do business with Luca Cross again either."

"Why do you care about him?" Titus asked, sounding amused.

DJ didn't answer, afraid to voice his fear that Keira wouldn't leave the man because she still loved him. Love was a fickle, foolish sentiment, one he avoided when it came to women. Family was another story, though, maybe especially family you didn't share blood with.

"I'll get your money. But you do realize that I'm going to have to put together a poker game to make it happen. That all right with you?"

Titus rocked forward in his chair, taking the bait quicker than DJ had expected. "I could suggest a couple of players with deep pockets I'd like to see cleaned. Let me know when and where."

"You're welcome to come play as well," DJ said with a grin.

The banker laughed. "I'm smarter than that. And Diamond? I'll need that money by the end of the week."

As he turned to leave, the banker called after him,

"So it's true. You're paying off your uncle's debts, too." Definite amusement in his voice.

DJ didn't trust himself to look back. If he saw that self-righteous look on Titus's face, he might just make good on his earlier threat.

As he left the building, he quit kidding himself that there was another way to solve this. He was going to have to pay, one way or another. He had the money in his savings account. Seventy-five grand wouldn't even make a dent. He could pay Titus off and walk away, but the very thought turned his stomach. He'd told Keira to stay put in Whitehall until this was settled. She'd be safe there—as long as she didn't do anything foolish like try to go to her husband.

DJ stopped for a moment as he tried to talk himself out of the plan that had come together the moment he'd walked into Grandville's office and seen Titus sitting behind his big desk. His good sense advised him to just pay the debt and forget it. Unfortunately, it wasn't just about the money. It hardly ever was.

He made the call to the one person he needed right now. "Sadie?" He hated the way his voice almost broke. It made him admit how much he wanted her help, as if a part of him worried that he couldn't do this without her, and that alone should have scared him. He'd come to depend on her. But even as he thought it, he knew it was a hell of a lot more than that. "I need you."

"I wondered how long it would take before you realized that," she joked.

"It's my sister. Her bad-choice soon-to-be hopefully ex-husband's fault. He's taken off and left her holding the bag."

"How heavy is this bag?"

"Seventy-five large."

"I can be on the next plane. Where am I headed?"

DJ closed his eyes for a moment, relief and something much stronger making his knees weak. "I'll pick you up at the airport outside of Bozeman. I'll be the cowboy in the hat," he said, needing to lighten the moment for fear he'd say something he couldn't take back. "I really appreciate this," he said, his voice rough with emotion. "Thank you."

"No problem, partner. I'm on my way."

Sadie disconnected, a lump in her throat. *DJ had a sister?* Why had she thought it was just him and the conman uncle who'd raised him? Not that DJ knew any more about her life than she did his. When they'd been thrown together, she'd just assumed that he was like her, from the same background, caught up in a world not to either of their making or liking. DJ had taken on his uncle's debt to the organization her godfather ran. The payments on that debt, which were almost paid, were what had kept them together.

She'd done her best to treat it like business, especially after her godfather had warned her against getting too close to DJ Diamond. But she'd gotten to know the man from sitting across a poker table from him all that time.

While she'd been shocked to learn that DJ had a little sister, she wasn't surprised that he would drop everything to bail her out. What worried her was that she'd never heard him sound like he had on the phone. Desperate? Anxious? Neither was good in this business, she thought as she quickly threw some clothing and money into a bag along with their decks of marked cards.

Two hours later, as she boarded a plane to Montana, she reminded herself that this might be the last time she saw DJ. Their "arrangement" was over. She'd told her godfather that she wanted out as soon as DJ's debt was paid. He'd been disappointed but not surprised.

"What will you do? You'll miss this," he'd said.

"I don't think so. I want a family." She didn't have to tell him that she also wanted to be as far away from criminal organizations as she could get.

"I understand," he'd said. "Your father was like that. Tell Diamond we're even. His uncle's debt is paid in full. My present to you since I can tell that you have a soft spot for him."

Sadie had only smiled. "Thank you."

"But you're not quitting because of him, right?"

"No, that partnership will be over," she said, hating how hard it would be to walk away from DJ Diamond. She'd grown more than fond of him. But she would walk away, she'd told herself.

"Good," her godfather said. "By the way, you're better at this than your father ever was, and he was pretty darned good." It had been her father who'd taught her that poker wasn't a game of chance. It was a game of skill, mental toughness and endurance.

"Never sit down at a table unless you know you can beat everyone there—one way or another," he'd said over and over. "You're going to lose sometimes, so never throw good money after bad. It all comes down to reading your opponents and knowing when to cash in and walk away."

Whatever DJ had going on in Montana, it was time to cash in and walk away. She would tell DJ when she got to Montana. She would also offer him the seventy-five grand so they wouldn't have to use the cards in her carry-on bag. He wouldn't take it, but she would offer. She feared that unlike her, he'd never be able to step away from the con. He enjoyed it too much. But eventually, his luck would run out. The thought made her sad. As her godfather had said, she had grown a soft spot for the cowboy.

Buck Crawford made the drive down to Casper, Wyoming, arriving in late afternoon. Luella Lindley lived in a small house in the older part of town. She was in her sixties, retired after being a telephone operator for years. She lived alone except for her three cats, George, Bob and Ingrid. She had a weakness for chocolate, her husband had been dead for almost twenty years, and she played bingo on Tuesday nights at the Senior Center.

He'd gotten all that information the first time he'd talked to her. Had she known Judy Ramsey? Yes. "We were like two peas in a pod," Luella had told him. "Sisters, that's what Judy called us, me being the older sister."

It took a good five minutes after ringing the doorbell for the woman to answer the door. She'd warned him that she used a walker and would be slow. Luella opened the door, leaning on her walker and smiling broadly. The smell of meat loaf wafted out, making his stomach growl.

"I hope you're hungry," she said, her blue eyes sparkling with excitement, giving him the feeling that she didn't get many visitors. "I made my famous meat loaf. Come on in. No need to stand out there on the front step." She turned and led the way into the house. "Have a seat." She went from the walker to a recliner. "Didn't expect a good-looking cowboy, although you did sound young on the phone. Are you really a private detective?"

"Yes, and you should have demanded proof of identification before you let me in," he said.

She laughed. "I saw you drive up. You didn't look that dangerous."

Buck knew he couldn't leave until he had meat loaf, so he let Luella talk about everything under the sun for a few minutes before he said, "What can you tell me about Judy Ramsey?"

"Sweet thing she was. Never had a lick of sense when it came to men, though," Luella said with a shake of her head. "Broke my heart every time she let some man hurt her."

"You knew her twenty-nine years ago. Did she tell you she was pregnant?"

The elderly woman nodded. "She was scared, but I could tell a part of her liked the idea of being a mother." She shook her head. "Turned out it was female problems. No baby. Never going to have one. By then, she'd realized she wasn't mother material."

"Did she tell you about meeting Maribelle Brookshire?"

"Read all about it in the paper. I have the Lonesome paper sent to me. The news is old by the time it arrives, but I don't care. It doesn't cost much and that is my hometown."

"So she told you about her deal with Maribelle to buy the baby if it was a girl?"

"No," she said after a moment. "I could tell something was going on, but no. She was devastated when she found out there was no baby. I didn't realize the main reason was because she'd already sold the baby to

Maribelle Brookshire. I thought her behavior was due to a man, but then she began asking questions about babies… I had to wonder why since I knew she wasn't having any of her own."

"What kind of questions?"

"Like what they ate, how to burp them, how to even put on a diaper and what you needed to buy for a baby. I thought she'd gone crazy."

"If you've read the news, then you know that Maribelle and Harrison Brookshire are awaiting trial for Judy's death. I'm engaged to their daughter they bought from Judy, Ansley Brookshire."

"My goodness, isn't that wonderful. That poor child needs a happy ending. Those so-called parents of hers, they deserve the electric chair for what they did to her, not to mention poor Judy."

"Ansley had a twin brother. Do you have any idea what Judy might have done with him?"

Luella shook her head. "I can understand why she did what she did. I mean, that's how we became such good friends—her moving in next door to me. She couldn't have done that without the money she got from that woman. Not that I approve of her means."

"Is it possible she gave the baby boy to someone she knew in Lonesome? I would think that she would have taken him to someone she trusted, someone with knowledge as to how to care for an infant."

The woman nodded sagely. "You're thinking me."

"The birth mother wasn't in any shape to take care of the baby. Also she thought both babies had died. So Judy had to have taken the baby boy to a friend."

Luella seemed to squirm a little in her seat. "Is talking to you like talking to a lawyer, anything I say is just between us?"

Buck hesitated, but only for a moment. "I just want to find him. I don't want to get anyone in trouble, especially you."

"That didn't quite answer my question."

"She brought you the baby, didn't she?"

Chapter 5

DJ had never been happier to see anyone. He stared at Sadie as she came down the stairs at the Yellowstone International Airport—his second time there in days. He blinked realizing he'd never seen her in normal clothes. Today, she wore designer jeans, a pale blue cashmere sweater and furry snow boots. She had her sheepskin coat thrown over one shoulder, her leather shoulder bag on the other and the expensive carry-on in her hand.

She looked like a million bucks. Everything fit like a glove, and she fit in here in the Gallatin Valley where the wealthy came to find paradise. She could have passed for any one of them because, he realized with a start, she was one of them. Sometimes he forgot that she'd been raised in Palm Beach, rubbing elbows with the rich and powerful.

He knew he wasn't the only man staring at this

breathtaking woman with her long blond hair resting around her shoulders. But when those honey-brown eyes found him, he felt like the only man in the world. She smiled, reminding him how amazing she was— and how unattainable.

His partner, Sadie Montclair, the smartest, funniest, sexiest woman he'd ever met, was off-limits in a big life-threatening way. Even if her godfather hadn't threatened him if he even thought about seducing her, DJ knew that she wouldn't look twice at someone like him. Not seriously, anyway.

"How was your flight?" he asked as he took her carry-on and led her outside into the cold, snowy December day to his rental SUV. "Thanks again for coming. You fly over so many mountains to get here. Sometimes the turbulence can get to you, but the view can be pretty spectacular."

"Are you really trying to make small talk, DJ Diamond?" she asked with a laugh as he climbed behind the wheel. She could tell he was nervous. He saw a flicker of concern in her gaze before she said, "Tell me about the people your sister owes this money to."

So like Sadie to get right to business. He tried to calm his nerves, having second thoughts about getting her involved in this. But while he kept thinking that he shouldn't have called her and she shouldn't have come, he was so glad that she was here. Maybe this was a mistake, but right now he couldn't help feeling relieved. Sadie balanced him; it's why they were such a good team.

He started the engine, stopped at the booth to turn in his parking ticket and drove out of the airport onto Interstate 90 headed west, mentally kicking himself for getting her involved in his family mess. "I shouldn't have called you."

"Of course you should have. If I hadn't wanted to come, I wouldn't have. I'm here for you. We're partners. It's just that you were acting like you'd picked up your girlfriend at the airport."

He nodded, swallowed and tried to relax. She was right. He wasn't himself around this version of Sadie. But he better pull it together. He cleared this throat and turned to business. "The men? Old money. Suits, ties, hired muscle. Grandville is a cocky bastard. Would they kill Keira? Probably not. Would they mess her up? Yeah."

Sadie saw that her words had hurt DJ. But she'd seen the way he looked at her as she'd come down the stairs at the terminal. It was going to be hard enough to walk away from this partnership as it was. She couldn't have him looking at her like that. Worse, she couldn't feel like she *was* his girlfriend he was picking up at the airport.

"Doesn't sound like anything we haven't dealt with before," she said as she took in the scenery as he drove, reminding herself that this was just another job.

She'd never been to Montana, but she could see the appeal. There was a winter wonderland outside her window. Everything was frosted with snow from the mountains to the pine trees, from houses to the fence posts they passed. Even the air seemed to sparkle with snow crystals. She couldn't help being enchanted as she saw a red barn with Christmas lights in the shape of a star on the side.

"I thought we'd make a big haul, pay off Grandville

and get out," DJ was saying. "He's supplying at least one of the players, someone's pockets he wants us to pick. I'll find someone to front the game who can bring in a local hard hitter or two to the mix."

"Whatever you think is best," she said as she saw a snowman in one of the yards. "Montana really is like the photographs I've seen. It's beautiful."

He glanced over at her. "You should see it in the spring. That's my favorite time of year, when everything greens up after a long, dull, colorless winter."

"I'd like that," she said. "I was thinking on the way up here. I have seventy-five thousand that I could—"

"Not a chance," he said quickly.

"It's my money, nothing to do with my godfather, and I wouldn't—"

"No," he said, shaking his head. "Thanks, but no. If you don't want to do this, just say so. No harm, no foul."

"I told you. I'm here. I'll do it. I just thought..." She could see that she'd offended him. "Sorry."

He shook his head. "I can't take your money."

"I get it." Sadie considered him for a moment. DJ saved what money he made when gaming legally. He was a hell of a poker player. She was betting that he had a whole lot more than seventy-five grand lying around. So if he wanted to, he could pay off his sister's creditor. This wasn't so much about money, she suspected. This was about getting even. With this Grandville he mentioned?

"Want to tell me what you have planned?"

"Just a friendly game of poker." He grinned as he looked over at her. She knew that look. He loved this. "I'm keeping you under wraps. Butte's an old mining town. I've got you a room at a local historic hotel that's been completely renovated. It's fancy—just like you. Room service, a bar, order whatever you want, any clothes you need."

"Sounds like you've thought of everything. So I'm the mark," she said, and shook her head in amusement. "A new role, huh?"

"One that clearly you were born into," he said, his gaze taking her in again.

She tried not to read too much into the look. She knew DJ. He couldn't help the charm. The man had an appreciation for women. All women—she couldn't let herself forget that.

Sadie told herself that this was just going to be another poker game like so many others they'd played together. She knew the drill. The two of them had it down pat. But as she studied him while he drove, she had to ask, "You sure about this? Once things get personal—"

"Like your godfather says, otherwise it is only money."

"Don't kid yourself. He likes the money just as much as the retribution."

They drove in silence for a few minutes. "It will be our last time." DJ tapped on the steering wheel, seeming lost in thought. "I know we're close to paying my uncle's debt. However much he owes for interest, I'll pay it from my own money. I'm done." He glanced at her as if to see how she was taking the news.

She nodded. "Talk about like minds. I was going to tell you the same thing. My godfather says you're paid in full." He turned to give her a suspicious look. "I had nothing to do with it. He says it's time."

DJ turned back to his driving and chewed on that for a while. She was wondering if he would miss it. If he would miss her. "One last big score." When she said nothing, he asked, "You're really up for this?"

"We're a team. If this is our last time… I wouldn't want to miss it for anything."

His gaze locked with hers for a few earth-shaking moments. She felt heat rush to her cheeks and quickly turned away. Was this really their last game? Her heart ached at the thought of never seeing DJ again as she watched the snowy landscape blur past her side window. Probably for the best, she thought, because she seemed to be losing her resistance to his charm. She couldn't let down her guard now when it was almost over. She knew how DJ was with women. She didn't want to be one of them.

It surprised her, though, that he'd been ready to end their relationship, even if it had been all business. Maybe like her, he'd decided it was time. Yet it made her uneasy, as if he was worried this was their last game for another reason. Just how dangerous was this going to be?

"You can still walk away," he said as if reading her mind.

He had to know her better than that. "Have I ever let you down?" she asked, still not looking at him.

"Never."

She heard something in his voice, an emotion she hadn't heard before. But by the time she dared look over at him, all his attention was back on the highway ahead.

Buck held his breath. This was the first decent lead he'd had on finding the missing twin. He couldn't help but think of Ansley. He had to find the last missing piece of her. She'd risked her life to find her birth mother, who had been told that both babies died.

"Can I go to prison for this?" Luella asked, her voice cracking.

"You aren't going to prison," he said. "Unless you harmed the baby."

"Oh, good Lord, no," she said, sounding shocked. "I'd never hurt a precious baby. He was so sweet, so tiny, so precious. I didn't care where Judy had gotten him. I should have. I know that was wrong. I just wanted to help her. She was beside herself, afraid he wasn't going to make it. I assured her I could help."

He saw her hesitate and suspected he knew where she was headed. "You knew someone who could take care of the baby."

"I'm not saying who, but yes. We took him over there and my…friend who'd just given birth six months before was still breastfeeding. He took right to it like the little champ he was and perked right up."

Buck thought how easy it would be to find out if Luella had a daughter or daughter-in-law who'd given birth that year—but only if it came to that. "So you left the baby with her?"

"Only for a few days. I still didn't know where Judy had gotten the little darling. Had I been younger, I would have kept him. I wanted to, but there would have been talk. Lonesome is a small town." She shook her head. "It wasn't possible. But it was so hard to give him back."

"Back to Judy?"

She nodded. "She knew someone who wanted a baby." Luella began shaking her head even before he asked who. "I didn't want to know. I'd involved people I cared about already. I knew not to push it."

He tried to hide his disappointment. "You must have some idea. You were Judy's best friend. You knew some of the same people."

She looked away for a moment and he felt hope resurface.

As DJ turned off the interstate and headed toward uptown Butte, Sadie took in the city sprawled across the side of the mountain—except for the right side, where much of the mountain was missing. "They still mine here?" she asked in surprise.

"Butte is a hard-core mining town," DJ said. "It started as a mining camp back in the 1860s and quickly grew to become Montana's first industrial city." They passed large abandoned old brick buildings, the windows either missing or covered in dust. "It's fallen on hard times since then, but the Continental pit is still active as an open-pit copper and molybdenum mining operation. Mining still pays better than any other industry in the state."

"Which is why we're here," Sadie said. "Aren't miners…a bit rough to deal with if things go south, though?"

"We aren't taking the miners' money. We're after the people above them who make the big money."

She was relieved to hear that. With her godfather, he handpicked the players in the games she and DJ relieved of their cash. Even so, there were some who often made her nervous. She'd learned that you could never tell what a person might do—especially if you'd just spent hours taking his money.

DJ headed up the mountainside, passing more old brick buildings in what was obviously the historic district. She couldn't help being fascinated just thinking of the history here as he pulled down an alley behind a large old brick hotel. The sign on the top floor read Hotel Finlen.

Sadie shot him a look as he stopped at the hotel's service entrance off the alley, but he didn't seem to notice. "Butte has an amazing history—and so does this hotel. Charles Lindbergh, Harry S. Truman and even JFK visited the Finlen," he said with an enthusiasm that was catching. "I love this hotel and this town. Butte was once the largest city between Chicago and San Francisco. You'll like this place. The Finlen was architecturally inspired by the Hotel Astor in New York and was built to impress in 1924."

She couldn't help smiling at him. Clearly this old mining town meant a lot to him. "How do you know all this?" she asked, hoping he would talk about his childhood here.

"The Finlen was my uncle's favorite hotel. He often paid the bill so we could come back. That wasn't true of most other hotels we stayed in."

She laughed. "Do you always use the back door off the alley?"

"Used to a lot. But today?" He shrugged. "I know people here." Of course he did. He knew people all over Montana and the northwest after growing up with a conman uncle. Not that DJ had ever offered anything about himself or his past. Just as she hadn't. But her godfather had told her a few things about the man before he'd asked her to work with him.

"I want to keep our partnership quiet. I hate to ask

you to walk around to the front of the building through the snow and slush, but we can't be connected," DJ said. "I need you to hang out here for a day or so. Like I said, buy expensive meals, shop, whatever. Throw money around. I'll contact you when I'm ready, but for this one you're a high roller."

"I think I'm going to enjoy being the mark," she said as he reached into the glove box and took out a thick envelope of money. She waved it away. "Thanks, but no. You don't get to be the only one to take the high road."

He looked as if he wanted to argue, before stuffing the envelope into his inside jacket pocket. "You'll get every penny back." He pointed up the street behind them. "It's easier to go that way. In this part of the older city, the streets and sidewalks are steep since they built the original city on the side of a mountain. I know how steep because I was the one who had to make the run for it so the employees chased me—and not my uncle."

His words hit her at heart level. She knew he'd had a rough childhood, but she hadn't known any details and now didn't know what to say. A cold silence seemed to surround the cab of the pickup for a moment. "It was a game for me," he said as if seeing her sympathy even though she tried hard to hide it. He grinned. "When we were flush, we ate lobster tail and steak from china plates on white linen tablecloths with real silver at the best places in town. True, when we were between scores, we ate whatever I could scrounge up—often from food trays left out in hotel hallways. But you'd be amazed what people leave. Like I said, as a kid it was a game. A scavenger hunt." He shrugged and she could tell that he wished he hadn't told her any of this. So why had he?

"Bet you could run fast." She smiled even though she felt more like crying as she thought about DJ as a boy outrunning hotel employees so his uncle didn't have to. "I can't wait to see this hotel that meant so much to you and your uncle." She met his gaze. "I like seeing this place through your eyes. Thanks for sharing. And don't worry about me. I'll do my part."

"I never doubt it. Thanks again, Sadie."

She hesitated, surprised how much she wanted to re-assure him. He seemed so vulnerable here in this place that had been such an important part of his younger life.

But she was the one who'd kept their relationship strictly business. While she couldn't *not* have regrets, it was almost over. The thought made a lump rise in her throat as she climbed out, closed the door and headed back down the alley. As she walked she couldn't help comparing his life to her own. Hers had been a fairy-tale princess's existence compared to his. There was no way she couldn't help him get the money for his sister. But she still felt uneasy. She didn't know this place or these people. Nor did she and DJ have the protection of her godfather. They were on their own.

At the front of the hotel, she pushed open the door, lifted her chin and strode in as if she owned the place. It was time to go to work.

Chapter 6

Buck watched Luella turn away to rinse out a cup in the sink. Stalling. He held his tongue although it was killing him. He could tell that she knew something he desperately needed. He thought of Ansley, his love for her, their upcoming wedding. *Please.*

"I honestly don't know for certain," Luella said. "I swear."

"I believe you, Luella," Buck said. "But anything you can tell me will help. My fiancée is desperate to have her missing twin brother give her away at our wedding."

The woman sighed as she turned back to face him. "That is so sweet." She hesitated, but only a moment longer. "There was this young woman that Judy had befriended when she worked at that old folks' home down in Missoula. Her name was Sheila. I saw her a few times when she came up to visit." Luella shook her head, lips pursed in disapproval. "I didn't like the look of her, but Judy was a sucker for anyone less off than she was. Sheila had had a hard life apparently and looked up to Judy."

He could see where that would have pleased Judy, who'd had a tough life herself. "Are you telling me Judy gave this young woman the baby?"

"I fear she did," Luella said, her voice cracking. "Broke my heart. That sweet innocent baby boy turned over to someone too immature, too irresponsible, too incapable of even taking care of herself let alone another life."

"How can I find Sheila?" he asked, hoping Luella had more than just the woman's first name to give him.

"I never knew her last name." His heart fell. "But I did hear from Judy that Sheila had gotten married. Said Sheila'd had a baby. Married some man named Grandville."

Buck knew the name. It was an old money Montana name. "You think the baby Sheila allegedly gave birth to was the baby boy Judy had given her?" Luella nodded. "You remember which Grandville she married?"

"Darrow Grandville," Luella said, not hiding her distaste for the man.

"I don't think I've ever heard of Darrow Grandville," Buck said, surprised.

"He was a cousin of the Grandvilles of Butte. Thought he was something, him and his fancy car, but I wasn't fooled." She shook her head. "I knew nothing good could come of it. Not a year later, Sheila was back—without the baby or the husband. Judy said Darrow had gotten into some kind of trouble and had to go underground, so to speak. I didn't ask about the baby. I didn't want to know."

"Underground?" he repeated.

Luella waved a hand through the air. "Some place outside of Butte, not really a ranch. The way Judy described it, the place was a hideout for outlaws. She always exaggerated, though. The ranch had a jewel in the name." She narrowed her eyes for a moment as if straining to come up with it. "Emerald Acres or something like that. I'm sorry. It's been too long."

"That will help," Buck said, hoping it was true.

"You think you can find him?" she asked, sounding as skeptical as he felt. "I mean for all we know, he didn't survive."

"I have to find him. Or at least find out what happened to him. If he's alive, his twin sister needs him at her wedding. As the groom, I'll turn over every rock looking for him."

As he left, he called the Colt Brothers Investigation office. "I need to find a ranch that existed near Butte almost thirty years ago. Might have been called Emerald Acres or something with a gemstone name."

"I'll put Tommy on it," James Colt assured him. "Anything else?"

"I'm also looking for a man named Darrow Grandville."

"Grandville? Like the Grandvilles of Butte?"

"A cousin apparently, a disreputable one possibly. He might have had my future bride's twin with him when he got into trouble and had to go to the ranch hideout."

"Great," James said. "I'd be careful with the Grandvilles."

Buck laughed. "Last I heard, they'd gone legit."

"Yeah. Crooks in high places are still crooks and even more dangerous. Also it's Butte. Tough town if you cross the wrong people."

"So I've heard."

"Let me guess," James said. "You're headed for Butte."

"Tell Tommy to call me if he finds anything on the ranch or Darrow. I might have to rattle some cages."

"I'll pay your bail," James said, and hung up.

DJ mentally kicked himself, wishing he hadn't told Sadie so much about his life with his uncle. He blamed it on being back in Butte. Memories assailed him the moment he started up the mountain to the old part of town. His uncle had loved Butte. He'd made a lot of money here and had been almost killed doing it several times. His uncle always said that he wouldn't have survived if it wasn't for DJ.

The two of them hadn't just been on the run from hotel managers and the dozens of people his uncle conned. "If anyone asks you why you aren't in school, you need to have a lie ready," Charley had warned. "Otherwise, they'll take you away from me, put you in a foster home, force you to go to school. Believe me, that's the last thing you want to happen."

Charley had grown up being kicked from home to home before he'd taken off on his own at sixteen and learned the grift from old codgers he met on the street. He taught everything he knew about the con to DJ. Everything else, DJ had learned when he was young from reading and television. Most hotels had books lying around that people had left behind. If desperate, there was usually a Gideon Bible in a motel room.

Once he was older, DJ got his GED and applied for college. Four years later he had a business degree and a legit job that he held on to for almost seven years. Poker night was just a way to pick up some spare change. Then he heard that his uncle Charley needed his help. He quit the job that he later admitted he hated, but before he could reach his uncle, Charley was arrested and sent to prison. That's when he met Sadie's godfather and went to work paying off his uncle's debt and buying him protection while inside. Charley died in prison two years ago of a heart attack.

DJ seldom looked back. That was something else his uncle had taught him. "Spend time looking behind you and you'll trip over your own two feet," Charley used to say. But being here brought so much of it back, the good, the bad and the downright ugly, he thought.

He tried to concentrate on setting up the poker game rather than going down a very bumpy memory lane. He'd picked up his phone to call Sadie a dozen times, needing to hear her voice, needing to know that he wasn't making a mistake, but he hadn't called.

He knew she was busy playing her part. She was a pro. Meanwhile, he'd been playing poker in penny-ante games around town, looking for a front for the game. He finally found Bob Martin, a small-time poker player with friends with deep enough pockets. It just couldn't be obvious that DJ was behind the game or that he needed players who had money to lose.

DJ told Bob that he knew of a woman with money to burn who liked to play poker but wasn't very good, and the game was set for Friday night. Bob said he even had the perfect place, a local poker spot in the back room of a Chinese restaurant in the older part of town. DJ called Titus with the time and place.

Then he called Sadie.

Buck was on the outskirts of Butte when he got the call. Up here, the snow was deeper, the day darker, as the sun would soon be disappearing behind the mountains that closed in the city.

"It was the Diamond Deluxe Ranch," Tommy Colt said. "It was owned by a man named Charley Diamond. Word is, it was an enclave for outlaws. Diamond lost it about fifteen years ago to back taxes."

"Charley Diamond? Why does that name sound familiar?" Buck asked. Tommy had no idea. "Think I'll see if Willie might recognize it. Anything on Darrow Grandville?"

"Dead. Killed in a bar fight twenty-four years ago."

Buck took the news like a blow. Ansley's twin would have been five years old. What had happened to him? "Tell me how to find the ranch."

"It's now part of a larger working ranch, so the place is probably not occupied." He gave him directions.

"Thanks." He disconnected and called Sheriff Willie Colt. "Charley Diamond," he said without preamble when Willie answered. "Ring a bell?"

"Charley Diamond? Nope, but if it's important I could ask around."

"If you wouldn't mind. He used to own a ranch up here outside of Butte. A place for outlaws to hide out apparently. Darrow Grandville might have been one of them. Grandville hooked up with a friend of Judy Ramsey's named Sheila. That's all I have on her. But she might have gotten Ansley's twin. Problem is, a year later, after hooking up with Grandville, she didn't have the kid anymore."

"I'll see what I can find out. Where are you?"

"On my way to visit the Grandvilles."

"Really bad idea from what I've heard about the family," Willie said, and disconnected.

Buck wasn't surprised that he had to push his way in to see Titus Grandville in his penthouse-floor office.

"I'm sorry, but if you don't have an appointment—"

He walked past the receptionist down the hallway. The views through the windows he passed were of historic Butte with its old mining rigs as well as decaying remnants of elaborate brickwork buildings from a time when it had been the largest city west of Chicago.

Titus Grandville was on his feet by the time Buck walked into his office. "I've already called security."

"I just need to ask you a couple of quick questions." He held out his hand as he approached the man. "Buck Crawford. I'm with Colt Brothers Investigation in Lonesome."

Titus raised a brow, but made no move to shake hands. "Private dick?"

Buck dropped his hand. "I prefer PI. I need to ask you about Darrow Grandville."

"I don't know anyone by that name. Had you called, I could have saved you the trip. Now if that's all."

"Darrow is your cousin. He was arrested in Butte about twenty-odd years ago and might have been staying out on the Diamond Deluxe."

"Before my time," Titus said.

"He might have had a woman with him. Sheila? And a little boy somewhere around one or two at the time."

Grandville was shaking his head. "I told you—"

"You don't remember, right. Well, I'm looking for the boy. He would be twenty-nine now."

"Why are you looking for him anyway?"

"Client confidentiality."

Titus smirked as he settled into his massive office chair. "He wanted for something?"

"A wedding. He needs to give the bride away."

Grandville laughed. "Quite the dangerous case you're on, PI."

"Maybe your father would remember," Buck said as he turned to leave. "I've got time. I'll drop by his place. Maybe his memory is better than yours. Shouldn't be hard to find him since your childhood home is on the historic register."

"Don't bother my father. He isn't well."

Buck was headed for the door.

Grandville was on his feet now. "I'm serious. Leave my father out of this. He doesn't know anyone named Darrow. Or Sheila or anything about a kid."

"I guess I'll see." He walked out with Grandville cursing after him.

Sadie had been getting into her new role by spending money. She'd ordered room service and then gone shopping. She'd bought her godfather a Western bolo tie as a gift. She'd picked up a pair of red cowboy boots for herself along with some boot-cut jeans and a large leather purse with a horse carved into it. The purse was plenty big enough for everything she needed.

After she'd returned from an outing, the hotel clerk had called to say that she had a package down at the main desk. Inside it, she'd found a handgun like the one she usually used and ammunition. She'd cleaned and loaded it, telling herself that the next time she saw DJ would be no different than any other night she'd worked with him. Except she was playing a different role and her godfather wouldn't have set up the place and the players.

While it had been dangerous the other times, she'd felt as if things had been under control. She feared that wouldn't be the case this time as she loaded the gun and put it in her new shoulder bag. DJ was too personally involved this time, and that worried her.

After DJ's call, she now had the time and place. All she had to do was wait. She'd already planned what she would wear, who she would be. She and DJ had signals so they could communicate if needed. Usually, it wasn't needed because they both knew the other person so well.

Just the thought that this would be their last game together made her sad. She knew she was being silly. When her godfather had come to her about working with DJ, she'd thought he'd lost his mind.

"This guy is one hell of a poker player," he'd said. "With you as his wingman, the two of you can't lose."

She'd been skeptical at best, especially after she'd met him. DJ was too handsome, too cocky, too much a cowboy even without the Stetson. He seemed like a wild card—the kind of man who could get her killed.

But after one game, she'd been a believer. He was as good as her godfather had said. And under all that cocky cowboy arrogance there was something special.

Isn't that why DJ had gotten to her? Why she knew she'd risk her life for this cowboy without a moment's hesitation?

Was that what she was about to do?

Chapter 7

Buck figured Titus Grandville would have called for security at his father's mansion. He decided to let security cool their heels for a few hours while he drove out to the old Diamond Deluxe Ranch first.

He drove south, down the mountain from historic Butte to a strip of newer businesses. Like a lot of towns in Montana, the old mining city had seen better days. Buck quickly found himself in the mountains.

Tommy had been right. There wasn't much left of the Diamond Deluxe Ranch and yet he could read the name branded into the weathered wood arch over the road in. A few outbuildings stood along the edge of the road. Through the pines he saw a dilapidated two-story farmhouse, the paint long peeled off, the porch rotted, little glass left in the windows. There was a chicken coop and what could have once been a bunkhouse.

Buck told himself there was nothing here to find, yet he knew he couldn't leave until he looked around. He had to climb up through a deep snowdrift that had blown in across the front porch. The front door was ajar, snow drifted across the weathered hardwood floor inside. He tested the floor. It creaked and groaned but didn't give way as he entered.

A stairway led up to the second floor. He could hear something moving around up there. Pack rats? He started up the stairs, more sounds of movement as small animals scrambled for cover. He found a few old mattresses, a pile of metal bed rails and a couple of broken-down dressers.

There was nothing here of DelRae's twin. For all Buck knew DJ had never even been here. The baby Sheila and Darrow Grandville had with them might not even be the missing twin. He coughed, aware of the dust and other scents in the air, none of them making him want to spend another minute here.

As he started for the top of the stairs, he saw something that made him stop. He recognized the painstakingly carved marks down one side of the door's wood frame. He still had those on the inside of his bedroom. It was a growth chart. Buck stepped closer and felt his heart bump in his chest. He crouched to read the crudely carved dates in the pine. A child had stood here to be measured. He leaned closer, running his finger over what appeared to be initials. DJ.

Buck broke into a grin. Ansley's missing twin had been here. His growth proved that he'd survived to live here at least until… He quickly did the math. His middle teens. That's when the dates on the marks stopped.

Frowning, he noticed that it wasn't just DJ's growth

chart carved into this piece of old pine. He tried to make out the name. Keira? A younger child from the dates. He took several photos, anxious to call his bride-to-be. He hadn't found her twin, but at least he knew that DJ had survived to his teens in this place.

Buck did the math, comparing the last date on the chart to when Tommy had told him that Charley Diamond had lost the ranch. What had happened to these kids? DJ had been in his middle to late teens, but whoever Keira was, that child had been much younger. Where would they have gone? Social services?

He called Tommy, then he headed for Old Man Grandville's. He told himself that he'd call Ansley later with the news, hoping he would know more by then.

The Grandville home had been a mansion in its day. Built in the late 1800s during the city's opulent past on what was known as the richest hill on earth, it was the home of one of the city's high society. Three stories with gingerbread brickwork, ornate wood filigree and leaded glass windows, it had stood the test of time.

Buck parked on the steep street. No sign of security. He climbed out and walked through the wrought iron gate, up the sidewalk and onto the wide front porch. At the massive wood door, he rang the bell.

To his surprise, an elderly man in apparently fine health answered the door. He was dressed in slacks and sweater, loafers on his feet. He wasn't tall or handsome, but there was an air about him of arrogant dominance. He could see where the son, Titus, had gotten it from.

"Marcus Grandville," Buck said. "I'm Buck Crawford, a private investigator with—"

"I know who you are," the man said. "You're here about Darrow. Titus called and warned me you might be stopping by. I have a few minutes before I need to leave." He waved him into what had once been the parlor. Now it felt more like a den. "This shouldn't take long, but if you'd like to sit…"

He took one of the chairs facing the elderly Grandville.

"Darrow," Marcus said. "What about him?"

"He's your nephew?"

The older man gave a nod. "*Was* my nephew. Why are you asking about him after all these years?"

"He married a woman named Sheila about thirty years ago and they moved up this way. I'm trying to find Sheila."

"I have no idea where she is after all this time."

"But you met her."

"I suppose I must have."

Buck tried not to grit his teeth. "Did she have a child with her?"

Marcus frowned. He could tell that the man was about to say no when Marcus surprised him. "A boy with dark hair and pale blue eyes. One look at him and I knew he was no Grandville. Any fool could tell that. Any fool except my nephew."

"He thought the boy was his?"

"Darrow took after the other side of our family," Marcus said in answer.

"Sheila returned to Lonesome without the boy after they split," Buck said. "What did Darrow do with the boy?"

The man shrugged. "Had him with him the last time I saw my nephew. He was hanging around some ranch outside of town."

"The Diamond Deluxe?"

Marcus's eyes lit up for a moment. "Charley Diamond's place, that's right. Haven't thought about that place in years. Look, I have an appointment." He started to get to his feet, but Buck stopped him.

"I know the young man I'm looking for lived out at that ranch," he said. "I suspect your nephew left him out there. What I need to know is what happened to the boy after that."

The elderly man sighed. "Charley lost that place, you know." Buck nodded. "I think I might know who you're looking for. After Charley lost the ranch, he and a teenage boy were running cons around the state. You think DJ Diamond was the kid Darrow thought was his? Mind if I ask why you're interested in Diamond?"

"It's a long story, but he has family looking for him."

"Family?" Marcus huffed, looking skeptical, as he rose, interview over.

"One more question," Buck said as he rose as well. "Have you ever heard of someone named Keira?"

He saw the answer in the man's face an instant before Marcus caught himself. "I really have to go. Sorry I couldn't have been more help."

"On the contrary, you have been very helpful. I can show myself out."

"Titus," Marcus said the moment his oldest son answered the phone. "That PI from Lonesome was just here."

Titus swore. "Where were Rafe and Butch? They were supposed to make sure he didn't bother you."

"I sent them away," Marcus said with a curse. "I'm quite capable of taking care of myself and I was curious why he would be asking about Darrow and that woman,

Sheila. Darrow's dead and who knows what happened to Sheila. Did the PI ask you about Keira?"

A worrisome silence, then, "No, why would he ask about her?"

"That's what I want to know. Didn't I hear that she owes us money?"

"I'd really like to know how you hear these things, Dad."

Marcus waved that off. "Why would the PI be asking about her?"

"I have no idea. Her husband, Luca, is the one who owes the money, but we've been putting pressure on her. But we're going to get it settled by the end of the week. She got her buddy from the ranch to come help her out."

"What buddy from the ranch?" Marcus asked, afraid he already knew the answer.

"DJ Diamond."

Marcus swore. "That's who the PI was looking for. Why didn't you tell me that DJ Diamond was in town?"

"I had no idea you'd care. He paid me a visit, threatened to throw me out the window. But he'll pay off Keira's debt. Calls her his sister."

He didn't like this. As much as he loved his son, Titus often made poor decisions. Soon he would be in charge of their family fortune. The thought terrified him. "How much does Luca owe us?"

"Seventy-five. Diamond's a conman. Offered to settle for half the price. He's an arrogant fool like his uncle."

"DJ was Charley Diamond's protégé," Marcus said. "I wouldn't underestimate him if I were you. The last thing you want him to do is move in on our territory. Settle this and let me know when he leaves town."

"I can handle him. I have a plan."

"That's what worries me," Marcus said.

James answered the phone when Buck called the office. "I'm staying in Butte." Since going out to the Diamond Deluxe and talking to the Grandvilles, Buck was more convinced that DJ Diamond was the missing twin.

"Find something?" James asked.

"A few pieces of the puzzle seem to be coming together," he said. "It looks like the baby that Sheila and Darrow Grandville had was called DJ. That's assuming that Sheila did name the boy Del Junior or at least call him DJ." He told James about what he'd found out at the ranch inside the farmhouse owned by Charley Diamond, then about his visit to Titus Grandville.

"Titus Grandville." James said the name like a curse. "Anyone from this part of Montana has nothing good to say about that man."

"He pretended he'd never heard of Charley Diamond or the ranch," Buck said.

"These guys all know each other. Might not have traveled in the same circles but they're all connected."

"After Grandville lied to me, I went to see his old man."

"He's still alive?"

"Titus told me he wasn't well. Another lie from what I could tell. Marcus was more up-front, confirming what I'd already found out. Said he did remember the boy being with his nephew. Also said he remembered the Diamond Deluxe Ranch and DJ running cons with his uncle when he was a teen. I got the impression that Marcus doesn't know what Titus is up to, though, but

I could be wrong. He definitely didn't want me talking to his father."

"Titus always was the worst of the bunch," James said. "And that was saying a lot."

"Marcus told me that after Charley Diamond lost the ranch, he and DJ traveled around Montana running cons." He didn't have to say that he was worried about the kind of man he was going to find.

"Buck, are you sure about this? Maybe finding him isn't the best idea."

"I can't stop now. I haven't told Ansley any of this. I'm thinking that I should wait until I find him."

"I think that's wise."

"I'm going to hang around and see what Titus is up to. I just have a feeling about him. I've rattled enough cages that I suspect he'll lead me to DJ if he knows where he is."

"Watch your back," James said. "You're in the Grandvilles' sandbox and we already know that they don't play nice."

Sadie told herself that she was ready. In the days since she'd arrived here, she hadn't seen DJ. She'd missed him. Knowing that this might be their last poker game together had her feeling melancholy. She'd known from the beginning that one day it would end. DJ would have paid off his uncle's debt. They would have no reason to see each other.

Her future felt hollow. She really hadn't realized how much she was going to miss that arrogant grin of his. Or the way she often found him looking at her. Every time, she saw that gleam in his eyes, it warmed her clear to her toes. She kept telling herself that she'd never fall for his charm. She didn't want to be one of his women. But now she could admit that the thought of never seeing him again made her ache with longing.

She was looking forward to tonight's game just to see him. Although she was nervous. She felt as if too much was riding on tonight. She'd taken an Uber part of the ride down the mountain and walked the rest of the way through the falling snow to get a feel for where she was. It appeared to be an even older part of the city, the area more industrial than residential or commercial. Even under a heavy blanket of the pristine new snow still falling, it looked as if this place hadn't seen better days in a very long time.

She didn't need to question why DJ might have agreed to this site. It was the kind of neighborhood where no one would hear a gunshot. But that was a double-edged sword when dealing with people you didn't know or trust.

As she stepped down the alley, she saw the door he'd described and the sign over it. It appeared to be the back entrance to a Chinese food restaurant—if still operational. She didn't see anyone else around, but knew she had the right place. DJ had been explicit in his directions.

The metal door was heavy as she pulled it open and looked down a long, dimly lit hallway. Time to get into character, she thought as she stepped in and let the door close loudly behind her. Swearing just loud enough to let the men know she was coming, she brushed snow from her coat and yelled, "Could you have found a darker place?"

The hall was long with several closed doors. She kept going, following the acrid scent of cheap cigars and the murmur of voices. At the end of the hall, she turned to the right toward another hallway. One of the doors was open a few yards farther. She could hear the men's voices more clearly along with the scrape of chair legs on a wood floor and the rattle of ice being dropped into a glass.

She stepped into the open doorway and, leaning against the jamb, she took in the men already starting to gather around the table.

"Why am I craving pot stickers?" she demanded, and laughed as they all turned toward her. As she entered the room, she removed her coat, sweeping in as if the place wasn't a dump. She'd worn designer jeans and a lightweight sweater that accentuated her curves but modestly. She wore a scarf loosely tied around her neck and diamond earrings that glittered every time she tucked a lock of her long blond hair back behind an ear. Her coat was a classic expensive wool. Nothing too flashy.

"Anyone save me a spot at the table?" she asked.

One of the men jumped up to pull out an empty chair for her. She wouldn't be sitting directly across from DJ, but she wouldn't be sitting next to him, either. "This should work," she said, and looked at each of the players as she sat down. "Good evening, gentlemen." She held her large leather bag in her lap.

"Buy-in is ten thousand dollars," said a florid-faced, heavyset man with the offending cigar in one hand and a drink in the other. He motioned to a makeshift bar set up over by a sad-looking couch. She saw a tray of mismatched glasses, a bucket of ice, several bottles of booze, a container with a dollar sign on the side, and a cooler on the floor with beer iced down. "Booze? Put your money in the kitty. I'm Bob. We're using cash, no chips. We're the Old West here. I'll need to see your money."

"I'm Whitney," she said as she met the man's gaze through the smoke, smiled and reached into her bag to pull out an envelope full of cash. She gave a tilt of her head. "Ten thousand. I'm betting you want to count it." She slid it over to him.

He thumbed through the hundreds, then passed it back with a lopsided grin.

Sadie took a thousand dollars from the envelope and laid it on the table in front of her. She wondered which players DJ had gotten into the game other than her and Bob. One of the men at this table was the real mark. Bob was the kind to have invited at least one of his buddies as well. The trick was figuring out who was who.

She'd never been more aware of DJ. Having him so close was like a separate pulse beating under her skin. She felt the heat of him and wanted more than anything to see that arrogant grin of his, to feel his eyes on her, to connect with the man who'd gambled his way into her thoughts and her heart.

Bob introduced everyone only by first name starting with the man to his right as he went around the table. Max, the large truck driver in the Kenworth jacket and T-shirt that read I Drop Big Loads. Her, then Lloyd in the canvas jacket and fishing shirt. Next to him was Keith, the youngest in a hoody, jeans and untied trainers. Then Frank, the oldest of the bunch with short gray hair and the air of an ex-military man or retired cop. He gave her a nod. She watched him line up his bills perfectly in front of him. And last but not least, DJ, sitting next to Bob.

Sadie tried to still the unease she felt as she looked around the table. It was an odd gathering. She noticed that only two of them were drinking, Bob and Lloyd, the fisherman. She had no idea who was the true mark. As she started to hook her purse over the back of the chair, it slipped and fell to the floor.

Lloyd started to reach down to pick it up.

"I have it," she said, and grabbed it before he could. He moved his chair over a little to make room.

"Sorry," he said, avoiding her gaze.

"Let's play some poker," Frank said impatiently. "I don't have all night."

"I agree with Frank. Let's play." Sadie bent down to retrieve her purse. As she did, she glanced under the table and saw Frank shift in his chair, his slacks riding up to expose the gun in his ankle holster—and froze.

Chapter 8

Sadie tried to stay calm, but her heart was pounding as she straightened. She could feel DJ's gaze on her and wasn't surprised when he spoke.

"Excuse me," he said. "Does anyone else have a new deck of cards? No offense, Bob." He looked around the table, his gaze lingering on her for just a few seconds longer than the others.

She pulled her purse up on her lap, reached inside, but instead of pulling out a deck of the marked cards, she took out her lipstick and applied a fresh coat before putting it away. Out of the corner of her eye she saw Bob roll his eyes. Frank said something rude under his breath.

But it was DJ's reaction to her "abort" signal that she was most interested in. He stared at her for a moment before shaking his head ever so slightly. He wasn't going to walk away.

"We're going old-school tonight," Bob said, opening one of the packs of cards he'd brought. "Five-card stud, jacks or better to open, minimum bid ten bucks, no pot limit." Bob grinned. "That ain't too rich for your blood, is it, cowboy?" he said to DJ. He began shuffling with practiced expertise. After a few more elaborate shuffles, he set down the deck and Trucker Max cut them.

Sadie could feel DJ's gaze on her and shook her head imperceptibly. She didn't have to look at him to feel his disapproval. She knew what was riding on this for him—and his sister. But she had also learned to follow her instincts. She'd felt uncomfortable the moment she'd walked into this room. After seeing that one of their opponents was armed—and possibly ex-military or a retired cop—there was no way she was going through with the original plan.

Unfortunately, DJ was ignoring her advice and now she had no idea what he was planning—except they wouldn't be using the marked deck of cards in her bag—and she hoped not the gun resting there, either.

So where did that leave them?

DJ had lived his life calculating the risk—and then playing the odds. But he'd never regretted it more than he did right now. He looked over at Sadie. He'd missed her. All the time he'd been putting things together, his thoughts had kept straying to her. He knew she was doing what he'd asked of her. That was Sadie. He could count on her. He just hoped she could count on him. She hadn't hesitated about coming to Montana to help him. He'd known she would fly up here to do whatever he needed done. He'd needed her, and of course she'd come.

What he couldn't understand was why. She didn't owe him anything. Half the time, he thought she didn't like him. It wasn't the first time he'd heard her call him an arrogant fool. He figured she'd be relieved now that they wouldn't be working together for her godfather. She was free.

He'd often wondered if there was a man in her life. He'd been glad that she'd never mentioned one—let alone let him see her with anyone. DJ knew he'd never think any man was good enough for her. Not that she would ask his opinion.

Now he tried to read her face. The woman had the best poker face he'd ever seen. She gave nothing away. But he knew that she'd been worried. He'd seen her concern. She'd heard it in his voice. She'd known this was personal. They all knew that when it got personal, it got more dangerous. He wasn't just taking a chance with his own life; he was jeopardizing hers. He had no idea why she'd wanted to abort. He'd known her long enough that he knew she wouldn't have done that unless she'd seen something she thought he hadn't.

His gaze locked with hers, but only for a moment before she looked away. She thought he was making a mistake. He could tell that she was angry with him. It wouldn't be the first time. She'd called him an arrogant fool, an arrogant cowboy and probably worse. But tonight was the first time she'd refused to use the marked cards.

He trusted her instincts. She'd seen or felt something that had made her change her mind. She wanted him to walk away. Had she sensed that one of the players was a wild card? Or had she seen something that scared her? Not that it mattered. He couldn't quit now.

Sorry, Sadie, no can do. He wanted to tell her to trust him. But he feared her trust might be misplaced tonight. Charley had taught him the con, always warning him to step away from the table if he didn't think he could win. Poker was a game of skill, one DJ had perfected. But most everything else was a crapshoot. You read the situation as best you could, but ultimately, you had no control over what other people did—or didn't do. All you had were your gut instincts and years of learning to read people.

DJ hoped to hell that he knew what he was doing tonight. He'd gotten Sadie into this. He signaled for her to walk away after a few hands. Leave not feeling well. Make up a lie. Just leave.

But when he met her eyes, he saw not just anger but stubborn determination. Damn the woman, she would see this through. It was up to him now. Play out the hand he'd been dealt or throw in his cards and walk. He didn't have to look at Sadie. They both knew he wouldn't walk away.

Sadie concentrated on the game and her opponents rather than DJ. She drew three cards on the first hand, picked up a couple of fours to go with the one she had, bet big and lost. The others noticed that she'd bet on a losing hand. She would play her part. But she would also be watching the table.

Frank had folded early in the betting, while Keith, slouching in his chair, was throwing good money after bad. Bob took the pot and passed the deal to trucker Max, and the game continued.

Sadie won and lost. So did DJ, although his pile of money kept growing. Keith, the kid, lost, got angry and stormed away from the table to crash on an old couch in the corner after Bob refused to spot him credit.

And then there were six of them and suddenly, the game turned serious. The pots got bigger, the smoke thicker, the smell of sweat stronger. Sadie felt the tension rise. She knew DJ felt it, too, but he looked calm, almost too calm.

Earlier, he had signaled for her to leave. *Cash out. Walk away.* She couldn't. She had tried to warn him. He hadn't listened. Her options were limited. Keep playing or quit and walk away from not only the game, but also DJ, and not look back. If she walked, that would be the end of them. He would never trust her again—even with him being the one to tell her to leave. Their time together was ending as it was. She couldn't bear the thought that she'd let him down when he needed her most.

No, she thought, there was no way she was leaving him here alone. There was nothing more she could do but stay in the game and see this to the end. She thought about the gun in her purse and hoped she wouldn't have to use it. The load wasn't enough to do much harm to DJ if he had worn his vest under his shirt and jean jacket. But it would stop someone. Problem was that she didn't want to use it any more than she had the marked cards.

All she could hope was that her instincts were wrong, that Frank wasn't the wild card she feared he was, and that DJ's stubborn determination would carry them through as the cards moved around the table. Bob opened a new deck after a short break, and they continued.

Bob was losing and getting drunker. His dealing was sloppy. Sadie watched him. If she hadn't been able to smell the booze wafting off him, she might have been worried that it was all an act, and he was dealing off the bottom of the deck. He lost the next pot and handed off the cards to Max.

The trucker had been playing well. He and DJ had about the same amount of money in front of them. Lloyd the fisherman had played a conservative game, folding early, and yet staying in the game. The armed Frank was good at the game. Maybe too good. He gave nothing away, including his money.

Her turn was coming up again to deal. She'd lost just enough so that the others didn't take her seriously. As it got later, she found herself getting more nervous. The trucker began losing badly, hemorrhaging money. He wasn't smart enough to stop. She could see him getting more anxious.

Bob had begun to sweat as his pile of bills dwindled. He'd been making bad bets on even worse hands. He kept rubbing the back of his neck, shifting in his chair, getting up to make himself another drink he didn't need. He knew he was going down and this had been his show. The pressure was clearly getting to him.

"Come on, we don't have all night," Bob kept complaining. The trucker, too, was restless. Only Frank seemed unperturbed when the game slowed. All of it put her on alert.

DJ must have noticed that things were coming to a head. On the next hand, he raised the bet. The others either thought he was bluffing or just didn't want to fold in defeat, so they stayed in, no doubt convinced that they had the better hand.

They'd come to the end of the night, one way or another. Even Frank was in deep with this hand. Bob would be broke if he didn't win the pot, and Lloyd was down badly. The game was about over.

Sadie stayed in with three queens. "I'll call your bluff," she said, and met DJ's gaze with a look that said, "I hope you know what you're doing."

He grinned as she tossed her money onto the growing pile. He was going to have to show his hand.

Buck had been parked down the street from the Grandville building for hours and was beginning to wonder if he'd missed Titus, when the man came out the back door and headed for a large SUV parked across the alley. He seemed in a hurry as he slid behind the wheel.

From down the block, Buck was glad that his instincts had been right. Now he feared that he'd wasted his time. Maybe Grandville would only go home for the night. But it didn't take long to realize that Titus wasn't headed home.

Instead, the man drove down the mountain to an older, more decrepit part of Butte. The streets became darker, the commercial buildings got more derelict looking before the banker pulled over, parked and after getting out, walked down the street to where he ducked into an alley.

Buck stopped down the block in front of an old gas station with a condemned sign out front. He checked his gun, put on his side holster and turned off his cell phone before tucking it into his coat pocket and getting out. It had been snowing off and on all day. Falling snow spun around him as he walked toward where he'd seen Grandville disappear. By the time he turned down the alley, huge lacy snowflakes were fluttering down, making it hard to see more than a few yards ahead.

His gut told him he was onto something even as his head said this might be a complete waste of his time. This nighttime adventure might not lead him any closer to DJ Diamond because it might be nothing more than a booty call. Titus might have a woman he was secretly meeting. Not that this appeared to be a residential area.

At the top of the alley, he could see footprints in the snow. The new flakes hadn't covered them yet. They led to a back entrance of what appeared to be a Chinese food restaurant. The sign was faded. He wondered if the place was even still in business. He moved down the alley through the falling snow, his footfalls cushioned by the new snow.

At the door, Buck grabbed the handle and pulled, half expecting it to be locked. It wasn't. He stood to the side for a few moments listening before he peered in, then stepped through into the semidarkness, closing the door quietly behind him. He stood stone still for a moment to let his eyes adjust to the lack of light.

There appeared to be a solitary bulb at the far end of the hallway. He headed for it, following the murmur of voices.

Sadie had been watching DJ closely. He hadn't cheated. But she could feel the tension in the room spark and sizzle. The pot was huge and DJ had already won a lot of money. Earlier he'd been playing with a stack of hundreds. A few minutes later, the stack had shrunk but not so noticeably that the others had seen him pocket the bills. He didn't want anyone to see how far ahead he was. He was playing smart, but she feared that wouldn't matter. Frank's being armed had her nerves frayed. Maybe he always came to games armed. Or not.

Sadie realized that she was holding her breath and told herself to breathe. She had to be ready if things went south. *When* things went south, she amended. The thing about carrying a gun was knowing when to pull it. The rule of thumb had always been: never pull a weapon unless you were going to use it—and quickly—before someone took it away and used it on you.

Her purse was hooked on the back of her chair, easily accessible—but not quickly. She had her gaze on DJ, but her true focus was on Frank, whom she was watching closely from the corner of her eye. If he reached down for the gun strapped on his ankle, she was going to have to pull hers. She would have only seconds to act.

For all she knew Frank wasn't a retired cop, but still an active-duty older cop. Even her godfather would have advised against shooting a cop—especially one with a loaded gun at a poker game. Ex-military or cop or just cop-looking older man with a gun, Frank was the wild card.

It had crossed her mind that Frank's true purpose here tonight might not be to play poker at all. She'd gotten the impression that DJ had enemies here in Butte. Her godfather had told her that teenage DJ had worked cons for years with his uncle until he went out on his own. She had no idea what kind of trouble DJ's sister was in, other than financially, or with whom. But if someone wanted to draw DJ out to even an old score, they now had him back in Montana on their home turf.

Sadie knew it was her fear making her think these things. But hadn't she, from the start, been worried that his concern for Keira had overridden his survival instincts?

She met his gaze across the table in those seconds as the last player threw his money into the pot and called to see DJ's hand. Her heart ached at the look in his eyes. He had known that this might be all about him. She held his incredibly blue eyes. *Tell me what you want me to do.* He gave a slight shake of his head. Nothing? He didn't want her to do *anything*? But it was what else she saw there that gutted her. *I'm sorry.*

No, she wanted to scream. DJ had to know her better than that. She wouldn't let Frank kill him in cold blood—not if she could prevent it. She could have heard a tear drop in the tense silence as DJ started to let his cards fall on the table.

Chapter 9

Buck reached the end of the hallway and saw a short hallway off to his right. One of the doors was partially open. The smell of cigar smoke wafted out. Quietly, he moved closer until he could look inside.

From what he could see through the haze of smoke, there was a poker game going on. He didn't see Titus, but he knew he was here somewhere. Even from the doorway, he could feel the tension in the room as thick as the cigar smoke.

There were five men and one woman at the table, another man on a couch in the corner. Past the woman he could see a pile of money in the middle of the table. High-stakes game, it appeared. He could smell the sweat and the booze. His anxiety rose. Where was Titus? Why had he driven down here tonight? The whole scene had Buck on edge. He'd seen gunplay break out over a game with a lot less at stake.

He heard the heavy man with the cigar say, "All right, DJ. Let's see what you've got." There was an edge to his voice.

Everyone seemed to be waiting on the cowboy who was about Buck's age. He had dark hair and even from here, Buck could see that he had pale blue eyes. DJ Diamond?

The room fell silent as if everyone in it was holding their breath. DJ shoved back his cowboy hat and grinned as he let the cards drop faceup on the table.

Even before DJ's cards hit the table, the room seemed to explode in a roar of voices and movement. Everyone was moving at once. Sadie had gotten only a glimpse of DJ's cards. He had a royal flush? No wonder everyone was yelling. She would have sworn that he hadn't cheated, but then again, DJ was a man of many talents.

She wanted to look at him, to see the truth in his eyes, but her gaze was on Frank. His chair scraped as he threw down his cards, one fluttering to the floor, and shoved back from the table.

Sadie reached into her purse, avoiding looking at DJ. If Frank came up with his gun, she'd be ready. Her hand dived into her purse, closing around the pistol's grip. She could feel movement all around her as players threw down their cards and rose, but her gaze stayed on Frank as he reached down. She gripped the gun tighter. She was about to bring it up when he straightened, coming up—not with a gun, but with the card he'd dropped.

As he threw the card on the table, his gaze locked with hers. But only for a second. Just long enough to tell her that she'd made a huge mistake. It wasn't Frank that she and DJ had to worry about.

* * *

DJ always expected trouble. So he wasn't surprised when cards went flying, chairs crashed to the floor, drinks spilled as all but a couple of players were on their feet and yelling.

The tension had been rising like the heat around the table. Too much money had changed hands and tempers were flaring. It was the name of these kinds of supposedly friendly card games.

But this one had gone south much quicker than he'd expected. Bob was on his feet and so was Max, the trucker, and Frank, the older man he figured Sadie had tagged as a retired cop. He'd figured both Bob and the trucker for poor sports if they lost too much. But it was the younger man in the fishing shirt who surprised him.

He watched in horror as Lloyd reached over and grabbed Sadie's wrist. She had her hand in her purse. Now he watched as Lloyd twisted her wrist, making her cry out and the gun drop from her fingers back into the large bag.

As he unarmed her, he rose to step behind her. Before DJ could move, Lloyd locked his arm around her neck, drew a gun and pulled her to her feet. DJ rose slowly, putting his hands into the air as the barrel of the gun was pointed at his chest. All he could think was that Sadie had tried to warn him and he'd ignored her. He thought he knew what he was doing. Arrogant fool.

"Everyone just stay where you are," Lloyd ordered as he motioned with the weapon in his hands. "This is between me and Diamond."

Max and Bob quickly stepped away from the table and the huge pile of money in the middle. "Easy," DJ said. "It's just a friendly game of poker."

"Like hell," Lloyd said as Keith left the couch with a bag in his hand. "Cash us out," Lloyd told him. Keith grinned as he began to scoop the money into the bag, taking not just the pot, but any money that had been in front of the players.

"What's the deal here?" Bob asked, sounding confused and scared. It seemed pretty clear to DJ what was happening. He'd been set up and was now being ripped off along with everyone else.

"I don't want any trouble," the trucker said, stepping even farther back. Bob and Frank had both frozen where they stood at the sight of the gun in Lloyd's hand. Bob looked jittery, as if he badly needed a drink. Frank on the other hand stood watching expressionless, seeming to be assessing the situation.

DJ expected someone in the room to do something stupid before this was over. But he figured Lloyd was expecting the same thing. The man still had Sadie in a headlock and his own gun pointed in the general direction of the three of them; Bob was to his right, Frank to his far left. The trucker had moved closer to the door.

Unfortunately, the table was between DJ and Lloyd, not to mention the gun or the man's arm cutting off Sadie's air.

"Got a message for you, Diamond, from Mr. Grandville," Lloyd said. "Pay up and get out of town. You're not welcome in Butte."

The tension in the room kicked up a few more notches. Frank swore and stepped farther back. "What the hell?" Bob said angrily. "DJ, you didn't tell me you were mixed up with the Grandvilles." He looked like he wanted to take a swing at him.

DJ felt the tension reaching a fevered pitch. Why

didn't Lloyd and Keith just take the money and leave
if that's what this was about? Because they'd come for
more than the money. He had to get Sadie away from
them. She wasn't part of this. Unless they knew differently. In that case, they were both as good as dead.

"Which Grandville in particular sent this message?"
he asked, surprised how calm he sounded. "Titus or
Marcus?"

"Does it matter?" Lloyd snapped.

"Actually, it does."

"They both want you gone, along with that PI from
Lonesome who's looking for you," Lloyd said. "Seems
you have family looking for you. You must owe them
money, too."

DJ frowned. He had a PI from Lonesome looking for
him? Something about family? That didn't sound right.
Actually, none of this felt right. According to Keira, her
husband, Luca, was staying just outside of Lonesome
in the mountains at Charley's cabin.

He met Sadie's gaze, his full of apology. She was
fighting to breathe but still looked angry and determined. He tried not to show how afraid he was for her.
All his instincts told him that this wasn't going to end
well, and he had only himself to blame. But he knew
that he would die trying to save her.

Sadie was filled with a cold dread as she watched
the scene unfold. Lloyd kept cutting off her air. She'd
leaned into him, trying to relieve some of the pressure
as she calculated what they could do to get out of this.
It wasn't her nature to give up. There was always a way
out of a mess, wasn't there?

She'd hoped that Lloyd and Keith would just take the

money and leave. But she could see that it wasn't going to happen. This was personal.

DJ had realized it, too. She saw it in those blue eyes of his. She couldn't bear seeing his regret. He thought he was about to get them both killed. She wasn't ready to give up so easily. Also she knew that he'd risk his life to save her. She couldn't live with his blood on her hands.

For a moment she was overwhelmed with her feelings for the cowboy. He'd gotten her into this, and she should have been furious with him. But instead, all she felt was love, and that alone made her angry with herself, with him and with this jackass who had her in a headlock.

The Grandvilles had apparently set them up, that much was clear. Lloyd had known about her and DJ. He'd known she had a gun. He'd also known that they were here to make money to pay back Titus Grandville.

When he'd grabbed her, twisting the gun from her hand and dropping it back into her shoulder bag as he pulled her to her feet, she'd been taken off guard. She'd been so sure that Frank was the one they had to fear.

Now as she watched the others, feeling the pressure rising to the point where everything was going to blow, she knew she couldn't wait much longer to do something. These men weren't through with her and DJ. She didn't think they would kill everyone in the room. But they weren't going to let her and DJ walk away. She would have to act.

For a moment, she'd been distracted by Bob, who definitely looked as if he wanted to pick a fight with DJ. So she hadn't seen how Frank had maneuvered himself out of her line of vision—and Lloyd's—behind DJ.

Keith had gone back to the old sofa and was busy counting the money.

She thought that no one had noticed Frank as he reached down and came up with the gun except her. If he fired, she feared Lloyd would shoot DJ. But before she could squeeze in her next breath, the door into the room was suddenly flung open.

"Everyone. Drop your weapons!" yelled a cowboy with a gun standing in the doorway. "Hands up! No one gets hurt!"

All she could think in that instant was *This is it. This is the game that will get me killed—and DJ, too.*

Chapter 10

Sadie had no idea who the man was. But the distraction was enough that she saw what might be her only chance—and so did DJ. He launched himself across the table toward her and Lloyd as she drove her elbow into Lloyd's ribs and grabbed for his gun. But not quickly enough. As DJ crashed into them, the gun went off, the sound of the shot deafening in the confines of the room.

Had DJ been hit? Her heart dropped.

The force of his attack sent all three of them to the floor, Sadie still grappling for the gun. DJ climbed on top of Lloyd, pulling back his fist to hit the man in the face so hard it knocked his head back, banging it on the worn wood floor. For a moment, he appeared to pass out. She managed to get the gun away. As she pointed it at Lloyd's head, her hands trembling, she saw the blood. Just as she'd feared, DJ had been hit.

Lloyd blinked and tried to rise. "Don't tempt me," she said to Lloyd over the pandemonium that had broken out in the room.

"Everyone just settle down," the cowboy in the doorway yelled. "I'm Buck Crawford. I'm a private investigator looking for DJ Diamond. I'm here on behalf of his family. I'm not interested in whatever else is happening here."

A restless quiet fell over the room. DJ pushed his forearm against Lloyd's throat as he took the gun from Sadie and pressed it into the man's side. He met Sadie's gaze. "Are you all right?"

She nodded, but he could tell that she was scared. He followed her widened gaze to his left arm, surprised to see that his shirt a few inches above his elbow was soaked with blood. His blood. He hadn't realized he'd been winged.

"We're going to get up," he said loud enough that the cowboy PI in the doorway could hear. He kept the gun against Lloyd's ribs as the three of them rose to their feet, Sadie next to him. She pulled off the scarf from around her neck and tied it around his wound as if she was nurse Nancy. DJ was both touched and amused. The woman never ceased to amaze him.

When he looked around the room, he saw that PI Crawford and Frank seemed to be in a standoff, both with weapons drawn and pointed at the other.

"I'm going to leave," Crawford was saying from the doorway. "But I need DJ Diamond to come with me. Then the rest of you can settle whatever this is all about."

"I want none of this," Max the trucker said, and headed for the door.

Keith, who'd been sitting on the sofa counting the money, looked to Lloyd as if asking what to do. DJ shook his head at the man and jabbed Lloyd hard in the ribs. The only way they were walking out of here was if neither Lloyd nor Keith put up a fight.

Crawford moved out of the doorway to let Max leave. Bob rushed out as well.

"I'm Diamond," DJ said to the PI, happy to have an escort out of here. "But I'm not coming without Sadie." He motioned to her. She quickly picked up her purse and coat to move toward the door. DJ just hoped they weren't jumping out of the frying pan into the fire by trusting the PI. But right now, it appeared he was their best bet.

Maneuvering Lloyd over to the sofa, he jabbed the man hard in the side with the barrel end of the gun and said, "Tell Keith to give me his gun."

"You won't kill me in front of witnesses," Lloyd challenged.

"Willing to bet your life on that?" DJ said. "You hurt my girlfriend. I'd just as soon shoot you as take my next breath." He dug the barrel into Lloyd's flesh, making him wince.

"Give him your gun."

Keith carefully took his weapon from between the sofa cushions where he'd apparently hid it when the PI had burst in armed.

"Now tell him to give me the money."

"You're a dead man, Diamond," Lloyd spat, but motioned for Keith to hand over the bag. The younger man did it with obvious reluctance. "You think you can get away with this? They'll be coming for you from every direction." Lloyd smiled. "Even those closest to you have already turned on you. Nothing can save you or your girlfriend."

DJ shoved Lloyd down on the couch. He held the gun on Keith and Lloyd as he reached into the bag of money, took a handful of bills and dropped them on the table before nodding to Frank. The older man slowly lowered his weapon as if to say, "Tonight never happened."

Then DJ backed over to Sadie and the PI. He took one last look at Lloyd and Keith. They weren't Grandville's real muscle. Just as Lloyd had said, Grandville would be sending the big guns after them before they got out of Butte. Meanwhile, these two thugs would be smart to get out of town before they had to face Grandville's wrath for what had gone down here tonight.

DJ grabbed the chair at the end of the table as the three of them walked out of the room. He closed the door, sticking the chair under the knob. It wouldn't keep the men from getting out, but it would slow them down.

Once outside in the alley, DJ breathed in the cold December night air. They'd dodged a bullet. Almost, he thought as he looked down at his arm and the blood-soaked scarf tied around it. With his uninjured arm, he pulled Sadie to him. She wrapped her arms around his waist, leaning into him, as they walked down the alley. He could feel her trembling. Or maybe it was him who was shaking inside. He was back in Butte and it was as if he'd never left.

"My truck is just up the street," the PI said. "I work for Colt Brothers Investigation out of Lonesome. We need to talk."

* * *

Through the falling snow, Buck saw that Titus Grandville's car was gone from where it had been parked earlier. He must have left when he thought his two men had everything under control. Or when the gunplay started. Buck hadn't heard him leave, but then again, he'd been busy.

He still couldn't believe they'd gotten out of that mess back there alive. Worse, he didn't know which side of the law Ansley's twin was on or what he'd just helped him do. All he knew was that Titus Grandville was up to his neck in this—and so was DJ Diamond.

"I appreciate what you did back there," DJ said. "But right now, you don't want to be anywhere near the two of us. When those two back there report to their boss—"

"Titus Grandville." DJ shot him a surprised look. "I followed him to the game earlier. I'm pretty sure he already knows what went down tonight and that's why he's taken off. As far as being involved, I'm already more involved than you know. You owe me at least time to explain why I've been looking for you. My truck's down here. Let's get out of the snowstorm."

"You said you work for DJ's family?" Sadie asked once she climbed in the front of the crew cab and DJ got in the back out of the weather. Buck started the engine, letting it run as the heater warmed up the car. The temperature hovered around zero as the storm cocooned them below a thick blanket of fresh snow.

Buck turned in his seat so he could see both DJ and Sadie. He wondered about their relationship. "What I have to tell you might come as a shock. I'm not sure how much you know about your birth." He glanced at Sadie. "Or how much you want anyone else to know.

I'm sorry, we haven't officially met." He held out his hand to her. "I'm—"

"Buck Crawford." She smiled. "I'm Sadie Montclair." She looked at DJ. "If he'd just as soon I not hear what it is you have to tell him—"

"No, she stays," DJ said as he looked from her to the PI. He'd kept so much of himself from the rest of the world, maybe especially Sadie because he hadn't wanted her to think the worst of him. But all that had changed tonight when he'd almost gotten her killed. He was still shaken at how close he'd come to losing her.

"Anything you have to say to me you can say in front of her," he said, his voice cracking as he shifted his gaze back to her and swallowed the lump that had risen in his throat. They had to make this quick. If the PI was right and Grandville already knew what had gone down here tonight, he would be sending more of his men for them.

"I'll give you the abbreviated version," the PI said, no doubt seeing how anxious he was. "About thirty years ago your mother was pregnant with twins, a girl and a boy. It was a rough delivery. She believed that you both had died. But you'd both been given away by a woman who thought she was doing the best thing for the two of you. I'm here on behalf of your twin sister, who is getting married at the end of this week. She didn't know about you until recently. Actually, she didn't know that the people who raised her weren't really her biological parents. Once she found out, she wouldn't stop until she found her birth mother. That's when she found out that she had a twin brother. I believe you are that missing twin."

DJ scoffed. Did he believe any of this? It sounded like a con. "That's quite a story."

"We won't know for sure until we get your DNA, but you look a lot like Ansley. The dark hair, the blue eyes… It's kind of incredible."

Incredible, DJ thought, feeling like he needed to ask what's the hitch. "So what's in it for you if I'm this missing twin?"

"I don't blame you for being suspicious. Other than finding my future bride's brother for her, I'm hoping you'll be at our wedding."

DJ felt his eyebrows shoot up as Crawford nodded.

"Ansley Brookshire is my fiancée."

"Brookshire?" That was a name he'd heard. It was right up there with Grandville—just not as old money. "Sorry if I'm having trouble believing this."

The PI pulled out his cell and flipped through the photos for a moment before handing the phone over to him. DJ stared down at the pretty woman with the dark hair and familiar blue eyes. His heart raced. Could this be true? "Other than I resemble her, what makes you think I'm the twin?"

"I've followed a trail from the birth mother to here," Crawford said. "I found your growth chart out at Charley Diamond's ranch. I'm pretty sure Darrow Grandville left you out there. It's a long story, but the sooner we get a DNA test the sooner we'll know for sure."

"If you're telling me that a Grandville was my father—"

"No," Buck said with a shake of his head. "If you're who I think you are, then your father is Del Ransom Colt, a former rodeo bull rider and the man who started Colt Investigations in Lonesome."

All DJ could think was that he couldn't trust this. Trust had always been an issue with him. Until he met Sadie. But hadn't he always wondered who he was, how he'd been left out at the ranch with Charley and if anyone had ever wanted him? He looked at Sadie as he handed her the phone with the picture of the young woman who could be his twin.

She glanced at the photo, her eyes widening in the same shock he'd felt. Maybe it *was* possible, but the timing couldn't have been worse.

A set of headlights bled through the falling snow that had accumulated on the windshield.

"All this is interesting, but we really need to get out of here," DJ said. "Grandville's men are going to be looking for us." He waited until the vehicle coming toward them passed before he started to open his door. "I'm going to have to get back to you."

Buck couldn't find Ansley's twin only to have him disappear again. "Look, I can see that you're in some kind of trouble," he said quickly. "Let me help you." He pulled out his business card with his cell phone number on it.

"Sorry, but you can't help," DJ said as he reluctantly took the business card and handed back Buck's phone. "A friend of mine is in danger. I have to get to her before they do."

"You might want to get some medical attention for that wound first," Buck said.

"I can see to it," Sadie said like a woman who'd done her share of patching up gunshot wounds. Buck had to wonder who this woman was and just how much trouble the two of them were in. But if Titus Grandville was involved, it was dangerous.

"I could help you more if you told me why Titus Grandville is after you—and your friend. If it's money, maybe I can—"

"It's more than money," DJ said. "But thanks for the offer. With me and Grandville it's apparently personal. My…friend's husband owes Titus money. He's pressuring her. I've got her hidden. After what went down tonight, I'm afraid of what they'll do to her if they find her, and I have no doubt that they are looking for her."

"DJ, if you go to her now, you'll lead them right to her," Buck said quickly. "I can keep all of you safe if you come back to Lonesome with me." He saw the answer and quickly added, "At least let me keep your friend safe until this is over. You can trust me."

DJ shook his head. He was clearly someone who'd been taking care of himself for so long that he was suspicious of help. But before he could decline the offer, the woman spoke.

"He's right. If you go to Keira now, you'll just be putting her in danger," she said, reaching back to take DJ's hand. "I trust him. He just saved us back there."

Keira. The name of the other child from the ranch. Buck could see that DJ was having a hard time trusting him. But there was something between these two, the woman he called Sadie and DJ himself. Apparently, DJ did trust her, because Buck saw him weaken.

DJ looked at Sadie, felt that lump form again in his throat as she nodded her encouragement. He'd almost gotten her killed tonight. He should have trusted her and aborted when she'd signaled for him to. But he hadn't. He'd been so sure he knew what he was doing. He'd trusted only a few people in his life. He realized that if there was one person he trusted with his life, it was Sadie. But did he dare risk Keira's life by trusting this PI?

He looked at Buck Crawford, reminding himself that Sadie was right—the man had just saved their lives back there. But it was Sadie's trust in the man that made him decide. "Her name's Keira Cross. She's in Whitehall at the Rice Motel. Tell her I sent you. She won't believe you, so you'll have to show her this."

He dug in his pocket and pulled out the tiny, tarnished gold bracelet with his initials on it. For a moment all he could do was rub his thumb over the *DJ* engraved in the gold. He'd had it from as far back as he could remember. It was why they'd called him DJ at the ranch.

He'd carried it for luck. He didn't even know who'd given it to him—just that it had been his talisman. He handed it to the PI. "Keira means a lot to me."

Crawford nodded as he took the bracelet and pocketed it. "I'll make sure she's safe." He handed his phone back to DJ. "Put your number in there. I'll call you when I have her." DJ took the phone again and keyed in his number, hoping he wasn't making a mistake. "The wedding is next Saturday."

DJ shook his head as he handed the phone back. "You aren't even sure I'm your future bride's missing twin."

"I'm not much of a gambler, but I'd put all my money on it. Next Saturday. It would mean everything to Ansley and me if you were there."

"Aren't you worried that I'm a wanted criminal who could be behind bars by then?" DJ asked, amazed by this PI.

"I'm a pretty good judge of character. Also, I know a good bail bondsman," Crawford told him. "I'll call you the minute I have Keira safe."

Chapter 11

"Can you ever forgive me?" DJ asked as he started the SUV's engine without looking at Sadie, and waited for the wipers to clear the windshield. He heard her buckle her seatbelt before she finally spoke.

"There's nothing to forgive," she said, her voice sounding hoarse.

His gaze swung to hers in disbelief. "I almost got you killed!"

"I'm fine." She wasn't. He could hear in her voice the scratchy sound of her bruised throat. It had to hurt since he could see the bruised area where Lloyd had held her too tightly. He gripped the wheel until his fingers turned white just thinking about Lloyd with his arm around her neck cutting off her air. "I should have listened to you and gotten out of there before—"

"I thought it was Frank. I saw his ankle holster and

gun right after I sat down. He looked like former military or an ex-cop. I panicked."

DJ shook his head. "It doesn't matter. I was wrong. You went with your instincts, and they were right. I'm so sorry."

"You have nothing to be sorry for."

He shifted the SUV into Drive and started down the street. "How can you even say that? If I had listened to you, we would have gotten out of there before Lloyd grabbed you."

"Would we have? I really doubt they were going to let us just walk out."

DJ didn't argue the point as he took a road out of Butte. It didn't matter which way he headed as long as it was out of town. "I thought I knew what I was doing. You were right. I was too personally involved. I believed that Grandville wanted his money bad enough that he'd let me win enough to pay him off. I underestimated him. I doubt now it was ever about the money."

Out of the corner of his eye, he saw Sadie nod. "Do the two of you have a history?"

"Back when we were kids," he said. "Just a couple of brief occurrences when our paths crossed. He was the rich kid. I was nobody. But I must have made an impression on him."

"You do have that ability," she agreed, and he saw her smile. "Do you think he might have used Keira to get you back in Montana?"

So like her to cut to the heart of it. For a moment, he couldn't answer. The thought hurt too bad. He refused to believe the kid he thought of as his little sister would betray him. "I'll ask her when I see her."

His words kind of hung in the air. Sadie didn't say

anything. The only sound was the swish of the windshield wipers as he drove through the falling snow. He saw that he was headed for Helena. He knew he was waiting to hear from Crawford and simply driving to stay one step ahead of the men after them.

It didn't matter what town they reached as long as it had an airport, where he planned to put Sadie on a plane home. It had been a mistake calling her and getting her up here. He'd selfishly wanted her with him, he could admit now. He hadn't really needed her. He'd been right about one thing, though…it had been their last game. He'd almost gotten her killed for nothing.

"You know that I have to finish this."

Sadie said nothing for a few moments. "What exactly is this?"

"I thought I was just coming back here to pay off Grandville and free Keira from the debt and her no-account husband. Now I'm not sure what this is. All I know is I never should have gotten you involved."

The drive to Whitehall took longer than Buck had expected because of the storm. He didn't think he'd been followed, but he'd still taken precautions just in case. The one thing he couldn't let happen was leading Grandville's thugs straight to Keira Cross's motel room. He'd gotten DJ Diamond to trust him. Now Buck just had to prove that his trust had been warranted. It was the only way he was going to get the missing twin to his and Ansley's wedding.

He tried not to worry about DJ and Sadie or speculate on just how much trouble the two were in with the Grandvilles. DJ was the missing twin. Didn't the bracelet prove it? But how to keep him alive was the problem. There was nothing he could do about that—at least not at the moment. Once he had Keira and knew she was safe...

The snow was falling harder as he pulled up in front of the Rice Motel in Whitehall. It was still dark, the hour late. The crack of dawn wasn't that far away. For a moment he just sat in his pickup watching the snow, watching the parking lot, hoping she was inside number nine and that he would soon be calling DJ with the good news.

Still, he couldn't help being a little leery. This felt almost too easy. That and the one man's words back in Butte about DJ not being able to trust those closest to him. He didn't see anyone else in the parking lot and there were only a couple of cars in front of two of the other motel rooms. On the surface, everything looked fine.

Still, as he got out of the pickup, he felt the hair spike on the back of his neck. He moved quickly to the motel unit door and knocked. No answer. He knocked again, then he tried the knob, his anxiety growing. The knob turned in his hand and with just a little push, the door swung open.

"Keira?" he called again. "Keira?" It was pitch-black inside the room, but as his eyes began to focus, he could see that there was someone in the bed. She was either a sound sleeper or... He raised his voice. "Keira?" He took a step in, his heart in his throat for fear that Grandville's men had already gotten to her.

Buck heard movement off to his right side. He turned, but not quickly enough. He caught a glimpse of Titus Grandville an instant before he was struck with something hard and cold. He staggered and went down hard.

* * *

After driving north toward Helena and the airport there, DJ tried Keira's cell. He couldn't risk the Butte airport. He'd already decided that he would get the PI to bring Keira to him. Somehow, he'd talk her into going to Florida with him. The Grandvilles might run Butte, their tentacles stretching even into the states around them, but they wouldn't come after them in Florida. If she wouldn't go, he'd know that she still loved Luca and had no intention of leaving him.

The call went straight to voicemail—just as it had earlier. Had trusting the PI been a mistake? Or had the Grandvilles been waiting for Crawford? If so, then they already had Keira. He tried Crawford. The call went to voicemail. Disconnecting, he felt worry bore deep into him. He told himself that he should have heard something by now.

"She could have stepped out to get something to eat," Sadie said, no doubt seeing his concern. She didn't sound any more convinced than he was.

He'd left a message for her to call, but his instincts told him she wasn't going to because she either couldn't or wouldn't. He'd been set up tonight at the poker game. Grandville had been two steps ahead of him the whole time. Keith and Lloyd had been low-rung thugs. Now Grandville would send his A-team after them, the men Keira had told him about, Butch Lamar and Rafe Westfall. Paying Grandville off was no longer an option. Maybe it never had been.

He'd had a bad feeling from the moment things had gone south at the poker game. Something was at play here, something that had him off-balance. He kept thinking about what Lloyd had hinted at, something about those closest to him turning on him. There was only one meaning he could get from that.

Keira.

If he couldn't trust her, Luca Cross was to blame, he told himself. Hadn't he worried that Keira was still in love with him, that she would go back to him, that he would get in trouble again? He told himself he shouldn't have ever let her marry the man, like he could have stopped her.

But even as he thought it, he knew he couldn't blame Luca. Keira had taken to life on the ranch even as a young girl, fascinated with the criminals who came and went. He'd caught her learning sleight of hand tricks by one of the cons when she was five. She'd been good at it. He'd seen the pride in her eyes.

"It's in her genes," Charley had always said with a laugh. "She was born to this life. As much as we don't want to be anything like our biological parents, we are part of that gene stew. Just need to make the best of the hand you've drawn. Remember that, DJ. Accept who you are."

He thought he had, even though he hadn't known his gene pool. But he had wanted to believe it didn't have to be Keira's future. He'd done his best to protect her, but he'd only been a boy himself back on the ranch. After that, he hadn't seen her much because he'd been trying to stay alive and not starve.

Thinking about his own biological stew, he wondered about this twin sister, if he really was her twin. Ansley Brookshire. She'd certainly landed in the lap of luxury, he thought uncharitably. By now she knew that if DJ was her twin, they weren't in the same league—not by a long shot. Maybe she would change her mind about meeting him—let alone having him stand up with her at her wedding. He wouldn't blame her if she did.

As Charley used to say, "It's all in the cards and how you play them." Isn't that what worried him? DJ thought. Was Keira in the game?

He refused to believe it. He called again and this time left a message. "Where are you?"

Buck opened his eyes to darkness. For a moment, he didn't remember anything—especially where he was. On the floor in a motel room. It took him a moment to adjust to the light coming through the partially cracked blinds. As his memory returned, he rolled over so he could see the bed. Empty. He pushed himself up into a sitting position, his head a little clearer.

He was surprised to realize that his gun was still in his holster. How long had he been out? He checked for his phone. Still in his coat pocket. He hadn't been out that long even though it was now daylight outside—and still snowing, and Keira was gone. He couldn't be sure she'd even been the body he'd seen covered in the bed.

The only thing he knew for sure was that he had a bump on the side of his head the size of a walnut. Nor was there any doubt that Titus Grandville was behind this. He hoped he'd get the chance to return the favor.

As he felt steadier, he got to his feet. Turning on a light, he checked out the motel room. No sign of a struggle. No blood. He checked the bed. It had been slept in, but also no blood. Keira had either been taken—or had walked out on her own.

But whoever had hit him had been expecting company. Had they thought it would be DJ? They must have been disappointed.

He peeked out at the parking lot. His truck was still right outside, but the rest of the parking lot was now empty. The two vehicles he'd seen earlier were gone. Either they had been early-rising guests, or they'd been Grandville's men.

As he started to turn out the light and leave, he felt something in his other coat pocket. He carefully pulled it out. The unsealed envelope had *To DJ* written on the outside.

Buck frowned as he opened the flap and quickly read the contents. Pulling out his phone, he called DJ.

DJ had driven as far as Helena last night. They'd parked in a Walmart lot, sleeping in the back of the SUV. This morning, he and Sadie had eaten breakfast at a local truck stop. Now, not even a mile from the airport, he knew he had to make a decision. He hadn't heard from either Keira or the PI. Both could be dead, although he doubted Grandville would kill Keira—not until he got whatever it was he wanted out of DJ.

Crawford was another story. He'd trusted the man, still did because Sadie did. He just hoped he hadn't gotten the man killed. He was mentally kicking himself for involving other people in this when his phone rang.

With a wave of both concern and relief, he saw it was PI Buck Crawford. He picked up. "Was my sister there?" he asked.

"No."

He listened as the PI told him what had happened when he'd reached the motel room. The news didn't come as a surprise. He'd already figured that Grandville's men had found her. "Are you all right?"

"I'll live," Crawford said. "But apparently she left you a note."

He listened as Crawford read: *"'I saw them looking for me in town. I barely got away. I have no choice. I'm going to meet Luca up at Charley Diamond's cabin in the mountains north of Lonesome.*

Thank you for trying to help me, but I know things didn't go well up in Butte or you would have been back by now. Luca and I are going to head for Alaska. It's only a matter of time before Grandville comes looking for us if we stay here.'"

Keira, no, DJ thought. She was making a huge mistake. He had to stop her, or she'd be running the rest of her life. "Any chance she left directions to the cabin?"

Silence, then Crawford said, "She did." What he didn't say, but DJ heard, were the words "almost as if she was hoping you'd go to the cabin to try to stop her." The PI continued reading. *"'I'd love to see you before we leave. In case you forgot where Charley's cabin is, here's the directions. If we miss each other, thank you again for everything.'"*

"DJ, you have to wonder why she'd leave you the directions to the cabin," Crawford said. "Are you sure you can trust her?"

He felt anger boil up inside him. "She's been like a little sister to me from the time she was just a toddler," he snapped. "Just give me the directions."

Again there was that slight hesitation before the PI read the directions.

"Thanks. Send me a bill," DJ said, hating that Crawford was thinking the same thing he was. If he went to Charley's old cabin outside of Lonesome, he could be walking into a trap—a trap set by someone he loved and thought he could trust with his life.

"You already know it isn't money I want," Crawford said. "Saturday at the only white church in Lonesome. Four o'clock."

He disconnected. He could feel Sadie's gaze on him and see the recrimination in her expression. The PI had done him a favor, gotten his head bashed in, and this was the way DJ repaid it. Of course she'd heard the entire conversation in the confines of the SUV. He could see that she agreed with the PI. Going up to the cabin was a mistake, maybe the last one he'd ever make.

But when she spoke, it was only to say, "So we're going up into the mountains to your uncle's cabin to meet her."

"Not *we*. Just me. I should never have gotten you involved in this. I'm putting you on the next plane to Florida."

"You know that isn't going to happen. I'm going with you because clearly you're determined to see her. You don't believe that she would turn on you and you could be right."

He held her gaze, but words stuck in his throat. He probably wasn't right; that's what hurt. Keira had betrayed him. He knew it and yet he refused to believe it until he heard it from her. And by then, it would be too late.

"I have to know," DJ said, fearing that the bond he and Keira had was never as strong as he'd thought. It was something he didn't want to think about right now. "I also have to try to save her if I can. Grandville will never let her go now."

* * *

Sadie felt her heart break for him. He and Keira weren't really brother and sister, but it didn't matter to DJ if they were blood or not. Some bonds were even stronger.

She could understand his loyalty and love for this girl he'd taken under his wing from an early age. Two children thrown together under strange if not terrifying circumstances. She thought of her own childhood. She'd been alone in an adult world that she knew wasn't normal. Her parents dead after their small private plane had crashed. If it hadn't been for her godfather, who knows what would have happened to her.

Ezra Montclair had taken her in, raised her, taught her the business as if she were the heir to his kingdom. She'd been all alone in that adult world. She would have loved to have another child to be there with her, let alone to watch her back. She'd learned to navigate through the many men who came to see her godfather. She'd learned to be invisible, to listen and learn, to not be a child.

"I envy the relationship you had with her," Sadie said at last. "I would have loved a big brother watching over me like you have Keira."

He said nothing, looking sick for fear he was wrong about her. Worse, that Keira had lied about the debt owed to the Grandvilles knowing he would come back to Montana to help her. If she'd deceived him, she had to know what Titus Grandville would do to DJ. She couldn't be that naive.

"I needed her as much as she needed me," he said. "She gave me a purpose."

Like paying off Uncle Charley's debt, she thought.

Now that debt was paid. Keira in need had become his new purpose. But what after that? she wondered, realizing how driven DJ had been. First it had been just the fight to survive in the world he'd found himself in. Later, it was repaying even a dead Charley for giving him a home, an occupation, a way to survive once he was on his own.

She realized that she and DJ weren't all that different. Both Charley and her godfather had taught them well. They were survivors.

Chapter 12

DJ made his decision. "I need you to go back to Florida." She started to speak, but he stopped her. "Sadie, I'm begging you. I'll take you to the airport so you can catch a flight home. It has to be this way. *Please*."

She shook her head, raising a hand and cutting him off. "I'm not letting you do this alone. You're wounded and you need me. We're partners, remember?"

He shook his head. "That's over. Your godfather and I are square. You and I are square, aren't we?" He held her gaze and saw something so soft and vulnerable that he had to look away. They were so much more than that, he thought as his heart lifted, then fell. Hadn't he wanted desperately to be with this woman—and not just as business partners. Now that they had a chance to be together... "You know I might be walking into a trap that could get me killed."

"Get us killed," she corrected. "But we stand a better chance together, always have. We check out the cabin. If it looks like a setup…" She drew his gaze back to her. "We walk away. Together. One last game. If we realize we can't win it, we throw in our cards and fold. There is no shame in walking away when the odds are against you."

He knew what she was saying. It didn't have to end this way. He had a choice. They had a choice. If he forced her on the plane… His heart ached at the thought that it would be over for them even if Keira hadn't betrayed him, even if he lived to tell about it. He couldn't imagine *never* seeing Sadie again. She would be walking away with a huge chunk of his heart he hadn't even realized he'd given her. But it would kill him if he got her hurt any more than he already had.

"I need to re-bandage that wound," she said as if the discussion was over. For her it was. "If you don't take me with you, I'll rent my own SUV," she said as if reading his mind. "I heard the directions to the cabin. I'm not leaving you, DJ. Not when you need me more than you ever have before. So don't even think about driving off and leaving me the first time I'm out of your sight."

He'd just been planning that exact thing. The thought made him sick inside that he would stoop to tricking her, since he'd always tried to be honest with her. She would go up to the cabin on her own. That kind of loyalty made the thought of Keira betraying him all the more painful. He saw her look around the SUV.

"Do you know what happened to the scarf I had tied on your wound?" she asked.

"I'm sorry. I must have lost it."

"It's not important." She met his gaze. "Keeping you alive is, though."

He couldn't take his eyes off her. The woman had always amazed him, but never as much as she did right now. Yet he couldn't help thinking that she'd picked the wrong horse to put her money on. "You seem to have some fool idea that you can save me from myself. What if you can't, Sadie? What if I've been a lost cause all along?"

She shook her head. "You have a twin sister who'll be standing at the altar soon waiting for her twin brother. You're going to show up and not let her down or die trying. She needs you and you just might need her and the family she's offering you. Now let me see your arm."

Buck called James back at Colt Brothers Investigation the minute he got off the phone with DJ. He quickly told him everything that had happened.

"The man you believe to be Ansley's twin is headed up in the mountains to confront a woman he grew up with and is probably walking into a trap?" James asked. "What is wrong with him?"

"Apparently, DJ and this young woman, Keira, were raised together there on the ranch. He considers her his sister. He doesn't believe she would betray him."

"You told him he might have a twin sister, a real sister by blood?"

"I think he's worried it's a scam," Buck said. "You have to understand, he isn't very trusting and given the way he grew up, I get it. I'm on my way back to Lonesome. I have a scarf I found in my pickup with his blood on it. I'm hoping Willie can get us a DNA sample from it to confirm that DJ Diamond is Ansley's lost brother.

He looks way too much like her not to be. Stubborn to a fault like her, too. Also I followed a trail from Lonesome and the woman who sold the babies to DJ Diamond. It's too much of a coincidence for him not to be the missing twin. The real kicker, though, is that he had the gold bracelet his birth mother had made for him with the initials DJ on it. I get the feeling it's his talisman, his good-luck charm. He's the real deal."

"Where are you headed now?" James asked as if he already suspected Buck's next move.

"As soon as I get back to Lonesome, I'm going to hook up to my snowmobile trailer and head up into the mountains. Keira Diamond Cross left directions to the cabin where she said she'd be waiting. DJ will be coming from the west side of the mountains. I plan to beat him to the cabin. I can't let him walk into a trap."

"Even without the blizzard, the freezing temps and killers possibly waiting at this cabin?"

"I can't let Ansley down." It was more than that. He liked DJ Diamond. He didn't want to see anything happen to him or to the woman with him.

"Getting yourself killed would be much worse than not having her brother at her wedding," James said. "There would be no wedding without you. That's why I'm going with you."

"Me, too," Tommy said, making Buck realize that he'd been on speaker.

"You have a pregnant wife," both Buck and James said at the same time.

"She's not due for a month," Tommy protested. "Stop by my place with the trailer. We'll throw on a couple more snowmobiles. Safety in numbers, you know."

Buck chuckled. "I'm on my way. But one more thing.

DJ has a woman with him, Sadie Montclair. See what you can find out about her."

Sadie checked DJ's wound, cleaned and bandaged his upper arm against his protests that it was just a flesh wound. It had been a clean shot, tearing through skin and flesh and fortunately missing the bone. It had to be painful, but he didn't show it. So like DJ, she thought. The man was the strongest, most determined man she'd ever known. He was also the kindest and surprisingly, the gentlest. His heart was so big, which she knew was why he was in so much emotional pain over Keira. The one thing he wasn't was a lost cause, no matter what he thought. She hoped she could prove that to him before it was too late.

The weather report they heard on the radio was dire. It was still blizzarding across the state. Residents were advised not to travel except in cases of an emergency. Sadie listened to the steady clack of the windshield wipers. They were doing their best but seeming to struggle to keep up. Because of the falling snow and the wind whipping it, visibility was only a matter of yards.

DJ seemed oblivious to the blizzard and the snow-covered road. She watched him drive, his strong hands on the wheel, his expression calm, maybe too calm, his amazing blue eyes intent on what road he could see ahead.

"Florida didn't seem to diminish your winter driving skills," she said, hating that the whirling snow outside the cab was making her nervous. She was born and raised in Florida. She hadn't even seen snow until she was in her teens. She'd never been in a storm like this one. How could something so beautiful be so treacherous?

"Driving in the snow is like falling off a bike," he said.

"I believe the expression is like riding a bike," she corrected, playing along.

He grinned over at her for a second. "We'll be fine. You trust me, don't you?"

She knew he meant more than with his driving in this storm. "I trust you with my life."

He shook his head almost ruefully. "That's what worries me."

A Christmas song came on the radio. He reached over and turned it off.

"What do you have against Christmas?" she asked, feeling a need to fill the silence, but also wanting to know more about this man. All the hours she'd spent with him and yet she knew little of his early life at Charley Diamond's ranch.

"Nothing against Christmas. Just never was something we celebrated at the ranch. Charley said it was a scam." DJ laughed. "He said a lot of things were a scam. He should know."

She laughed. "See, we have even more in common. My godfather didn't celebrate holidays either. Said they were businessmen's trick to play on people's emotions so they felt guilty if they didn't spend more money than they had. I never cared about the present part of Christmas."

For a moment, she watched snow flying around them in a dizzying blur. "But I did love the lights and the decorations. I always felt that there was something special about the season beyond all the commercialism. We

were far from a religious family, but there was something spiritual that I felt at Christmas." She fell silent
before adding with a laugh, "I always wanted a real
Christmas tree. Did you have a Christmas tree at the
ranch?"

"No."

Sadie felt him turn toward her for a second before
going back to his driving.

After a few minutes, she realized she wasn't getting
any more out of him. They drove through the whiteout
with only the clack of the wipers and the hum of the
heater. She kept losing sight of the road ahead. She felt
as if they were driving into a wall of white with no idea
of what was on the other side. The snow had a claustrophobic quality, no longer as beautiful as she'd first
thought. It now felt dangerous.

The weather report on the radio continued to get
worse. Many of the highways were closed due to a lack
of visibility. The snow kept getting deeper on the highway. She realized that she couldn't remember the last
time she'd seen a car go by, let alone a snowplow.

Through a break in the whirling snow, she saw a
sign. DJ slowed and turned onto a narrower road. This
one led up higher into the mountains. The snow quickly
got deeper. The SUV broke through the drifts that the
wind had sculpted, sending a shower of white flakes
up over the windshield.

Sadie was relieved that DJ seemed to know how to
maneuver in the deep snow filling the narrow road.
That wasn't what had her worried, though. It was why
he was driving in a blizzard when roads were closing,
drivers were told to stay home, plows couldn't keep up.

This part of the state was closing down and yet DJ kept going as if racing toward his destiny.

She'd seen determination in him many times before, but not like this. She could only hope that Keira had been telling the truth. She and her husband might already be on their way to Alaska. What would DJ do if he missed them? Would that be enough proof that Keira hadn't betrayed him?

The road wound up the mountain. The wind was reduced with the thick pines on each side of the road so the snow wasn't as drifted. They kept climbing. Sadie remembered being in awe of the winter wonderland DJ had brought her to. Now it had a lethal quality that unnerved her. It was bad enough that they were probably driving into a trap—and that's if they survived the blizzard and the drive up this mountain.

You trust me, don't you? DJ had asked.

I trust you with my life.

"It should be right up here," DJ said as they topped a small hill and he turned up an even more narrow road. He started up it. They hadn't gone far when she heard a spinning sound as the tires fought to find traction—and failed.

The SUV came to a stop. DJ tried to get it going again, but the whine of the tires told her that they weren't going any farther. DJ backed up and made a run at the hill. The same thing happened: tires spun, no traction. Only this time, the pickup slid off the road, and the driver's side dropped into what appeared to be a narrow ditch—not that she could tell with the snow so deep.

"Stay here." He jumped out, leaving the engine running, the heater cranked. He was out of the SUV, cold rushing in as he exited, then he disappeared into the storm. Sadie hugged herself and waited, not sure where he had gone. To see how stuck they were? But when he didn't return, she began to worry. What if something happened and he didn't come back? The thought raced past, kicking up her pulse and making her stomach churn. She was completely out of her element. How long could she survive out here? She quickly shoved the thought away. DJ would come back. If he could.

She checked to see how much gas they had. Less than half a tank. She reached over and turned the key. The engine stopped and so did the heater. An eerie, deafening quiet filled the vehicle. She felt the cold surround the SUV and begin making its way in. Moments ago, it had been almost too warm. She shivered, realizing she wouldn't survive long if DJ didn't make it back.

The air inside the truck was getting colder by the second. How long had she been sitting here? How long had DJ been gone?

She tried to see outside. The wind would occasionally part the falling snow enough that she could see pine trees. Had they reached the cabin where he was to meet Keira? Surely he wouldn't have gone in to face Keira alone knowing he could be walking into a trap! She should have jumped out and gone with him, but he hadn't given her a chance.

But even as she thought it, she knew that was exactly what he would do to protect her. She buttoned up her coat and reached for her scarf before she remembered that she'd used it to put over DJ's wound and he'd lost it somewhere. She must not have tied it tight enough.

She dressed as warmly as she could manage; still, she hesitated. Should she go after him? She wasn't even sure which way he'd gone or if this was the road to the cabin. Leaving the pickup seemed like a bad idea since the alternative was to go out into the snow and cold. Snow had accumulated on the windshield. Soon she wouldn't be able to see out.

She reached for the door handle and stopped. Through a break in the falling snow, she caught movement. She held her breath, unsure what was up here in these woods. Animal? Or human?

Her heart bumped hard against her ribs as DJ appeared out of the storm. Relief made her weak for a moment as he opened the door and climbed in.

For a startled moment, she didn't recognize him with his hair and coat covered with snow. Flakes clung to his long dark lashes. "Are we— Is this—"

He must have seen her relief and her fear. "Sorry, I didn't mean to leave you alone for so long. Charley's cabin is on up the road about halfway up the mountain."

"Keira?"

He shook his head. "But someone's been here. There is food and firewood. I found a branding iron with the Diamond Deluxe, a diamond shape with a D inside. I hurried up and built a fire so it would be warmer for you once we climb up the mountainside. It's a pretty good hike up."

"No problem," she said without hesitation. Anywhere was better after sitting here thinking the worst might have happened.

"We'll be warm and dry. I saw older tracks in the snow. I might have already missed her. Otherwise..."

Otherwise, she could be coming once the storm passed, he didn't say, but she knew what he meant. He pulled the SUV key and met her gaze. "Don't worry. I've got everything covered."

She'd heard these words before, so they didn't give her much assurance. The thing about DJ Diamond, though, was when things went south, he always came up with a backup plan. Whether he'd thought of it before things went bad or not was debatable. But he'd always managed to save them. She just hoped he hadn't met his match this time as she climbed out into the Montana blizzard.

Buck heard the relief in Ainsley's voice the moment she answered the phone. "Are you all right? I've been so worried about you."

"I'm fine. I'm sorry I haven't called sooner." There was no way he was getting into everything that had happened since he'd last seen her. Eventually, Ansley would know most of it.

"Did you find him?" Her voice cracked. He could hear the hope and felt his heart break for her. He'd wanted so badly to have good news for her.

"I think I've found him, but we won't know for sure until we get the DNA results."

"That's wonderful news," she cried. She sounded so relieved. She really did have her heart set on him giving her away at the wedding. He wished he could have talked her into putting off the ceremony until spring, but she'd wanted a Christmas wedding and he would give her anything.

He told her what he'd learned and about going out to the Diamond Deluxe Ranch and what he'd found out there.

"His name is DJ Diamond?" she said. "It has to be

him if he had the gold bracelet our mother had made for him. And he grew up on a ranch, that's great."

He didn't know how to tell her. It was one reason he hadn't called until now. He'd put it off, telling himself he wanted to be sure that DJ Diamond was indeed her twin. But the truth was he didn't know how to tell her about the life her twin might have lived.

"It wasn't that kind of ranch," he told her now. They were about to start their lives together. He didn't want there to be any lies between them. She needed to know the truth, as hard as it was going to be to tell her—let alone for her to hear. He told her about everything that he'd learned. For a moment there was only silence on the line. "Ainsley, are you there?"

"You're saying he's a criminal?"

"No. Maybe. I'm not sure. He was raised by an uncle who was a conman who apparently taught him everything he knows. From what I can tell he makes his living gambling."

"What aren't you telling me, Buck?"

He sighed. "Right now DJ's on the run after a poker game went badly. He has a friend who's in trouble and he's determined to save her. James, Tommy and I are going after him, but we aren't the only ones anxious to catch up to him and this friend of his he grew up with. There are some powerful men also after him. I don't want to upset you, but I think we should postpone the wedding."

Chapter 13

On the climb up the mountainside to the cabin, DJ mentally kicked himself. Sadie should be winging her way to the sunny shores of Florida right now—not trudging through thigh-high snow with him. He should have been more insistent. As if that would have changed her mind. He imagined himself physically putting her on a plane home. That was just as ridiculous as thinking he could make her do anything she didn't want to do.

But bringing her up here… A gust of wind whirled fresh snow around him. He caught a glimpse of the cabin above them almost hidden in the tall pines.

"A little longer and we'll be there," he said to her as he stopped to let them both catch their breath. They were used to Florida and sea level. He looked at her, trying to gauge how she was doing—and not just from the climb. He'd gotten her into this, something he deeply regretted. It was bad enough that he'd been possibly tricked into coming back here—let alone that he'd dragged Sadie into it. He couldn't bear the thought that Keira had purposely drawn him back to Montana on a lie so that Grandville could get retribution for some old grudge.

Pushing the nagging thought away, he said, "You doing okay?"

"I'm good," she said, and flashed him a smile. It wasn't one of her brilliant, knock-a-man-for-a-loop smiles. This one was part worry, part sympathy. He wanted to tell her that he'd be fine no matter what he found out, but he couldn't lie to her because she would see right through it. If Keira had turned on him... He hated to think of the pain it would cause. That's if she didn't get him killed.

"It's not far now," he said.

"Lead the way, partner."

A few minutes later, they waded through the drifted snow up onto the porch. As he opened the front door of the cabin, he gave a slight bow and waved her inside. He had no idea how long they would be here. At least until the storm passed. Where was Keira? Had she gotten caught in the storm? And what about the Grandvilles? Were they on their way as well?

Keira had chosen the perfect isolated place in the mountains for her husband to hide out. It was also a perfect place to get rid of someone. Bodies often didn't turn up for years in these woods. He tried not to think about what might happen if Keira showed up. If she was telling the truth, she and Luca might already be headed for Alaska. He realized he might never see her again if that was the case.

Or she and Luca might be planning a visit to the cabin—just waiting for him to arrive. Keira knew him. She would know that he would come to the cabin. Wasn't that why she'd left the note?

His head hurt thinking about it. He could no more see the future than flap his arms and fly. Yet his gut told him he couldn't trust her. Maybe he never could.

He looked over at Sadie, fighting the feeling that they were sitting ducks and hunting season was about to open.

Sadie stepped into the cabin and glanced around as DJ closed the door behind them. She'd caught the scent of smoke the last half dozen yards up the mountain and now welcomed just being out of the storm.

A fire crackled in an old rock fireplace against the right wall, but from what she could tell, it wasn't putting out all that much heat yet. She beat the snow off her boots before she stepped toward the heat and took in the rest of the cabin.

It was compact and open. The living area consisted of the fireplace, two upholstered chairs and a kindling box sitting open. Inside it, she could see twigs and pine cones, old newspapers and matches. Turning behind her, she saw what served as the kitchen. It consisted of a sink with a bucket under it. A propane stove and an old icebox-type refrigerator. Pots and pans hung over a small cabinet that she assumed held utensils and possibly flatware.

DJ was right. It appeared someone had been here recently. She saw a package of store-bought cookies open on the top of the cabinet. "No electricity, right?" she asked as she peeled off her gloves to hold her hands up to the fire. Her fingers ached from the cold. So did her cheeks.

"No electric, no cell service, no internet," DJ said, "but there is a root cellar–type enclosure in the back against the mountainside with canned food that isn't frozen. There is also a stove with a propane tank and a pile of dry wood under a shed roof on the side of the cabin. We won't starve and we won't freeze."

She couldn't help but smile at him as she took in the rest of the cabin. She suspected DJ often looked for a silver lining in even the darkest of clouds. There was a back door with some storage along the wall. To the right of that was a double bed taking up the corner of the room near the fireplace.

As she began to warm up, she took off her coat and dropped it into one of the chairs. She saw that they had tracked in snow, but she wasn't ready to take off her boots. Her toes were just starting to warm up.

DJ threw some more wood on the fire. She could feel the heat go to her face. Her fingers and toes began to tingle, then sting. Her cheeks ached, but she began to relax. They were safe for the moment and as he'd said, they wouldn't starve or freeze. That was enough for now.

"Not bad, huh," DJ said, and grinned.

Partners to the end, she thought. "Not bad."

He turned toward the cupboard over the stove. "Let's see what there is to eat. I don't know about you, but I'm hungry after that hike."

Titus Grandville stared out at the snowstorm in disgust before spinning his office chair back around to face the two men standing there with their hats in their hands.

"Let me see if I've got this straight," Titus said, trying to keep his voice down. "You lost Diamond, you lost the money and now…" His voice began to rise. "You say you can't go find him and the money and finish this because it's snowing too much?"

Rafe Westfall looked at him wide-eyed. "It's a *blizzard*. Some of the roads are closed. How are we supposed to—"

"We'll find him," Butch Lamar said. "We know Diamond's headed up into the mountains. Keira left him a note with directions to Charley's old cabin. She swears that Diamond will show. If she isn't worried, why should we be?"

Titus swore. "Because you're standing in my office, dripping melted snow all over my floor instead of being up in the mountains waiting for him."

"We're going to need snowmobiles," Butch said. "There's no way anyone is driving very far in the mountains right now. We'll find him. We're taking Lloyd with us. But what do you want us to do about the woman with him?" The banker gave him an impatient look. "We'll take care of all of it," Butch said quickly. "Don't we always?"

Titus could have argued further, but it would have been a waste of time. "Diamond thinks he can come into my town and make a fool out of me? I don't want him or his girlfriend coming out of those mountains. Is that understood? By spring there should be not enough left of his body to know how he died, right?"

Rafe nodded. "The animals will see to that."

"Make sure you dump the remains where some horn hunter doesn't stumble across them this spring."

"You got it," Butch said. "We'll let you know when it's done."

Titus shooed them out of his office and told his secretary to get maintenance to come up and clean up the mess the two had made. Then he sat back and looked out at the whirling snow again.

His father wasn't going to like this. Then again, Marcus didn't like the way he ran much about the business. It was time for Marcus to step down, but the old fool was healthy and stubborn and still thought he was running things.

"This kid was Charley Diamond's protégé. His legacy. Hell, practically his flesh-and-blood heir," Marcus Grandville had said on the call this morning. "So he outsmarted you last night and walked away with the poker money. Cut your losses. I'm warning you. We don't want him coming back to Butte. From what I've heard, he's in a position where he could do great harm to our business."

Titus still didn't believe that. Diamond was a cheap conman. But even if he did believe it, things had progressed such that it was too late. He had Keira Cross right where he wanted her and thus he had DJ. He couldn't tell his father that the reason he wanted DJ dead had little to do with the money lost last night or even the embarrassment of DJ getting the better of him. No, this went way back to when he was a kid. Humiliation was something that had stuck with him all these years—and DJ Diamond had witnessed it.

Now it was just a matter of finishing this. Then he

would run the business as he saw fit. But he wondered if it would be possible as long as his father was alive.

"Are you sure I can't help?" Sadie asked as she heard DJ banging pots and pans in the tiny kitchen behind her. He'd told her to just take a seat in front of the fire, warm up and relax. He was going to cook.

"You cook?" she'd questioned.

"I can cook," he'd assured her. "But this will be more a case of opening canned goods.

"I've got everything under control," he called back now.

She stared into the flames, wondering how true that was. If what Lloyd had told him was true, Keira had set DJ up. Meeting her up here in the mountains seemed like a death wish. Was DJ really that sure he could trust this girl he'd called his little sister?

She thought about PI Buck Crawford. She didn't doubt that it was true, DJ had a twin sister. She knew there was more to the story. Hadn't the PI said that DJ and his twin's mother had thought both babies had died? That they'd later been given away? Sadie just hoped there was some good news to be had with his biological family. She wasn't sure how much more bad DJ could take—especially if Keira betrayed him.

"I hope you're hungry," he said from behind her, startling her out of her thoughts. She caught a whiff of something that smelled wonderful and felt her stomach rumble. "It's my own concoction. I hope you like it."

He handed her a bowl and spoon. "It's a can of spaghetti mixed with a can of chili. I added a few spices I found." He sounded so eager as he waited for her to take a bite.

She breathed in the rather unusual mixed scents, filled her spoon and took a bite. Surprisingly the canned spaghetti and the chili actually went together. "This is delicious."

"Don't sound so shocked," he joked.

She took another bite. "Seriously, it's really good."

He laughed, shaking his head before returning to the kitchen to load his own bowl. He joined her in front of the fire in the opposite chair. "You really like it?"

"I love it. I hadn't realized how hungry I was until I tasted it."

She could see that he was pleased as he began to eat his. They ate in a companionable silence. The only sound the occasional crackle of the fire. Outside, the snow continued to fall as if it were never going to stop. She could see flakes fly by the window, whirling through the pines outside. Sometimes she heard the soft moan of the wind. Outside there was only white. With a start she realized something. They were snowed in here. Trapped.

The thought startled her until she reminded herself that if they couldn't leave, then no one could get to them. The rental SUV was down the mountain, blocking the road. She couldn't help but wonder. Where was Keira?

As she finished her dinner, DJ offered her more, but she shook her head, pleasantly full. He took her spoon and bowl and went to finish off what he'd made. She found herself lulled by the crackling fire, the warmth, the fullness in her stomach.

It felt so pleasantly domestic that she could almost forget why they were here in this cabin and what they would be facing when the storm stopped. As she glanced over at DJ, she wanted to pretend that they had stumbled onto a magical cabin and they could stay here forever, safe from a dangerous outside world. In here, no one could hurt them.

Childish wishing, she thought. There were no magical cabins, no place safe from the dangerous outside world because of the life they both had lived—and were still living. Was she kidding herself that she could stop doing this? Just get off, like climbing from a merry-go-round? Could DJ?

Otherwise, *they* were that dangerous world.

Marcus Grandville kept going over his morning conversation with his son. The fool had authorized a poker game with DJ Diamond and two of Titus's men. The PI Marcus had met got involved. DJ walked away with the money after besting Titus's men.

"What kind of foolishness was this?" Marcus had demanded. "I told you to settle and get him out of town. What about that didn't you understand, Titus?"

"I couldn't just let this bastard come into town, set up a poker game, take us to the cleaners and walk away. One of your associates, Frank Burns, was in the game. DJ was thumbing his nose at us."

"So what?"

"You're beginning to get soft in your old age if you'd let a Diamond come into our town and do whatever he damned well pleases."

"Oh, and you handled it so much better? DJ Diamond did exactly what he planned and now he's left town after rubbing your face in it. Isn't that why you're so upset? You thought you could outsmart him and you failed."

"He hasn't gotten away," Titus said. "I have him right

where I want him. I have Keira Cross, the woman he calls his little sister. I have her and therefore, I have Diamond."

"What are you talking about?"

"I'm using her to get DJ. I know exactly where he's headed and when he gets there, I'm going to make sure that he never comes back to Butte again."

Marcus shook his head, thinking now that he should have tried to talk his son out of this plan. Titus had always been a hothead. He didn't understand business, legit business; he never would. He wanted to be the tough guy, the schoolyard bully. He didn't even know how to pick his fights.

Now he'd sent Rafe, Butch and Lloyd into the mountains. Marcus knew what that meant. Titus wouldn't be happy until Diamond was dead. He swore under his breath as more of the conversation got under his skin.

"You used to let Charley run all over you. I'm not going to let DJ Diamond run roughshod over me."

Marcus shook his head. Titus could never understand the respect he and Charley Diamond had for each other. "I let him run his small-time cons in my town. Because I knew that he could never hurt me unless I did something stupid and tried to keep him from making a living here. You never learned how to make deals because you always have to win. You think I've gone soft? I'm washing my hands of this whole mess. You're on your own just like you've always wanted. If you're looking for my blessing, you're not getting it. You're making a huge mistake. Probably your last."

Now he regretted his words. He feared for his son. Worse for what this might do to the Grandville name—and their business. Titus was a fool, and he was about to prove it to the world.

DJ finished eating the rest of what he'd made, then cleaned up the dishes in the water he'd heated on the stove. He couldn't help smiling. He could see Charley in this cabin. It was comfortable and yet simple, like Charley himself. Why his uncle had never told him about the place still surprised him. Especially since Keira knew about it.

He pushed the thought away as he finished the dishes, dried them and put them away. Returning to the fire, he found Sadie sound asleep. He stared down at her, feeling a wave of affection for her that threatened to drop him to his knees. When had he fallen in love with her?

He felt blindsided. All that time when he'd been flirting and joking with her knowing she only saw him as an arrogant fool, she'd somehow sneaked into his heart and made a home there. She was right. He was a fool.

Leaning down, he kissed her forehead, then carefully, he picked her up and carried her the few feet to the double bed. He took off her boots and covered her with several of the extra quilts on a rack by the bed. She stirred a little but went right back to sleep. It had been a long, exhausting day, after a long, uncomfortable night in the back of the SUV.

For a moment, he watched her sleep. She looked so peaceful, as if she didn't have a care in the world. He realized that he didn't know if she had a man in her life. He knew she lived in a penthouse condo next to the ocean, that she drove a nice car that she'd bought with money she'd earned herself, that she had Sunday dinner with her godfather each week and that she didn't like the mustache DJ had grown shortly after they'd first met. He'd shaved it off before the next time he saw her. But that's about all he knew about her.

Turning away, he went back to the fire. He was exhausted but knew he wouldn't be able to sleep. His heart ached for so many reasons. Now he felt as if he'd come to a crossroads in his life. He could keep looking back at the paths he'd taken or he could look to the future— a far different future than he had ever imagined.

Was it possible that he had a twin sister? Ansley Brookshire. A blood relative. And he had a mother who'd believed that both he and Ansley had died at birth. And family, half siblings.

For so long he'd wondered who he was and why no one had wanted him, thankful that Charley had taken him in when he had no one else. If true that Ansley was his twin, it brought up a lot of questions. Like what had happened to separate them? Where was their mother? Why hadn't someone come looking for him sooner?

He realized he wasn't all that sure he wanted to know the answers. Maybe it would be better not to know the truth.

He glanced over at Sadie sleeping on the bed. Partners. More than partners. Did she feel the same way about him that he felt about her?

His beating heart assured him she had to. Why else was she here risking her life to help him?

He thought about Keira and questioned why he had to know the truth. Why he had to face her. He would be facing his past. If she'd betrayed him, then nothing had been as he'd thought.

Once the storm stopped, he would know the truth.

If Keira had betrayed him, she might not even come to the cabin. Instead the Grandvilles' thugs, Butch Lamar and Rafe Westfall, would. He told himself that right now they would have the same problem he did, so he didn't expect them until the storm blew through. According to the weatherman the last they'd heard on the radio, the storm wasn't supposed to let up until the day after tomorrow.

So they had time, he told himself. He had time to decide what to do.

He'd always had a different idea about what made up family. Not blood. Not love. Not even loyalty. Family had been Charley and Keira. At best, he'd hoped they would have his back. Now, he feared both would have sold him out to save their own skins. And that could be exactly what Keira had done.

Either way, he couldn't worry about it now, he thought as he rose and stepped out on the porch. He listened as the snow blew past. Absolute silence. No sound of a vehicle. Nothing but the whisper of wind blowing the falling snow. He could feel the temperature dropping as he went around the side of the cabin to get more firewood. It would be a long night.

He was just glad he'd found this cabin. He didn't think they would have survived in the pickup even with the engine running and the heater going. They would have run out of gas, run out of hope, fairly soon. He told himself he could relax a little as he went back inside. Sadie was safe.

Now all he had to do was keep her that way.

Chapter 14

Buck had been sure he could beat DJ and Sadie up to the cabin. He and the Colts had the shorter drive if they were anywhere around Butte, but DJ had also gotten a head start. But as they had just started up in the mountains a tire blew on the snowmobile trailer. They had to take the machines off to fix it. They'd lost any chance they had at getting to the cabin before DJ, and now it was getting dark.

The conditions had been worse than even he and Tommy and James had thought they would be—especially in the dark, but no one suggested turning back. It became apparent quickly that once they reached the mountains, they wouldn't make it all the way to Charley's cabin.

"Don't Francis and Bob Reiner have a cabin up here?" James had asked.

Buck tried to calculate where they were. "Not far ahead." His pickup was bucking snowdrifts. It wouldn't be that long before they couldn't go any farther by truck. They'd have to take the snowmobiles, but not in this storm in the dark. In his headlights, he could barely make out the narrow road through the pines.

"Watch for the sign," he said. "We can spend the night there and try again in the morning. DJ is going to be having the same problem on the other side."

They'd gone a few miles when Tommy said, "There's the sign."

Buck turned and drove up the road toward the cabin, but he didn't get far before the truck high-centered on a huge drift. The wind whipped snow around them as he shut off the engine.

"That's as far as we're going," he said, afraid this had been a mistake. He hadn't been surprised when James and Tommy had insisted on coming along. Sheriff Willie Colt was standing by, offering a helicopter when the storm stopped, if needed. So far no crime had been committed. Buck was hoping to end this without gunplay, but that would depend on what they found up here on this mountain.

They grabbed their gear and started up through the whirling snow, breaking through drifts, until they reached the front door of the cabin. The Reiners never locked the front door, saying they'd rather not have anyone break in. They didn't keep guns or liquor, and nothing worth carting out of the mountains to pawn. They'd never had a break-in or anything stolen.

James opened the door as Buck grabbed a load of firewood from the overhang on the porch. Within minutes they had a fire going in the woodstove.

"I can tell you're having second thoughts," James said after they'd eaten one of the sandwiches Lori had sent.

"I should have come alone," Buck said.

"Wasn't going to happen, so get over it. If you feel really bad, you can take one of the kid bunk beds. I'm going for the double bed in the only adult-sized bedroom," James said with a grin. "Looks like Tommy has already taken the couch." Tommy was sprawled out trying to get a bar on his phone.

"You can take the truck back in the morning," Buck told him.

"I'm not worried about Bella," Tommy denied. "Baby's not due for a month and you know Bella, she wouldn't want me worrying. Just wanted to check in, that's all." Buck and James exchanged a look.

"Just in case you are worried in the morning, take the truck. Charley's cabin isn't that far by snowmobile. I am wondering if Keira Diamond Cross didn't get us all up here on a fool's errand while she's on her way to Alaska."

"That could be the best scenario," James said.

"Maybe for her. That still leaves DJ to deal with the Grandvilles if I'm right and this woman he calls his little sister set him up."

"I guess we'll find out tomorrow," James said, and yawned. "Try to get some sleep. Tomorrow could be a busy, eventful day."

Sadie woke to the smell of something frying. She opened her eyes to see DJ at the small stove. It felt too early to wake up and yet there was DJ with a pancake turner in his hand humming softly as he cooked whatever was sizzling in that huge cast-iron skillet.

Next to the bed, she could see that there was fresh wood on the fire. How long had he been up? Or had he ever come to bed? She tried to remember going to bed and couldn't.

Had DJ put her under the covers last night? She threw back the heavy quilts covering her, not surprised to see that she was fully clothed. DJ wouldn't have taken advantage of her exhaustion. No, he had a code of honor that he followed. The thought touched her, warming her heart.

If he wanted to bed her, he'd seduce her. The thought made her swallow as she saw her boots were positioned next to each other beside the bed and slipped them on.

"Is that breakfast I smell?" she said, walking the few yards into the kitchen. It was still storming outside. She couldn't see anything but snow through the windows, as if the cabin had been wrapped in cotton.

"Hey, sleeping beauty. I wondered if you planned to sleep all day." He was grinning, those blue eyes of his bright in the white light coming through the windows. Looking at him, it was as if he didn't have a care in the world except what to cook next. She could see that he felt at home here as basic as the place was. That, too, made her smile.

"What is that?" she asked, taking in what was frying in the skillet.

"Are you telling me that you've never had Spam?"

"I've never heard of it," she said skeptically.

"Well, then you are in for a treat."

He was giving her the hard sell, which was making

her even more skeptical. *"You made flour tortillas?"* This man continued to amaze her.

His grin broadened. "I found flour in an airtight canister and canned shortening and salt. Voilà! Flour tortillas and Spam and canned salsa. This morning, we feast. Shall I make you a Diamond burrito?"

She nodded, laughing as she did. "I'm guessing this isn't your first time eating canned meat."

His grin faded a little as he shook his head. "We could sit at the kitchen table," he suggested, nodding toward a folding table and chairs that he'd set up near the front door.

She hadn't noticed. But she did notice that it looked like fresh blood on his shirtsleeve. "Right after breakfast, I need to re-bandage your arm." He started to argue but she talked over him. "I'm sure I can find something to use here in the cabin."

"There's a first aid kit in the top drawer over there," he said, nodding in the direction of the cabinets along the wall to the back door. She marveled at how he'd made himself at home. It made her wonder about the man he called Uncle Charley. Apparently they had a lot in common.

Buck awoke in the middle of the night to snow. He'd hoped that the storm would have stopped. It hadn't. He heard Tommy and James moving somewhere in the cabin. He tried his cell phone. No service. According to his calculations, they still had a way to go before they reached Charley Diamond's cabin. He had no idea if DJ and Sadie had made it there. Or what they had found if they had. His stomach churned at the thought that he might be too late.

James had been subdued last night. Tommy seemed restless. Was he worried about Bella? Bringing them along had been a mistake, Buck told himself, then was reminded how much trouble he would have had changing that tire last night in the storm if he'd been alone.

"You two okay?" he asked as they began to put on their warm clothes to leave.

"Let's do this," James said, and looked at his brother. Tommy nodded.

"It's only a half mile up the road before the turn to the cabin. I doubt we'll get that far before we have to unload the snowmobiles and go the rest of the way on them. With luck, DJ and Sadie are still okay."

Both looked solemn as he glanced outside. All he could see was white. Out of the corner of his eye, he saw James check his weapon. Tommy did the same. Buck had already made sure his was loaded, even though he didn't want any gunplay.

But he'd heard stories about the Grandvilles and the men who worked for the family. DJ had already been shot. Guns were a part of this world—and the one Buck now considered his new career as a PI. Most private investigators, though, didn't even carry guns. Few had ever been forced to use them.

Unfortunately, Buck feared today would not be one of those days.

That's when he heard the buzz of snowmobiles. More than one. All headed their way.

DJ handed Sadie a plate with her burrito on it. "I gave you extra salsa. I know how you love your hot peppers." His grin was back and she tried to relax, telling herself that they wouldn't be up here in the mountains all that long. Once they reached civilization again, she'd insist he have his wound checked out. She worried it would get infected. Better to worry about a flesh wound than what might happen before they got off this mountain.

If she had to, she'd call her godfather. He'd know someone who knew someone who knew someone who would check out the gunshot wound and not report it. Not that she wanted her godfather to know where she was and why. He wouldn't like it, that much she knew.

"Keep it professional," he'd warned her. "DJ Diamond will make a great partner for what I have him doing, but beyond that…" He shook his head. "He's not boyfriend material, so don't get too attached."

At that time, she hadn't met DJ yet and had rolled her eyes. "You don't have to worry. I won't touch him with a ten-foot pole."

Her godfather, who had already met DJ, had said, "Keep it that way. I've been told he has an irresistible charm that's like catnip for women. I hear you're falling for his routine, and I'll put someone else with him."

She'd been fine with that at the time. Now she knew that no one could have done the job she and DJ had for her godfather. Her godfather knew it, too. He'd just assumed now that DJ had paid off his uncle Charley's debt that his goddaughter wouldn't be seeing the young Diamond again. She'd let her godfather believe that because she'd thought it was probably true. Once she told DJ that his bill was paid in full, he'd be gone.

Sadie hadn't admitted to herself, let alone DJ or her godfather, that it was the last thing she wanted. She had more than a soft spot for the cowboy.

"Well?" DJ asked. When she didn't immediately respond, he glanced at her plate and the half-eaten burrito on it. She hadn't even realized that she'd taken a bite. Half of it was already gone.

"Delicious. Sorry, I was just enjoying it. Do you need me to tell you that you're a great cook?"

He was eyeing her as if he'd seen that her mind had been miles away. "Great, huh?"

"Great," she said and ducked her head to take another bite. "I'm a Spam fan now."

"Good to hear, since we might be eating a lot of it, depending on when this storm lets up. But I hope you know that I can see through any lie that comes out of that mouth of yours," he said quietly, his gaze on her mouth.

She swallowed the bite of burrito, her cheeks heating under the directness of his look.

Sadie heard it about the same time as DJ did. He set down his plate and was on his feet in an instant. By the time he reached the front window, she was beside him. "Someone's coming, aren't they?"

"Stay here." He pulled on his coat, one of the weapons in his hand as he went out the front door, closing it behind him, before he stepped off the porch and disappeared into the falling snow.

DJ didn't go far before he stopped to listen. He could hear the whine of the snowmobiles somewhere on the mountain. It didn't sound close, but it was hard to tell.

Who was it? Keira? Or someone else foolish enough to try to get to their cabin in this storm? Someone like Butch Lamar and Rafe Westfall? Not Titus. He didn't do his own dirty work.

It had sounded as if the machines were busting through snowdrifts. He waited for the buzz to get louder, signifying that they were headed this way. But that didn't happen. The sound died off. They weren't headed here. At least not yet, he thought as he went to the woodpile.

But now he was on alert. It had felt as if they were alone on the mountain. Just the two of them. And he'd liked it. Liked it a lot more than he'd wanted to admit. Now he feared they didn't have that much more time together.

Sadie looked up expectantly when he came through the door. She'd taken their plates to the sink and was washing them. But next to her on the counter was her gun, fully loaded, he knew.

"Whoever it was didn't come this way." He was relieved. He wanted this time before seeing Keira. He realized that he also wanted this time with Sadie.

"You think they were looking for us?" she asked.

"Didn't sound like it. Our tracks would have been covered and they wouldn't have been able to see the SUV up here hidden in the pines and snow. As long as it's snowing, I doubt they'd be able to see the smoke from our fire." Unless they stopped, got out and smelled it.

He saw her visibly relax as he took off his boots and coat and hung them up, his gun tucked in the back of his jeans. The other gun he'd taken from Rafe and Butch was on the mantel behind a large wooden vase. Both were loaded if needed. He hoped it wouldn't come to that, but then again he couldn't imagine any other way out of this. If the Grandvilles' thugs showed up, then Keira had to be in on the setup—even if she didn't show herself.

"Thanks for breakfast," Sadie said, drying her hands

on a paper towel. "Where did you say I could find that first aid kit?"

"First, I brought you something."

She frowned quizzically. "At the local convenience store you stopped at on your way back in the cabin?"

"Something like that. It's right outside the door on the porch."

Sadie was still giving him a questioning look as she stepped to the door, opened and saw a small evergreen tree leaning against the side of the cabin.

"I thought it was small enough that we could find something to decorate it with around the cabin."

She turned to stare at him. "A real Christmas tree."

He shrugged. "You said you never had one. I found an axe near the woodpile and since it is the season…"

Tears welled in her eyes, and he felt his heart ache. It had been impulsive and such a small thing to him, but so much more to her. "DJ."

He heard so much in those two letters. He cleared his throat. "I'll make a stand for it."

"Thank you."

He could only shrug again, half afraid of what he'd say—let alone do—seeing the emotion in her eyes.

He'd cut her a Christmas tree. Sadie feared she would cry if she tried to speak so she could only nod as she closed the door. His thoughtfulness was almost her undoing. She went back to the fire, warmed her hands and steadied herself before she asked, "Where did you say that first aid kit was?"

She was surprised to find that her hands were trembling as she opened the box with the red cross on it. DJ had taken off his shirt. She'd seen him without one enough times, but seeing him half-naked in the close confines of the small cabin made it much more intimate.

Sadie tried to concentrate as she took off the old makeshift bandage. She could feel DJ watching her closely. She cleaned and gently put antiseptic on the wound before she re-bandaged it. Closing the first aid kit, she started to stand to return it to the cabinet when DJ laid a hand on her arm.

She froze as his touch sent a bolt of electricity charging through her at the speed of lightning before it settled in her center. She tried to breathe but it made her chest hurt.

"Sadie." He'd never said her name like that. Low, husky, loaded with a jolt of emotion that she recognized even though she'd never felt it with such intensity.

She slowly raised her gaze to his. What she saw in those unusually pale blue eyes made her heart kickstart. She let out the breath. She hadn't realized that she'd still been holding the first aid kit as DJ took it from her and set it aside.

Her mouth went dry as he locked eyes with her. She tried to swallow as he rose and gently pulled her closer. She wanted to drag her gaze from his. She wanted to pull away, but all the reasons this was a bad idea evaded her. She wanted this, and from the look in his eyes, he wanted it just as desperately.

Drawing her closer, he bent to tenderly kiss her. Her lips parted of their own accord and she heard a soft moan escape him. He dragged her to him, the look in his eyes telegraphing the message *Stop. Me. At. Any. Time.*

But stopping him was the last thing she wanted. He pulled her against him, her soft to his hard, and then they were kissing like lovers. His hands slid down her back to her behind. He cupped her, pulling her against him. She heard his moan.

He drew back to look at her. She could see he was begging her to stop him. He didn't want to hurt her. He didn't want her to just be another of the women he'd bedded and walked away from.

"If you stop now, I will never forgive you," she said, her voice breaking.

He shook his head. "You have no idea how long I have wanted this. Wanted you."

"So what's stopping you?"

He chuckled. "Your godfather will kill me. But he'll have to wait in line." He swept her up into his arms and carried her over to the bed. The moment he set her down, she pulled him down with her. The kiss was all heat. Their tongues met, teased, then took. They tore at each other's clothes in reckless abandonment.

There was no turning back as he bent over her breasts, sucking, nipping, teasing with his tongue. Outside the wind howled at the eaves, the snow fell as if never going to stop, and inside DJ made love to her as if there might not be a tomorrow. Later, after they were curled together trying to catch their breaths, he whispered next to her, "You intrigued me from the first time I laid eyes on you. Then I got to know you."

She chuckled as she turned to him. "I could take that a number of ways."

"You were pretty and smart and sexy as all get-out. Sitting across from you all those nights, I wanted you, but I also wanted more than anything I'd ever had with another woman." His gaze met hers and held. "When you got off that plane the other day... I knew. I love you, Sadie Montclair."

"You don't have to say that."

"I've never said it to another woman—even at gunpoint. I wasn't sure how much longer I could work with you and not…step over a line that would end it."

She'd never seen him this serious. "DJ," she whispered as she moved to kiss him.

He looked uncomfortable, as if he'd opened his heart, laid it out in front of her and now felt too vulnerable. "If I'd just known that all it would take was a misshapen little evergreen tree to get you into bed…" he joked.

Sadie knew this man so well. "I didn't sleep with you because you brought me a Christmas tree. I've wanted this for a very long time too." She smiled and said, "I fell in love with you as hard as I tried not to. I love you, DJ. Do I need to tell you that's the first time I've said those words to a man?"

He shook his head. "So it wasn't my imagination? This has been building for some time?" She nodded.

"I never thought…" He didn't have to finish. She knew what he was saying. He never thought the two of them would ever be together like this. "I did think about you and me, though. But I saw us in a fancy hotel with silken sheets and room service. Nor did I ever think it could be so amazing, not even in my wildest dreams." He traced a finger along her cheek to her lips.

She smiled. Her gaze locked with his. "The room service here is quite good and I don't need expensive sheets with a high thread count. Just being here with you like this…" She touched the washboard of his stomach. "I feel I'm never going to get enough of you."

He laughed as he grabbed her and rolled her over so she was flat on the bed and he leaned above her. "Let me see what I can do about that." He bent down to kiss her gently on the lips before he trailed kisses down her neck. She closed her eyes, remembering that his favorite song was something about a slow hand.

Chapter 15

When DJ woke beside Sadie, he was afraid that earlier had been nothing more than a dream. In the corner was the small Christmas tree they'd taken a break from love-making to decorate together with the silly things they'd found in the cabin. It made him smile it was so ugly and yet so beautiful all at the same time. Then they'd gone back to bed to make love and had fallen asleep.

He glanced over at Sadie and wanted to pinch himself. He'd never thought he'd even get to kiss her. The woman had captivated him for so long, but it had been strictly hands-off, all business. He ran his gaze down the length of her naked body, memorizing it the way he had earlier with his fingertips, with his tongue, with his lips—as if he could ever forget.

Remembering made his heart beat faster. He'd never experienced this kind of pleasure and pain, and knew it was why he'd never put his heart in jeopardy before. The emotions he was experiencing were the most joyous he'd ever known—and the most terrifying. Yet his pulse drummed with more than desire as he realized he couldn't bear to ever walk away from this woman. He felt as if he would die with the longing. As if he wouldn't be able to breathe—and wouldn't care if he did.

He'd never felt anything like this, and it scared him more than having killers after them. This woman had stolen not just his heart, but his body and soul. He'd always felt protective of her, but now—

Her brown eyes opened, her gaze on his face as if she'd felt him looking at her. He smiled, not in the least embarrassed to be caught. "I'll never get tired of looking at you."

He saw the heat in her eyes as she reached for him, but just as quickly, she froze. Her gaze shot over his shoulder to the front of the house. He felt himself tense and quickly estimated how long it would take him to get to the weapon behind the vase on the mantel.

"It stopped snowing," she said in a whisper filled with regret.

He felt it, too. Being here like this, he'd forgotten the outside world for a while. Now it came rushing back in. With the storm stopped, someone could get to them. He felt both dread and regret. "We'd better get up."

She nodded but didn't let go of his forearm. Looking into her eyes, he knew she was afraid this might be their last time together. He bent toward her for a kiss, and she cupped the back of his head, drawing him closer.

He wanted this so badly, and not just for today but always. He knew he would do whatever it took to make sure that happened as he lost himself in her. One way or another, they would be together. Partners to the end, he thought.

By the time they were out of bed and dressed, the sun had come out. The sunshine lit up the freshly fallen snow. It glittered like diamonds, so bright that it was blinding. Even the pine needles under the cover of snow caught the rays and glistened.

"It's so beautiful," Sadie said from the window. "Like a field of diamonds." She turned as DJ came in through the back door, reminding herself how dangerous it could be.

"I found a shovel in the shed behind the cabin," DJ said. "I'm going to dig out the SUV and then we're getting out of here."

She stared at him in surprise. "What about Keira?"

He shook his head. "Hopefully she's on her way to Alaska."

"Are you sure about this?" She couldn't bear the thought that he'd have regrets. That their lovemaking had been the cause of him wanting to leave.

DJ's look was heartbreaking. "I don't need to look her in the eye to know the answer. I just didn't want to believe it." He shrugged. "At some point, you have to quit trying to save a person."

She wasn't sure he was still talking about Keira. She quickly stepped to him and put a finger to his lips. She shook her head slowly until his gaze met hers and held. She kissed him, wanting desperately to be in his arms, to assure him that she wasn't ever going to give up on him. But even as she had those thoughts, she realized how much she needed this man.

She'd always been independent, determinedly so. While her godfather had raised her and made sure she had anything she wanted, she'd been on her own since she was eighteen. She could take care of herself, something she prided herself on. She'd never needed a man to take care of her.

Nor had she ever wanted one badly enough to even consider giving up her independence, let alone admitting that need. Until DJ Diamond. Neither of them had relationships that had lasted. The two of them as partners had been the longest for both of them.

Her need for DJ filled her with panic that she might lose him. They'd finally admitted how they felt about each other. She'd kept it bottled up for so long. It was unbearable even letting him go down to get the SUV unstuck. That need was an excruciating ache, so physically painful that she wanted to beg him not to leave for fear of what would happen.

But as she met his eyes, she saw that they couldn't stay up here on this mountain forever. Eventually they would have to leave and go back to the real world. If their love for each other couldn't withstand that, then there was no future for them.

She stepped back, feeling bereft. Love hurts. The words from a song now resonated in her heart, in the pounding of her blood.

"That vehicle we heard before," she asked. "Keira?"

He shrugged. "Could have been Grandville's men. Could have been anyone."

She knew it could also be PI Buck Crawford—with more of the PIs from Colt Brothers Investigation. Crawford was determined to get DJ to his twin's wedding.

She could only hope that was the case and that DJ made it. He had family waiting for him.

Buck woke to the sound of the snowmobiles. He sat up, banged his head on the upper bunk and swore. What time was it?

Climbing out of the bed, he hurriedly pulled on his boots since he'd slept in his clothes in the cold cabin.

Before he got his second boot on, James opened the door. "You hear that?"

He nodded. "Sounds like more than one."

"Sounds like they're headed our way."

"Willie?"

James shook his head. "The sheriff's department doesn't move that quickly, especially in a snowstorm. You think it's DJ?"

"I doubt he had access to a trailer and snowmobiles. Grandville's men."

"That's what I'm afraid of," Tommy said from the doorway. "They must have seen your truck and the snowmobile trailer outside the cabin. Sounds like there are three of them coming up the mountain. What do you want to do?"

"They aren't looking for us, right?" James asked.

"Guess we'll have to find out." Buck pulled on his second boot and rose.

By the time they reached the cabin's front door, all three snowmobiles and their drivers were sitting outside. Buck opened the door and stepped out, James and Tommy following.

"Where's DJ Diamond?"

"Who wants to know?" Buck asked over the rumble of the three snowmobile engines.

"Butch, it's that PI I told you about." Buck recognized the man's voice who'd spoken. Lloyd from the poker party. He seemed nervous, his hand on the weapon at his side.

But it was Butch Lamar he kept his eye on. He'd met other men like Butch. Grandville's lead thug was a big man, with a face that had met too many other men's fists and an unfriendly attitude. They were always looking for a fight. They liked beating people up. They constantly were looking for someone to knock that chip off their shoulder. Butch Lamar was one of them.

Buck assumed the third man was Rafe Westfall. Both Butch and Rafe had AKs hanging across their chests and pistols at their hips over their winter clothing.

"We have business with Diamond," Butch said.

He knew what kind of business. "So do we. Also we have the sheriff on his way just in case your business includes hurting Diamond or the woman with him," Buck said.

Butch wagged his head as if amused. "I don't think you know who you're dealing with."

"Trust me, I do," Buck said.

"And where's this law? I don't see any law. Rafe, do you see any law?" He turned back to Buck. "From the looks of it, we have the upper hand here. He touched the AK-47 strapped to his chest. This is a dangerous place to be for you boys. Anything can happen up here this time of year. A man could get himself killed really easy."

Butch's words hung in the air. An open challenge.

James saw Lloyd go for his pistol before Buck did. He drew his weapon from behind him and fired at the same time Lloyd did. Buck was drawing his gun as well when Butch gunned his snowmobile, the others following suit as they sped off, Lloyd hunched over his machine in pain, the snow where he'd been sitting on his machine dotted red with blood.

Buck turned quickly to James, who was holding his side. He looked at Tommy who hadn't had a chance to go for his gun. He was thankful since it could have been worse if they had pulled their weapons. "Get inside. Let's see how bad you're hit."

"Not bad," James said as he was helped inside the cabin to a chair.

"I'll be the judge of that," Buck said. "Tommy, disconnect the snowmobile trailer from the truck."

"Aren't we going after them?"

"No, you're taking James down the mountain so Willie can get a helicopter to take him to the hospital."

As soon as Tommy went outside, Buck looked to see how badly James had been hit. There was a lot of blood. He did what he could to stop the bleeding and prepare the wound for traveling. "Keep this on the wound," he said of the gauze and bandage he'd found in the bathroom cabinet.

"I know what you're thinking," James said. "But you can't go after those three alone."

"You need to get to the hospital," Buck said. "Tommy needs to take you. Once you're where you can use your phone, get Willie to send up deputies and Feds. Don't worry about me. I'll be fine," Buck said.

James shook his head as Tommy came back in. "The truck's ready. How's James?"

"He needs to get to the hospital. You're taking him," Buck said, expecting more argument. But one look at how pale James had gone and Tommy nodded. "He's lost a lot of blood. I did what I could. Get him off this mountain."

James grabbed Buck's arm. "I'm planning to stand up with you at your wedding, man. Don't let me down."

Buck smiled. "I'll be there. Now go. They might decide to circle back. I want them to think we all left. Tommy, drive the truck down following their tracks to their vehicle. They would have busted through the drifts. It should make the going easier."

"You do realize that we are going to have to disable their vehicle, right?" James said.

"You need medical attention. Tommy, don't listen to him. Just get him to the hospital. Tell the sheriff hello."

"Willie will be coming like gangbusters," Tommy said. "Just keep yourself safe until he and the troops arrive."

Ansley had been waiting anxiously by the phone. She'd wrapped the rest of the Christmas presents she'd purchased and put them around the tree. She'd cleaned the kitchen, made a batch of cookies and was just about to ice them when her phone finally rang.

Hurriedly, she scooped up her cell. "Buck?"

"Sorry, it's me," Bella said. "I'm in labor."

It was the last thing she'd expected to hear.

"Don't panic," her friend said quickly. "I called my doctor. He said not to come in until my contractions were more consistent and much closer together. I've called Lori. She just put the twins down for a nap. She assured me that I might not be having this baby for hours—or maybe not even today. She called Ellie while I called Carla. Ellie's in Seattle at her law firm. Carla didn't pick up."

"I'll be right there," Ansley said, knowing that Bella had to be wishing she'd reached someone with at least pregnancy experience. She checked to make sure that the stove was off. The cookies could wait. "I'm leaving now."

Bella laughed. "I know I'm being silly, but this is all new and I'm nervous."

"I am a great hand-holder," Ansley assured her. "Have you been able to reach Tommy?"

"No, that's the other thing. I haven't heard a word since they went up into the mountains yesterday. I know he doesn't want to miss this. He better not miss this." Her voice broke.

"I'm sure he'll be back before you even have to go to the hospital," she said, not sure of that at all. She knew nothing about giving birth or babies. But after she and Buck were married, she couldn't wait to learn. "Sit tight. I'll be there before you know it."

The moment she disconnected, she tried Buck's number. It went straight to voice mail. "Hey, it's me. Bella's in labor. Hope you're all right. Come back. Bella needs us all. I need you. I should never have sent you on this ridiculous mission." She hung up close to tears. Maribelle was right. She was a spoiled rich girl. Even as she thought it, she knew that wanting to have her twin at her wedding wasn't outrageous. It was her deepest desire. Unless, of course, her twin was a possible, even probable, criminal on the run and this ended up getting the people she loved killed.

DJ took the shovel down the mountain to the snow-bound SUV and began digging. He needed the physical exertion. He went to work, shoveling as his mind raced.

He kept thinking about Keira. Had he really been ready to jeopardize everything just to know whether or not she had betrayed him?

His thoughts rushed back to Sadie and the time they'd spent in the cabin. He didn't want to leave here for fear the bubble would pop. He'd told her that he loved her, but he wasn't sure that was enough. She'd said she loved him, too. But what would happen when they got back to the real world? If they got back?

He stopped to listen, hearing snowmobiles but far off in the distance; he glanced back up the mountain. He knew Sadie had taken the SUV keys the moment he couldn't find them. She didn't trust him and with good reason. He would do anything to protect her, even leave her behind if it came to that. But right now, he wasn't sure that Keira wouldn't show up. The cabin was no longer safe since the storm had passed. Keira might not be the only one coming for them.

Going back to his shoveling, he thought about Ansley Brookshire, his alleged twin sister, who was going to all this trouble so he'd be at her wedding. She really could be his twin, he thought with a chuckle. She was determined enough and they did look like they could be fraternal twins.

But how would she feel when she met him? She was a Brookshire. The name meant money. He was willing to bet that her childhood had been nothing like his own. She probably didn't realize who she might be inviting not only to her wedding but also into her life.

He tried to imagine being part of this family Crawford had told him about. He would have been a complete fool not to realize that this was the fork in the road, the crossroads he'd felt coming. His deal with Sadie and her godfather had come to an end, but that didn't mean that he and Sadie couldn't have a future. A twin sister was offering him a family. And then there was Keira, who was either going to Alaska to live with her no-account husband or setting him up for a fall.

DJ stopped shoveling. With luck, he should be able to drive the SUV out now. He leaned on the shovel as he tried to catch his breath. He'd made a decision about his future. He and Sadie were leaving.

Glancing back up the mountain, he smiled to himself. It was a no-brainer. Let go of the past, let Keira go to Alaska, leave the poker game money for the Grandvilles and walk away. One call to Marcus Grandville once they got off this mountain could end this.

He took a deep breath of the cold mountain air. It was almost Christmas. He thought of their Christmas tree back in the cabin. He was ready to experience the magic of the holiday through Sadie's eyes.

At the whine of a single snowmobile high on the mountain, he dropped the shovel. Whoever it was, they were headed this way and fast. Sadie. He had to get to her. He took off through the deep snow as he raced up the mountain, knowing that he would never reach the cabin before the snowmobile did.

Chapter 16

Sadie had felt a chill as she stood on the porch and looked down the mountainside to where she had seen DJ shoveling. The breeze dislodged the fresh snow from the pines, sending it streaming through the sunlight, making the flakes gleam like glitter. The mountainside was so quiet it was eerie. DJ had said that they were leaving. He wasn't going to wait for Keira. He wasn't going to leave her, either. She had the keys to the SUV in her pocket, so she knew he'd be back. But if she hadn't taken the keys, would he have left?

If so it would have been to find his sister. He still wanted the truth, she knew that. No matter what he said, he had to know if Keira had betrayed him, set him up to die. Sadie shuddered at the thought. How could anyone want to hurt DJ? Once you looked into his heart and saw what was there, it seemed impossible.

She thought of their lovemaking. He'd been so gentle with her, as if he was afraid she would break. Yet she'd sensed the urgency in him. He'd wanted her for a long time. The man had amazing control, she thought with a wry smile. All the time they'd worked together, he'd joked, but he'd never let it go past that.

Sadie wouldn't have known how he felt if she hadn't seen it in his eyes. She'd thought she'd caught glimpses of it over their time together, but she'd never trusted it until now. DJ had said he loved her, something he'd never told another woman, and she believed him. Their lovemaking had been more than sex. There was a connection between them that felt so strong. The thought of losing it, losing DJ, made her stomach roil. They needed to get out of here, she thought urgently.

She hugged herself, shaken by that sudden almost warning. A part of her never wanted to leave this cabin, never wanted to go back into that world where things were complicated. Here, life was simple. But she knew they couldn't stay for so many reasons; Keira and Grandville's men were only part of it. DJ would never be happy with a life like this.

That was the problem, she thought, as she watched the breeze send the new snow into the cold morning air. She wasn't sure what it would take to make DJ happy. She wasn't sure he even knew himself. Could she make him happy once they left here?

Sadie just knew that it was important for him to make it back for his twin sister's wedding. She had no doubt after looking at Ansley's photo that it was true. He was the missing twin. He was born into a family that would love him. They'd gone to a lot of trouble to find him. It appeared to be the kind of family neither of them had ever had.

She silently urged DJ to hurry and get the SUV unstuck. The woods seemed too quiet. She felt a chill as she thought of Keira. Where was she? Had this been a trap? Sadie couldn't imagine what was in the woman's heart to do such a thing to DJ. She'd been glad to hear DJ say he wasn't staying around to wait for her. If not for the storm, she feared they would already know Keira's true intentions.

After everything that had happened between her and DJ since she met him, she would risk her life for his. She might have to let him go once they got off this mountain, but she couldn't live without knowing he was alive somewhere. She wanted to be able to think about him and imagine him in his Stetson sitting at a poker table. He'd be grinning, holding the winning cards in his hand because he was the best player at that table, and nothing was going to keep him from proving it.

Sadie heard the sound of a snowmobile. At first it was distant, but it was coming this way and fast. Her heart lurched. She looked down the mountain and didn't see DJ. He must have heard it, too.

She hurriedly stepped back inside the cabin and started for the mantel and the gun there when she heard the snowmobile engine stop. The silence was deafening. Until the back door of the cabin flew open, and she reached for the gun.

Ansley found Bella pacing the floor, her hand on her swollen abdomen, looking close to tears. "It's going to be fine," she assured her the moment she walked into the large ranch lodge. "I called Buck and left a message. I know they will turn back the moment they get it."

Bella didn't look any more convinced than Ansley. Who knew when they would get the message? Or if they would, since there was spotty cell service at best in the mountains and with this storm...

"Did you hear the avalanche report on the radio this morning?" Bella asked, sounding scared. "They're warning people to stay out of the mountains. The new snow on the old is too unstable. They said it is like a powder keg about to go off."

"Let's sit down," Ansley said. She'd heard the report. Like Bella, she was worried, but she couldn't show it. Bella was already upset enough. It couldn't be good for the baby. "I'm sure the men know what they're doing."

She didn't know the mountains around here, but she'd skied at both Bridger Bowl and Big Sky. There, though, the ski patrol cleared the cornices before letting skiers on the slopes. Cornices formed high in the mountains could be kicked off by anything– even a sound.

"I hope you're right," Bella said. "All this fresh snow, it just makes me so nervous."

Ansley felt the same way. Every year backcountry skiers and snowmobilers were caught in avalanches, many of them not surviving. Once the snow began to shift... The mountains would be extremely dangerous right now and Tommy, James and Buck had all gone up there.

"How far apart are your contractions?" She led Bella over to the living room couch, anxious to change the subject.

"They're sporadic," she said with a sigh. "But this

girl is kicking like crazy. She is ready to come out of there."

"Why don't you put your feet up?" Ansley suggested. "Relax as much as you can. Your Christmas tree is beautiful. Tell me you didn't climb up on a ladder to decorate it yourself."

Bella rolled her eyes, seeing what she was trying to do. Still, Bella explained that Tommy had insisted she hire a crew to decorate the house. "He didn't want me overdoing it. Now I'm afraid maybe I did anyway and that's why the baby is coming early." She was clearly fighting tears.

"You don't know that," Ansley said, getting her some tissues. "We aren't even sure the baby is coming today." They sat in silence for a few minutes. "I feel like this is all my fault. If I hadn't been so determined to have my twin at my wedding…"

"Don't be silly," her friend said, sniffling as she wiped her eyes. "It's your determination that got you to us. None of this is your fault. We all just want your wedding to be perfect. Buck won't let you down, trust me. Anyway, this is what our men do. We wouldn't love them so much if they weren't the way they are."

Ansley nodded, knowing it was true. Buck was as driven as the Colt brothers in righting wrongs, helping people, finding out the truth. She loved that about him. All of them had helped her find her family and now they were doing their best to help the man Buck was convinced was her twin.

"So who do you think this woman is with DJ?" Bella asked.

"Sadie Montclair? I'm not even sure Buck knows. But he says there's something between them."

"Romantically?" Bella's eyes lit, making Ansley laugh.

"You are such a sucker for a happy ending," she teased. "I heard Davy is manning the office. I'll call him and see if he knows anything about her."

As she gave Davy what few details she knew about Sadie Montclair, Bella had another contraction. Ansley had been timing them, knowing that she might have to take her to the hospital soon. "Davy's going to call back."

They talked about baby names, baby clothes—"Have you seen the little overalls they make for girls?" Bella had cried. "I couldn't resist. I got the denim ones and the Western shirts that match."

"For a newborn?" Ansley asked in surprise.

"No, that would be silly. I got the twelve-month size and while I was at it, picked up the twenty-four month size as well." Bella laughed. "Tommy is actually worried that I might go overboard on baby clothes. Can you imagine?"

Ansley's phone rang. She quickly picked it up, hoping it was Buck. "Davy," she said trying not to sound disappointed since she was the one who'd asked him for the favor.

"If she is the Sadie Montclair of Palm Beach, Florida," Davy said, "then she has quite the mob connection. I found a socialite photo online that tagged her as the goddaughter of Ezra Montclair, Palm Beach business mogul. He's her godfather, all right."

Bella was waving her hand. "Well? Who is she?"

"Any word from the others?" Ansley had to ask before she hung up.

"Nope. Not yet. Don't worry. They know those mountains. They'll be fine."

"Thanks." She disconnected, even more worried. Davy was worried, too, but who wouldn't be given the weather?

"What?" Bella demanded after breathing through another contraction.

"I think we should get you to the hospital," Ansley said, rising. "Your contractions are more consistent and are now ten minutes apart."

Her friend looked surprised that she'd been timing them. "What about Sadie?" she asked as she lumbered to her feet.

Ansley helped her. "Seems Sadie's godfather might be the head of the mob in Palm Beach, Florida."

"Get out of here," Bella cried.

"Which is exactly what we are doing," she said, steering her toward the door. "Should we call your doctor to let him know we're coming in?"

Bella shook her head. "He's on call. He knows." Her face crumpled. "What if Tommy doesn't make it?"

"I'm sure he'll show up at the hospital as soon as he's out of the mountains," she said, and realized Bella meant what if Tommy doesn't make it out of the mountains. "Do you have a bag packed for the hospital?"

"It's by the door. Tommy insisted."

"I'll grab it." As Ansley picked it up and turned, she saw Bella standing by the door looking back at the house as if she might never see it again.

"Let's go see if this baby is coming today or not," Ansley said too brightly as Bella turned to look at her, tears in her eyes as her water broke.

* * *

Sadie turned, not sure who she would find standing in the doorway as her hand closed around the grip of the gun. She blinked, startled by the tiny, slim blonde who stared back. But she was more startled by the gun in the angelic-looking woman's hand. She took a wild guess. "Keira."

"Who are you?" the blond woman demanded.

Sadie was debating whether or not she could pull the gun from behind the vase, let alone shoot this woman who DJ considered his little sister. She eased her hand off the grip and pretended to hold on to the mantel for support. "I'm Sadie."

"Sadie, of course. You're that mobster's daughter DJ's been working with down in Florida."

That pretty much summed it up, she thought. Although her father and her godfather considered themselves businessmen who played the odds and used the system to their benefit.

"Where's DJ?" Keira asked, taking in the small cabin and seeing for herself that he wasn't there.

"The last time I saw him, he was headed for the outhouse out back. Actually, I thought you were him returning. He must have heard you coming and took off."

The blonde stepped deeper into the cabin, letting the back door close as she moved away from it. "He wouldn't leave you behind," Keira said, smirking. "I know how he feels about you." Sadie stayed by the fire, turning her back on Keira to warm her hands, and considered her chances if she went for the gun. "Get over here so I can see you."

The gun was in reach, but she could feel the blonde's sights on her back. It was clear that this wasn't the first time Keira had held a gun. There was no reason to believe that she wouldn't use it, Sadie thought as she turned to look at the woman. Sadie had talked herself out of tough spots before, but her instincts told her that trying to reason with this woman would be a waste of breath. There was something in Keira's eyes, something dark, something soulless. She'd seen the look before in some of the men she and DJ had played poker with. It was a terrifying pit to look into, seeing raw greed and hate, knowing there was violence there.

"Sit down," Keira ordered. "In that chair there." She pointed with the gun as she moved closer. "We'll just sit here and wait, although I don't believe he went to the outhouse."

Sadie shrugged as she took the chair as Keira had instructed while her would-be killer stood next to the fireplace wall so she could see both the back as well as the front door. DJ would have heard the snowmobile. He wouldn't just come walking in unaware of what might be waiting for him.

But he would come back to the cabin. He would know it was Keira. He had thought he could leave without facing her. But now that she was here… He wouldn't be able to help himself. He'd want to hear it from her.

Sadie just hoped that this woman didn't kill DJ as he came in the door. Her instincts told her that Keira wouldn't. She would want him to realize what she'd done, for whatever reason. She would want to make him suffer first.

Counting on that, Sadie considered what she could do to stop Keira. Unfortunately, it would be hard to disarm the woman from this chair in front of the fire. Sadie felt tense, waiting for the sound of DJ's boots outside on one of the wooden porch boards. He would be armed, but she really doubted he would fire a weapon before he would ask questions. Keira would know that. Maybe that's what she was counting on.

Sadie caught sight of the Christmas tree DJ had cut for her and they'd had so much fun decorating. They'd laughed so hard as they tried to outdo each other, finding the wildest things to put on that puny tree's limbs. Yet when they'd finished, it looked wonderful to Sadie.

"This is the best real Christmas tree I've ever had," she told DJ.

He'd hugged her and said, "And I thought my childhood was bad."

A sob rose in her throat. She pushed it back down. Now more than ever she needed that poker face that DJ said she was famous for. She couldn't let Keira see what she was feeling. It would make her and DJ more vulnerable.

"He probably went looking for you," Sadie said, wishing it were true. He could have taken off on foot. Or he could still be down digging out the SUV. Now she wished she'd let him take the keys so he could have left in search of his sister. But she doubted he would have. Things had changed between them. She knew DJ was somewhere outside this cabin. He would soon be opening one of the doors and walking into a trap—just as Sadie had feared and Keira had no doubt planned.

By the time DJ neared the cabin, he could no longer hear the snowmobile's engine. Heart lodged in his throat, he slowed as climbed up to the back door. Sounds in the mountains were often amplified and hard to pinpoint exactly where they were coming from. But there had been no doubt about this earlier sound, he thought as he caught sight of a snowmobile sitting in the pines above the cabin.

He stayed to the trees, keeping the cabin in sight as he approached. He told himself that Sadie was all right. It wasn't like he'd heard anything coming from the cabin. Anything like a scream. Or a gunshot. Yet he knew she was no longer safe, as if his heart now beat in time with hers.

As he reached the side of the cabin, he saw the footprints from the snowmobile sitting in the nearby pines to the back door. He looked around for other tracks. Only one person had gotten off the machine and entered the cabin. Could be PI Crawford.

All his instincts told him it wasn't. Just as he knew it wasn't one of the Grandville men either. The tracks in the snow were too small.

It was Keira.

DJ stood for only a moment considering his best play. He knew the odds. They weren't to his liking. Sadie was in there. He told himself that she was still safe. He would have heard a gunshot. He would have heard a scream. All he heard even now was silence.

Even if Sadie hadn't been inside with Keira, there was no walking away from this. There hadn't been since getting the call drawing him back to Montana. Keira was either here to tell him goodbye before she left for Alaska or she'd come here to earn whatever Grandville had paid her.

He thought about her as a little girl. She'd been so skinny, so pale. He remembered her eyes that first day. He'd had trouble meeting them, afraid of what horrors she'd already been through. Like him, she had no one.

Whoever had dropped her off wouldn't be coming back for her and he thought she'd known it.

He'd thought he could protect her, erase whatever had happened to her before Charley's ranch. He'd been a fool. Sometimes you can't save a person. That was a lesson Sadie had never learned.

Tucking the gun into the back of his jeans, he walked to the back of the cabin, hesitated only a moment and opened the door.

Chapter 17

DJ stepped into the cabin. His gaze went to Sadie first. She was sitting in the chair in front of the fire. She gave him a look that said she was all right. He shifted his gaze to Keira, the woman he'd called his little sister since the day she'd arrived at the Diamond Deluxe Ranch.

She stood over Sadie, holding a gun on her. He remembered her wanting to learn to shoot when she was about nine. She'd been so determined that he'd taught her. She'd been a natural, knocking off the cans he'd put on the fence one after another. He remembered the joy in her expression now and felt sick.

When he spoke, his voice was much calmer than he felt. "Keira, want to tell me what's going on?"

"Seems pretty obvious, doesn't it?" she said.

"Sorry, you're going to have to spell it out for me. Talk slowly, you know I never was as quick at catching onto things as you were. Bet you excelled at college."

She shook her head, anger flaring in her eyes. He feared he'd taken it one step too far. "Right, you worked, you paid for my college. Subtle reminder, big brother. You think that made up for what you did?"

"I'm sorry, what exactly was it that I did, Keira, that you would betray me?" he demanded. "Why would you do this to me? I've always been there for you."

"Not always," she snapped. "You let Charley put me in foster care. You and Charley just left me."

"Keira, I was a kid myself. You were a child much younger than me. There was no way you could have gone with us. That life was no picnic. I was terrified most of the time because people were chasing us, some trying to kill us. There were days when we had nothing to eat, no place to stay but out in the woods."

She shook her head stubbornly. "You abandoned me."

"That's not true. Once I went out on my own, I started sending you money. When it came time for you to go to college—"

"I didn't go to college, DJ. All I ever wanted was what you got—to live the con. I would have been better at it than even you. Look how I conned you."

He stared at her, still disbelieving. "This was Luca's idea, wasn't it?"

"See, that's why you fell for it. You wanted to believe an idea like this could only have come from a man. Keira couldn't have come up with this on her own." She huffed. "It was all my idea, DJ, and it worked." She looked so satisfied that he felt even sicker inside. He'd thought he'd protected her from this life, but he'd been wrong. She'd done this to show him but also to get even for him leaving her all those years ago.

"What did you do with the college money?" he asked.

She smiled. "Taught myself a few tricks of the trade. You wouldn't know, living down there in Florida working for the mob."

"I've been paying off Charley's debt. It's not the glamorous life you think it is." He hated that she'd grown into a hardened woman already, so hard that she'd sold him out to Grandville. "How much do you get for delivering me to them?"

Her smile was all greed and misplaced glory. "Two hundred grand. Like you, Grandville wanted to treat me like a child, or worse, a woman who doesn't know what she's doing. But he sees me differently now."

DJ was sure that Titus did see her differently now. "You can't trust him. He'll turn on you like the venomous snake he is, Keira." But even as he said the words, he could see that she didn't believe him. She'd thought that she'd won Titus Grandville's respect and there was no telling her different.

She tilted her head, listening, but not to him. He heard it too. The whine of snowmobiles in the distance. Grandville was coming with his thugs to get retribution, as if he and his ilk needed a reason. Charley was at the heart of this. Years ago, he remembered his uncle embarrassing Titus on the street in Butte with a card trick. At the time, DJ had looked into the young Grandville's furious red face and worried Titus would go to his father and make things harder for them. He seriously doubted that Titus had ever forgotten the humiliation—or the young threadbare-dressed boy who'd witnessed it. Titus had felt small in front of DJ, a kid he'd ridiculed and felt superior to.

Suddenly DJ felt tired and defeated. He was sick of old grudges and feuds. He'd come up here to save Keira.

Worse, he'd gotten Sadie involved. For that, he would never forgive himself. Not that he would have long to regret his mistakes. Titus planned to kill him, but what Keira didn't realize was that the banker wouldn't leave any witnesses.

DJ looked at Sadie. He saw that familiar glint in her eye. She knew the score, but clearly she wasn't ready to give up yet. How had he ever gotten involved with such an optimist?

Sadie had taken in the situation. She knew DJ had a weapon on him, but she doubted, even after everything he'd heard, that he was capable of shooting Keira. But Sadie now didn't have that problem. She saw the woman as a product of her own greed, using her childhood as her excuse, blaming everyone but herself for the way her life had turned out so far.

The problem was how to play this and not get DJ or herself killed. She couldn't do anything from this chair, though. She had to take a gamble, something she was apparently born to do.

As she began to clap, Sadie got to her feet to face Keira. "Thank you for this wonderful reminder of how lucky I am not to have a sibling. What a heartrending moment to have witnessed. To think I used to want a little sister."

Just as she'd hoped, her act caught Keira off guard.

"I told you to sit down there and not move," the woman cried, swinging the gun in Sadie's direction.

Holding up her hands, she'd stepped back toward the fireplace and the gun now within reach behind the vase. She'd also distracted Keira, who was having trouble keeping her gun on both of them.

DJ had moved toward the kitchen, putting the two of them on each side of Keira.

"You move again and I'll shoot you," Keira cried. "That goes for you, too, DJ."

"Other than to get me killed, what is it you want?" he asked, sounding bored.

She took a few steps back, bumping into the bed as she tried to keep them both within sight. "For starters, I want the money you took from the poker game in Butte and any other money you might have on you."

"It's yours," he said. "But I'm going to have to move to get it."

Keira raised the gun so it was pointed at Sadie's head. "Try anything and I kill her."

The sound of the snowmobiles made all three of them freeze for a moment. The sound grew louder, closer. Time was running out. Sadie looked at DJ. *Tell me what you're thinking. Give me a sign.* Otherwise, Sadie was going to do whatever she had to.

The moment Tommy and James left in the truck, Buck climbed on one of the snowmobiles, drove it off the trailer and went after Grandville's thugs. He hadn't gone far when he saw the blood on the fresh snow and remembered that James had wounded one of them. A little farther, following the tracks the three had left, he saw a snowmobile sitting without a rider, idling. As he drew closer he saw the body lying next to it on the far side. He cautiously approached. Within a few feet, he saw that it was Lloyd, and he was dead. He appeared to have been shot not once, but twice, the last time between the eyes.

Buck looked to the dark pines ahead, feeling sick

to his stomach as he thought about the kind of men he was dealing with. He knew where Rafe and Butch were headed. Charley Diamond's cabin. Were DJ and Sadie there? What about Keira Cross? He gunned his engine; the snow machine roared past the abandoned one as he followed the tracks that he knew would lead him into more trouble than he'd know what to do with.

Ahead, he could see the snowmobile tracks where they had crossed the mountain above the tree line. He'd been following three, now two. But now he saw another track. It, too, had gone in the same direction. His heart sank, as he knew it must belong to the other person on this mountain DJ and Sadie had to fear. Keira.

He just hoped that Tommy and James got word to Willie and the rest of the law in time. He could use all the help he could get since he had a bad feeling Keira had already found DJ and Sadie.

The buzz of the approaching snowmobiles got louder. DJ could see that Sadie was planning something. He wasn't sure it would make any difference if he was right about who was coming. If it was Grandville's men, they were toast. Keira would be the least of their problems. "You hear those snowmobiles approaching?" he asked his sister, and saw her self-satisfied expression. She thought like he did that they were Grandville's men. "They're going to take the money away from you and kill you. You'll never see the two hundred grand. You'll never see Alaska."

She laughed. "I was never going to Alaska."

"Luca will be so disappointed," he said, wondering if Luca wasn't on one of the snowmobiles headed this way.

"I dumped Luca. He's history. He was just dragging me down. I should have known he'd never get me the start-up money I needed. I realized I'd have to do it myself."

"So you went to Titus. I actually thought he was the one who'd suggested you betray me. But it had been your idea. Good to know. Let me get you that money," he said as he moved toward the bed.

"You can't shame me, DJ," she said angrily. "This life is about doing what needs to be done no matter who it hurts."

He chuckled. "It doesn't seem to be hurting you, Keira. In fact, as smug as you're acting, I get the feeling you're enjoying this."

"So what if I am?" she demanded, waving the gun in his direction as he started across the room.

It was just what Sadie had been hoping for.

Sadie moved quickly, deciding at the last moment not to go for the gun behind the vase. She'd already figured out that Keira was cold enough that she might shoot DJ just out of meanness rather than drop her gun. So instead, Sadie went for the woman with the gun.

Even as she launched herself at Keira, she figured the woman would be expecting it. That's why she stayed low, hitting her in the knees, taking her down with a thud that seemed to rattle the entire cabin. Keira managed to get off one shot. Sadie heard it whiz by over her head as she landed on top of the skinny and yet feisty woman. She was already going for the gun when DJ put his boot down on Keira's wrist before she could fire again.

Almost casually, he leaned down and took the weapon from her. Keira kicked at Sadie, grabbing for her hair like a street fighter. Sadie punched her in the face, Keira's head flopping back and smacking the floor. She went still but didn't pass out.

Not that Sadie trusted her. "Please get me something to tie her up with," she said to DJ.

"Let me," he said, handing her the gun as he reached for a dish towel and began to rip it into strips. By the time he'd tied Keira's hands she was kicking and screaming, then pleading with him to let her go. "I'll split the money with you," she cried in desperation.

He shook his head, looking at her with pity. "I don't need the money. I have plenty. I could have paid Titus off without making a dent in my savings."

She stared at him. "Then why didn't you?"

"Because he knew I would try to make the money in a poker game. He would have his ear to the ground making sure that at least one of his men was in the game—and that it would end badly. I wanted to beat him at his own game. Now I wish I'd paid him off and walked away. I won't make that mistake again."

"DJ, let me leave with the money," she pleaded. "I need a new start and you're probably right about Titus double-crossing me."

"Sorry, little sis. It's too late," he said as he dragged her over to a chair and shoved her into it. He appeared to be listening as he tied her to the chair.

Sadie heard it, too. Silence. No sound of the snowmobiles. They both looked toward the back door.

Keira began to laugh. "What did you do to make Titus Grandville hate you so much?"

* * *

"Anyone hungry besides me?" DJ asked as he stepped into the kitchen and began to bang around in the pots and pans.

Sadie stared at him and so did Keira. He'd heard the snowmobiles stop on the mountain behind the cabin. Whoever it was had probably already surrounded the cabin. Any moment they would come busting in.

"Sadie, would you mind helping me?" he asked without looking at her.

She moved to stand next to him. "DJ?"

He handed her the opened container of canned meat and a sharp knife, the size that might fit in the top of a boot. "Why don't you cut the ham into slices," he said, still without looking at her. She saw that he had the larger of the two cast-iron skillets on the stove, the grease he'd put in it getting hot.

She glanced behind her at Keira, who was trying to get to her feet as the back door slammed open with a crash. The man in the doorway was big and rough-looking. He was carrying an AK.

"Now isn't this a cute little domestic scene," he said.

"Help me, Butch, they were going to kill me," Keira cried. "Cut me loose," she yelled louder when he didn't move. "I have the money. Hey, I'm talking to you."

Butch started over to the chair and Sadie saw another man standing just outside. He also carried an AK.

"Could you move any slower?" Keira demanded of the thug.

Out of the corner of her eye, Sadie watched Butch walk over to the woman. "Where's the money?"

"I'll get it for you as soon as you untie me," she snapped.

He pulled a knife and began cutting the strips of dish towel from her ankles and wrists.

"Hey, watch it with the knife, you big dumb—"

He raised the butt of the rifle and brought it down hard on her head. The sound reverberated through the small cabin. Sadie's gaze shot to DJ. His eyes were closed; he was gripping the edge of the counter.

"Your sister's taking a nap," Butch said from behind them. "Now where's the money?"

DJ's fingers loosened on the counter. His blue eyes flashed open. "Don't you want breakfast first?" he asked without turning around. His voice sounded strained as he took the ham she'd sliced from her and dumped it into the hot skillet, where it quickly began to sizzle and brown. The skillet was smoking hot. "Toast? What do you think?" he asked Sadie.

Her mouth felt dry. She didn't know what to say, let alone think. DJ was making her nervous. These two thugs were armed with weapons that could saw them in half and he was cooking breakfast?

She heard Butch come up behind them. "I'm sure you're one hell of a chef, but I didn't come here for breakfast, and you know it. Where's the money?" Butch swung the gun toward the front of the cabin and pulled the trigger on the AK, turning the front door into kindling. "Unless you want some of this, you'd better get me my money."

Buck stopped in the shelter of the trees and shut down his sled. He couldn't hear the two on the snowmobiles in front of him. He figured he must be close to Charley Diamond's cabin because the machines hadn't been silent for long. He could see the trail the two had left to a spot high on the side of the mountain.

As he followed its path, he saw a huge cornice that the blizzard had sculpted high on the peak above the cabin. The cornice hung over this side. He felt a chill.

He'd been caught in a small avalanche as a teenager on a backcountry ski trip. He'd been terrified and fascinated by the power of snow when it started moving. New snow was 90 percent air, yet one foot of it covering an acre weighed more than 250,000 pounds.

In an instant, that cornice could break off and slide. Thousands of tons of snow could come roaring down that mountain at the speed of a locomotive and with the same impact.

He could see the old avalanche chute where trees and rocks had been wiped out next to Charley Diamond's cabin. It wouldn't be the first time a cornice high on the peak had avalanched down. But this time, the cabin might not be so lucky.

The sound of gunfire inside the cabin made him jump as he swung off the snowmachine, lunging through the deep snow. While the snowmobiles had busted a trail, there was still a good two feet of snow below their tracks he had to break through as the gunshots echoed across the mountainside.

Reaching the cabin, he saw three snowmobiles parked outside. Two belonged to Grandville's muscle; the other must belong to Keira since he didn't think DJ and Sadie had brought any.

He moved toward the back door where the machines were parked, weapon drawn, knowing he would be outgunned. Just as he reached the door, all hell broke loose inside.

Chapter 18

The contractions were coming only a few minutes apart when Tommy walked into the hospital room. Ansley felt her heart float up at the sight of him. He went straight to the bed to take his wife's hand. "Heard our girl is coming early," Tommy said, and smiled at Bella, who, in the middle of a contraction, growled at him.

"Buck?" Ansley asked hopefully.

"He's still up on the mountain," Tommy said, his smile fading. "I had to bring James down."

She felt a start. "What happened to James? Is he all right?"

"He's going to live, the doc said." He turned back to his wife. "Lori was on her way up here to check on Bella when I brought James in. She's in the waiting room while he's in surgery. The bullet went straight through. Doc said that was good."

Bella was oblivious to their conversation as she panted through yet another contraction.

"I'll just be down the hall," Ansley told her friend, and hurried out. James had been shot? Buck was still up on the mountain? She found Lori in the waiting room on the surgical floor.

"What happened?" she cried as she rushed to her.

"James was shot."

"But he's going to be all right?"

"He lost a lot of blood." She sounded close to tears. Ansley was close to them herself. "Willie's headed up there with a helicopter, deputies and EMTs. The Feds aren't far behind, he said."

She nodded but couldn't speak. "I never should have asked them to find my twin," Ansley said.

Lori took her hand. "None of this is your fault. This is what they do."

"You sound like Bella."

"Welcome to being a wife of a private investigator."

"I want to be a wife of a private investigator," Ansley wailed as Lori pulled her into her arms.

"I've known Buck Crawford my whole life," Lori said. "He'll be standing next to you on Saturday. He might be bruised and battered, but he'll be there. Sorry, not funny." She drew back to look at Ansley. "Buck will be there and if there is any way on this earth, your twin brother will be with him."

Ansley desperately needed to believe that finding her missing twin wouldn't cost her everything.

"How's James?"

She looked up to see Davy Colt coming through the door.

"He's in surgery," Lori said.

Davy glanced at his half sister. "Just got the preliminary DNA report from the blood Buck found on that scarf left in his pickup," he said. "DJ Diamond is definitely your twin."

Ansley began to cry. Buck had done just what he'd said he would do—find her missing twin even if it killed him. She couldn't lose them both.

"Settle down," DJ said to Butch as the sound of gunfire died off. "I'll get your money." He knew the money was only an excuse. "Let me take this off the fire." He picked up the pot holder next to the stove, grabbed the handle of the largest skillet and swung around fast.

The sizzling canned ham hit Butch first so he was already screaming when the blistering-hot cast-iron skillet slammed into his face, not once but twice as the AK was wrenched from his hand. The first strike stunned him, the next knocked him to his knees. DJ was about to hit him again when he saw Rafe raising his AK and heard Sadie scream a warning.

Everything seemed to happen too fast after that. DJ saw the winter-clad figure come up behind Rafe. Crawford. The butt end of the PI's handgun came down on the thug's head hard. Rafe dropped, but as he did he pulled the trigger on the AK. Bullets sprayed across the cabin.

When DJ saw what was happening, he grabbed Sadie and threw her down, landing on top of her. As he threw her to the floor, he saw Keira's body jump with each shot before the bullets arced toward him and Sadie on the floor. He'd felt Sadie take one of the bullets even as he tried to shelter her from them. It was as if the bullet punctured his heart. For a moment he couldn't move, couldn't breathe. Beneath him, Sadie wasn't moving, either. His worst fears had come true. He'd gotten Sadie killed.

In the silence that followed, the earth seemed to move. He heard a whump sound, then Crawford yelling. He rolled off Sadie, praying he was wrong, that she was fine. But one look at her and he knew she wasn't. More yelling. He wasn't even sure it wasn't him yelling as he scooped an unconscious Sadie up into his arms.

"We have to get out of here." Crawford was shaking his shoulder. "We have to get out of here. Now!"

He could hear a roar, thinking it was in his ears, but it appeared to be outside as if a runaway train was headed for the cabin.

"This way," Crawford said, dragging him through the demolished front door, off the porch and into the pines away from the cabin. "Keeping going. Don't stop."

He could hear what sounded like trees being snapped off as the roar grew closer. Looking back he could see nothing but a cloud of white. He kept going until Crawford yelled for him to stop. DJ fell to his knees, still holding Sadie in his arms, and the PI rushed to him. Buck took off his coat and spread it on the snow. "Put her down here."

DJ didn't want to let her go.

"Let me check her wound," the PI said.

He slowly released her, laying her on the coat in the snow. He could see that she was still breathing but losing blood from a wound in her side. He stripped off his coat and put it over her, then removed his bloody shirt to press it against her side. He didn't feel the cold. He didn't feel anything as the cloud of snow around him began to dissipate.

"Stay here. I'll get a snowmobile. Help is coming. We just need to get to a spot where a chopper can land," Crawford said.

DJ looked back toward the cabin. It was gone. All he could see was a few boards and one wall sticking up out of the snow farther down the mountain. Charley's cabin was gone and everything in it. Keira. He closed his eyes and pulled Sadie closer as he heard the PI coming with the snowmobile.

Chapter 19

Dressed in his Western suit, Buck rode the elevator up to the recovery floor. He found DJ next to Sadie's hospital bed. He was sitting in a chair, his elbows on his knees, his head in his hands. The anguish he saw there was nothing like what he saw in the man's eyes when DJ lifted his head.

"How is she doing?"

DJ swallowed, nodding, dark circles under his eyes. "The doctor said she should recover—once she's conscious. If she regains consciousness."

"I'm sorry. I know you don't want to leave her, even for a minute," Buck said. "But your twin sister needs you."

DJ shook his head. "She's better off without me. Can't you see that I'm trouble? The people closest to me get hurt. Ansley doesn't need that."

"She needs you, flaws and all. You have no idea how much trouble she's gone through trying to find out the truth about her birth parents," Buck said. "She is no shrinking violet. She's strong. She can handle just about anything, even you." He smiled to soften his words.

"What if my past comes back and I put her life in jeopardy?"

"You'll have family." Buck reached into his pocket, took out the gold bracelet and handed it to DJ. "You'll want this back. Your birth mother had it made for you. She called you Del Junior before you were born, and Ansley DelRae. She wanted you to know your father. You have more than just your twin, though she is definitely a force to reckon with. You're a Colt. You have four half brothers. One's a sheriff, the others are PIs. You also have your birth mother, who is just as anxious to meet you as Ansley is. She didn't know the truth until Ansley came to town looking for her. But you'll hear all about it from your mother, from your twin, from the rest of the family. DJ, you'd be a fool to pass up a chance to be part of this family. You won't be alone. We have you covered."

DJ put his head in his hands for a moment. "I don't want to disappoint her. I've already disappointed two people I swore to protect and got one of them killed."

He could have argued that Keira got herself killed, but he knew that wouldn't help right now. "Believe me, I know what you're feeling. I don't want to let Ansley down, today especially. I promised her I would find you and if at all possible get you to our wedding."

DJ raised his head, took in Buck's suit, and then looked down at his bloodstained clothing. "Do I look like I'm dressed for a wedding?"

"You will. Like I said, we have you covered. The wedding will be short and once it's over, you can come right back here. Your family is waiting."

"Family, huh." Buck could tell that he was thinking about Keira. "Charley always said you can't overcome your genes," DJ said. "I never knew what that meant until now. Now that my DNA makes me officially a Colt, I guess I don't have much choice."

"You always have a choice," Buck said. "But you'd be a fool to pass up accepting the rest of the Colts as family. Hell, I've been trying to get them to adopt me for years. DJ, I promise I'll have you back here as fast as possible. I brought you some clothes."

"I don't have a present."

"You are the best wedding present either of us will get today. Trust me, once she sees you…"

DJ rose and went to Sadie's side. He leaned down to kiss her forehead, then turned to Buck. "I need to meet my twin before the wedding," he said. "I know you ran the DNA test, and it proves I'm her brother, but I need to know here." He tapped his chest just over his heart.

Buck nodded, hearing the determination in his soon-to-be brother-in-law's voice. "You got it. She can't wait to meet you, either."

Ansley stared into the mirror. Today was her wedding day. Brushing her dark hair back, she promised herself she wouldn't cry even as her eyes filled with tears.

"You are going to ruin your makeup," her mother said, and handed her a tissue. "Buck will show. Nothing on this earth can keep him from marrying you today."

She took the tissue, dabbed at her eyes and nodded.

"I know it's bad luck to see each other on your wedding day but—"

"Buck called you. He told you he made it out of the mountains. He's going to be here."

"Have you heard how James is doing?" Ansley asked.

"He came through surgery fine. The doctor said he was lucky. The bullet missed vital organs. It was just the loss of blood they were worried about, but you know Lonesome. Once word was out that blood was needed, people turned out to help. Bella and the baby are doing great. It's all good news."

She shook her head. When she'd talked to Davy, he'd told her that Willie and deputies from the sheriff's department had gone up to help search for bodies. Buck could have been one of them. She still worried that he'd been injured and didn't want to tell her. "I shouldn't have put so much pressure on Buck to find my brother. What was I thinking? Me and my perfect Christmas wedding. Without Buck—"

"Oh, honey." Her mother took her in her arms. "Buck will be here and if I know him, he'll have your twin brother with him. That man will move heaven and earth to give you the wedding you've always wanted." She drew back to look at her daughter. "You just have to believe."

Ansley nodded. She did believe in Buck, trusted him with the rest of her life. But she was set to get married in less than an hour and there had been no word from Buck since that one phone call. She couldn't help being terrified that something horrible had happened up there, that she would die alone because Buck Crawford was the only man for her.

Her cell phone rang. She grabbed it up. "Buck?"

"Hey, honey."

"Are you all right?" she cried.

"I'm fine. I'll tell you all about it when I see you. Actually, after the wedding, if that's okay. I know I'm calling it close." Tears of relief began streaming down her face. "There's someone here who wants to meet you before the wedding. He's right outside."

She heard the tap at the door and quickly wiped at her tears, her mother handing her another tissue. The door opened and standing there was her twin brother. She would have known him anywhere. Their gazes met and locked. As tears filled his eyes, she began to cry in earnest as she ran into his arms.

Chapter 20

DJ was beside Sadie's bed when she opened her eyes. She blinked, her eyes focusing on his face for a moment before she said, "Tell me you made it to the wedding."

He laughed; it felt good. Sadie was awake. She was going to make it. He couldn't remember ever feeling this overjoyed. "You just made my day and I've already had the most amazing day."

She smiled. "Tell me." She sounded weak, but back from wherever she'd been. He never wanted to come that close to losing her ever again.

So he told her about wanting to see Ansley before the wedding. "It was…incredible," he said, his voice cracking. "I was afraid. I didn't know what to expect. I had no idea what she was like and yet when I saw her…" He shook his head. Sadie reached for his hand, squeezing it, tears glistening in her eyes.

"She told me that she always felt as if a part of her was missing," he said after a moment. "I understood at once. How can a person yearn for something they didn't even know existed? I realized at the cabin that I'd tried to fill that need with Keira. The problem was, she never saw me as family. She never felt the immediate closeness I felt when I saw my twin. It was like a bolt of lightning."

"And the wedding?"

He chuckled. "Of course you'd want to know about that. It was perfect. All of the Colts were there except for James, who's still recovering. I'll fill you in later. But Lori had him on her phone so he got to be there via the internet. I met all my half brothers."

"And your mother?"

He nodded. "It was strange. She's nice. Buck was right. I like all of them. They made me feel like…family."

She smiled. "I figured as much."

"It's a complicated story about my mother and father. He was Del Ransom Colt, one hell of a bronc rider and one hell of a private eye, according to the family. I was named for him. Del Ransom Jr., thus the DJ. Apparently, I come from a long line of rodeo cowboys." Sadie laughed, then winced in pain. "You need to rest."

"So do you. I'm so glad you made the wedding."

"Me, too." She squeezed his hand and closed her eyes. He stayed there watching her breathe, thinking about everything. He didn't move until the sheriff popped his head in and motioned that he was needed out in the hall.

He kissed Sadie on the forehead and went out to

talk to his half brother Willie Colt. They'd met on the mountain in passing.

"How is she?"

"She's conscious," DJ said. "The doctor said she should have a complete recovery."

"Good," Willie said. "I'm going to need to ask both of you some questions about what happened up on that mountain. If now isn't a good time for you…"

"No, I'd just as soon get it over with."

After DJ left her hospital room, Sadie found herself in tears. She hardly ever cried. But seeing DJ, seeing the change in him since meeting his twin and the rest of the family, filled her heart with joy. It would take him a while to get used to it. He'd already lost so much. It would be hard for him to accept this gift of family, but in time, he would and he'd be better for it.

Sadie thought of the pain she'd seen in his eyes on the helicopter ride to the hospital. He'd held her hand, begging her to stay awake. "I can't lose you," he said again and again, his voice rough with emotion, his blue eyes swimming in tears. "I can't lose you."

She remembered little after that until she opened her eyes and saw DJ beside her bed wearing a Western suit and bolo tie. He looked so handsome in the suit, so different from the Montana cowboy she'd known. Wiping her tears, she closed her eyes, surprised how exhausted she felt.

When she woke again, her room was filled with women all about her age. They introduced themselves as Carla, Davy's wife; Ellie, Willie's wife; Lori, James's wife; and Bella, Tommy's wife. The Colt women had brought her gifts, wanting to meet her. Ansley was with them.

"Shouldn't you be on your honeymoon?" Sadie had asked.

"Buck and I aren't going anywhere until all of you are out of the hospital," the pretty dark-haired woman told her. "It's my fault since I desperately wanted my twin at the wedding. I could have gotten you all killed."

Sadie shook her head. "Your search for DJ actually saved our lives. We wouldn't be here now if it wasn't for your husband."

Bella had just given birth to a little girl with dark hair and Colt blue eyes. "She's precious," Sadie said after looking at the photo, since the infant was still down the hall in the nursery after coming a month early.

The women were fun, laughing and bringing cheer to the hospital room. They were all so excited about DJ being found, commenting on how much he looked like Ansley.

"We brought you a few things you might like," Lori Colt told her.

Bella had produced a dusty-rose-colored nightgown. "DJ said dusty rose was your color. I promise it's more comfortable than a hospital gown."

They also brought her flowers, candy, lip balm, lotion, a scented candle. They promised that their next visit they'd bring ice cream and small fried pies from Lori's former sandwich shop.

True to their word, they showed up the next day with the treats and lots of laughter and stories, often about the Colt brothers and growing up around Lonesome.

Sadie couldn't imagine, not after growing up in Palm Beach. Here the mountains came right down to the small western town. Pine trees grew everywhere. She wondered what it was like when it wasn't covered in a thick blanket of snow. She thought about what DJ had said about his favorite season, spring in Montana. She had never lived in a place that had seasons.

"How is DJ doing?" she'd asked. She didn't need to explain herself. They knew at once what she was asking since they knew that he had practically been camped out at the hospital.

"It's like he's always been part of the family," Carla, Davy's wife, said. "I think at first he was nervous, but once he met his brothers, I think he realized how much they all have in common."

"If you're asking if he plans to stay," Bella said, always the one to get to the heart of things, Sadie had realized, "he knows he's welcome. The brothers told him that there's a section of the ranch that is his for a house, if he wants it. They also told him that the ranch is as much his as theirs. I heard them talking about raising more cattle."

"It's the way Del would have wanted it, all of his offspring together," Lori said.

"I'm sure DJ is overwhelmed by all of your generosity. I certainly am," Sadie said, wondering why DJ hadn't mentioned any of this to her. Because he was going to turn it down? Or because he was going to take their offer? Probably because it was all overwhelming and he hadn't made up his mind yet.

"Bet you're ready for a nice juicy burger," Carla said. "We'll bring you one tomorrow."

"When are you blowing this joint?" Bella inquired. "We want you and DJ to come out to the ranch for dinner. I'm also throwing a New Year's Eve bash if you feel up to it by then."

"We've worn her out enough for one day," Lori said. "She doesn't have to make any big decisions right now."

"Except about the burger," Ellie said. "You want that loaded?"

She laughed and nodded. "Fries?"

"Of course fries," Bella cried. "What do you think we are?"

They'd all left laughing and Sadie found herself looking forward to their next visit even as she realized the visits would soon be ending. The doctor said she was healing nicely and would be able to leave soon—long before New Year's Eve.

Titus Grandville hated his father butting into his business. Worse was when his old man showed up unannounced at his office. He'd had no word on what had transpired up in the mountains. Butch had promised to call the moment it was done. He hadn't called. The storm had stopped. The plows were running, the roads opening up.

Nerves on end already, looking up and seeing Marcus walk in only angered him. "What are you doing here?"

His father didn't answer, merely came in, pulled out a chair and sat down across the desk from him.

"Hello?" Titus snapped. "I really don't need this right now. I'm busy. I have work to do. What are you doing here?"

"This used to be my office," his father said. "You probably don't remember when you and your brother

Jimmy used to play on the floor in here. You always took Jimmy's toys."

"Why are we talking about my dead brother?" Titus demanded. He knew his father still blamed him for the car crash that had killed Jimmy. He'd felt enough guilt over it; he didn't need the old man to rub it in, especially today.

"I always wondered why you didn't cry at the funeral."

Titus was on his feet. "Would love to wade through the past with you, Dad, but not today. You need to leave."

"Things didn't go like you planned them, did they?"

He felt the hair rise on the back of his neck. "Why would you say that?"

"Because I saw the cops as I came up the back way."

It was the smugness on his father's face. All of his life, his father had tried to tell him what to do. "You never trusted my instincts," Titus snapped. "Not even once. You never said, 'Good job, son.'"

"You never gave me reason to," Marcus said as two uniformed officers filled his office doorway.

"Titus Grandville?" one of the officers said as he stepped in. "We need you to come with us."

"What's this about?" Titus asked innocently as he saw his father get to his feet.

"We're arresting you for the murder of Keira Cross and attempted murder of DJ Diamond and Sadie Montclair as well as the deaths of Lloyd Tanner, Butch Lamar and Rafe Westfall and the shooting of PI James Colt."

"Is that all?" Marcus Grandville said with a laugh as he moved out of the cops' way.

"You realize that you can't prove any of this, right?" Titus said.

Titus looked around for a way out, his gaze going to his father who was standing back, smiling as if to say, "Told you so." It was something he'd heard all his life. He'd killed the good son, his father's favorite, and Marcus had never let him forget it.

"Enjoying this, old man?" Titus said as one of the cops began reading him his rights and the other cuffed him. Soon he would be doing the perp walk through the Grandville building out to a squad car. "You've been waiting for this day, haven't you?"

His father nodded, then grimaced, his hand going to his chest as he fell back against the wall and slumped to the floor. One of the cops hurried to him and quickly called 911 to report that the elderly man appeared to be having a heart attack.

"Go ahead and take him down to headquarters," the cop said to the other cop as he began to do CPR on Marcus.

Titus stared at his father, wondering why the cop was bothering. "You're wasting your time. He has a bad heart. It's rotten to the core. There's no saving him."

The cop jerked on his arm, dragging him to the door.

"I want to call my lawyer," Titus said. "I'm going to sue you and the police department for false arrest. You have no proof that I've done anything." On the way out of his office he saw two men in suits coming toward him. The one in the lead flashed his credentials. FBI. He waved a warrant.

"When it rains, it pours," Titus said, and smirked at agents demanding to see all records and confiscating all computers and phones.

Before they reached the street, EMTs raced past them on the way up to the top floor. Titus looked out at dirty snow in the street and told himself he'd be out of jail before the EMTs reached the top floor. He was a Grandville, the last of them, finally. All of this was his. He was finally taking his rightful place. These people had no idea who they were dealing with.

When Sadie woke later that evening, the nurse told her that she had another visitor. She was glad to see Buck Crawford enter her room. "I heard you were getting better. I had to see for myself."

She smiled at him, sitting up a little. She knew little of what had happened up on the mountain. DJ had glossed over it when she'd questioned him on one of his many visits. Clearly, he hadn't wanted to relive it—not that she could blame him. "Tell me what happened after I was shot. It's all such a blur." She listened as he told her about the avalanche.

"Keira?" Buck shook his head. "She took one of the bullets. She was gone before the cornice broke and fell. We barely got you out before the avalanche hit the cabin. Her body will be recovered and when it does, DJ said he plans to have her buried next to Charley Diamond on the mountainside cemetery back in Butte."

"And the Grandvilles?" she asked.

"Titus was arrested earlier today in Butte. One of the men from the poker game, Keith Danson? He's turning state's evidence against Titus. He might never get out of prison. The FBI has been investigating him for some time apparently. They raided his office earlier. I suspect whatever they find added to murder and attempted murder…" He shrugged. "I'd say the reign of the Grandvilles is over, since his father died of a heart attack during Titus's arrest."

Sadie shook her head. It all sounded too familiar. "How is DJ?" she finally had to ask.

"He won't have any trouble with the law," Buck said. "Both Butch Lamar's body and Rafe Westfall's bodies have been retrieved from the avalanche. I'm sure their connection to Titus Grandville will be of interest to the Feds, but DJ is in the clear."

"So it's over," Sadie said, thinking of DJ.

"It doesn't have to be," Buck said as if reading her thoughts.

She smiled, wishing it were true. She was DJ's past. These people and this town, they were his future. He'd come by the hospital constantly to see how she was doing. Each time, she asked about his new family and each time, he would smile and tell her. She saw that he was indeed overwhelmed by their acceptance and even more so by their love.

When the doctor told her that she was being released in a few days, she knew it would be best if she didn't see DJ again once she left. He had to learn a lifetime about himself, about his mother and his father, about the family he had only recently found. But he was fortunate that he had people to tell him the stories, to fill in the gaps in his life, to share memories of his father. He also had his mother, who was now part of the Colt family circle. She, too, had missed out on so much, but at least she'd gotten to watch the Colt brothers grow up.

Sadie had no idea what DJ's future held—just that he needed to sort it all out. She wanted him to have this time. They both needed it. She could admit it now. She loved DJ Diamond and always would. Which was why she couldn't say goodbye. It would hurt too bad. She also knew that he would try to get her to stay and she might if he asked. She couldn't imagine ever loving anyone as much as she did him. Her heart couldn't take a long goodbye.

On the day she was to be released, the nurse came in to tell her that she couldn't leave until a wheelchair was brought up for her. "Then please hurry," Sadie had said. "I have a plane to catch." The nurse gave her a disapproving look but turned and left.

Sadie pulled out her phone and called her godfather before she could change her mind. It was a call she'd been putting off and was grateful when he didn't answer. She left a voice mail. "Headed home. Will see you soon."

Chapter 21

DJ told himself that he was ready to look toward the future as he hurried up to Sadie's floor at the hospital. Yesterday, he'd put Keira to rest in the cemetery next to Charley. He still couldn't help feeling as if he'd failed her even though he knew Charley would have told him that it all came down to genes.

He'd been rediscovering his own genes. He was a Colt from his dark hair to his blue eyes. The more he was around his twin and his half brothers, the more he saw himself in them. They'd taken a different path in life, but they weren't that different. The Colt brothers risked their lives at their jobs—just as they'd risked them in the rodeo. It seemed something in their blood craved adventure. They were all gamblers at heart.

Pushing open Sadie's hospital room door, he couldn't contain his excitement. He couldn't wait to tell Sadie what he had planned. He'd never bought flowers for a woman before, and he felt uncomfortable holding the large bouquet. There was so much he had to say to her, words that had been stacking up, ready to burst out of him since he'd admitted how he felt about her.

Just the thought terrified him. He'd told Sadie that he loved her at the cabin, something he'd never said to another woman because he'd never felt love like that before her. Over the time they'd worked together they'd become more than colleagues. They'd become friends. It was no wonder that he'd fallen for her.

But she'd never taken him seriously. She thought he chased more women than he did. He'd let her believe it, a mistake, he realized some time into their relationship. From the beginning, she'd made it perfectly clear that it was hands-off. If he needed a reminder there was her godfather, who'd also warned him with the threat of violence not to fall in love with Sadie. Their arrangement had been strictly business.

Until Montana. Until they were snowed in at the cabin high in the mountains just before Christmas. Until they'd let their true feelings out.

Now, though, they had to decide about their future. He knew what he wanted, but he wasn't sure Sadie would. He knew that wouldn't be a deal breaker for him. He loved her. He'd go and do whatever she wanted. It would be hard though to leave Montana, to leave the family he'd found, especially to leave his twin. He and Ansley had bonded instantly.

As he stepped into Sadie's room, he stopped cold when he saw the stripped bed and the woman from housekeeping readying the room for the next patient. For just an instant he thought the worst.

"She...she...tell me she didn't..."

The woman looked up. "Leave? She checked out this morning."

That wasn't possible. "But she wasn't supposed to check out until this afternoon."

"She checked out early."

She'd just checked out without letting him know? "Where did she go?"

The woman shrugged. "You might ask downstairs."

He looked down at the bouquet of flowers. "That's you, Diamond, a dollar short and a day late," he whispered to himself as he turned around and left the room. Uncle Charley used to say that when he messed up. He'd really messed up this time.

Downstairs he inquired as to where Sadie Montclair had gone and found out that she had been trying to catch a flight to Florida. Without saying goodbye? Maybe something urgent had happened to her godfather. Otherwise... Otherwise, she'd gone home, back to Florida, back to the life she was born into. Their partnership over, she felt there was nothing keeping her in Montana?

He thought about their time together in the cabin. His chest felt hollowed out, his heart crushed. She'd said she loved him. Clearly, she'd changed her mind. Otherwise, why would she just leave without even saying goodbye?

It wasn't like he'd asked her to stay, he reminded himself. But how could he? He not only had little to offer her, but also he'd put her life in danger and might again if she stayed with him. Wasn't it better to let her walk away? It wasn't like he was a prize. Why would she want to marry him?

"What are you doing?"

He recognized the voice calling to him. As he came out of the hospital, he turned to see Buck Crawford on his way in. "Shouldn't you be on your honeymoon?" he asked Buck.

"Ansley postponed it until we knew that James and Sadie were going to be okay. Wasn't Sadie being released this afternoon?"

"Apparently she left early. She's gone."

"I take it you missed her. So go after her," Buck said.

DJ hesitated, feeling lost. "She apparently already made her decision about me."

Buck sighed. "I'm going to give you some unsolicited advice, brother-in-law. When you find the woman who makes you doubt everything about yourself and at the same time makes you believe you're superhuman, you hang on to her."

He shook his head. "I'm not sure she feels the same way."

"One way to find out," Buck said. "Press your luck. Love is a gamble, but when you win…" He broke into a huge grin.

As he started to go inside, DJ said, "Did Ansley send you?"

His brother-in-law just laughed. "She said it's a twin thing."

Sadie had planned to take a taxi home, so she was surprised when her godfather picked her up at the airport.

"Is everything all right?" she had to ask as she climbed into the back of the town car beside him.

"That's what I want to know," he said. "When I heard you were flying home, I was worried."

"I'm fine. The doctor said I will have a scar but other than that…"

He took her hand. "I'm sorry."

She turned slowly to look at her godfather, frowning in confusion.

"I shouldn't have brought DJ Diamond into your life."

Sadie shook her head. "I was the one who followed him to Montana."

"When I met him, I knew he was trouble. I just thought the two of you would be a good match. I had no idea that you would fall for him."

"I never said I—"

"You don't have to. I know you, Sadie. What I want to know now is what are you going to do about it?" She stared at him. "Don't tell me that you're going to let him get away with breaking your heart."

"It wasn't like that. I was the one who left. It's better this way."

"For whom? You look like someone kicked your dog. You've never backed down from a challenge. Why are you running now?"

Sadie shook her head, thinking about the small cozy cabin, making love in front of the fire with the snow falling outside. It had been magical—but it hadn't been real life. It was a fantasy few days in a snowstorm. To read any more into it was beyond foolish.

"Please don't insult my intelligence by trying to tell me that you aren't still in love with him."

"Even if I was, I can't believe you'd want me to marry him," she said, shocked by this conversation. "You're the one who warned me not to fall in love with him."

Her godfather shook his head. "But you did anyway

and now you come back here looking like you let him steal your heart and you're afraid to go get it back. No goddaughter of mine would give up so easily."

"I'm your only goddaughter." She frowned. "Aren't I?"

He smiled, something he seldom did. "You are indeed. Does he love you?"

How did she answer that? She thought of him beside her hospital bed. She thought of the way he'd looked in her eyes, the way he'd held her, kissed her, made love to her. But how did she know that she was any different from the other women DJ had seduced?

As if reading her mind, her godfather said, "Don't be a fool. That cowboy has been smitten with you from the start. But if you don't believe it, go back there and ask him. He'd be a fool if he wasn't and DJ Diamond is a lot of things, but he's not a fool."

"You make it sound so simple."

"Love?" He chortled a laugh. "It's the most complicated and confusing, excruciatingly painful and exasperating emotion there is. But it's what makes life worthwhile. Stop being a coward and find out how that man feels about you. How can it be any worse than the way you're feeling right now?"

"Want to tell me about the woman who broke *your* heart?" she asked.

"No, I don't," he snapped. "And Sadie? Take the private jet, if you want. And if he says he doesn't love you, shoot him. I have people who will take care of the body."

"I wish you were joking," she said, but had to smile. "Thank you."

* * *

DJ couldn't believe it when he got the text from Sadie.

I'm sorry I left the way I did. I love you. If you can forgive me, I'll be flying into Yellowstone International Airport tomorrow afternoon at 4. I'll be the one wearing the red cowboy boots.

He read the text twice. He'd really thought that he'd never hear from her again. He'd been telling himself that he had to let her go. A part of him believed that she loved him, but maybe love couldn't conquer all—no matter what his twin said. His heart had been breaking since finding her gone. Now he was almost afraid to trust she'd be back again.

Except this was Sadie. This was the woman he loved. He'd had to let her go even though he'd been planning to go after her. He read the message again—just in case he'd misread it.

He smiled and tried to still his pounding heart before he responded with his own. I'll be wearing my hat.

Then he headed for the airline ticket counter to cancel his flight to Florida that was leaving in an hour. Sadie loved him. His smile was so big it hurt his face. Sadie loved him. Love had brought her back. Just as love had him wearing his lucky boots as he planned to fly to Florida and try to get her back.

Okay, maybe Ansley was right. Maybe love could bring two very different people together. Just as it had brought him to this family of his. He pulled out his phone. He couldn't wait to tell his twin.

"Didn't I tell you that nothing can stop true love?"

Ansley cried. "You two were meant for each other. It is high time you told her what's in your heart. But first here's what we need to do."

Sadie wore her red cowboy boots. The first time she met DJ, he'd been wearing a pair of worn cowboy boots. She'd commented on them, suggesting he buy a new pair.

He'd laughed. "Sorry, sweetie, but these are my lucky boots."

"Call me sweetie again and not even your lucky boots can save you."

She could laugh about it now. Especially since she was wearing her boots because she needed all the luck she could get as she got off the plane.

"He needs time with you and the rest of his family," she'd told Ansley when she'd called.

"He needs you. He loves you and you love him. That makes you family. You need to come back. He's hurting."

"So am I."

"Do you love him?"

"I do." Her voice had cracked. "I just don't know where we go next."

Ansley had laughed. "You think there's a road map? It's a leap of faith. None of us can see the future. We just have to believe that something amazing is ahead and enjoy each day. DJ told me you were an optimist."

"He did, did he?"

"All he talks about is you," Ansley said. "He wants to make a life with you. He has a plan."

She'd laughed. She was familiar with his plans. "A plan?"

"He'll tell you all about it when he sees you. He isn't going to let you go. My brother is no fool, even though sometimes he acts like one." They'd laughed. "Tell me you'll give him a chance. You know he loves you."

She did know, she thought as she looked around for DJ in the crowd at the Yellowstone International Airport. She spotted him standing against a nearby wall, his Stetson cocked on his dark hair, those blue eyes taking her in as if she was a cold drink of water in the desert. He pushed off the wall and headed toward her as she descended the stairs.

The way she'd left without saying goodbye and having been gone for a couple of days, she thought they'd be awkward with each other. That they no longer had anything to say. That they would realize not even love could sustain this relationship.

She watched him approach, her pulse hammering.

"Sadie." That one word filled her heart like helium. DJ looped his arm around her waist and picked her up before she reached the bottom step. He swung her around, taking her in his arms as he put her down. For a moment, he just looked at her, then he kissed her passionately.

She heard cheers and clapping, but they were a distant sound. Her heart was beating too loudly in her ears as DJ drew back.

"I love you, Sadie Montclair. Marry me." He dropped to one knee. "Love your boots, by the way," he whispered, then said, "Be my wife, be my partner, be mine."

She smiled. She knew this man. This wasn't such a leap of faith. Yet she couldn't speak as she looked into his eyes. All she could do was nod and fall into his arms as he rose. There were more cheers and clapping than before as some of the crowd joined in along with the entire Colt and Crawford clan.

All she could think was that from now on these would be her lucky boots as she was swept up in this large, gregarious, loving family.

Did it matter what the future held? Not as long as she and DJ faced it together. She was putting her money on the two of them. It wasn't a safe bet, but she was ready to play the odds.

Chapter 22

It was their first Christmas holiday together. Also their first with DJ's family. Sadie had never seen anything like it and she could tell that DJ was just as overcome by it all. The Colts had a variety of holiday traditions—including all getting together at Bella and Tommy's because they had the largest space. There was a mountain of food and holiday treats, games and prizes, and more presents than she'd ever seen.

Because of everything that had happened, even the holiday had been put off until they could all be together.

"Ansley," Buck cried as he finished bringing in all the presents his new bride had purchased.

"I might have gone a little overboard," she admitted. "But it's our first Christmas, the first with my family, the first with my twin."

Buck smiled and raised his hands in surrender.

"Given all that, I'm surprised you exhibited such self-control."

Sadie and DJ had gone shopping even though everyone told them it wasn't necessary. "The two of you are our presents," Ansley had said, and the others had agreed.

"It's just because you don't know us very well," DJ had joked. "By next year, you'll feel entirely different."

Still, they'd shopped together. It had been fun. Even DJ had enjoyed it. Sadie could tell that he'd never had anyone to buy for, other than Keira, and they'd never celebrated holidays together.

They went to Bozeman, hitting all the shops, and then had lunch in a quaint place along Main Street.

This large, exuberant family was something so new for them both that they grew quiet after they ate. Sadie thought that it was all just starting to sink in. When DJ spoke, she knew he'd been thinking the same thing.

"Can we do this?" he asked, meeting her gaze.

She didn't have to ask what he meant. The two of them, she felt, were solid together because they knew each other given everything they'd been through. "We can do anything we set our minds to."

"Are you sure we aren't too broken?" DJ asked.

Sadie chuckled. "Isn't everyone in one way or another?"

He shook his head. "What worries me is that I really like them. I don't want to let them down. Especially Ansley."

"You won't." She reached across the table to take his hand. "We have the rest of our lives yet to live. Our pasts are…unique, but they have also made us stronger. We're survivors. We can do this."

He smiled then, squeezing her hand, and she let go. "I've never asked you what you wanted out of life."

"To be like everyone else." She said it quickly and shrugged. "Promise you won't laugh?" He nodded solemnly and crossed his chest above his heart with his finger. "I want a family. I want what the Colt women have."

"To be married to private eyes?"

She shook her head. "They have a sense of community I've never had. They're all excited about their kids growing up together. Bella is convinced the kids will rule the school. I have no doubt hers will." She laughed. "I want Montana." She saw his surprised expression.

"I never thought you'd leave Florida."

"I want to see spring here," she said, glancing toward the restaurant window. Christmas decorations hung from the streetlights. Snow was piled up along the edge of the street. Everyone outside was bundled up against the cold. "I want to see the grass turn green, to feel the sun bring back life. I want to grow a garden and catch a fish out of the river." Her voice broke. "I want an ordinary house with a swing set in my backyard and a couple of kids out there playing on it."

He laughed. "You want a lot," he joked. "Just a couple of kids?"

"I'd discuss more," she said with a grin.

DJ turned serious. "You haven't mentioned this husband of yours."

She smiled. "I want him to be anything he wants. Lover, father, best friend. You want to raise cattle to go with that Stetson of yours, I'm all for it."

His eyes seemed to light up. "My brothers want to make the Colt Ranch a true ranch. There's plenty of land and they've offered me a section for our house. I have money to buy whatever we'll need."

"You know I have my own money, so we can pretty much do anything we want." She met his gaze, her heart in her throat. Was it possible? Could they do this? "Wouldn't you miss the grift?"

"Sounds like raising cattle might be enough of a gamble."

"I'm serious. You love what you do."

"I used to, but I've lost my taste for it. I'm like you. I look around Lonesome and I feel the need to put down roots. I want a swing set in my backyard. I want a couple of blond towheads out there who look just like you but are trying to see how much higher they can swing. You do realize that if you and I had kids they'd get some of my genes."

She smiled. "Would that be so bad? I happen to love your jeans. Especially the way they fit you."

He locked eyes with her. "We could do this, you and me. We could make a good life here in Montana. You'd have to learn to ride a horse."

"You know how to ride? You never told me that."

"I was raised on a ranch."

"Charley had a horse?"

"A couple of wild ones that Keira and I used to try to ride." At the mention of Keira a shadow crossed his face for a moment. "Our kids will have horses. Apparently rodeoing is in my blood."

"So I've heard. Let's cross that bridge when we get to it," she said. "But I'd love to have a horse of my own. Bella rides all the time. I know she'd teach me."

He nodded. "I can see us here."

"Me, too." She felt her smile widen. "I love you, DJ.

I have for a very long time. You do realize that my god-father will want to give me away."

"Yes, your godfather. You sure he's good with this, you and me?"

She nodded. "He gave me his blessing." She didn't mention what else he'd said as DJ leaned across the table to steal a quick kiss.

They both grinned. They'd found not only their way to each other, but to a family and a place to make a home and a life neither of them had ever expected.

They could do this. Together. Partners forever.

Just before midnight on New Year's Eve, Sheriff Willie Colt stood, raising his glass as he looked around the table. As the oldest of the Colt brothers and prodded by his wife Ellie, it was up to him to speak before they rang in the new year. Bella and Tommy had thrown quite the party as usual. The whole family was here, and it had grown considerably since last year.

"It's been quite the year, wouldn't you say?" Everyone laughed.

"What a couple years this has been," Willie said as he looked around the huge table. "When James got hurt on his last bronc ride and came home, we all expected him to do what we usually did, heal up and go back. But instead he started digging into Dad's last case, the one he'd never solved before his death. We couldn't have known where that was going to lead."

There were murmurs around the table. "James gave up rodeoing to reopen Dad's private investigative business. It was the beginning of Colt Brothers Investigation. Tommy was lured back and then Davy. I was determined not to join this ragtag bunch," he said, and laughed.

"Instead, I joined the sheriff's department as a deputy to find out what had really happened to Dad that night when he was killed on the railroad tracks. I ended up finding something that I loved more than rodeo, law enforcement, and that led me to Seattle, and we all know how that ended."

More laughter around the table.

"We got Ellie," Bella said, and the other women all joined in with cheers. "Turned out to be a great deal."

"It wasn't like we ever expected you to fall in love, let alone get married," James said.

"We figured you would be Lonesome's old cranky bachelor," Tommy said.

"He's still cranky," someone said.

Willie waited until the laughter died down. "The four of us are now married, some of us fathers. There's been a few surprises along the way." He looked in the direction of Ansley and DJ and smiled. "Happy surprises," he added. He watched Ansley hug her brother and Sadie, tears in her eyes.

"We hadn't wanted to believe Dad's pickup being hit by the train was an accident. We now know it was. Also, we learned a lot about our mother, who was a mystery to us all." He glanced down the table at Beth. "I know Dad loved our mother, Mary Jo, but I also know that she made his life very hard. He found true love the second time with Beth, Ansley and DJ's mother. Sometimes we don't get the happy endings we want, but in the end we're so thankful for family. I wish Dad were here to see this. I like to think he'd be proud. I know I am at what you've all accomplished."

He cleared his voice. "Now we're about to start another year and I for one can't wait to see what this amazing family has in store for it." A cheer went up. He looked over at his wife. Ellie was glowing.

"Are you kidding me?" Bella cried. "Ellie?"

Her sister-in-law smiled and nodded. "There is a little Willie in the works." That brought on more cheering along with groans from some of the brothers and remarks like, "Never thought you had it in you, bro."

"It's almost time," someone called out, and everyone looked to the clock on the wall. They rose from the table as the countdown began. "Ten, nine, eight, seven…" The joy in the room rose as their voices joined to ring in the new year.

"Six, five, four, three, two… Happy New Year!"

Willie took Ellie in his arms and kissed her. All around him he watched his brothers and their wives and girlfriends kiss and hug. Noisemakers came out and confetti filled the air along with balloons. Bella never did anything halfway, he thought. This year she had a lot of help from the family since she had a new baby girl.

Willie laughed, hoping his father was watching all of this. This was the family he'd started. Willie hoped he'd be proud.

Epilogue

Ansley felt as if her feet weren't touching the ground as she looked out past the American flag flapping in the backyard breeze to her husband standing with the Colt men by the barbecue grill. Her husband. She would never get tired of staying that.

"You have been smiling way too much for a woman about to turn thirty," Bella said as she put her daughter down in the playpen in the shade. Daisy immediately began cooing and waving her arms at the bird mobile hanging over her head. Her twin boy cousins were in another playpen, also in the shade. Both were sacked out. Their older sister, Jamie, was playing in the kiddie pool not far from where the men were grilling lunch.

"Isn't it wonderful to have so much family?" Ansley said, knowing that Bella had also been an only child. So had Lori and Carla and Ellie. Probably why all of them wanted numerous children. "Just think, Daisy will grow up with all these cousins. Won't that be fun?" Carla and Ellie were both pregnant. When Ansley had gone looking for her birth mother she could never have imagined finding this much family.

"Don't try to change the subject." Bella looked down to where Tommy was standing. As if feeling her gaze on him, he looked up and smiled. She smiled back and glanced down at their daughter. Ansley knew Bella had to be thinking about how close she'd almost come to losing him the day their baby was born.

"What's going on with you?" Bella said. "I can tell you're holding out on me."

Ansley smiled as she saw her twin standing with the other men. Just the sight of DJ brought her such joy. She'd been so afraid that they would never find him and when Buck had, she'd been so afraid that she would lose them both. When he'd walked in before her wedding…

Tears filled her eyes at the memory. She made a swipe at them, embarrassed at how emotional she'd been lately. "I'm happy, that's all," she said. "I love my life and you're a part of that."

Bella made a rude sound. "Okay, fine. Just keep it to yourself, but I have to tell you, you should never play poker. Your face gives everything away."

She laughed as she scanned Bella's backyard. Soon she would have a backyard of her own. Her brothers and Buck's father and brother had been helping with the new houses being built on the Colt Ranch for her and Buck—and for DJ and Sadie. She couldn't wait until theirs was finished.

Past the men at the barbecue grill, Lori and Ellie were uncovering the salads and desserts on the table under the umbrella. Sadie was busy putting serving spoons in everything. Ansley could tell they were laughing and was amazed how Sadie had become one of them so quickly. Having all of these women come into her life was a joy she'd never anticipated when she'd come looking for her birth mother.

Speaking of her birth mother, where was she? Running late probably, because she was working even on a holiday. Being the mayor of Lonesome was a full-time job, one Beth took seriously—just as she did motherhood. She was going to make a wonderful grandmother. Ansley started to go help with the other women when Bella stopped her.

"Ansley!" Bella demanded. "No one is this excited for her thirtieth birthday, not even you."

She couldn't help but smile. Her happiness just seemed to overflow these days. "It's my birthday! Mine and DJ's. It also just happens to be the Fourth of July." They were also celebrating Davy's birthday as well since his was only a few days ago.

Bella was giving her a side-eye when suddenly her eyes widened. "Oh, you are not." She was laughing and smiling. "Does Buck know yet?"

"No, and don't you dare tell him. I want to surprise him tonight during the fireworks show."

Her friend's eyes filled with tears. "I am so happy for you. So happy for all of us. I never imagined that our children would be raised together on this ranch. We're all going to get sick of each other," she joked.

She pulled her into a hug. "I'm so glad you came into our lives and brought DJ and Sadie. You know they'll be getting married soon. I love weddings. Can you imagine what it is going to be like when all of our kids go to school?" Bella asked as she looked down at her daughter, who'd fallen asleep. "The Colt kids will rule the school. Along with the Crawfords and Diamonds, of course. The teachers won't know what hit them."

Ansley saw Buck look up at her. Their gazes met and she realized that he knew. He gave her a wide grin. So much for waiting until the fireworks. They'd already had their fireworks and now they were going to have a baby.

DJ pulled Sadie aside. "It's not too late. You can change your mind about marrying me." He waved a hand, taking in all the family gathered today. "I suspect it will always be like this."

"I certainly hope so," she said, stepping into his arms. "Happy birthday." She kissed him and let him lead her into the cool of the pines and out of sight of the others.

He held her at arm's length as he studied her. "I wouldn't be here if it wasn't for you. I almost lost you because of it."

She shook her head. "We *are* here now. Together. There is no looking back anymore. You changed my life...don't you realize that?"

DJ smiled. "How did I ever get so lucky?"

"I guess you played to your strengths."

"Whatever the reason, thank you for being my partner. I'm sure you had your doubts when your godfather suggested we work together."

Sadie laughed. "It was when I met you that I really had my doubts. What was I supposed to do with this arrogant Montana cowboy?"

"Save him from himself," DJ said, and pulled her closer for another kiss.

"Do you think we could sneak away during the fireworks show?" he asked.

"You're incorrigible," she said with a laugh.

"I just can't seem to get enough of you." He kissed her and drew back. "Okay, we should go back to the barbecue. Everyone will be talking about us."

"Everyone is already talking about us. They wonder what a man like you is doing with a woman like me."

He drew her close again so that their bodies were molded together. "I hope you told them."

Laughing she pulled away. "I love your family."

"*Our* family. They are pretty fantastic, aren't they? Ansley is nothing short of amazing. Do you know that she started her own jewelry business without the help of her rich family? Talk about determination."

Sadie nodded, smiling. "She's a lot like her twin. She just wouldn't give up hope that Buck would find you and bring you to the wedding."

"Thanks to you I made it. I wish you could have been there."

"All that matters is that you made it and just in time."

"You know me, I like to call things close to the wire," DJ said.

"Yes, I do know that about you."

He met her gaze. "I'll be early to our wedding. Are you sure you want to be the wife of a rancher? Us living on the Colt Ranch. Me, raising cattle."

"After all those years of being all hat and no cattle?" she joked. "I suspect you were born to ranching. You love a gamble."

He grinned. "You know me so well."

"Don't I, though," she said as he put his arm around her waist and led her back toward the barbecue and their new family.

"Your godfather still coming to our wedding this spring?" he asked, sounding a little worried.

"He's going to give me away. He said he wouldn't miss it for anything. He wants to ride a horse while he's in Montana and eat steak, he said."

"So he isn't coming just to make sure I'm good enough for his goddaughter?"

She smiled over at her fiancé. "Oh, he's definitely doing that. But I wouldn't worry too much if I were you. He's the one who brought us together, so he only has himself to blame for the way it turned out."

DJ pulled her closer. "Thanks, I feel so much better." He grinned. "Have I told you how much I love you and that I can't wait to marry you?"

"I believe you have mentioned it." She matched his grin.

"You did save me, you know," he said quietly. "The odds were against you and me, and yet you bet on me."

She cupped his handsome face in her hands. "I'd bet on you any day, DJ Diamond. I love you and I always will."

They heard their family calling to them. The barbecued ribs were ready.

"Hungry?" DJ asked.

"Starved," she said. He put his arm around her, and they headed back toward the Fourth of July picnic birthday party. "Ansley asked me what your favorite cake was. When I wouldn't tell her, she said, 'Fine. Lori will make my favorite then.' Wanna guess what it is?"

"Chocolate?" DJ asked with a grin.

"Chocolate."

"Did she mention that we are twins?" he joked as they joined the party. "You are aware that twins run in my family, right?"

"How else can we keep up with all these Colts otherwise?" Sadie said, and laughed. She couldn't wait to have babies with this cowboy. "In fact, I was thinking. After the party… I mean, it is your *birthday*."

* * * * *

DELIVERANCE AT
CARDWELL RANCH

Chapter 1

Snow fell in a wall of white, giving Austin Cardwell only glimpses of the winding highway in front of him. He'd already slowed to a crawl as visibility worsened. Now on the radio, he heard that Highway 191 through the Gallatin Canyon—the very one he was on—was closed to all but emergency traffic.

"One-ninety-one from West Yellowstone to Bozeman is closed due to several accidents including a semi rollover that has blocked the highway near Big Sky. Another accident near West Yellowstone has also caused problems there. Travelers are advised to wait out the storm."

Great, Austin thought with a curse. *Wait out the storm where?* He hadn't seen any place to even pull over for miles let alone a gas station or café. He had no choice but to keep going. This was just what this Texas boy needed, he told himself with a curse. He'd be lucky if he reached Cardwell Ranch tonight.

The storm appeared to be getting worse. He couldn't see more than a few yards in front of the rented SUV's hood. Earlier he'd gotten a glimpse of the Gallatin River to his left. On his right were steep rock walls as the two-lane highway cut through the canyon. There was nothing but dark, snow-capped pine trees, steep mountain cliffs and the frozen river and snow-slick highway.

"Welcome to the frozen north," he said under his breath as he fought to see the road ahead—and stay on it. He blamed his brothers—not for the storm, but for his even being here. They had insisted he come to Montana for the grand opening of the first Texas Boys Barbecue joint in Montana. They had postponed the grand opening until he was well enough to come.

Although the opening was to be January 1, his cousin Dana had pleaded with him to spend Christmas at the ranch.

You need to be here, Austin, she'd said. *I promise you won't be sorry.*

He growled under his breath now. He hadn't been back to Montana since his parents divorced and his mother took him and his brothers to Texas to live. He'd been too young to remember much. But he'd found he couldn't say no to Dana. He'd heard too many good things about her from his brothers.

Also, what choice did he have after missing his brother Tag's wedding last July?

As he slowed for another tight curve, a gust of wind shook the rented SUV. Snow whirled past his windshield. For an instant, he couldn't see anything. Worse, he felt as if he was going too fast for the curve. But he was afraid to touch his brakes—the one thing his brother Tag had warned him not to do.

Don't do anything quickly, Tag had told him. *And whatever you do, don't hit your brakes. You'll end up in the ditch.*

He caught something in his headlights. It took him a moment to realize what he was seeing before his heart took off at a gallop.

A car was upside down in the middle of the highway, its headlights shooting out through the falling snow toward the river, the taillights a dim red against the steep canyon wall. The overturned car had the highway completely blocked.

Chapter 2

Austin hit his brakes even though he doubted he stood a chance in hell of stopping. The SUV began to slide sideways toward the overturned car. He spun the wheel, realizing he'd done it too wildly when he began to slide toward the river. As he turned the wheel yet again, the SUV slid toward the canyon wall—and the overturned car.

He was within only a few feet of the car on the road, when his front tires went off the road into the narrow snow-filled ditch between him and the granite canyon wall. The deep snow seemed to grab the SUV and pull it in deeper.

Austin braced himself as snow rushed up over the hood, burying the windshield as the front of the SUV sank. The ditch and the snow in it were much deeper than he'd thought. He closed his eyes and braced himself for when the SUV hit the steep rock canyon wall.

To his surprise, the SUV came to a sudden stop before it hit the sheer rock face.

He sat for a moment, too shaken to move. Then he remembered the car he'd seen upside down in the middle of the road. What if someone was hurt? He tried his door, but the snow was packed around it. Reaching across the seat, he tried the passenger side. Same problem.

As he sat back, he glanced in the rearview mirror. The rear of the SUV sat higher, the back wheels still partially up on the edge of the highway. He could see out a little of the back window where the snow hadn't blown up on it and realized his only exit would be the hatchback.

He hit the hatchback release then climbed over the seat. In the back, he dug through the clothing he'd brought on the advice of his now "Montana" brother and pulled out the flashlight, along with the winter coat and boots he'd brought. Hurrying, he pulled them on and climbed out through the back into the blinding snowstorm, anxious to see if he could be of any help to the passengers in the wrecked vehicle.

He'd waded through deep snow for a few steps before his feet almost slipped out from under him on the icy highway. No wonder there had been accidents and the highway had closed to all but emergency traffic. The pavement under the falling snow was covered with glare ice. He was amazed he hadn't gone off the road sooner.

Moving cautiously toward the overturned car, he snapped on his flashlight and shone it inside the vehicle, afraid of what he would find.

The driver's seat was empty. So was the passenger seat. The driver's air bag had activated then deflated. In the backseat, though, he saw something that made his pulse jump. A car seat was still strapped in. No baby, though.

He shined the light on the headliner, stopping when he spotted what looked like a woman's purse. Next to it was an empty baby bottle and a smear of blood.

"Hello?" he called out, terrified for the occupants of the car. The night, blanketed by the falling snow, felt too quiet. He was used to Texas traffic and the noise of big-city Houston.

No answer. He had no idea how long ago the accident had happened. Wouldn't the driver have had the good sense to stay nearby? Then again, maybe another vehicle had come from the other side of the highway and rescued the driver and baby. Strange, though, to just leave the car like this without trying to flag the accident.

"Hello?" He listened. He'd never heard such cold silence. It had a spooky quality that made him jumpy. Add to that this car being upside down in the middle of the highway. What if another vehicle came along right now going too fast to stop?

Walking around the car, he found the driver's side door hanging open and bent down to look inside. More blood on the headliner. His heart began to pound even as he told himself someone must have rescued the driver and baby. At least he hoped that was what had happened. But his instincts told him different. While in the barbecue business with his brothers, he worked as a deputy sheriff in a small town outside Houston.

He reached for his cell phone. No service. As he started to straighten, a hard, cold object struck him in the back of the head. Austin Cardwell staggered from the blow and grabbed the car frame to keep from going down. The second blow caught him in the back.

He swung around to ward off another blow.

To his shock, he came face-to-face with a woman wielding a tire iron. But it was the crazed expression on her bloody face that turned his own blood to ice.

Chapter 3

Austin's head swam for a moment as he watched the woman raise the tire iron again. He'd disarmed his fair share of drunks and drugged-up attackers. Now he only took special jobs on a part-time basis, usually the investigative jobs no one else wanted.

Even with his head and back aching from the earlier blows, he reacted instinctively from years of dealing with criminals. He stepped to the side as the woman brought the tire iron down a third time. It connected with the car frame, the sound ringing out an instant before he locked an arm around her neck. With his other hand, he broke her grip on the weapon. It dropped to the ground, disappearing in the falling snow as he dragged her back against him, lifting her off her feet.

Though she was small framed, she proved to be much stronger than he'd expected. She fought as if her life depended on it.

"Settle down," he ordered, his breath coming out as fog in the cold mountain air. "I'm trying to help you."

His words had little effect. He was forced to capture both her wrists in his hands to keep her from striking him as he brought her around to face him.

"Listen to me," he said, putting his face close to hers. "I'm a deputy sheriff from Texas. I'm trying to help you."

She stared at him through the falling snow as if uncomprehending, and he wondered if the injury on her forehead, along with the trauma of the car accident, could be the problem.

"You hit your head when you wrecked your car—"

"It's not my car." She said the words through chattering teeth and he realized that she appeared to be on the verge of hypothermia—something else that could explain her strange behavior.

"Okay, it's not your car. Where is the owner?"

She glanced past him, a terrified expression coming over her face.

"Did you have your baby with you?" he asked.

"I don't have a baby."

The car seat in the back of the vehicle and the baby bottle lying on the headliner next to her purse would indicate otherwise. He hoped, though, that she was telling the truth. He couldn't bear the thought that the baby had come out of the car seat and was somewhere out in the snow.

He listened for a moment. He hadn't heard a baby crying when he'd gotten out of the SUV's hatchback. Nor had he heard one since. The falling snow blanketed everything, though, with that eerie stillness. But he had to assume even if there had been a baby, it wasn't still alive.

He considered what to do. His SUV wasn't coming out of that ditch without a tow truck hooked to it and her car certainly wasn't going anywhere.

"What's your name?" he asked her. She was shaking harder now. He had to get her to someplace warm. Neither of their vehicles was an option. If another vehicle came down this highway from either direction, there was too much of a chance they would be hit. He recalled glimpsing an old boarded-up cabin back up the highway. It wasn't that far. "What's your name?" he asked again.

She looked confused and on the verge of passing out on him. He feared if she did, he wouldn't be able to carry her back to the cabin he'd seen. When he realized he wasn't going to be able to get any information out of her, he reached back into the overturned car and snagged the strap of her purse.

The moment he let go of one of her arms, she tried to run away again and began kicking and clawing at him when he reached for her. He restrained her again, more easily this time because she was losing her motor skills due to the cold.

"We have to get you to shelter. I'm not going to hurt you. Do you understand me?" Any other time, he would have put out some sort of warning sign in case another driver came along. But he couldn't let go of this woman for fear she would attack him again or worse, take off into the storm.

He had to get her to the cabin as quickly as possible. He wasn't sure how badly she was hurt—just that blood was still streaming down her face from the contusion on her forehead. Loss of blood or a concussion could be the cause for her odd behavior. He'd have to restrain her and come back to flag the wreck.

Fortunately, the road was now closed to all but emergency traffic. He figured the first vehicle to come upon the wreck would be highway patrol or possibly a snowplow driver.

Feeling he had no choice but to get her out of this storm, Austin grabbed his duffel out of the back of the SUV and started to lock it, still holding on to the woman. For the first time, he took a good look at her.

She wore designer jeans, dress boots, a sweater and no coat. He realized he hadn't seen a winter coat in the car or any snow boots. In her state of mind, she could have removed her coat and left it out in the snow.

Taking off his down coat, he put it on her even though she fought him. He put on the lighter-weight jacket he'd been wearing earlier when he'd gone off the road.

In his duffel bag, he found a pair of mittens he'd invested in before the trip and put them on her gloveless hands, then dug out a baseball cap, the only hat he had. He put it on her head of dark curly hair. The brown eyes staring out at him were wide with fear and confusion.

"You're going to have to walk for a ways," he said to her. She gave him a blank look. But while she appeared more subdued, he wasn't going to trust it. "The cabin I saw from the road isn't far."

It wasn't a long walk. The woman came along without a struggle. But she still seemed terrified of something. She kept looking behind her as they walked as if she feared someone was out there in the storm and would be coming after her. He could feel her body trembling through the grip he had on her arm.

Walking through the falling snow, down the middle of the deserted highway, felt surreal. The quiet, the empty highway, the two of them, strangers, at least one of them in some sort of trouble. It felt as if the world had come to an end and they were the last two people alive.

As they neared where he'd seen the cabin, he hoped his eyes hadn't been deceiving him since he'd only gotten a glimpse through the falling snow. He quickly saw that it was probably only a summer cabin, if that. It didn't look as if it had been used in years. Tiny and rustic, it was set back in a narrow ravine off the highway. The windows had wooden shutters on them and the front door was secured with a padlock.

They slogged through the deep snow up the ravine to the cabin as flakes whirled around them. Austin couldn't remember ever being this cold. The woman had to be freezing since she'd been out in the cold longer than he had and her sweater had to be soaked beneath his coat.

Leading her around to the back, he found a shutterless window next to the door. Putting his elbow through the old, thin glass, he reached inside and unlocked the door. As he shoved it open, a gust of cold, musty air rushed out.

The woman balked for a moment before he pulled her inside. The room was small, and had apparently once been a porch but was now a storage area. He was relieved to see a stack of dry split wood piled by the door leading into the cabin proper.

Opening the next door, he stepped in, dragging the woman after him. It was pitch-black inside. He dropped

his duffel bag and her purse, removed the flashlight
from his coat pocket and shone it around the room. An
old rock fireplace, the front sooty from years of fires,
stood against one wall. A menagerie of ancient furniture formed a half circle around it.

Through a door, he saw one bedroom with a double
bed. In another, there were two bunk beds. The bathroom was apparently an outhouse out back. The kitchen
was so small he almost missed it.

"We won't have water or any lavatory facilities, but
we'll make do since we will have heat as soon as I get a
fire going." He looked at her, debating what to do. She
couldn't go far inside the small cabin, but she could find
a weapon easy enough. He wasn't going to chance it
since his head still hurt like hell from the tire iron she'd
used to try to cave in his skull. His back was sore, but
that was all, fortunately.

Because of his work as a deputy sheriff, he always
carried a gun and handcuffs. He put the duffel bag down
on the table, unzipped it and pulled out the handcuffs.

The woman tried to pull free of him at the sight of
them.

"Listen," he said gently. "I'm only going to handcuff
one of your wrists just to restrain you. I can't trust that
you won't hurt me or yourself if I don't." He said all of
it apologetically.

Something in his voice must have assured her because she let him lead her over to a chair in front of the
fireplace. He snapped one cuff on her right wrist and
the other to the frame of the heaviest chair.

She looked around the small cabin, her gaze going to
the back door. The terror in her eyes made the hair on
the back of his neck spike. He'd once had a girlfriend

whose cat used to suddenly look at a doorway as if there were something unearthly standing in it. Austin had the same creepy feeling now and feared that this woman was as haunted as that darned cat.

With the dried wood from the back porch and some matches he found in the kitchen, he got a fire going. Just the sound of the wood crackling and the glow of the flames seemed to instantly warm the room.

He found a pan in the kitchen and, filling it with snow from outside, brought it in and placed it in front of the fire. It wasn't long before he could dampen one end of a dish towel from the kitchen.

"I'm going to wash the blood off your face so I can see how badly you've been hurt, all right?"

She held still as he gently applied the wet towel. The bleeding had stopped over her eye, but it was a nasty gash. It took some searching before he found a first aid kit in one of the bedrooms and bandaged the cut as best he could.

"Are you hurt anywhere else?"

She shook her head.

"Okay," he said with a nod. His head still ached, but the tire iron hadn't broken the skin—only because he had a thick head of dark hair like all of the Cardwells— and a hard head to boot.

The cabin was getting warmer, but he still found an old quilt and wrapped it around her. She had stopped shaking at least. Unfortunately, she still looked confused and scared. He was pretty sure she had a concussion. But there was little he could do. He still had no cell phone coverage. Not that anyone could get to them with the wrecks and the roads the way they were.

Picking up her purse, he sat down in a chair near her.

He noticed her watching him closely as he dumped the contents out on the marred wood coffee table. Coins tinkled out, several spilling onto the floor. As he picked them up, he realized several interesting things about what was—and wasn't—in her purse.

There was a whole lot of makeup for someone who didn't have any on. There was also no cell phone. But there *was* a baby's pacifier.

He looked up at her and realized he'd made a rooky mistake. He hadn't searched her. He'd just assumed she didn't have a weapon like a gun or knife because she'd used a tire iron back on the highway.

Getting up, he went over to her and checked her pockets. No cell phone. But he did find a set of car keys. He frowned. That was odd since he remembered that the keys had still been in the wrecked car. The engine had died, but the lights were still on.

So what were these keys for? They appeared to have at least one key for a vehicle and another like the kind used for house doors.

"Are these your keys?" he asked, but after staring at them for a moment, she frowned and looked away.

Maybe she had been telling the truth about the car not being hers.

Sitting back down, he opened her wallet. Three singles, a five—and less than a dollar in change. Not much money for a woman on the road. Not much money dressed like she was either. Also, there were no credit cards.

But there was a driver's license. He pulled it out and looked at the photo. The woman's dark hair in the snapshot was shorter and curlier, but she had the same intense brown eyes. There was enough of a resemblance that he would assume this woman was Rebecca Stewart. According to the ID, she was married, lived in Helena, Montana, and was an organ donor.

"It says here that your name is Rebecca Stewart."

"That's not my purse." She frowned at the bag as if she'd never seen it before.

"Then what was it doing in the car you were driving?"

She shook her head, looking more confused and scared.

"If you're not Rebecca Stewart, then who are you?"

He saw her lower lip quiver. One large tear rolled down her cheek. "I don't know." When she went to wipe her tears with her free hand, he saw the diamond watch.

Reaching over, he caught her wrist. She tried to pull away, but he was much stronger than she was, and more determined. Even at a glance, he could see that the watch was expensive.

"Where did you get this?" he asked, hating that he sounded so suspicious. But the woman had a car and a purse she swore weren't hers. It wasn't that much of a leap to think that the watch probably wasn't hers either.

She stared at the watch on her wrist as if she'd never seen it before. The gold band was encrusted with diamonds. Pulling it off her wrist, he turned the watch over. Just as he'd suspected, it was engraved:

To Gillian with all my love.

"Is your name Gillian?"

She remembered *something,* he saw it in her eyes.

"So your name *is* Gillian?"

She didn't answer, but now she looked more afraid than she had before.

Austin sighed. He wasn't going to get anything out of

this woman. For all he knew, she could be lying about everything. But then again, the fear was real. It was almost palpable.

He had a sudden thought. "Why did you attack me on the highway?"

"I... I don't know."

A chill ran the length of his spine. He thought of how she'd kept looking back at the car as they walked to the cabin. She had thought someone was after her. "Was there someone else in the car when it rolled over?"

Her eyes widened in alarm. "In the trunk."

He gawked at her. *"There was someone in the trunk?"*

She looked confused again, and even more frightened. "No." Tears filled her eyes. "I don't know."

"Too bad you didn't mention that when we were down there," he grumbled under his breath. He couldn't take the chance that she was telling the truth. Why someone would be in the trunk was another concern, especially if she was telling the truth about the car, the purse and apparently the baby not being hers.

He had to go back down anyway and try to put up some kind of flags to warn possible other motorists. He just hated the idea of going back out into the storm. But if there was even a chance someone was in the trunk...

Austin stared at her and reminded himself that this was probably a figment of her imagination. A delusion from the knock on her head. But given the way things weren't adding up, he had to check.

"Don't leave me here," she cried as he headed for the door, her voice filled with terror.

"What are you so afraid of?" he asked, stepping back to her.

She swallowed, her gaze locked with his, and then she slowly shook her head and closed her eyes. "I don't know."

Austin swore under his breath. He didn't like leaving her alone, but he had no choice. He checked to make sure the handcuff attached to the chair would hold in case she tried to go somewhere. He thought it might be just like her, in her state of mind, to get loose and take off back out into the blizzard.

"Don't try to leave, okay? I'll be back shortly. I promise."

She didn't answer, didn't even open her eyes. Grabbing his coat, he hurried out the back door and down the steep slope to the highway. The snow lightened the dark enough that he didn't have to use his flashlight. It was still falling in huge lacy flakes that stuck to his clothing as he hurried down the highway. He wished he'd at least taken his heavier coat from her before he'd left.

His SUV was covered with snow and barely visible. He walked past it to the overturned car, trying to make sense of all this. Someone in the trunk? He mentally kicked himself for worrying about some crazy thing a delusional woman had said.

The car was exactly as he'd left it, although the lights were starting to dim, the battery no doubt running down. He thought about turning them off, but if a car came along, the driver would have a better chance of seeing it with the lights on.

He went around to the driver's side. The door was still open, just as he'd left it. He turned on the flashlight from his pocket and searched around for the latch on the trunk, hoping he wouldn't have to use the key, which was still in the ignition.

Maybe it was the deputy sheriff in him, but he had a bad feeling this car might be the scene of a crime and whoever's fingerprints were on the key might be important.

He found the latch. The trunk made a soft *thunk* and fell open.

Austin didn't know what he expected to find when he walked around to the back of the car and bent down to look in. A body? Or a woman and her baby?

What had fallen out, though, was only a suitcase.

He stared at it for a moment, then knelt down and unzipped it enough to see what was inside. Clothes. Women's clothing. No dead bodies. Nothing to be terrified of that he could see.

The bag, though, had been packed quickly, the clothes apparently just thrown in. That in itself was interesting. Nor did the clothing look expensive—unlike the diamond wristwatch the woman was wearing.

Checking the luggage tag on the bag, he saw that it was in the same name as the driver's license he'd found in her purse. Rebecca Stewart. So if Rebecca Stewart wasn't the woman in the cabin, then where was she? And where was the baby who went with the car seat?

He rezipped the bag and hoisted it up from the snow. Was the woman going to deny that this was her suitcase? He reminded himself that she'd thought there was *someone* in the trunk. The woman obviously wasn't in her right mind.

He shone the flashlight into the trunk. His pulse quickened. Blood. He removed a glove to touch a finger to it. Dried. What the hell? There wasn't much, but enough to cause even more concern.

Putting his glove back on, he closed the trunk and

picked up the suitcase. He stopped at his rented SUV to look for something to flag the wreck, hurrying because he was worried about the woman, worried what he would find when he got back to the cabin. He was digging in the back of the SUV, when a set of headlights suddenly flashed over him.

He turned. Out of the storm came the flashing lights of a Montana highway patrol car.

Chapter 4

"Let me get this straight," the patrolman said as they stood in the waiting room at the hospital. "You handcuffed her to a chair to protect her from herself?"

"Some of it was definitely for my own protection, as well. She appeared confused and scared. I couldn't trust that she wouldn't go for a more efficient weapon than a tire iron."

The patrolman finished writing and closed his notebook. "Unless you want to press assault charges...that should cover it."

Austin shook his head. "How is she?"

"The doctor is giving her liquids and keeping her for observation until we can reach her husband."

"Her husband?" Austin thought of the hurriedly packed suitcase and recalled that she hadn't been wearing a wedding ring.

"We tracked him down through the car registration."

"So she *is* Rebecca Stewart? Her memory has returned?"

"Not yet. But I'm sure her husband will be able to clear things up." The patrolman stood. "I have your number if we need to reach you."

Austin stood, as well. He was clearly being dismissed and yet something kept him from turning and walking away. "She seemed…terrified when I found her. Did she say where she was headed before the crash?"

"She still seems fuzzy on that part. But she is in good hands now." The highway patrolman turned as the doctor came down the hallway and joined them. "Mr. Cardwell is worried about your patient. I assured him she is out of danger," the patrolman said.

The doctor nodded and introduced himself to Austin. "If it makes you feel better, there is little doubt you saved her life."

He couldn't help but be relieved. "Then she remembers what happened?"

"She's still confused. That's fairly common in a case like hers."

The doctor didn't say, but Austin assumed she had a concussion. Austin couldn't explain why, but he needed to see her before he left. The highway patrolman had said they'd found her husband by way of the registration in the car, but she'd been so sure that wasn't her car.

Nor had the highway patrolman been concerned about the baby car seat or the blood in the trunk.

"Apparently the baby is with the father," the patrolman had told him. "As for the blood in the trunk, there was so little I'm sure there is an explanation her husband can provide."

So why couldn't Austin let it go? "I'd like to see her before I leave."

"I suppose it would be fine," the doctor said. "Her husband is expected at any time."

Austin hurried down the hallway to the room the doctor had only exited moments before, anxious to see her before her husband arrived. He pushed on the door slowly and peered in, half fearing that she might not want to see him.

He wasn't sure what he expected as he stepped into the room. He'd had a short sleepless night at a local motel. He had regretted not taking a straight flight to Bozeman this morning instead of flying into Idaho Falls the day before. Even as he thought it through, he reminded himself that the woman would have died last night if he hadn't come along when he did.

Austin told himself he'd been at the right place at the right time. So why couldn't he just let this go?

As the door closed behind him, she sat up in bed abruptly, pulling the covers up to her chin.

Her brown eyes were wide with fear. He was struck by how small she looked. Her unruly mane of curly dark hair billowed out around her pale face, making her look all the more vulnerable.

"My name's Austin. Austin Cardwell. We met late last night after I came upon your car upside down in the middle of Highway 191." He touched the wound on the back of his head where she'd nailed him. "You remember hitting me?"

She looked horrified at the thought, verifying what he already suspected. She didn't remember.

"Can you tell me your name?" He'd hoped that she would be more coherent this morning, but as he watched her face, it was clear she didn't know who she was any more than she had last night.

She seemed to search for an answer. He saw the moment when she realized she couldn't remember anything—even who she was. Panic filled her expression. She looked toward the door behind him as if she might bolt for it.

"Don't worry," he said quickly. "The doctor said memory loss is pretty common in your condition."

"My *condition?*"

"From the bump on your head, you hit it pretty hard in the accident." He pointed to a spot on his own temple. She raised her hand to touch the same spot on her temple and winced.

"I don't remember an accident." She had pulled her arms out from under the covers. He noticed the bruises on her upper arms. They were half-moon shaped, like fingerprints—as if someone had gripped her hard. There was also a cut on her arm that he didn't think had happened during her car accident.

She saw him staring at her arms. When she looked down and saw the bruises, she quickly put her arms under the covers again. If anything, she looked more frightened than she had earlier.

"You don't remember losing control of your car?"

She shook her head.

"I don't know if this helps, but the registration and proof of insurance I found in your car, along with the driver's license I found in the purse, says your name is Rebecca Stewart," he said, watching to see if there was any recognition in her expression.

"That isn't my name. I would know my own name when I heard it, wouldn't I?"

Maybe. Maybe not. "You were wearing a watch…"

"The doctor said they put it in the safe until I was ready to leave the hospital."

"It was engraved with: 'To Gillian with all my love.'" He saw that the words didn't ring any bells. "Are you Gillian?"

She looked again at the door, her expression one of panic.

"Don't worry. It will all come back to you," he said, trying to calm her even though he knew there might always be blanks that she could never fill in if he was right and she had a concussion. He wished there was something he could say to comfort her. She looked so frightened. "Fortunately a highway patrolman came along when he did last night."

"Patrolman?" Her words wavered and she looked even more terrified, making him wonder if he might be right and that she'd stolen the car, the purse and the watch. She'd said none of it belonged to her. Maybe she *was* telling the truth.

But why was she driving someone else's car? If so, where was the car's owner and her baby? This woman's fear of the law seemed to indicate that something was very off here. What if this woman wasn't who they thought she was?

"Where am I?" she asked, glancing around the hospital room.

"Didn't the doctor tell you? You're in the hospital."

"I meant, where am I...?" She waved a hand to encompass more than the room.

"Oh," he said and frowned. "Bozeman." When that didn't seem to register, he added, "Montana."

One eyebrow shot up. *"Montana?"*

It crossed his mind that a woman who lived in Helena, Montana, wouldn't be confused about what state she was in. Nor would she be surprised to find herself still in that state.

He reminded himself that the knock on her head could have messed up some of the wiring. Or maybe she'd been that way before.

Her gaze came back to him. She was studying him intently, sizing him up. He wondered what he saw and couldn't help but think of his former girlfriend, Tanya, and the argument they'd had just before he'd left Texas.

"Haven't you ever wanted more?*"* Tanya hadn't looked at him. She'd been busy throwing her things into a large trash bag. When she'd moved in with him, she'd moved in gradually, bringing her belongings in piecemeal.

"I'm only going to be gone a week," he'd said, watching her clean out the drawers in his apartment, wondering if this was it. She'd threatened to leave him enough times, but she never had. Maybe this was the time.

He had been trying to figure out how he felt about that when she'd suddenly turned toward him.

"Did you hear what I said?"

Obviously not. *"What?"*

"This business with your brothers..." She did her eye roll. He really hated it when she did that and she knew it. *"If it isn't something to do with* Texas Boys Barbecue...*"*

He could have pointed out that the barbecue joint she was referring to was a multimillion-dollar business, with more than a dozen locations across Texas, and it paid for this apartment.

But he'd had a feeling that wasn't really what this particular argument was about, so he'd said, *"Your point?"* even though he'd already known it.

"You're too busy for a relationship. At least that is your excuse."

"You knew I was busy before you moved in."

"Ever ask yourself why your work is more important than your love life?" She hadn't given him time to respond. *"You want to know what I think? I think Austin Cardwell goes through life saving people because he's afraid of letting himself fall in love."*

He wasn't afraid. He just hadn't fallen in love the way Tanya had wanted him to. *"Glad we got that figured out,"* he'd said.

Tanya had flared with anger. *"That's all you have to say?"*

And he'd made it worse by shrugging, something he knew *she* hated. He hadn't had the time or patience for this kind of talk at that moment. *"Maybe we should talk about this when I get back from Montana."*

She'd shaken her head in obvious disgust. *"That is so like you. Put things off and maybe the situation will right itself. You missed your own brother's wedding and you don't really care if they open a barbecue restaurant in Montana or not. But instead of being honest, you ignore the problem and hope it goes away until finally they force you to come to Montana. For once, I would love to see you just take a stand. Make a decision. Do something."*

"I missed my brother's wedding because I was on a case. One that almost got me killed, you might remember."

Tears welled in her eyes. *"I remember. I stayed by your bedside for three days."*

He sighed and raked a hand through his hair. *"What I do is important."*

"More important than me." She'd stood, hands on hips, waiting.

He'd known what she wanted. A commitment. The problem was, he wasn't ready. And right then, he'd known he would never be with Tanya.

"This is probably for the best," he'd said, motioning to the bulging trash bag.

Tears flowing, she'd nodded. *"Don't bother to call me if and when you get back."* With that, she had grabbed up the bag and stormed to the door, stopping only long enough to hurl his apartment key at his head.

"Where are my clothes?"

Austin blinked, confused for a moment, he'd been so lost in his thoughts. He focused on the woman in the hospital bed. "You can't leave. Your husband is on his way."

Panic filled her expression. She tried to get out of the bed. As he moved to her bedside to stop her, he heard the door open behind him.

Chapter 5

Austin turned to see a large stocky man come into the room, followed by the doctor.

"Mrs. Stewart," the doctor said as he approached her bed. "Your husband is here."

The stocky man stopped a few feet into the room and stood frowning. For a moment, Austin thought there had been a mistake and that the man didn't recognize the woman.

But the man wasn't looking at his wife. He was frowning at Austin. As if the doctor's words finally jarred him into motion, the man strode to the other side of the bed and quickly took his wife's hand as he bent to kiss her forehead. "I was so worried about you."

Austin watched the woman's expression. She looked terrified, her gaze locking with his in a plea for help.

"Excuse me," Austin said as he stepped forward. He

had no idea what he planned to say, let alone do. But something was wrong here.

"I beg your pardon?" said the alleged husband, turning to look at Austin before swinging his gaze to the doctor with a *who the hell is this?* expression.

"This is the man who saved your wife's life," the doctor said and introduced Austin before getting a page that he was needed elsewhere. He excused himself and hurried out, leaving the three of them alone.

"I'm sorry, I didn't catch your name," Austin said.

"Marc. Marc Stewart."

Stewart, Austin thought, remembering the name on the driver's license in the purse he'd found in the car. "And this woman's name is Rebecca Stewart?" he asked the husband.

"That's right," Marc Stewart answered in a way that dared Austin to challenge him.

As he looked to the woman in the bed, Austin noticed that she gave an almost imperceptible shake of her head. "I'm sorry, but how do we know you're her husband?"

"Are you serious?" the man demanded, glaring across the bed at him.

"She doesn't seem to recognize you," he said, even though what he'd noticed was that the woman seemed terrified of the man.

Marc Stewart gave him the once-over, clearly upset. "She's had a *concussion.*"

"Old habits are hard to break," Austin said as he displayed his badge and ID to the alleged Marc Stewart. "You wouldn't mind me asking for some identification from you, would you?"

The man looked as if he might have a coronary. At least he'd come to the right place, Austin thought, as the alleged Marc Stewart angrily pulled out his wallet and showed Austin his license.

Marc Andrew Stewart, Austin read. "There was a car seat in the back of the vehicle she was driving. Where is the baby?"

"With my mother." A blood vessel in the man's cheek began to throb. "Look Deputy… Cardwell, is it? I appreciate that you supposedly saved my wife's life, but it's time for you to butt out."

Austin told himself he should back off, but the fear in the woman's eyes wouldn't let him. "She doesn't seem to know you and she isn't wearing a wedding ring." He didn't add that the woman seemed terrified and had bruises on her upper arms where someone had gotten rough with her. Not to mention the fact that when he'd told her that her husband was on his way, she'd panicked and tried to leave. Concussion or not, something was wrong with all this.

"I think you should leave," the man said.

"If you really are her husband, it shouldn't be hard for you to prove it," Austin said, holding his ground— well, at least until Marc Stewart had hospital security throw him out, which wouldn't be long, from the look on the man's face. The woman in the bed still hadn't uttered a word.

For a moment, Marc Stewart looked as if he was about to tell him to go to hell. But instead, he dug into his pocket angrily and produced a plain gold band that caught the light as he reached for the woman's left hand.

"My wife left it by the sink yesterday," Marc Stewart said by way of explanation. "She always takes it off when she does the dishes. Sometimes she forgets to put it back on."

Austin thought, given the bruises on the woman's upper arms, that she had probably thrown the ring at him as she took off yesterday.

When she still didn't move to take the ring, the man snatched up her hand lying beside her on the bed and slipped the ring on her finger.

Austin watched her look down at the ring. He saw recognition fill her expression just before she began to cry.

Even from where he stood, he could see that the ring, while a little loose, fit close enough. Just as the photo ID in Rebecca Stewart's purse looked enough like the woman on the bed. He told himself there was nothing more he could do. Clearly she was afraid of this man. But unless she spoke up…

"I guess I'll leave you with your husband, unless there is something I should know?" Austin asked her.

"Tell the man, Rebecca," Marc Stewart snapped. "Am I your husband?" He bent down to kiss her cheek. Austin saw him whisper something in her ear.

She closed her eyes, tears leaking from beneath dark lashes.

"We had a little argument and she took off and apparently almost got herself killed," Marc said. "We both said and did things we regret, isn't that right, Rebecca? Tell the man, sweetheart."

Her eyes opened slowly. She took a ragged breath and wiped away the tears with the backs of her hands, the way a little kid would.

"Is that all there is to this?" Austin asked, watching her face. Across from him, he could see Marc gritting his teeth in fury at this interference in his life.

She nodded her head slowly, her gaze going from her

husband to Austin. "Thank you, but he's right. It was just a foolish disagreement. I will be fine now."

Feeling like a fool for getting involved in a domestic dispute, Austin headed for Cardwell Ranch. Last night, a wrecker company had pulled his rental SUV out of the ditch and brought it to the motel where he was staying. Fortunately, his skid into the ditch hadn't done any damage.

Highway 191 was now open, the road sanded. As he drove, Austin got his first real look at the Gallatin Canyon or "the canyon" as his cousin Dana called it. From the mouth just south of Gallatin Gateway, fifty miles of winding road trailed the river in a deep cut through the mountains, almost all the way to West Yellowstone.

The drive along the Gallatin River was indeed breathtaking—a snaking strip of highway followed the Blue Ribbon trout stream up over the Continental Divide. This time of year, the Gallatin ran crystal clear under a thick cover of aquamarine ice. Dark, thick snowcapped pines grew at its edge, against a backdrop of the granite cliffs and towering pine-clad mountains.

Austin concentrated on his driving so he didn't end up in a snowbank again. Piles of deep snow had been plowed up on each side of the road, making the highway seem even narrower, but at least traffic was light. He had to admit, it was beautiful. The sun glistening off the new snow was almost blinding in its brilliance. Overhead, a cloudless robin's-egg-blue sky seemed vast and clearer than any air he'd ever breathed. The canyon looked like something out of a winter fairy tale.

Just before Big Sky, the canyon widened a little. He spotted a few older cabins, nothing like all the new construction he'd seen down by the mouth of the canyon. Tag had told him that the canyon had been mostly cattle and dude ranches, a few summer cabins and homes— that was, until Big Sky resort and the small town that followed at the foot of Lone Mountain.

Luxury houses had sprouted up all around the resort. Fortunately, some of the original cabins still remained and the majority of the canyon was national forest so it would always remain undeveloped. The "canyon" had remained its own little community, according to Tag.

Austin figured Tag had gotten most of his information from their cousin Dana. This was the only home she'd known and, like her stubborn relations, she apparently had no intention of ever leaving it.

While admiring the scenery on the drive, he did his best not to think about Rebecca Stewart and her husband. When he'd left her hospital room, he'd felt her gaze on him and turned at the door to look back. He'd seen her take off the ring her husband had put on her finger and grip it in her fist so tightly that her knuckles were white.

Trouble in paradise, he thought as he reached Big Sky, *and none of my business.* As a deputy sheriff, he'd dealt with his share of domestic disputes. Every law enforcement officer knew how dangerous they were. The best thing was to stay out of the middle of them since he'd seen both husbands and wives turn on the outsider stepping in to try to keep the peace.

Cardwell Ranch was only a few miles farther up the highway from Big Sky. But on impulse, he swung onto the road to Big Sky's Meadow Village, where he suspected he would find the marshal's department.

His cousin Dana's husband, Marshal Hud Savage, waved him into his office and shook his hand. "We missed you at the wedding." The wedding, of course, had been his brother Tag's, to Lily McCabe, on July 4. He knew he would never live it down.

"I was hoping to get up for it, but I was on a case..." He hated that he'd missed his own brother's wedding, but hoped at least Hud, being a lawman, would understand.

"That's right. Deputy sheriff, is it?"

"Part-time, yes. I take on special cases."

"As I recall, there were extenuating circumstances. You were wounded. You're fine now?"

He nodded. He didn't want to talk about the case that had almost gotten him killed. Nor did he want to admit that he might not still be physically a hundred percent.

"Well, have a seat," Hud said as he settled behind his desk. "And tell me what I can do for you. I suspect this isn't an extended family visit."

Austin nodded and, removing his hat, sat down, comfortable at once with the marshal. "You might have heard that I got into an accident last night. My rental SUV went into the ditch."

"I did know about that. I'm glad you weren't hurt. We couldn't assist because we had our hands full down here with a semi rollover."

"I was lucky I only ended up in the ditch. What made me hit my brakes was that I came upon a vehicle upside down in the middle of the highway last night."

Austin filled him in on the woman and everything that had happened up to leaving her about thirty minutes ago at the hospital in Bozeman.

"Sounds like she and her husband were having some marital issues," the marshal said.

Austin nodded. "The trouble is I think it's more than that. She had bruises on her arms."

"Couldn't the bruises have been caused by the accident?"

"No, these were definitely finger impressions. More than that, she seemed scared of her husband. Actually, she told me she wasn't Rebecca Stewart, which would mean this man wasn't her husband." He saw skepticism in the marshal's expression and admitted he would have felt the same way if someone had come to him with this story.

"Look," Austin said. "It's probably nothing, but I just have this gut feeling…"

Hud nodded, as if he understood gut feelings. "What would you like me to do?"

"First, could you run the name Marc Stewart. They're apparently from Helena."

"If it will relieve your mind, I'd be happy to." The marshal moved to his computer and began to peck at the keys. A moment later, he said, "No arrests or warrants. None on Rebecca Stewart either. Other than that…"

Austin nodded.

Hud studied him. "There's obviously something that's still worrying you."

He couldn't narrow it down to just one thing. It was the small things like the older-model car Rebecca had been driving, the baby seat in the back, the woman's adamant denial that she was Rebecca Stewart, the look of fear on her face when he'd told her that her husband was on his way to the hospital, the way she'd cried when he'd put that ring back on her finger.

Then there was that expensive diamond watch. *To Gillian with all my love.*

He mentioned all of this to the marshal and added, "I guess what's really bothering me is the inconsistencies. Also she just doesn't seem like the kind of woman who would leave her husband—let alone her baby—right before Christmas, no matter what the argument might have been about. This woman is a fighter. She wouldn't have left her son with a man who had just gotten physical with her."

Hud raised a brow as he leaned back in his chair. "You sure you didn't get a little too emotionally involved?"

He laughed. "Not hardly. Haven't you heard? I'm the Cardwell brother who never gets emotionally involved in anything. Just ask my brothers, or my former girlfriend, for that matter." He hesitated even though common sense told him to let it go. "There's no chance you're going into Bozeman today, is there?"

Hud smiled. "I'll stop by the hospital and give you a call after I talk to her and her husband."

"Thanks. It really would relieve my mind." Glancing at his watch, he saw he was late for a meeting with his brothers.

He swore as he hurried outside, climbed behind the wheel of his rental SUV and drove toward the small strip shopping mall in Meadow Village, all the time worrying about the woman he'd left in the hospital.

The building was wood framed with stone across the front. It looked nothing like a Texas barbecue joint. As Austin climbed out of the SUV and walked through the snow toward the end unit with the Texas Boys Barbecue sign out front, he thought of their first barbecue joint.

It had been in an old small house. They'd done the

barbecuing out back and packed diners in every afternoon and evening at mismatched tables and chairs to
eat on paper plates. Just the smell of the wonderfully
smoked meats brought people in. He and his brothers
didn't even have to advertise. Their barbecue had kept
people coming back for more.

Austin missed those days, sitting out back having a
cold beer after the night was over and counting their
money and laughing at what a fluke it had been. They'd
grown up barbecuing so it hadn't felt like work at all.

As he pushed open the door to the building his brothers had bought, he saw by the way it was laid out that
the space had started out as another restaurant. Whatever had been here, though, had been replaced with
the Texas Boys Barbecue decor, a mix of rustic wood
and galvanized aluminum. The fabric of the cushy red
booths was the same as that on the chairs, and red-
checked tablecloths covered the tables. The walls were
covered with old photos of Texas family barbecues—
just like in their other restaurants.

Through the pass-through he could see a gleaming
kitchen at the back. Hearing his brothers—Tag, Jackson,
Laramie and Hayes—visiting back there, he walked in
that direction.

"Well, what do you think?" Tag asked excitedly.

Austin shrugged. "It looks fine."

"The equipment is all new," Jackson said. "We had
to add a few things, but other than that, the remodel
was mostly cosmetic."

Austin nodded. "What happened to the restaurant
that was here?"

"It didn't serve the best barbecue in Texas," Tag said.

"We'd hoped for a little more enthusiasm," Laramie said.

"Sorry."

"What about the space?" Hayes asked.

"Looks good to me." He saw them share a glance at each other before they laughed and, almost in unison, said, "Same ol' Austin."

He didn't take offense. It was actually good to see his brothers. There was no mistaking they were related either since they'd all inherited the Cardwell dark good looks. A curse and a blessing. When they were teens they used to argue over who was the ugliest. He smiled at the memory.

"Okay, we're opening a Texas Boys Barbecue in Big Sky," he said to them. "So buy me some lunch. I'm starved."

They went to a small sandwich shop in the shadow of Lone Mountain in what was called Mountain Village. As hungry as he was, Austin still had trouble getting down even half of a sandwich and a bowl of soup.

During lunch, his brothers talked enthusiastically about the January 1 opening. They planned two grand openings, one on January 1 and another on July 4, since Big Sky had two distinct tourist seasons.

Apparently the entire canyon was excited about the Cardwell brothers' brand of barbecue. His brothers Tag, Hayes and Jackson now had all made their homes in Montana. Only he and Laramie still lived in Texas, but Laramie would be flying back up for the grand opening whenever that schedule was confirmed. None of them asked if Austin would be coming back for that one. They knew him too well.

Austin only half listened, too anxious for a call from

the marshal. When his cell phone finally did ring, he quickly excused himself and went out to the closed-in deck. It was freezing out here, but he didn't want his brothers to hear. He could actually see his breath. He'd never admit it, but he couldn't imagine why they would want to live here, as cold and nasty as winter was. Sure, it was beautiful, but he'd take Texas and the heat any day.

"I just left her hospital room," the marshal said without preamble the moment Austin answered.

"So what do you think?"

"Apparently she has some loss of memory because of the concussion she suffered, according to her husband, which could explain some of your misgivings."

"Did you see the bruises on her arms?"

The marshal sighed. "I did. Her husband said they'd had a disagreement before she took off. He said he'd grabbed her a little too hard, trying to keep her from leaving, afraid in her state what might happen to her. As it was, she ended up in a car wreck."

"What does she say?"

"She doesn't seem to recall the twenty-four hours before ending up upside down in her car in the middle of the highway—and even that is fuzzy."

"You think she's lying?" Austin asked, hearing something in the marshal's voice.

Hud took his time in answering. "I think she might remember more than she's letting on. I had some misgivings as well until Marc Stewart showed me a photograph of the four of them on his cell phone."

"*Four* of them?"

"Rebecca and her sister, a woman named Gillian Cooper, Marc and the baby. In the photo, the woman in the hospital is holding the baby and Marc is standing next to her, his arm around her and her sister."

Austin sighed. Gillian Cooper. Her sister. That could explain the watch. Maybe her sister had lent it to her. Or even given it to her.

"The doctor is releasing her tomorrow. I asked her if she wanted to return home with her husband."

Austin figured he already knew the answer. "She said yes."

"I also asked him to step out of the room. I then asked her if she was afraid of him. She said she wasn't."

So that was that, Austin thought. "Thanks for going by the hospital for me."

"You realize there is nothing we can do if she doesn't want to leave him," Hud said.

Austin knew that from experience, even though he'd never understood why a woman stayed in an abusive marriage. Disconnecting, he went back into the restaurant, where his brothers were debating promotion for the new restaurant. He was in no mood for this.

"I really should get going," he said, not that he really had anywhere to go, though he'd agreed to stay until the opening.

Christmas was only a few days away, he realized. Normally, he didn't do much for Christmas. Since he didn't have his own family, he always volunteered to work.

"Where are you going?" Tag asked.

"I've got some Christmas shopping to do." That, at least, was true.

"Dana is planning for us all to be together on Christmas," Tag said as if he needed reminding. "She has all kinds of plans."

Jackson laughed. "She wants us all to try skiing or snowboarding."

"There's a sledding party planned on Christmas Eve behind the house on the ranch and, of course, ice skating on an inlet of the Gallatin River," Hayes said with a laugh when he saw Austin's expression. "You really have to experience a Montana Christmas."

He tried to smile. Anything to make up for missing the wedding so everyone would quit bringing it up. "I can't wait."

They all laughed since they knew he was lying. He wasn't ready for a Montana Christmas. He'd already been freezing his butt off and figured he'd more than experienced Montana after crashing in a ditch and almost getting killed by a woman with a tire iron. However, never let it be said he was a Scrooge. He'd go Christmas shopping. He would be merry and bright. It was only for a few days.

"You know what your problem is, Austin?" his brother Jackson said as they walked out to their vehicles.

Austin shook his head although he knew what was coming. He'd already had this discussion with Tanya in Houston.

"You can't commit to anything," Jackson said. "When we decided to open more Texas Boys Barbecues in Texas—"

"Yes, I've been told I have a problem with commitment," he interrupted as he looked toward Lone Mountain. The peak was almost completely obscured by the falling snow. Huge lacy flakes drifted down around them. Texas barbecue in Montana? He'd thought his brothers had surely lost their minds when they had suggested it. Now he was all the more convinced.

But they'd been right about the other restaurants they'd opened across Texas. He wasn't going to stand in their way now. But he also couldn't get all that excited about it.

"Can you at least commit to this promotion schedule we have mapped out?" Hayes asked.

"Do what you think is best," he said, opening the SUV door. "I'll go along with whatever y'all decide." His brothers didn't look thrilled with his answer. "Isn't that what you wanted me to say?"

"We were hoping for some enthusiasm, *something*," Jackson said and frowned. "You seem to have lost interest in the business."

"It's not that." It wasn't. It was his *life*. At thirty-two, he was successful, a healthy, wealthy American male who could do anything he wanted. Most men his age would have given anything to be in his boots.

"He needs a woman," Tag said and grinned.

"That's *all* I need," Austin said sarcastically under his breath and thought of Rebecca and the way she'd reacted to her husband. What kind of woman left her husband and child just before Christmas?

A terrified one, he thought. "I have to go."

"Where did you say you were going?" Hayes asked before Austin could close his SUV door.

"There's something I need to do."

"I told you he needed a woman," Tag joked.

"Dana is in Bozeman running errands, but she said to tell you that dinner is at her house tonight," Jackson said before Austin could escape.

All the way to the hospital in Bozeman, all Austin could think about was the woman he'd rescued last night. Rescued? And then turned her over to a man who terrified her.

Austin thought of that awful old expression: she'd made her bed and now she had to lie in it.

Like hell, he thought.

Chapter 6

When he reached the hospital, Austin was told at the nurses' station that Mrs. Stewart had checked out already. His heart began to pound harder at the news, all his instincts telling him he had been right to come back here.

"I thought the doctor wasn't going to release her until tomorrow?"

"Her husband talked to him and asked if she was well enough to be released. He was anxious to get her home before Christmas."

Austin just bet he was. "He was planning to take her straight home from the hospital?" he asked and quickly added, "I have her purse." He'd forgotten all about putting it into his duffel bag last night as the highway patrolman helped the woman down to his waiting patrol car.

"Oh, you must be the man who found her after the accident," the nurse said, instantly warming toward him. "Let me see. I know her husband stayed at a local motel last night. I believe they were going to go there first so she could rest for a while before they left for Helena."

"Her husband got in last night?" Austin asked in surprise. Helena was three hours away on Interstate 90.

"He arrived in the wee hours of the morning. When he came by the hospital to see his wife, he thought he'd be able to take her home then." She smiled at how anxious the husband had apparently been. "He left the name of the motel where he would stay if there was any change in her condition," the nurse said. "Here it is. The Pine Rest. I can call and see if they are still there."

"No, that's all right. I'll run by the motel." He realized Rebecca Stewart wouldn't have been allowed to walk out of the hospital. One of the nurses would have taken her down to the car by wheelchair. "You don't happen to know what Mr. Stewart was driving, do you?" She remembered the large black Suburban because it had looked brand-new.

The Pine Rest Motel sat on the east end of town on a hill. Austin spotted Marc Stewart's Suburban at once. Austin had to wonder why Marc's "wife" had been driving an older-model car.

That didn't surprise him as much as the lack of a baby car seat in the back of the Suburban. Marc had had the vehicle for almost a month according to the sticker in the back window. The lack of a car seat was just another one of those questions that nagged at him. Like the fact that Marc Stewart had gotten his wife out of the hospital early just to bring her to a motel in town.

That made no sense unless he'd brought her there to threaten her. That Austin could believe.

The black Suburban was parked in front of motel unit number seven—the last unit at the small motel.

Austin didn't go anywhere without his weapon. But he knew better than to go into the motel armed—let alone without a plan. He tended to wing things, following his instincts. It had gotten him this far. But it had also nearly gotten him killed last summer. He had both the physical and mental scars to prove it.

Glancing at the purse lying on the seat next to him, he wondered if all this wasn't an overreaction on his part. Maybe it had only been an argument between husband and wife that had gotten out of control. Maybe once Rebecca Stewart's memory returned, she wouldn't be afraid of her husband.

Maybe.

He picked up the purse. It was imitation leather, a knockoff of a famous designer's. He pulled out the wallet and went through it again, this time noticing the discount coupons for diapers and groceries.

He studied the woman in the photo a second time. It wasn't a great snapshot of her, but then most driver's license mug shots weren't. Montana only required a driver to get a license every eight years so this photo was almost seven years old.

If it hadn't been for the slight resemblance… He put everything back into the purse, opened the car door and stepped out into the falling snow.

Every cop knew not to get in the middle of a domestic dispute. This wasn't like him, he thought as he walked through the storm to the door of unit number seven and knocked.

At his knock, Austin heard a scurrying sound. He knocked again. A few moments later, Marc Stewart opened the door a crack.

He frowned when he saw Austin. "Yes?"

"I'm Austin Cardwell—"

"I know who you are." Behind the man, Austin heard a sound.

"I forgot to give Rebecca her purse," he said.

Marc reached for it.

All his training told him to just hand the man the damned purse and walk away. It wasn't like him to butt into someone else's business—let alone a married couple's, even if they had some obvious problems—when he wasn't asked.

"If you don't mind, I'd like to give it to her myself," he heard himself say. Behind the man, Austin caught a rustling sound.

"Look," Marc Stewart said from between gritted teeth. "I appreciate that you found…my wife and kept her safe until I could get here, but your job is done, cowboy. So you need to back the hell off."

Rebecca suddenly appeared at the man's side. "Excuse my husband. He's just upset." She met Austin's gaze. He tried to read it, afraid she was desperately trying to tell him something. "But Marc's right. We're fine now. It was very thoughtful of you to bring my purse, though."

"Yes, thoughtful," Marc said sarcastically and shot his wife a warning look. "You shouldn't be up," he snapped.

She was pale and a little unsteady on her feet, but she had a determined look on her face. Behind her, he saw her open suitcase—the same one he'd found in the overturned car's trunk. The scene looked like any other married couple's motel room.

Even before Marc spoke, Austin realized they were about to pack up and leave.

"We were just heading out," Marc said.

"I won't keep you, then," Austin said, still holding the purse. Rebecca Stewart looked weak as she leaned into the door frame. He feared her husband had gotten her out of the hospital too soon. But that, too, was none of his business. "I didn't want you leaving without your purse."

"Great," Marc said and turned to close her suitcase. "We have a long drive ahead of us, so if you'll excuse us…" Austin stepped aside to let him pass with the suitcase. "You should tell him our good news," he called over his shoulder.

"Good news?" Austin asked, studying the woman in the doorway. He realized that even though her suitcase had been open, she was still wearing the same clothing she'd had on last night. That realization gave him a start since there was a spot of blood on her sweater from her head injury the night before.

"We're pregnant again," Marc called from the side of the Suburban, where he was loading the suitcase.

Austin was watching her face. She suddenly went paler. He thought for a moment that she might faint.

"Marc, don't—" The words came out like a plea.

"Andrew Marc, our son, is going to have a baby sister," Marc said as if he hadn't heard her or was ignoring her. "Isn't that right, Rebecca? I think we'll call her Becky."

Austin met her gaze. "Congratulations." He couldn't have felt more like a fool as he handed her the purse.

She took it with trembling fingers, her eyes filling with tears. "Thank you for bringing my purse all this way." Her fingers kneaded the cheap fabric of the bag. He saw she was again wearing the wedding band that her husband had put on her finger at the hospital. That alone should have told him how things were.

"No problem. Good luck." He meant it since he knew in his heart she was going to need it. He started to step away when she suddenly grabbed his arm.

"Wait, I think this must be your coat," she said and turned back into the room.

"That's okay, you should keep it," he said.

She returned a few moments later with the coat.

"Seriously, keep it. You need it more than I do."

"Take the damned coat," Marc called to him before slamming the Suburban door.

Austin shook his head at her. "Keep it. Please," he said quietly.

Tears filled her eyes. "Thank you." She quickly reached for his hand and pressed what felt like a scrap of paper into his palm. "For everything." She then quickly pulled down her shirtsleeve, which had ridden up. He only got a glimpse of the fresh red mark around her wrist.

Austin sensed Marc behind him as he helped her into his coat. It swallowed her, but the December day was cold, another snowstorm threatening.

"Well, if we've all wished each other enough luck, it's time to hit the road," Marc said, joining them. "Hormones." He sounded disgusted as he looked at his wife. "The woman is in tears half the time." He put one arm around her roughly and reached into his pocket with the other. "Forgive my manners," he said, pulling out a crinkled twenty. "Here, this is for your trouble."

Austin stared down at the twenty.

Marc thrust the money at him. "Take it." There was an underlying threatening sound in his voice. The man's blue eyes were ice-cold.

"Please," Rebecca said. Austin still couldn't think of her as this man's wife. There was pleading in her voice, in her gaze.

"Thanks," he said as he took the money. "You really didn't have to, though."

Marc chuckled at that.

"Have a nice trip, then. Drive carefully." Austin turned and walked toward his rental SUV.

Behind him, he heard Marc say, "Get in the car."

When he turned back, she was pulling herself up into the large rig. He climbed into his own vehicle, but waited until the Suburban drove away. He caught only a glimpse of her wan face in the side window as they left. Her brown eyes were wide with more than tears. The woman seemed even more terrified.

His heart was already pounding like a war drum. That red mark around her right wrist. All his instincts told him that this was more than a bossy husband.

He tossed down the twenty and, reaching in his pocket, took out the scrap of paper she'd pressed into his palm. It appeared to be a corner of a page torn from a motel Bible. There were only four words, written in a hurried scrawl with an eyeliner pencil: "Help me. No law."

Chapter 7

Austin looked down the main street where the black Suburban had gone. If Marc Stewart was headed for Helena, he was going the wrong way.

He hesitated only a moment before he started the engine, backed up and turned onto the street.

Bozeman was one of those Western towns that had continued to grow—unlike a lot of Montana towns. In part, its popularity was because of its vibrant and busy downtown as well as being the home of Montana State University.

Austin cursed the traffic that had him stopped at every light while the black Suburban kept getting farther away. What he couldn't understand was why Marc Stewart was headed southwest if he was anxious to get his wife home. Maybe they were going out for breakfast first.

He caught another stoplight and swore. The Suburban was way ahead and unfortunately a lot of people in Bozeman drove large rigs, which made it nearly impossible to keep the vehicle in sight. He was getting more nervous by the moment. All his instincts told him the woman hadn't been delusional. She was in trouble.

From the beginning, she'd said the car wasn't hers, the purse wasn't hers and that her name wasn't Rebecca Stewart. What if she had been telling the truth?

It was that thought that had him hitting the gas the moment the light changed. Determined not to have to stop at the next one, he sped through the yellow light and kept going. He sped through another yellow light, barely making it. But ahead, he could see the Suburban. It was headed southwest out of town.

That alone proved something, didn't it?

But what? That Marc Stewart had lied about wanting to get his wife home to Helena as quickly as possible. What else might he be lying about? The pregnancy?

Austin used the hands-free system in the SUV to put in a call to the doctor at the hospital who'd handled the case. He knew he couldn't ask outright about the patient's condition. But…

Dr. Mayfield came on the line.

"Doctor, it's Austin Cardwell. I'm the man who found Rebecca Stewart—"

"Yes, I remember you, Mr. Cardwell. What can I do for you?"

"I ended up with Mrs. Stewart's purse after last night's emergency." He was counting on the doctor not knowing he'd already stopped by the hospital earlier. "I wanted to drop it by if Mrs. Stewart is up to it."

"I'm sorry, but her husband checked her out earlier today."

"I noticed she has prenatal vitamins in her purse when I was looking for her identification."

A few beats of silence stretched out a little too long. "Mr. Cardwell, I'm not sure what Mrs. Stewart told you, but I'm not at liberty to discuss her condition."

"Understood." He'd heard the surprise in the silence before the doctor had spoken. "Oh, one more thing. I just wanted to be sure she got her watch before she left the hospital. She was worried about it."

"Just a moment." The doctor left the line. When he came back, he said, "Yes, her husband picked it up for her."

Her husband picked up the watch with the name Gillian on it?

"Thank you, Doctor." He disconnected. Ahead, he could see the black Suburban still headed west on Highway 191. Marc had lied about her being pregnant, but why?

Austin thought about calling Marshal Hud Savage, but what would he tell him? That Marc Stewart was a liar. That wasn't illegal. Even if he told the marshal about the note the woman had passed him or about the diamond watch with the wrong name on it, Austin doubted Hud would be able to do more than he already had. Not to mention Rebecca had specified, *No law.*

Her name isn't Rebecca, just as she'd said, he realized with a jolt.

It's Gillian. Gillian Cooper. Rebecca's sister? The thought hit him like a sledgehammer. That was the only thing she had reacted to last night other than the man who was pretending to be her husband. It was the name on the expensive watch. It was proof—

Austin groaned as he realized it proved nothing. If she was Rebecca, she could have a reason for wearing her sister's watch. He thought of a woman he knew who wore her brother's St. Christopher medal. Her brother had died of cancer a few years before.

So maybe there was no mystery to the watch. But the woman in that black Suburban was in trouble. She'd asked for his help. Even if she was Rebecca and Marc Stewart was her husband, she was terrified of him. Terrified enough to leave her child and run.

That was the part that just didn't add up. Maybe Marc wouldn't let her take the child. All this speculation was giving him a headache.

Austin saw the four-way stop ahead. The black Suburban was in the left-hand turn lane. Marc Stewart was turning south—back up the Gallatin Canyon where Austin had found her the night before. So where was he going if not taking her home?

Instead of taking the highway south, though, the Suburban pulled into the gas station at the corner. Austin slowed, hanging back as far as he could as he saw Marc pull up to a gas pump and get out. The woman climbed out as well, said something to Marc and then went inside.

Austin saw his chance and pulled behind the station. He knew he didn't have much time since he wasn't sure why the woman had gone into the convenience store. If he was right, the man would be watching her, afraid to let her out of his sight. All he could hope was that the Suburban's gas tank was running low. He knew from experience that it took a long while to fill one.

Once inside the store, he looked around for the woman, anxious to find her since this might be his only chance to talk to her. There were several women in the store. None was the one he'd rescued last night.

It had only taken a few minutes for him to park. Surely she hadn't already gone back out to her vehicle. He glanced toward the Suburban from behind a tall rack of chips. Its front seats were both empty. Marc was still pumping gas into the tank, his gaze on the front of the store. The glare on the glass seemed to keep him from seeing inside. The woman was in here. Austin could think of only one other place she might be.

He found the restrooms down a short hallway. As she came out of the ladies' room, she saw him and froze. Eyes wide with fear, she looked as if she might turn and run. Except there was nowhere to run. He was blocking her way out.

He rushed to her. "Talk to me. Tell me who you are and what is going on."

She shook her head, glancing past him as if terrified Marc Stewart would appear at any moment.

"You gave me the note. You obviously are in trouble. Let me help you."

"I'm sorry. I shouldn't have involved you," she said. "Please forget I did. You can't help me." She tried to step past him, but he grabbed her arm. She flinched.

"He hurt you again, didn't he?"

"You don't understand. He has my sister."

"Your *sister*?"

Tears welled in her eyes. "Rebecca. If I don't go with him—" Her eyes widened in alarm again and he realized a buzzer had announced that someone had entered the store. Fortunately he and the woman couldn't be seen where they were standing, though. At least not yet.

"Your name is Gillian, isn't it? The watch—"

"Where are your restrooms?" he heard Marc ask the clerk.

Gillian gripped his arm, her fingers digging into his flesh. "If you tell anyone, he'll kill her."

There wasn't time to reassure her. "Where's he taking you?"

"A cabin in Island Park."

"Here, take this. If you get a chance, call me." He pressed one of his business cards into her palm and then pushed into the men's restroom an instant before he heard Marc's voice outside the door.

"It took you long enough," Marc snapped. "Come on."

Austin waited until he was sure they were gone before he opened the door and headed for his SUV. He had no idea what Island Park was or how to get there. All he knew was that he had no choice but to go after her.

Chapter 8

As Gillian climbed into the Suburban, she could feel Marc watching her, his eyes narrowed.

"It took you long enough in there," he said, studying her. "You didn't try to make any calls while you were in there, did you?" he asked, his voice low. She knew how close he was to hitting her when his voice got like that.

"How would I have made a call? You have my cell phone, I have no money and, in case you haven't noticed, there aren't pay phones around anymore."

He narrowed his eyes in warning. She knew she was treading on thin ice with him, but kowtowing to him only seemed to make him more violent.

Marc was still staring at her as if searching for even a hint of a lie. "I figure if anyone could find a way, it would be you. I've learned the hard way what you're capable of, sister-in-law. Let's not forget that you've

managed to get some local marshal sniffing around—
not to mention a deputy from *Texas*."

"I told you that wasn't my doing. The deputy was
merely worried about me." She looked away, wishing
he would start the engine. He was looking for any excuse to hurt her again.

"*Worried about you?* That Texas cowboy took a
shine to you after you told him you weren't my wife.
You take a shine to him, too? The patrolman said the
cowboy had you in some cabin handcuffed to a chair.
He have his way with you?"

"You disgust me," she said and turned to look out
the side window. A pickup had pulled up behind them,
the driver now waiting for the gas pump.

"Gave you his coat. How gallant is that?" he said,
his voice a sneer. "You must have done something to
keep him coming back."

She wished he would just start the engine. "You
know I didn't know what I was saying. I have a concussion. Or don't you believe that either?" She turned
to face him, knowing it was a daring thing to do. He
was just looking for an excuse. He hated everything
about her and her sister.

"Right, your head injury from an accident that would
never have happened if you hadn't—"

"Been running for my life?"

His face twisted into a mask of fury. "You—"

She braced herself for the smack she knew was coming. The only thing that saved her was the driver behind
them honking loudly.

Marc swore and flipped the man off, but started the
engine and pulled away from the pump and onto the
highway headed south toward West Yellowstone.

Gillian breathed a small sigh of relief. All she'd done was buy herself a little time. She'd be lucky if Marc didn't kill her. Right now, she was more worried about what he'd already done to Rebecca.

"What are you looking at?" Marc snapped.

"Nothing," she said as she turned toward him.

"You were looking in your side mirror." He hurriedly checked his rearview. "Is that cowboy following us?"

She realized her mistake. "What cowboy?"

"Don't give me that what cowboy bull. You know damned well. That *Texas* cowboy. Did you see him back there?"

"In the ladies' room?" She scoffed at his paranoia. "I was only looking out the window." It was a lie and she feared he knew it.

He kept watching behind them as he drove. "If you said something to him back at the motel—"

"You were there. You know I didn't say anything. Why did you say Rebecca was pregnant with a baby girl?" She held her breath for his answer.

Marc let out a snort. "I figured it would just get the guy off my back once he thought you were pregnant." He chuckled as if pleased with himself and seemed to relax a little, although he kept watching his mirror.

She hated that she'd involved Austin Cardwell in all this, but she'd been so desperate... Now she prayed that if he really was following them, that he didn't let Marc see him. There was no telling what Marc would do.

"What did you tell him last night?"

Gillian didn't need to ask whom he was talking about. "I didn't even know who I was last night, so how was I going to tell him anything?"

"That was convenient. But you recognized *me* when you saw me, didn't you?"

She'd been so confused, so terrified and yet she hadn't known of what or whom. But once Marc had come into her hospital room, she'd remembered, even before he'd whispered in her ear, "I'll kill your sister if you don't go along with what I say."

It had all come back in a wave of misery that threatened to overwhelm her. When Marc had slipped her sister's wedding band onto her finger... She hadn't been able to hold back the tears. She'd made matching rings for her sister and Marc when they'd married. Marc had lost his almost at once, but Rebecca... She felt a sob try to work its way up out of her chest. If Marc was carrying Rebecca's wedding ring in his pocket, was she even still alive?

Austin stayed back, letting the black Suburban disappear down Highway 191 toward Big Sky, while he called Hud.

"I need a favor," he said. "Does Marc Stewart own a cabin in a place called Island Park?"

Silence, then, "I'm sure you have a good reason to ask."

"I do."

"Want to tell me what's going on?"

"I wish I could."

"I hope you know what you're doing," the marshal said.

Austin hoped so, as well.

More silence, then the steady clack of computer keys.

"Funny you should ask," Hud said when he came

back on the line. "Marc Stewart has been paying taxes on a place in Island Park."

Austin leaned back, relieved, as he drove out of the valley and into the canyon. The traffic wasn't bad compared to Houston. Most every vehicle, other than semis, had a full ski rack on top. The roads had become more packed with snow, but at least he had some idea now where Marc Stewart might be heading.

"Where and what is Island Park?"

Hud rattled off an address that didn't sound like any he'd ever heard. "How do I find this place?" he asked frowning. "It doesn't sound like a street address in a town."

"Finding it could be tricky. Island Park is a thirty-three-mile-long town just over the Montana border from West Yellowstone. Basically, it follows the highway. The so-called town is no more than five hundred feet wide in places. They call it the longest main street in the world."

"Seriously?"

Austin was used to tiny Texas towns or sprawling urban cities.

"Owners of the lodges along the highway incorporated back in 1947 to circumvent Idaho's liquor laws, which prohibited the sale of liquor outside city limits."

"So how do I find this cabin?"

"In the middle of winter? I'd suggest by snowmobile unless it is right off a plowed road, which will be doubtful. Have you ever driven a snowmobile?"

"No, but I'll manage." He'd deal with all that once he knew where to look for the cabin.

"I don't know Island Park at all so I can't help you beyond the address I gave you. I should warn you that you're really on your own once you cross the border into

Idaho. I would imagine any help you might need from law enforcement would have to come out of Ashton, a good fifty miles to the south. Where you're headed is very isolated, with cabins back in heavily wooded areas. They get a lot of snow over there."

"Great." He'd already known that he was on his own. But now it was clear there would be no backup should he get himself in a bind. He almost laughed at that. He couldn't be in a worse situation right now, headed into country he didn't know and into a possible violent domestic dispute between Marc Stewart and his real wife.

"I suppose you won't be able to join us for dinner tonight?"

Austin had forgotten about dinner. "I'll try my best, but if things go south with this…"

"Not to worry. Dana is used to having a marshal for a husband. Just watch your back. And keep in touch," Hud said.

Austin didn't see the black Suburban again on the drive through the canyon. When the road finally opened up, he found himself on what apparently was called Fir Ridge. Off to his left was a small cemetery in the aspens and pines. Then the highway dropped down into a wooded area before crossing the Madison River Bridge and entering the small tourist town of West Yellowstone.

Had Marc stopped here to get Gillian something to eat? Buy gas? Or was he just anxious to get to wherever he was going?

Austin had no way of knowing. He only knew that he couldn't cross paths with him if he hoped to keep Gillian alive. All his training told him to bring the law into this now. Going in like the Lone Ranger was always a bad idea—especially when you weren't sure what you were getting into.

And yet, he couldn't make himself do it. Gillian did not want the law involved. She was terrified of Marc Stewart, and with her sister in danger, Austin couldn't chance that calling in law enforcement would push Marc into killing not only her, but also her sister, as well.

Not that he wasn't worried about getting her killed himself. If only he'd had more time with Gillian at the convenience store. There was so much he needed to know. Such as where was Rebecca's young son, Andrew Marc? Was he really with his grandmother? Or was that, too, a lie?

West Yellowstone was a tourist town of gas stations, curio shops, motels and cafés. Austin took the first turn out and headed for the Idaho border. He still hadn't seen the black Suburban. He could only hope that Gillian was right about where Marc was taking her.

Last night, Gillian had been driving her sister's car. He suspected the registration, the purse, the baby car seat, even the suitcase in the back belonged to her sister, Rebecca.

From the way the clothes had been thrown into the suitcase, he was assuming Rebecca had tried to leave her husband. So how had Gillian ended up in her sister's car?

He had many more questions than he had answers. No wonder he felt anxious. Even if he hadn't been shot and almost died just months ago when a case had gone wrong, he would have been leery of walking into this mess. No law officer in his right mind wanted to go in blind.

His cell phone rang. He snatched it up with the crazy thought that somehow Gillian Cooper had gotten away from Marc and was now calling.

"Where the hell are you?" his brother Tag demanded. "You did remember that we're supposed to have dinner with Dana, didn't you?"

Austin swore under his breath. "Something has come up."

"*Something?* Like something came up and you couldn't make my wedding?"

"Do we have to go through this again? I'm sorry. If it wasn't important—"

"More important obviously than your family."

"Tag, I'll explain everything when I get back. I'm sure you can go ahead with…" He realized his brother had hung up on him.

Not that he could blame his brother. He disconnected, feeling like a heel. He had a bad habit of letting down the people he cared about. He blamed his job, but the truth was he felt more comfortable as a deputy than he did in any other relationship.

"Maybe I'm like my dad," he'd said to his mother when she'd asked him why of the five brothers, he was the one who was often at odds with the others. *"Look how great Dad is with* his *sons,"* he'd pointed out.

His parents had divorced years ago when Austin was still in diapers. His mother had taken her five boys to live in Texas while their father had stayed in Big Sky. Austin had hardly seen his father over the years. He knew that his brothers had now reconciled with him, but Austin didn't see that happening as far as he was concerned. He wouldn't be in Montana long enough, and the way things were going…

It amazed him that his mother always stood up for the man she'd divorced, the man who had fathered her boys. *"I won't have you talk about your father like that,"* his mother had said the last time they discussed it. *"Harlan and I did the best we could."*

Austin had softened his words. *"You did great, Mom. But let's face it, I could be more like Harlan Cardwell than even you want to admit."*

"Tell me, is there anything you care about, Austin?" she'd asked, looking disappointed in him.

"I care about my family, my friends, my town, my state."

"But not enough to make your own brother's wedding."

"I was on a case."

"And there was no one else who could handle it?"

"I needed to see it through. I might not be great at relationships, but I'm damned good at my job."

"Watch your language," she'd reprimanded. *"A job won't keep you warm at night, son. Someday you're going to realize that these relationships you treat so trivially are more important than anything else in life. I thought almost losing your life might have taught you something."*

As he dropped over the Idaho border headed for Island Park, he thought no one would ever understand him since he didn't even understand himself. He just knew that right now Gillian Cooper needed him more than his brothers or cousin Dana did. Just as the woman he'd tried to save in Texas had needed him more than Tag had needed another attendant at his wedding.

He'd failed his family as well as that woman in Texas, though, and it had almost cost him his life. He couldn't fail this one.

"You look like hell."

Gillian didn't bother to react to Marc's snide comment as they drove into West Yellowstone. He wanted to argue with her, to have an excuse to hit her. His anger was palpable in the interior of the Suburban. She'd outwitted him—at least for a while before she'd lost control of Rebecca's car and crashed.

Her head ached and she felt sick to her stomach. How much of it was from the accident? The doctor had discussed her staying another night, but Marc had told her that her sister would be dead if she did. She wasn't sure if her ailments were from her concussion solely or not. She'd often felt sick to her stomach when she thought of the man her sister had married.

"I'll get you something to eat," Marc said. "I don't want you dying on me. At least not yet." He pulled into a drive-through. "What do you want?"

She wasn't hungry, but she knew she needed to eat. She would need all her strength once they reached the cabin.

Marc didn't give her a chance to answer, though. "Give us four burgers, a couple of large fries and two big colas." As he dug his wallet out, she felt him looking at her. "You're just lucky you didn't kill yourself last night. As it is, you owe me for a car."

Just like Marc to make it about the money.

"I'm sure my insurance will pay for it," she said drily. "If I get to make the claim."

He snorted as he pulled up to the next window and

paid. A few moments later, he handed her a large bag of greasy smelling food.

Just the odor alone made her stomach turn. She thought she might throw up. "I need to go to the bathroom." The business card Austin Cardwell had given her was hidden in her jeans pocket. She knew she should have thrown it away back at the convenience store, but Marc hadn't given her a chance.

He shook his head. "You just went back at Four Corners."

"I have to go again." She had to get rid of the business card. If Marc found it on her—

She regretted telling Austin where they were headed. Not only had she put him in danger and possibly made things even worse, but she wasn't sure he would be able to find the cabin anyway. She'd stolen glances in the side mirror and hadn't seen his SUV. He was a deputy sheriff in Texas. What if he contacted law enforcement here?

No, she couldn't see him doing that. Just as she couldn't see him giving up. He was back there somewhere. He'd saved her life last night. But she wasn't so sure he could pull it off again. Worse, she couldn't bear the thought that she might get him killed.

If she could get to a phone, she could call the number on the card and plead with him not to get involved. Even as she thought it, she knew he wouldn't be able to turn back now. She'd seen how determined he was at the hospital and later at the motel room. Her heart went out to him. Why couldn't her sister have married someone like Austin Cardwell?

"You'll just have to hold it," Marc was saying. "Hand

me one of the burgers and some fries," he said as he drove onto the highway again.

She dug in the bag and handed him a sandwich. The last thing she wanted was food, but she made herself gag down one of the burgers and a little of the cola. Marc ended up devouring everything else. She prayed her sister was still alive, but in truth she feared what was waiting for her at the cabin.

As they drove up over the mountain and dropped down into Idaho, she stared out the window at the tall banks of plowed snow on each side of the road. Island Park was famous for its snow—close to nine feet of it in an average winter. And where there was snow…

Three snowmobiles buzzed by like angry bees on the trail beside the highway and sped off, the colorful sleds catching the sunlight.

She stole a glance in the side mirror. The highway behind them was empty. Her stomach roiled at the thought that Austin was ahead of them because of their food stop, that he might be waiting at the cabin, not realizing just how dangerous Marc was.

Gillian closed her eyes, fighting tears. She'd been so afraid for her sister she'd been desperate when she'd asked for his help. If only she could undo what she'd done. The man had saved her life last night and this was how she repaid him, by getting him involved in this?

There was no saving any of them, she thought as more snowmobiles zoomed past, kicking up snow crystals into the bright blue winter sky. It wasn't until they passed a cabin with a brightly decorated tree in the front yard that she remembered with a start that Christmas was only a few days away.

Chapter 9

Not long after the Idaho border, the terrain closed in with pines and more towering snowbanks. Austin started seeing snowmobilers everywhere he looked. They buzzed past on brightly colored machines, the drivers clad in heavy-duty cold-weather gear and helmets, which hid their faces behind the black plastic.

Even inside the SUV, he could hear the roar of the machines as they sped by—all going faster on the snow track next to him than he was on the snow-slick highway.

Just as Hud had told him, he began to see cabins stuck back in the pines. He would need directions. He figured he was also going to need a snowmobile, just as Hud had suggested, if the cabin was far off the road.

When he reached the Henry's Fork of the Snake River, he pulled into a place alongside the highway called Pond's Lodge. The temperature seemed to be dropping, and tiny snowflakes hung around him as if suspended in the air as he got out of the SUV. He shivered, amazed that people lived this far north.

Inside, he asked for a map of the area.

"You'll want a snowmobile map, too," the older woman behind the counter said.

He thought she might be right as he stepped back outside. Snow had begun falling in huge lacy flakes. He wasn't all that anxious to get out in it on a snowmobile for the first time. But after a quick perusal of the map, he knew a snowmobile was his best bet.

As the marshal had told him he would, he could see the problem of finding the cabin—especially in winter. He figured a lot of the dwellings would be boarded up this time of year. Some even inaccessible.

He had to assume that Marc Stewart's family cabin would be open—but possibly not the road to it. What few actual roads there were seemed to be banked in deep snow. Clearly most everyone traveled by snowmobile. He could hear them buzzing around among the trees in a haze of gray smoke.

Back in his rented SUV, he drove down to a small out-of-the-way snowmobile rental. The moment he walked in the door, he caught the scent of a two-stroke engine and the high whine of several others as two snowmobiles roared out of the back of the shop. Even the music playing loudly from overhead speakers behind the counter couldn't drown them out. Beneath the speakers, a man in his late twenties with dozens of tattoos and piercings glanced up. The name stitched on his shirt read "Awesome."

"My man!" he called. "Looking for the ultimate

machine, right? Are we talking steep and deep action or outrageous hill banging to do some high marking today?"

The man could have been speaking Greek. "Sorry, I just need one that runs."

Awesome laughed. "If it's boondocking you're looking for, chutes, ridges, big bowls, I got just the baby for you." He shoved a map at him. "We have an endless supply of cornices to jump, untouched powder and more coming down, mountainsides just waiting for you to put some fresh tracks on them."

"Do you have one for flat ground?"

Awesome looked a little disappointed. "You seriously want to pass up Two Top, Mount Jefferson and Lion's Head?"

He seriously did. "I see on your brochure that you have GPS tours. It says here I can pinpoint an area I want to go to with the specific coordinates and you can get me there?"

"I can." Awesome didn't seem all that enthusiastic about it, though. "We have about a thousand miles of backwoods trails."

"Great. Here is where I need to go. You have a machine that can get me there?"

He looked at the map, his enthusiasm waning even faster. "This address isn't far from here. I suppose you need gear? Helmet, boots, bibs, coat and gloves? They're an extra twenty. I can put you in a machine that will run you a hundred a day."

"How fast do these things go?" Austin asked as one sped by in a blur.

"The fastest? A hundred and sixty miles an hour. The ones we have? You can clock in at a hundred."

Austin had no desire to clock in at a hundred. Even the price tag shocked him. The one sitting on the show-room floor was on sale for fourteen thousand dollars and everyone around here seemed to have one. He figured Marc Stewart would have at least one of the fastest snowmobiles around. He tagged the guy as someone who had done his share of high marking. "What is high marking, by the way?"

Awesome laughed and pointed at a poster on the wall. "You try to make the highest mark on the side of a mountain." On the poster, the rider had made it all the way up under an overhanging wall of snow.

"It looks dangerous."

Awesome shrugged. "Only if you get caught in an avalanche."

Austin didn't have to worry about avalanches, but what he was doing was definitely dangerous. Gillian was terrified for her sister. Austin wouldn't be trying to find them if he didn't believe she had good reason for concern.

But he was smart enough to know that a man like Marc Stewart, when trapped, might do something stupid like kill an off-duty state deputy sheriff who was sticking his nose where it didn't belong.

Gillian looked out through the snow-filled pines as Marc drove. She couldn't see the cabin from the road. She'd been here once before, but it had been in summer. The cabin sat on Island Park Reservoir just off Centennial Loop Trail. While old, it was charming and pictur-esque. At least that's what she'd thought that summer she and her sister had spent a week here without Marc.

That had been before Rebecca and Marc had married, back when her sister had been happy and foolishly naive about the man she'd fallen in love with.

Gillian hugged herself as she remembered her sister's text message just days before.

On way to your house. I've left Marc.

She'd tried her sister's number, but the call went straight to voice mail. She'd texted back. Are you and Andy all right?

No answer. Helena was a good two hours away from Gillian's home in Big Sky. Even the way her sister drove, Rebecca wouldn't have arrived until after dark. Gillian had paced, checking the window anxiously and asking herself, "What would Marc do?" She feared the answer.

It was night by the time she finally saw her sister's car pull up out front. Relieved to tears, she'd run outside without even a coat on. But it hadn't been Rebecca in the car.

By the time she'd realized it was Marc alone and furious, it was too late. He'd grabbed her and thrown her into the trunk. She'd fought him, but he'd been so much stronger and he'd taken her by surprise. He'd slammed the trunk lid and the next thing she'd known the car was moving.

"Did you really forget your name?" Marc asked, dragging her out of her thoughts. He sounded amused at the idea. "Sometimes I'd like to forget my name. Hell, I'd like to forget my life."

She didn't tell him that pieces of memory had her even more confused. She'd remembered there was someone in the trunk of the car she'd been driving, but she hadn't remembered it was her.

When Austin had returned to the cabin with the patrolman, he'd told her that the only thing he'd found in the trunk of the car was a suitcase. She'd been more confused.

It wasn't until she'd laid eyes on her alleged *husband* that she'd remembered Marc forcing her into the trunk. When he'd stopped at a convenience mart in the canyon, she'd shoved her way out by kicking aside the backseat.

She hadn't known where they were when she'd crawled out. He'd left the car running because of the freezing cold night. Not knowing where she was, she'd just taken off driving, afraid that he would get a ride or steal a car and come after her.

The next thing she remembered was waking up in a hospital with vague memories of the night before and a tall Texas cowboy.

"I'm curious. Where was it you thought you were going?" Marc asked. He sounded casual enough, but she could hear the underlying fury behind his words.

"I have no idea." She'd been running scared. All she'd been able to think about was getting to a phone so she could call the police. Her cell phone had been in her pocket when she'd rushed out of her house, but Marc had taken it.

"You should have waited and run me down with the car." Marc glanced over at her. "Short of killing me, you should have known you wouldn't get away."

She shuddered at the thought, but knew he was right. She had managed to get away from him, but not long enough to help herself or her sister. Maybe that had been a godsend. He'd told her at the hospital that if they didn't get back to her sister soon, she would be dead.

Gillian hadn't known then where he'd left Rebecca. But she'd believed him. He'd had her sister's wedding band in his pocket. It wasn't until Marc headed out of Bozeman that she'd figured out where he was taking her.

Now Marc slowed the Suburban as he turned down a narrow road with high snowbanks on each side. He drove only a short distance, though, before the road ended in a huge pile of snow. She glanced around as he pulled into a wide spot where the snow had been plowed to make a parking area. Other vehicles were parked there, most of them with snowmobile trailers.

"Here." He tossed her a pair of gloves. A snowmobile buzzed past, kicking up a cloud of snow. "If you want to see your sister alive, you will do what I say. Try to make another run for it—"

"I get it." As angry and out of control as he was, she feared what kind of shape her sister was in. Marc had told Austin that their son, Andrew Marc, was with his grandmother. That had been a lie since Marc's parents were both dead and he had no other family that she knew of.

So where was Andy? Was he with his mother at the cabin? She didn't dare hope that they were both safe.

Marc backed up to where he'd left his snowmobile trailer. Both machines were on it, Gillian noticed, and any hope she'd had that her sister might have escaped evaporated at the sight of them. Even if Rebecca was able to leave the cabin, she had no way to get out. The snow would be too deep. One step off the snowmobile and she would be up to her thigh in snow. As she glanced in the direction of the cabin, Gillian could see the fresh tracks that Marc had made in and back out again from the cabin on the deep snow. Neither trip had packed down the trail enough to walk on.

Marc cut the engine. She could hear the whine of snowmobiles in the distance, then an eerie quiet fell over the Suburban.

"Come on," he said as he reached behind the seat for his coat. "Your sister is waiting."

Was she? Gillian could only pray it was true as she pulled on the coat Austin had given her and climbed out into the falling snow. Even as she breathed in the frosty air, she prayed they hadn't arrived too late. Marc had told her last night that if Rebecca was dead, it was her fault for taking off in the car and causing him even more problems.

The only thing that made her climb onto the back of the snowmobile behind her brother-in-law was the thought of her sister and nephew. Whatever was going on, Marc had brought her here for a reason. She couldn't imagine what. But if she could save Rebecca and Andy…

Even as she thought it, Gillian wondered how she would do that against a man like Marc Stewart.

Austin was pleased to find that driving a snowmobile wasn't much different from driving a dirt bike. Actually, it was easier because you didn't have to worry as much about balance. You could just sit down, hit the throttle and go.

With the GPS in his pocket, along with a map of the area, and his weapon strapped on beneath his coat, he headed for Marc Stewart's cabin. The area was a web of narrow snow-filled roads that wove through the dense pines. From what he could gather, the Stewart cabin was on the reservoir.

He followed Box Canyon Trail until it connected

with another trail at Elk Creek. Then he took Centennial Loop Trail.

He passed trees with names on boards tacked to them. Dozens of names indicating dozens of cabins back in the woods. But he had a feeling that the Stewart cabin wasn't near a lot of others or at least not near an occupied cabin.

Snowmobiles sped past, throwing up new snow, leaving behind blue exhaust. It was snowing harder by the time he reached the spot on the GPS where he was supposed to turn.

He slowed. The tree next to the road had only four signs nailed on it. Three of them were Stewart's. Off to his right, Austin saw a half dozen vehicles parked at what appeared to be the entrance to another trailhead that went off in the opposite direction from the Stewart family cabins.

The black Suburban was parked in front of a snowmobile trailer with one machine on it. There were fresh snow tracks around the spot where a second one must have recently been unloaded.

Austin double-checked the GPS. It appeared the cabin at the address the marshal had given him was a half mile down a narrow road.

As he turned toward the road, he saw that there were several sets of snowmobile tracks, but only one in the new snow—and it wasn't very old based on how little of the falling snow had filled it.

Marc and Gillian weren't that far ahead of him.

Chapter 10

The road Austin had taken this far was packed down from vehicles driving on it. But the one that went back into the cabins hadn't been plowed since winter had begun so the snow was a good five or six feet deep.

Austin had to get a run at it, throttling up the snowmobile to barrel up the slope onto the snow.

Fortunately, the snowmobile ahead of him had packed down the new snow so once he got up on top of it, the track was fairly smooth. Still, visibility was bad with the falling snow and the dense trees. He couldn't see anything ahead but the track he was on. According to the map, the road went past the Stewart cabins for another quarter mile before it ended beside the lake.

His plan was to go past the cabin where the snowmobile had gone, then work his way back. As loud as the snowmobile motor was, it would be heard by anyone inside the cabin. His only hope for a surprise visit would be if those inside thought he was merely some snowmobiler riding around.

A corner of a log cabin suddenly appeared from out of the falling snow. Austin caught glimpses of more weathered dark log structures as he continued on past. The shingled roofs seemed to squat under the layers of snow, the smaller cabins practically disappearing in the drifts.

No smoke curled out of any of the rock chimneys. In fact as he passed, he saw no signs of life at all. Wooden shutters covered all the windows. No light came from within.

He would have thought that the cabins were empty, still closed up waiting for spring—if not for the distinct new snowmobile track that cut off from the road he was on and headed directly for the larger of the three cabins.

Austin kept the throttle down, the whine of his snowmobile cutting through the cold silence of the forest as he zoomed past the cabins huddled in the pines and snow. He stole only a couple of glances, trying hard not to look in their direction for fear of who might be looking back.

Marc pulled around the back of the cabin and shut off the snowmobile engine.

Gillian could barely hear over the thunder of her heart. Her legs felt weak as she slipped off the back of the machine and looked toward the door of the cabin. The place was big and rambling, dated in a way that she'd found quaint the first time her sister had invited her here.

"Isn't this place something?" Rebecca had said, clearly proud of what she called Stewart Hall.

The main cabin reminded Gillian of the summer lodges she'd seen on television. All of it told of another time: the log and antler decor, furniture with Western print fabric, the bookshelves filled with thick tomes and board games, and the wide screened-in front porch with its wicker rockers that looked out over a marble-smooth green lake surrounded by towering pines.

"It is *picturesque,"* Gillian had said, not mentioning that it smelled a little musty. *"How often does Marc's family get up here?"*

"There isn't much family left. Just Marc and me." Rebecca's hand had gone to her stomach. Her eyes brightened. *"That's why he wanted to start our family as soon as possible."*

"You're pregnant?*"* Her sister and Marc had only been married a few months at that time. But Gillian had seen how happy her sister was. *"Congratulations,"* she'd said and hugged Rebecca tightly as she remembered how she'd tried to talk her out of marrying Marc and her sister had accused her of being jealous.

Now as she watched Marc pocket the snowmobile key, she wished she'd fought harder. Even when they were only dating, Gillian had seen a selfishness in Marc, a need to always be the center of attention, a need to have everything his way. He was a poor sport, too, often leaving games in anger. They'd been small things that Rebecca had ignored, saying no man was perfect.

Gillian wished she had fought harder. Maybe she could have saved Rebecca from a lot of pain. But then there would be no baby. No little Andy…

"You know what you have to do," Marc said as he reached in another pocket for the key to the door.

She nodded.

"Do I have to remind you what happens if you don't?" he asked.

Gillian looked into his eyes. It was like looking into the fires of hell. "No," she said. "You were quite clear back at the motel."

Austin rode farther up the road until he could see another cabin in the distance. He found a spot to turn the snowmobile around. The one thing he hadn't considered was how hard it would be to hike back to the Stewart cabins.

The moment he stepped off the machine, his legs sank to his thighs in the soft snow. His only hope was to walk in the snowmobile track—not that he didn't sink a good foot with each step.

He checked his gun and extra ammunition and then headed down the track. The falling snow made him feel as if he were in a snow globe. Had he not been following the snowmobile track, he might have become disoriented and gotten lost in what seemed an endless forest of snow-covered trees that all looked the same.

An eerie quiet had fallen around him, broken only by the sound of his own breathing. He was breathing harder than he should have been, he realized. It had been months now since he'd been shot. That had been down on the Mexico border with heat and cactus and the scent of dust in the air, nothing like this. And yet, he had that same feeling that he was walking into something he wouldn't be walking back out of—and all because of a woman.

A bird suddenly cried out from a nearby tree. Austin started. He couldn't remember ever feeling more alone. When he finally picked up the irritating buzz of snowmobiles in the distance, he was thankful for a reminder of other life. The snow had an insulating effect that rattled his nerves with its cold silence. That and the memory of lying in the Texas dust, dying.

It seemed he'd been wrong. He hadn't put it behind him, he realized with a self-deprecating chuckle. And now here he was again. Only this time, he didn't know the area, let alone what was waiting for him inside that cabin, and he wasn't even a deputy doing his job.

The structure appeared out of the falling snow. He realized he couldn't stay on the track. But when he stepped off into the deep snow, he found himself laboring to move. It was worse under the trees, where it formed deep wells. If you got too close… He stepped into one and dropped, finding himself instantly buried. He fought his way to the surface like a swimmer and finally was able to climb out. The snow had chilled him. He'd never been in snow, let alone anything this deep and cold.

But his biggest concern was what awaited him ahead. He had no idea what he was going to do when he reached the main cabin. He needed to know what was going on inside. Unfortunately, with the shutters on all the windows, he wasn't sure how to accomplish that.

As he neared the side, he saw an old wooden ladder hanging on an outbuilding and had an idea. It was a crazy one, but any idea seemed good right now. The snow was deep enough where it had drifted in on this side of the cabin that it ran from the roof to the ground. If he could lay the ladder against the snowdrift, it was possible he could climb up onto the roof. The chimney stuck up out of the snow only a few feet. With luck, he might be able to hear something.

The snowmobile that had made the recent tracks to the cabin was parked out back—just as he'd suspected. Steam was still coming off the engine, indicating that whoever had ridden it hadn't been at the cabin long.

Austin took the ladder and, working his way through the snow, leaned it against the house and began to climb.

It was like a tomb inside the cabin with the shutters closed and no lights or heat on. Gillian stood in the large living room waiting for Marc to turn on a lamp. When he did, she blinked, blinded for a moment.

In that instant, she saw the cabin the way it had been the first time she'd seen it. The Native American rugs, the pottery and the old paintings and photographs on the walls. The vintage furniture and the gleam of the wood floors.

She'd felt back then that she'd been transported to another time, one that felt grander. One she wished she'd had as a child. She'd envied Marc his childhood here on this lake. How she'd longed to have been the little girl who curled up in the hammock out on the porch and read books on a long, hot summer day while her little sister played with dolls kept in one of the old trunks.

If only they could have been two little girls who swam in the lake and learned to water-ski behind the boat with her two loving parents. And lay in bed at night listening to the adults, the lodge alive with laughter and summer people.

For just an instant, Gillian had heard the happy clink of crystal from that other time. Then Marc stepped on a piece of broken glass that splintered under his snowmobile boot with the sound of a shot. He kicked it away and Gillian saw the room how it was now, cold, dark and as broken as the lonely only child Marc Stewart had been.

Most of the lighter-weight furniture now looked like kindling. Anything that could be broken was. Jigsaw pieces of ceramic vases, lamps and knickknacks littered the floor, along with the glass from the picture frames.

The room attested to the extent of Marc Stewart's rage—not that Gillian needed a reminder.

She looked toward the large old farmhouse-style kitchen. The floor was deep in broken dishes and thrown cutlery.

Past it down the hall, she saw drops of blood on the worn wood floor.

"Where's my sister? Rebecca!" Her voice came out too high. It sounded weak and scared and without hope. *"Rebecca?"*

"She's not up here," Marc said as he kicked aside what was left of a spindle rocking chair.

The weight of the fear on her chest made it hard to even say the words. *"Where is she?"*

"Down there." He pointed toward the old root cellar door off the kitchen.

Gillian felt her heart drop like a stone. She couldn't get her legs to move. Just as she couldn't get her lungs to fill. "You left her down there all this time?"

"We would have been here sooner if it wasn't for you." Marc looked as if he wanted to hit her, as if it took everything in him not to break her as he had everything else in this cabin. "Are you coming?"

* * *

Austin climbed across the roof to the chimney. The snow silenced his footfalls, but also threatened to slide in an avalanche that would take him with it should he misstep. He knelt next to the chimney to listen just as he heard Gillian call out her sister's name.

He waited for an answer.

He heard none.

"Can't you bring her up here?" Austin heard the fear in Gillian's voice. Bring her up? Was there a basement under the cabin? He didn't think so. A root cellar possibly? Then he felt his skin crawl as he remembered a root cellar one of his friends had found at an old abandoned house. He was instantly reminded of the musky smell, the cobwebs, the dust-coated canning jars with unidentifiable contents and the scurry of the rats as they'd opened the door.

"I thought you understood that we were doing this my way," Marc said, his tone as threatening as the smack that followed his words and Gillian's small cry of pain. "Come on."

Austin heard what sounded like the crunch of boot heels over gravel, then nothing for a few moments.

Chapter 11

Gillian peered down the steep wooden stairs into the dim darkness and felt her stomach roil. Only one small light burned in a black corner of the root cellar. The musty, damp smell hit her first.

"Rebecca?" she called and felt Marc shove her hard between her shoulder blades. She would have tumbled headlong down the stairs if she hadn't grabbed the door frame.

"Move," Marc snapped behind her.

Gillian thought she heard a muffled sound down in the blackness, but it could have been pack rats. What if Marc had lied? What if Rebecca was dead? Then the only reason Marc had come after her and brought her back here was to kill her, too.

She took one step, then another. There was no railing so she clung to the rough rock wall that ran down one side of the stairs. With each step, she expected Marc to push her again. All her instincts told her this was a trap. She wouldn't have been surprised to hear him slam and lock the door at the top of the steps behind her. Leaving her to die down here would be the kind of cruel thing he would do.

To her surprise, she heard the steps behind her groan with his weight as he followed her down. It gave her little relief, though. The moment she reached the bottom, she turned on him. "Where is she? Marc, where is my sister?"

Gillian heard another moan and turned in the direction the sound had come from. Something moved deep in the darkest part of the root cellar. "Oh, God, what have you done to her?"

Marc pushed her aside. An instant later, a bare overhead bulb turned on, blinding her. Gillian blinked, shielding her eyes from the glare as she tried to see—all the time terrified of what Marc had done to her sister.

In the far reaches of the root cellar, Gillian saw her. Rebecca was shackled to a chair. He'd left her water and a bucket along with at least a little food. But there was dried blood on her face and clothes. Her face was also bruised and raw, but her eyes were open.

What Gillian saw in her sister's eyes, though, sent her heart plummeting. Regret when she saw her sister, but when her gaze turned to her husband, it was nothing but defiance. Gillian tried to swallow, but her mouth felt as if filled with cotton balls.

"You're her last hope, big sister," Marc said as he looked from his wife to her. "Get her to tell you what she did with my ledger, my money and my son…" He met her gaze. "Or I will kill her and then I will beat it out of you since I know she tells you everything."

Not everything, Gillian thought. She swallowed again, her throat working. "I already told you that I don't know."

He nodded, his facial features distorted under the harsh glare of the single bulb hanging over his head. How could such a handsome man look so evil…?

"Either you get it out of her or I will beat her until her last scream." He handed her a key to the lock on the shackles.

Gillian moved to her sister, falling on her knees in front of her. She worked to free her, her hands shaking so hard she had trouble with the lock. "She needs water and food and help out of this chair." She turned to glare back at him. "It's too cold and damp down here. I think she is already suffering from hypothermia. She's going to die before you can kill her."

He took a step toward her. "Who the hell do you think you are, telling me what I *have* to do?"

It took all of her courage to stand up to him knowing the kind of man he was. But if she and Rebecca had any chance, they had to get out of this root cellar.

"If she dies, then what she knows dies with her," Gillian said quickly. "I told you. I don't know. She didn't tell me because she knows I'm not as strong as she is. I would tell you."

He seemed to mull that over for a moment, his gaze going to his wife. Marc looked livid. He raised his hand and Gillian tried not to cower from his fist.

To her surprise, he didn't strike her. "Fine," he said with a curse.

Rebecca didn't move, didn't seem to breathe. If it

weren't for the movement of her eyes, Gillian would have sworn she was already dead.

"I hope you don't think you're going to get away again," Marc said, meeting her gaze. "I have nothing to lose and I'm sick of both of you."

Austin heard the sound of footfalls and murmured voices. He froze, listening, and was relieved when he heard Gillian's voice. He hadn't been able to hear anything for a while.

"We need to get her warm." Her voice was louder. So were the footfalls. They'd come up from the root cellar. He also heard another sound, a slow shuffling, almost dragging, gait.

"Maybe you could build a fire or turn on the furnace."

Marc swore at Gillian's suggestion. The footfalls stopped abruptly. Gillian let out a small cry. Austin cringed in anger, knowing that Marc had hit her.

"Enough wasting time," Marc snapped.

"You want her to talk? Then give me a chance. But first we need to warm her up. Can you get some quilts from the bedroom?"

Marc swore loudly, but Austin heard what sounded like him storming away into another room. "Move and I'll—" he said over his shoulder.

"I'm not going to move," Gillian snapped. "My sister can barely stand, let alone run away. I'm going to put her in the living room in front of the fireplace. Maybe you could build a fire?"

Austin didn't catch what Marc said. He could guess, though. Marc was an abusive SOB. But Austin still had no idea why he'd brought Gillian and her sister here, nor where the child was. From what he had surmised, Marc thought Gillian could get her sister to talk, but talk about what?

Austin decided it didn't matter. Marc had forced Gillian to come here against her will. He had abused her and her sister and had apparently held Rebecca captive here. It was time to put a stop to this.

Working his way back off the roof, he walked around to where Marc had left the snowmobile. All Austin's instincts warned him not to go busting in. He couldn't chance what Marc would do.

He moved carefully back the way he'd come until he was at the far side of the cabin complex. He found an old door with a single lock and waited until he heard the sound of several snowmobiles nearby. Hoping they would drown out the noise, he busted the lock and carefully shoved open the door.

Gillian helped her sister into a straight-backed chair from the dining room and gently wiped her sister's face with the hem of her sweater. "Oh, Becky."

Rebecca's gaze locked with hers, her voice a hoarse whisper. "I thought I could do this without getting you involved."

Marc returned with the quilts and dropped them next to the chair.

"We're going to need a fire," Gillian said, not looking at him as she rubbed life back into her sister's hands and arms.

After a moment, she glanced over her shoulder to see what Marc was doing. He was busy building a fire in the rock fireplace using some of the furniture he'd destroyed. He struck a match to the wadded-up newspaper under the stack of wood. The paper caught fire. The dried old wood of the furniture burst into flames and began to crackle warmly.

"She needs something to drink. Is there any water in the kitchen?"

"What do you think?" Marc snapped. "It's winter. Everything is shut off."

"Maybe you could melt some snow." She motioned with her head for him to go as if the two of them were in collaboration. The thought made her sick.

He glanced from her to her sister and back again. "Don't do anything stupid," he said as he walked into the kitchen and came back out with a pot in one hand.

Marc had both women in an old cabin in the woods, far enough from the rest of the world that they would never be found if he killed them and buried them in the root cellar. So what was the stupid thing he thought she might do?

He gave her a warning look anyway and left, going out the back door where he'd left the snowmobile. She let go of her sister's arms and to her surprise Rebecca fell over in the chair, catching herself before she fell on the littered floor.

Gillian helped her sit up straighter, shocked at how weak her sister was and terrified she wasn't going to survive this.

Marc came back in, shot them a look, but said nothing as he headed for the kitchen with the cooking pot full of fresh snow. She heard him turn on the stove. She could feel time slipping through her fingers.

"Becky, what's going on?" she whispered. "What is this about some ledger of Marc's? And where is Andy?"

Her sister shook her head in answer as she glanced

toward the kitchen, where Marc was cussing and banging around.

"Tell him what he wants to know—otherwise he is going to kill you," Gillian pleaded.

"So sorry to get you—" her sister said from between cracked and cut lips.

"Becky—"

"Remember when we were kids and that big old tree blew over?"

Gillian stared at her. Had her brain been injured as a result of Marc's beating? Gillian's heartbreak rose in a sob from her throat as she looked at what that bastard had done to her sister.

Rebecca suddenly gripped her arm, digging in her fingernails. "Tell me you remember," her sister said.

"I remember."

Her sister's eyes filled with tears. "Love you." She licked her lips, her words coming out hoarse and hurried. "Save Andy. Make Marc pay." Pain filled her sister's eyes. "Can't save me."

"Stop talking like that. I'm not leaving here without you."

Her sister smiled, even though her lips were cut and bleeding, and then shook her head. "Get away. Run. He'll hurt you." She stopped talking at the sound of heavy footfalls headed back in their direction.

Gillian stared at her sister. "What are you going to do?" she whispered frantically. She could feel Marc closing the distance.

"Get ready to run," her sister said under her breath as Marc's shadow fell over them.

"What's all the whispering about?" Marc demanded as he handed Gillian a cup of melted snow.

She held it up to her sister's swollen lips. Her gaze met Rebecca's in a pleading gesture. Her sister was talking crazy. Worse, she seemed about to do something that could get them both killed.

Without warning, her sister knocked the cup out of her hand. It hit the floor, spilling the water as it rolled across the floor.

"You stupid—" Marc shoved Gillian out of the way. She fell backward and hit the floor hard. From where she was sprawled, she saw him pull his gun and crouch down in front of Rebecca. He put the end of the barrel against his wife's forehead. "Last chance, Rebecca."

With horror, Gillian saw Becky's expression—and what she had picked up from the floor and hidden in her hand. "No!" she screamed as her sister swung her arm toward Marc's face. The shard of sharp broken glass clutched in her fingers momentarily flashed as it caught the dim light.

Blood sprouted across Marc's cheek and neck as Rebecca raked the glass down his face. He bucked back and then shoved the barrel of the gun toward Rebecca's head as Gillian scrambled to her feet and launched herself at him.

The sound of the gunshot boomed, drowning out Gillian's scream as she careened into him, knocking them both to the floor.

The doorknob turned in Austin's hand as he heard the scream. He charged into the cabin, running toward the echoing sound of the scream and the gunshot, his heart hammering in his chest.

His lungs ached with the freezing-cold musty smell of the cabin. He had his gun drawn, his senses on alert, as he burst into the room and tried to take in everything at once. He saw it all in those few crucial seconds. The large wrecked living room; the small glowing fire crackling in the huge stone fireplace; snowy, melting footprints on the worn wood floor; and three people—all on the floor.

"Drop the gun!" Austin ordered as he saw Gillian and Marc struggling for the weapon. The other figure—Rebecca Stewart, he assumed—lay in a pool of blood next to them.

There was no way he could get a clear shot. He rushed forward an instant before the sound of the second gunshot ripped through the room. The bullet whistled past him. Marc wrestled the gun from Gillian and scrambled to his feet, dragging her up with him as a shield, the barrel of his gun against her temple.

"You drop *your* gun or so help me I will put a bullet in her head," Marc said, sounding in pain. Austin saw that he was bleeding from a cut down his cheek and neck.

"You can't get away," Austin said his weapon aimed at Marc's head.

Marc chuckled at that as he lifted Gillian off her feet and backed toward the door where he'd left his snowmobile. "Drop your gun or I swear I will kill her!" Marc bellowed. His eyes were wide, blood streaming down his face, but the gun in his hand was steady and sure.

"The police are on their way. Let her go!" Austin doubted the bluff would work and it was too risky to try a shot since Marc was making himself as small a target as possible behind Gillian.

Marc kept backing toward the door. His snowmobile was just outside. If he could manage to get to it… Austin couldn't stand the thought of the man getting away, but his first priority had to be the safety of the women. Austin knew Marc wouldn't try to take Gillian with him. He needed to get away quickly. If he could make him let her go… He wouldn't be surprised, though, if at the last moment Marc put a bullet in her head.

Gillian was crying, the look on her face one of horror more than terror. She was looking at her sister crumpled on the floor in front of the fireplace. Rebecca wasn't moving.

Marc dragged Gillian another step back. He would have to let Gillian go to open the door. Austin waited as the seconds ticked by.

As Marc reached behind him to open the door, Austin knew he would have only an instant to take his shot. Moving fast, Marc shoved Gillian away, turned the gun and fired as Austin dove to the side for cover—and took his own shot.

He heard a howl of pain and then a loud crash, looking in time to see Marc grab a large old wooden hutch by the door and pull it down after him. The hutch crashed down on its side, blocking the door as Marc made his escape.

Austin raced toward the door but couldn't see Marc or the snowmobile to get off a shot. As he started to scramble over the downed hutch, he heard the engine, smelled the smoke as the man roared away.

Behind him, Gillian, sobbing hysterically, pushed herself up from the littered floor and rushed to her sister.

His need to go after Marc blinded him for a moment. He'd wounded Marc, but it hadn't been enough to stop him. He couldn't bear the thought of Marc getting away after what he'd done. He swore under his breath. But as badly as he wanted the man, he couldn't leave Gillian and her sister to chase after him.

"Help her," she pleaded from where she was kneeling on the floor. "My sister—"

He holstered his gun and knelt down next to Rebecca to feel for a pulse. "She's alive." Just barely. He checked his phone. Still no service.

"Go for help. I'll stay here with her," Gillian said. "Go."

Chapter 12

Marc couldn't believe this. He was bleeding like a stuck pig. Reaching the road and his Suburban, he stumbled off the snowmobile and lurched toward his vehicle. He couldn't tell how badly he was wounded, but his movements felt too slow, which he figured indicated that he was losing blood fast.

He thumbed the key fob, opened the Suburban's door and pulled himself inside. The last thing he wanted to do was take the time to check his wounds for fear the cowboy would be coming after him, but something told him if he didn't stop the bleeding, he was a dead man either way.

The Texas deputy had said he'd already called the cops. Marc couldn't risk that the man was telling the truth. His hand shook as he turned the rearview mirror toward him and first inspected the cut.

"Son of a bitch!" He couldn't believe what Rebecca had done to him. The cut ran from just under his eye, down his cheek to under his chin and into his throat. He took off his gloves and pressed one to the spot that seemed to be bleeding the most.

After a few moments, the bleeding slowed—at least on his face. He could feel blood running down his side, chilling him as it soaked into his clothing. He became aware of the pain. His shoulder felt as if it were on fire. Unzipping his coat, then unbuttoning his shirt, he inspected the damage.

Again, he'd been lucky. The bullet had only grazed his shoulder. He stuck the other glove on the wound and zipped his coat back up. He would have to get more clothes. He couldn't wear a coat drenched in blood with a bullet hole in it—especially given the way his face looked.

He swore again, furious with Rebecca but even more furious with himself. She'd purposely pushed him so he would pull the trigger. Now he was no closer to finding his ledger and his money—or his son—than he had been at first.

Starting the Suburban, he pulled away. He would have to ditch this rig and pick up another. That was the least of his problems. He knew someone who could stitch up his wounds and get him another vehicle.

But now he was a man on the run from the law.

Gillian was cradling her sister's head in her arms when Austin returned with local law enforcement. Rebecca was breathing, but she hadn't regained consciousness. Gillian had wanted to go in the ambulance with her sister, but the officer had needed her to answer questions about what had happened.

"I'll take you to the Bozeman hospital to see your sister," Austin said when the interrogation had finally ended and they were allowed to go.

Gillian was still shaken and worried about her sister as she climbed into Austin's SUV. The officers who'd questioned them had taken them to a local station to talk. She'd been grateful to get out of the cold cabin.

"We have to make sure Marc doesn't get to Becky," she said as Austin pulled onto Highway 191, headed north.

"That isn't going to happen. There will be a guard outside her room at the hospital, not that I suspect Marc will try to see her. There is a BOLO out on your brother-in-law. He can't get far in that large black Suburban. Also, he's wounded and needs medical attention. Law enforcement has thrown a net over the area. When he shows his face, they will arrest him."

She glanced at the Texas cowboy. "You don't know Marc. He has access to other vehicles. He's resourceful. He'll slip through the net. He has nothing to lose at this point. He will be even more dangerous."

"You don't have any idea where your brother-in-law might go?"

She shook her head, then winced in pain. "The man is crazy. Who knows what he'll do now."

"Whatever information he was trying to get out of your sister…he didn't get it, right?"

"No," she said, her eyes filling with tears. "Apparently Rebecca would rather die than tell him."

"I'm trying to understand all of this. Marc Stewart

brought you to the cabin to make your sister talk, right? He thought she would tell you. Did she?"

Gillian wiped her tears. "No. Rebecca knew the moment I saw what he'd done to her that I would have told him anything he wanted to know. She didn't tell me *anything*. I didn't know about any ledger or about Andy being gone until Marc told me. I'm just praying she regains consciousness soon and tells us where we can find Andy. My nephew is only ten months old...."

"Maybe Marc will turn himself in given that he's wounded and now wanted by the law."

She scoffed at that. "I highly doubt that since whatever is in this ledger Rebecca took would apparently put Marc behind bars for years. He'd never go down without a fight."

"A lot of criminals say that—until it comes time to die and then they find they prefer to turn state's evidence," Austin said. "Your sister never even hinted what Marc might be up to?"

"No. I knew they were having trouble. I couldn't understand why she stayed with the man. He was domineering and tight with the money, and treated Rebecca as if she was his property. But I never dreamed something like this would happen. When Rebecca texted me that she had left Marc, I was shocked since there had been no warning."

Austin glanced over at her as he drove. Gillian looked numb. Her face was still pale, her eyes red from crying. He hated to ask, but he needed to know what they were up against. "Would you mind telling me how all this began?"

She sat up a little straighter, drawing on some inner

strength that impressed him. He knew given what she'd been through, she must be exhausted let alone physically injured and emotionally spent.

"I had no idea what was going on. Rebecca and Andy had been at my house just a week before and everything seemed to be fine. Then I got the text. When I saw her car pull up to my house last night, I ran out thinking it was her."

He listened to her explain that instead of it being her sister in the car, it had been Marc. She told him how Marc had thrown her into the trunk and she'd escaped partway down the canyon.

"So there *had* been someone in the trunk," he said. It all made sense now. Even as confused as she'd been after her car accident, she'd recalled someone in the trunk.

"I wasn't thinking clearly when I took off. I just knew I had to get away from Marc and find my sister."

"You did everything you could to save her without any thought to your own life," Austin said. "This is on Marc, not you. But there is one thing I don't understand. Why did your sister choose now to leave him? I mean, had something happened between them?"

Gillian sighed. "I don't know. All I can figure is that Rebecca got her hands on Marc's business ledger, saw what was inside and realized she was married to a criminal—as well as an abuser. Apparently there was a reference to all the money Marc had stashed in the ledger and that's why she went to the Island Park cabin and he followed her there." She shook her head. "I don't know what she was thinking. How could she not know what Marc would do?"

"It sounds as if she was just trying to keep her son

safe from him," Austin said. "She was also trying to protect you by not telling you anything." He felt Gillian's gaze on him.

"I'm sorry I dragged you into this."

"We're past that. As I told you before, I'm a deputy sheriff down in Texas. I'm glad I can help."

"I wish you could help, but I have no idea where my sister hid her son, let alone this ledger that Marc is losing his mind over. Marc will only be worse now. He's dangerous and desperate. I'm afraid of what he will do—especially if he finds his son."

Austin hated the truth he heard in her words. He'd known men like Marc Stewart. "Which is another reason I don't want to let you out of my sight. It won't make any difference if he believes your sister told you anything or not. He'll blame you."

"He already does for involving you in this. I'm so sorry. But I can't ask you—"

"I'm in this with you," he said, reaching over to take her hand. He gave it a squeeze and let go.

Gillian met his gaze. Her eyes shimmered with tears. "If you hadn't shown up when you did…" She looked away. He could tell she was fighting tears, worried about her sister and her nephew, and maybe finally realizing how close she had come to dying back there. "I have to find Andy and this notebook, ledger, whatever it is, before Marc does. If he finds it first, he'll skip the country with Andy. I know him. I wouldn't be surprised if he doesn't have a new identity all set up."

Marc avoided looking in the mirror as he drove. His friend had fixed him up. But when he saw his bandaged face in the mirror, it made him furious all over again. And when he was furious, he couldn't think straight.

He'd just assumed that Rebecca would cave at some point and tell him what he wanted to know. Frankly, he'd never thought her a strong woman. Boy, had she proven him wrong, he thought as he silently cursed her to hell. If she had just told him what he wanted to know all this would be over by now. She might even still be alive. Or not. But at least he would have made her death look like an accident.

Word was going to get out about Rebecca's murder. His DNA would be found at the scene. Not to mention he'd shot at a Texas deputy. Gillian would swear he'd kidnapped her… How had things gotten so out of hand? He had a target on his back now. Even with an old pickup and a change of identity, he couldn't risk getting stopped even for a broken taillight—not with this bandage down the side of his face.

His cell phone rang. "What?"

"You don't have to bite off my head."

Marc rolled his eyes, but bit his tongue. He needed his friend's help. "Sorry, Leo. What did you find out?"

"They took your wife to the hospital in Bozeman. I couldn't get any information, though, on her condition."

Rebecca was *alive?*

"As for your sister-in-law? She and some cowboy left together after spending a whole lot of time talking to the cops. I suspect they're headed to Bozeman and the hospital. You want me to keep following them?"

"The man with her? He's a sheriff's deputy from Texas. He'll know if he is being followed, so no. I'll call you if I need you."

He disconnected, not sure what to do next. When his cell rang, he thought it was Leo again. Instead it was his…so-called partner. In truth, Victor Ramsey ran the show and always had. Marc began to sweat instantly as he picked up.

"What the hell is going on, Marc? Why are there cops after you?"

At the hospital in Bozeman, Gillian was told that her sister was stable and resting. She hadn't regained consciousness, but the doctor promised he would call when she did.

Gillian tried not to let the tidal wave of relief drown out the news. Becky was alive and stable. Once she woke up, she could tell them what they needed to know. But in the meantime…

Down the hallway, she saw Austin on his cell phone and overheard the last of what he was saying as she approached. She felt awful as she realized that he'd come to Montana to see his family and Christmas was just days away…. She didn't know what she would have done without him, though, but she couldn't have him missing a family Christmas because of her.

"Hey," he said, smiling when he saw her. "Good news?"

She nodded. "Becky's still unconscious but stable. Listen, Austin, I already owe you my life and my sister's. Aside from almost getting you killed, now I'm keeping you away from your family who you came all the way to Montana to see and it's almost Christmas."

"I came up for the grand opening of our first Texas Boys Barbecue restaurant in Montana."

"Barbecue?"

He nodded at her surprise. "My brothers and I own a few barbecue joints."

"I thought you said you were a deputy sheriff?"

"I am. My brother Laramie runs the company so the rest of us can do whatever we want." He gave a shrug.

"Cardwell?" Why hadn't she realized who he was? "You're related to Dana Savage?"

"She's my cousin. She and her husband own Cardwell Ranch. My brothers came up to visit her, fell in love with Montana and all but one of them has fallen in love with more than the state and moved here."

"You can't miss this grand opening...."

"Believe me, my family can manage without me. Actually, they're used to it. I'm not good at these family events and I'm not leaving you until Marc is behind bars. You're stuck with me." He smiled. He had an amazing smile that lit up his handsome face and made his dark eyes shine.

She hadn't realized how handsome he was. Maybe because she hadn't taken the time to really look at him. "Are you trying to tell me that you're the black sheep of the family?" she asked as they took the elevator down to the hospital parking area.

He laughed at that. "And then some. I missed my brother Tag's wedding last summer. I was on a case. I'm often on a case. I'm only here now because they all ganged up on me and made me feel guilty."

"When is the grand opening?"

"The first of January. See? Nothing to worry about."

"You're that confident Marc will be caught by then?" she asked.

He turned that smile on her. "With my luck, he will and I won't have any excuse not to attend not only the grand opening but also Christmas at my cousin's house with the whole family."

"You aren't serious."

"On the contrary. I usually volunteer to work the holidays so deputies with families can spend them at home. I'm the worst Scrooge ever when it comes to Christmas. So trust me when I say my family won't be surprised I'm not there, nor will they mind all that much."

"I think you're exaggerating," she said as they reached his SUV.

He shook his head. "Nope. It's the truth. What do you suggest we do now?"

She turned to look at him. "I can't ask you—"

"You aren't asking. I already told you. I'm not leaving you alone until Marc is behind bars."

Tears filled her eyes. She bit down on her lower lip for a moment. "Thank you. I need to go to my house."

"Where is that?"

"I have a studio at Big Sky."

"A studio?"

"I'm a jeweler."

"The watch." He frowned and she could see he was wondering who'd made it for her.

"My father was the one who taught me the craft. I lost him five years ago. Before that, my mother. I can't lose my sister."

He put an arm around her and pulled her close. "You won't. The doctor said she is stable, right? She's a strong woman and she has every reason to pull through."

Gillian nodded against his strong chest. He smelled

of the outdoors, a wonderful masculine scent that reminded her how long it had been since a man had held her. She reminded herself why Austin Cardwell was here with her and stepped away from his arms.

"I need to figure out what my sister was thinking," she said as Austin opened the door to the SUV. "It was one thing to hide the ledger, but another to hide my nephew."

As he slid behind the wheel, he asked, "Those few moments you had with your sister before Marc returned, did she say anything that might have been a clue where either might be?"

"I'm not even sure she was in her right mind at the end. Marc told me she was taking some kind of pills for stress before all this happened."

Austin shook his head as he started the engine. "She got her son away from Marc and she hid a book that can possibly get her husband put away for a long time. On top of that, she wounded Marc in a way that makes him easy to spot. That doesn't sound like a woman who wasn't thinking straight."

Gillian's eyes filled with tears. "But why didn't she tell me where to find Andy and the ledger?"

"Maybe she mailed you something. Or said something that didn't make sense at the time, but will later. You've been through so much, not to mention Marc taking you out of the hospital too soon after a head injury. You say you live at Big Sky?"

"Before you get to Meadow Village. I have an apartment over my studio and shop." She rubbed her temples with her fingers.

"Headache?"

Gillian nodded. "Maybe Becky *did* send me something in the mail. If that's the case…" She turned to look at him. "Then we need to get to my house before Marc does."

They were only a few miles out of Big Sky when Gillian fell into an exhausted sleep. Austin's heart went out to her. He couldn't imagine what the past forty-eight hours had been like for her. He worried about her even though she was holding up better than he would have expected. The woman was strong. Or maybe it hadn't really hit her yet.

What drove him was the thought of Marc Stewart not just getting away with kidnapping and attempted murder, but possibly finding his son and taking him out of the country. If that happened, Austin doubted either Rebecca or her sister would ever see the child again.

The man had to be stopped, and Austin was determined to do what he could to make that happen.

When Gillian woke near the outskirts of Big Sky, she looked better, definitely more determined. There was so much more he needed to know about the situation he'd found himself in and he was anxious to ask. But first they had to reach her studio. There was the chance that Marc Stewart had been there—was even still there.

Chapter 13

Marc held the phone away from his ear for a moment as he considered how much to tell Victor. The first time Marc had met Victor Ramsey, he'd been amused by the man's clean-cut appearance that belied the true man underneath. That was five years ago. Victor still had one of those trustworthy faces, bright blue eyes and a winning smile. But if you looked deeper into those blue eyes, as Marc had done too many times, you would see a cold-blooded psychopath.

"What's going on, Marc?" Victor asked now as if he'd just called to catch up.

The two had met through a mutual friend, something Marc later suspected had been a setup from the start.

Want to make more money than you've ever dreamed

possible? his friend had said one night after they'd consumed too much alcohol.

His answer had been, *Hell yes*. The auto body shop he'd taken over from his father was a lot of work and for average income, not to mention he hated it.

His friend, now deceased under suspicious circumstances, had made the introduction. At first Marc had been in awe of Victor, a self-made man with a lot of charm and ambition. It wasn't until he was in too deep that he'd begun to regret all of it.

"Just having a little domestic trouble," Marc answered now.

"Attempted murder is a little more than domestic trouble. I want to see you. Where are you?"

He'd been expecting this, but the last person he wanted to see him like this was Victor. "Right now isn't a great time."

"I'm staying at my place in Canyon Creek. I'll give you two hours. Don't be late. You know how I hate anyone who wastes my time." Victor hung up.

Marc swore. After Victor saw his face—and found out everything else—Marc knew he would be lucky to walk out of that meeting alive.

With a curse, he realized he had really only one choice. Get out of the country—or at least try. But it would mean leaving without his son—or settling the score with his wife, his sister-in-law and the Texas deputy who'd stuck his nose in where it didn't belong.

He would prefer to find the ledger and his son, take care of all of them and then get out of the country. Rebecca had discovered some of his money, but he had more hidden.

Unfortunately the clock was ticking and if he hoped

to live long enough to do what had to be done, he would have to meet with Victor and try to talk his way out of this mess.

Austin parked behind a three-story building with a sign that read Gillian Cooper Designs. As she led the way up the back steps, Austin kept an eye out for Marc Stewart. There was no sign of his black Suburban, but Austin figured he would have gotten rid of it by now.

There were no other buildings around Gillian's. The studio and apartment sat against the mountainside with only one parking spot in back. The building was unique in design. When he asked her about it, he wasn't surprised to find out that she'd designed it herself.

As she led him into the living area, he saw that the inside was as uniquely designed as the outside with shiny bamboo floors, vaulted wood ceilings, arches and tall windows. He could see that she had more than just a talent for jewelry. The decor was a mixture of old and new, each room bright with color and texture.

Remembering how Marc had torn up the Island Park cabin, he was relieved to see that the man hadn't been in Gillian's apartment. From what he could gather, nothing had been disturbed. Maybe Marc had been wounded badly enough that he'd been forced to get medical attention before anything else. Once an emergency room doctor saw the bullet wound, the law would be called and Marc would be arrested. At least Austin could hope.

He stood in the living area, taking in the place. He found himself becoming more intrigued by Gillian Cooper as he watched her scoop up the mail that had been dropped through the old-fashioned slot in the antique front door.

"I love your house," he said, hoping he got a chance to see the jewelry she made.

"Thanks," she said as she sorted through the mail. He could tell by her disappointed expression that there was nothing from her sister. She looked up at him. "Nothing." Her voice broke as she shook her head.

"Why don't you get a hot shower and a change of clothes," he suggested.

She nodded. "There is a shower in the guest room if you…"

"Thank you." They stood like that for a moment, strangers who knew too much about each other, bound together by happenstance.

He moved first, picking up his duffel bag, which he'd brought up from the car. She pointed toward an open door as if no longer capable of speech. He'd seen it often in people who were thrown into extraordinary circumstances. They often found an inner strength that made it possible for them to do extraordinary things. But at some point that strength ebbed away, leaving them an empty shell.

The shower was hot, the water pressure strong. Austin stood under it, spent. He'd had little sleep last night and then today… He was just thankful he'd burst into the cabin when he had. He didn't want to think what would have happened otherwise. Nor did he want to think about what he'd gotten himself into and where it would end.

Clean and warm and dressed in clean jeans and a long-sleeved T-shirt, Austin went back out into the living room. Where was Marc now? Austin could only imagine. Hopefully he'd been arrested, but if that were the case, Austin would have received a call by now. The officer who'd responded to his call had promised to let him know when Marc Stewart was in custody.

Which meant Marc Stewart was still out there.

A few minutes later, Gillian emerged from the other side of the house. Her face was flushed from her shower. She wore a white fluffy sweater and leggings. Her long dark hair was still damp and framed the face of a model.

For a moment, she looked nervous, as if realizing she was now alone with a complete stranger.

"If you don't mind talking about it, could you tell me more about this ledger Marc is looking for?" he said, finding ground he knew would ease the sudden tension between them.

"I only know what Marc told me," she said as she walked to the refrigerator, opened it and held up a bottle of wine. He nodded and she poured two glasses, which they took into the living room.

Gillian curled up at one end of the couch, tucking her feet under her. Austin took a chair some distance away. He watched her take a sip of her wine and she seemed to relax a little.

"I gathered Marc wrote down some sort of illegal business dealings in a black ledger that he never let out of his sight," she said after a moment. "Marc is dyslexic so he has trouble remembering numbers, apparently. He wrote everything down. According to him, my sister drugged him and took the book."

"What do you know about your brother-in-law's business?"

"Nothing really. He owns an auto body shop, repairs cars."

"That doesn't sound like something that would force

him to go to the extremes he has to recover some ledger he kept figures in."

"I'm not sure what's in it other than where he hid large amounts of money, but I gathered, from Marc's terror at the ledger landing in the wrong hands, that there is enough in it to send him to prison."

"I don't understand why she didn't take it to the police or the FBI. Marc would be in jail now and none of this would have happened."

Gillian shook her head. "Apparently she thought she could force him into giving her a divorce and custody of Andrew Marc in exchange for the ledger. She also needed money. I guess she didn't realize just how dangerous that would be."

"Or she didn't get a chance to before Marc realized the ledger was missing. He figured out she was headed for the Island Park cabin fairly quickly."

She nodded. "He'd stashed money there." She grew quiet for a moment. "Apparently she hid the ledger. I know it's not at their house. He said he tore the place apart looking for it."

"You and your sister were close. Any ideas where she could have hidden it?"

"None. Becky and I…" She hesitated, turning to glance out the side window. "We weren't that close recently. Marc thought I was a bad influence on her. I didn't want to make things worse for her but I couldn't stand being around him. He kept her on a short leash. The last time we were together before this, I begged her to leave Marc. She kept thinking he was going to change."

Austin heard the worry in her voice. "A lot of women have trouble leaving."

"I always thought my sister was smarter than that," she said as she got up to refill their glasses.

"Intelligence doesn't seem to have much to do with it." He doubted this helped at the moment. Marc Stewart was out there somewhere, wounded and still obsessed with finding not only the ledger, but also his son. Which meant Gillian wasn't safe until Marc was behind bars and maybe not even then, depending on just what Marc Stewart was involved in.

She met his gaze as she filled his glass. "You saw what Marc's like. Just out of spite, he might do something to Andy if he finds him." Her voice cracked, and for a moment, she looked as if she might break down.

Austin rose to take her in his arms. She felt small but strong. It was he who felt vulnerable. He'd never met anyone like her, and that scared him. Not to mention the fact that Gillian felt too good in his arms.

He let go of her and she stepped away to wipe her tears.

"We'll find your nephew," he said to her back. He had no idea how, but he agreed with her. Marc was a loose cannon now. Anyone in his path was in danger. "Your sister was living in Helena? Where would she stash her son that she thought he would be safe? Marc said the boy was with his grandmother."

Gillian shook her head. "No grandparents are still alive."

"Maybe a babysitter? A friend she trusted?"

Again Gillian shook her head. "Marc didn't allow her to leave Andy with anyone, not that she had need of a babysitter because he would check on her during the day to make sure she hadn't gone anywhere."

Austin hated the picture she was painting of her sister's

life. "Then how did your sister manage to not only get possession of Marc's ledger, but hide their son?"

Gillian shook her head again. "I suspect she'd been planning it for weeks, maybe even months. Rebecca did tell me when I was trying to get her to leave him that time in Helena that Marc had threatened to kill her and Andy if she did."

He guessed that Rebecca had believed her husband. But then she'd taken the ledger and thought she had leverage. "You said your sister visited a while back. Is there a chance she left you a note that you might have missed?"

Gillian shook her head and stepped to one of the windows to look out. Past her, he caught glimpses of the Gallatin River and the dense snowcapped pines. It was snowing again, huge flakes drifting down past the window. How could his brothers live in a place where it snowed like this?

"Apparently my sister found quite a bit of money that Marc kept hidden in his locked gun cabinet." She turned toward him. "It is missing, as well."

He thought of the ransacked Island Park cabin. "Your sister had gone to the cabin to get more money he had stashed there?"

She nodded. "So foolish. I guess she wanted to keep him from skipping the country and taking his money, and she thought that would work. She apparently didn't think she could keep him in jail long enough to do whatever she had planned."

He watched her look around the room as if remembering her sister's last visit. She frowned. "If Becky was well into her plan when she came to see me, why didn't she say something? Why didn't she tell me so I would know what to do now?" She sounded close to tears again.

"While she was here, where did she stay?"

"In the spare bedroom. You don't think she might have hidden the ledger in there?"

He followed her, thinking there was a remote chance at best. Still, they had to look. Like the rest of the place, it was nicely furnished in an array of colors. The wall behind the bed was exposed brick. Several pieces of artwork hung from it.

Gillian searched the room from the drawers in the bedside tables to under the mattress and even under the bed. Austin went into the bathroom and looked in the only cabinet there. No note or a ledger of any kind.

As Gillian finished, she sat down on the end of the bed. She looked pale and exhausted, like a woman who should be in the hospital.

"Are you sure you shouldn't have seen a doctor while we were at the hospital? I don't mind taking you back."

"I'm fine," she said with a sigh. "Just disappointed. I knew it was doubtful that Becky left anything. She would have been afraid I would find it and try to stop her. Rebecca never wanted to be a bother to anyone, especially me, her older sister. She hid a lot of things from me, like just how bad it was living with Marc."

"Why don't you get some rest? We can talk more in the morning and figure out what to do next."

She nodded. "I can't even think straight right now."

He reached out and took her hand to pull her up from the bed. "You still have that headache?"

She smiled at him. "It's nothing to be alarmed about. I'm fine. Really." Suddenly she froze. "Becky *did* leave something." Her voice rose with excitement. "I didn't think anything about it at the time. Since Andy had been playing with an old key ring of hers that had a dozen keys on it. She left a key on the night table beside the bed. I thought it must have come off Andy's key ring so I just tossed it in the drawer for when he came back."

She opened the drawer beside the bed and took out the key.

Austin had hoped for a safety deposit key. Instead, it appeared to be an ordinary house key. He realized that Gillian's first instinct on finding it was probably right.

"You didn't find anything else?"

She shook her head, her excitement fading. "It's probably nothing, huh?"

"Probably," he said, taking the key. "But we'll hang on to it just in case." He pocketed it as Gillian started to leave the room.

"You can have this room," she said over her shoulder. She stopped in the doorway and turned to look back at him. "That is, if you're staying."

"As I told you, I'm not going anywhere until Marc is behind bars. I'm a man of my word, Gillian."

She met his gaze. "Somehow I knew that."

"No matter how long it takes, I'm not leaving you." Austin knew even as he made the promise that there would be hell to pay with his family. But they were used to him letting them down. She started to turn away.

"One more thing," he said. "Did your sister have a key to this house?"

"No." Realization dawned on her expression. She shivered.

"Then there is nothing to worry about," he said. "Try to get some sleep."

"You, too."

He knew that wouldn't be easy. An electricity seemed to spark in the air between them. They'd been through so much together already. He didn't dare imagine what tomorrow would bring.

She hesitated in the doorway. "If you need anything…"

"Don't worry about me." As he removed his jacket, her gaze went to the weapon in his shoulder holster. He saw her swallow before she turned away. "Sweet dreams," he said to her retreating back.

Chapter 14

It had begun to snow. Large lacy flakes fell in a flurry of white as Marc pulled up to Victor's so-called cabin in the mountains overlooking Helena, Montana. The "cabin" was at least five thousand square feet of luxury including an indoor pool, a media center and a game room. At his knock, one of Victor's minions answered the door, a big man who went by only Jumbo.

"Mr. Ramsey is in the garden room." Oh, yeah, and the house had a garden room, too.

There was no garden in the glassed-in room, but there was an amazing view of the valley below and there was a bar. Victor was standing at the bar pouring himself a drink. Marc got the feeling he'd seen him drive up and had been waiting. Today he wore a velour pullover in the same blue as his eyes.

"What would you like to drink?" he asked as he motioned to one of the chairs at the bar. Victor seemed to take in his bandaged face and neck, but said nothing.

Marc took one of the chairs. "Whatever you're having."

"Wise man," Victor said with a disarming smile. "I only drink the best. Isn't that the reason you and I became friends to begin with?"

Friends? What a joke. Marc didn't need him to spell things out. "I like the best things in life like anyone else."

"But you aren't like anyone else," Victor said as he pushed what looked like three fingers of bourbon in a crystal glass over to him.

"No, I'm unique because I know you." He knew it was what the man wanted to hear, and right now he was fine with saying anything that could get him out of here. He took a gulp of the drink. It burned all the way down. As he set the glass down, he said, "Okay, I screwed up, but I'm trying to fix it."

Victor lifted a brow. "You think? And how is it you hope to do that?"

He wasn't surprised that his mess was no secret to the man. Victor had someone inside law enforcement. There was little he didn't know about.

"I didn't mean to almost kill her."

"The her you're referring to being your *wife?*"

"Who else?"

"Who else indeed. With you I never know." Victor took a sip of his drink, studying him over the rim of the glass. "Attempted murder, kidnapping, assault?" Victor leaned on the bar like one friend confiding in another. "Tell me, Marc. What's going on with you?"

He knew this tone of voice. He'd seen it used on other

men who'd messed up in their little…organization. He also knew what had happened to those men. Victor was most dangerous when he was being congenial.

"The bitch drugged me and took my ledger—you know, where I kept track of the business."

Victor leaned back, his expression making it clear that his concern had shifted to himself rather than Marc's future. "By the business, you mean your automotive business."

Marc didn't answer.

"You wrote down *our* business transactions?"

"It was a lot of names and numbers, and I do better if I can write it down."

"You mean like names of our associates and their phone numbers." His voice had dropped even further.

"Yeah, that and a few transactions just so I could remember whom I'd dealt with. You have a lot of associates."

Victor looked as if he might have a coronary. "This… ledger? I'm assuming you got it back. Tell me you got it back."

"Why do you think I tried to kill her? She hid it *and* my kid. I was trying to get the information out of her…."

"That's why you involved her sister." Victor closed his eyes for a moment. He was breathing hard. Marc had never seen him lose his cool. Victor was the kind of man who didn't do his own dirty work. He prided himself on never losing control, but he seemed close right now.

"So you don't have the information and you don't know where it is," Victor said.

That about sized it up. "But I'm going to find it."

"She could have mailed it to the FBI."

Marc hadn't thought of that. Probably because he was still caught up in his old belief that Rebecca wasn't all that smart. "I don't think she'd do that."

Victor looked at him, aghast. "You don't *think* so?"

"She's just trying to use the ledger to get a divorce and custody of my kid."

"Let me guess." Victor didn't look at him. Instead, he turned his glass in his hands as if admiring the cut crystal. "You refused to give her what she wanted."

"She isn't taking my kid." The blow took him by surprise. The heavy crystal glass smashed into the side of his face, knocking him off his stool. The crystal shattered, prisms flying across the Italian rock flooring of the garden room an instant before Marc joined them.

Jumbo appeared, as if he had been waiting in the wings, expecting trouble. "You all right, Mr. Ramsey?"

Marc swore. Victor wasn't the one on the floor surrounded by glass. As he rose, he saw Victor picking glass out of his hand. Jumbo rushed around the bar to get a rag.

"No harm done. Isn't that right, Marc?" Victor said.

Blood was running down into his eye. He reached up and pulled a shard of glass from his temple.

"Get Marc a bandage to go with his other bandages, will you, Jumbo?" their boss said. "Sorry about that," he said after Jumbo had left. "I seldom lose my temper."

Marc said nothing. His head hurt like hell and this was the second time in twenty-four hours that he'd been cut. The blow had opened his other cut, and it, too, was now bleeding. First his wife had tried to kill him, now this.

Jumbo returned with a first aid kit. "Let him see to it," Victor ordered when Marc tried to take the kit from the man. It was all he could do to sit still and let an oaf like Jumbo work on him. "Here, be sure there isn't any glass in the cut first." Victor handed the man a bottle of Scotch. "Pour some of the good stuff on it."

Marc gritted his teeth as Jumbo shoved his head to the side and poured the alcohol into the wound. The Scotch ran into Rebecca's handiwork as well, sending fiery pain roaring through him. He swore, the pain so intense he thought he might black out. Jumbo patted the spot on his temple dry with surprising tenderness before carefully applying something to stop the bleeding.

"There, all better," Victor said. "Thank Jumbo. He did a great job."

"Thanks, Jumbo," Marc mumbled.

After Jumbo had cleaned up the mess and left, his boss refilled Marc's glass and got himself a new one. "Now," he said, "I don't need to tell you what needs to be done, do I?"

"No. I'm going to get the ledger." He knew better than to mention his son. Victor didn't give a crap about Andy.

The man frowned. "The sister, is she going to be a problem?"

"Naw." He tried to keep his gaze locked with Victor's, but he broke away first even though he knew it was a mistake.

"The sister isn't the only problem, is she? Who is this Texas deputy who got involved?"

Marc swore under his breath. It amazed him how Victor got his information and so quickly. He must have "associates" everywhere. The thought did nothing to make him feel better.

"I'll take care of them."

Victor shook his head. "You just get this…ledger you lost back. And what are you going to do with it?"

"Destroy it."

Victor looked pained. "Wrong, you're going to bring it to me. I'll take care of it. There are no copies, right?"

"No, I'm not a fool." From Victor's expression, it was clear he thought differently. Marc should have been relieved. What Victor was saying was that they were finished. No more money. It was over. Their relationship was terminated.

Marc searched his emotions for the relief he should have been feeling. Instead, all he could think was that he would kill them. First Rebecca. Then her sister and the cowboy. "I'll fix everything."

Victor didn't look convinced. "Just find the ledger. That's all I ask."

But Marc knew nothing in his life had ever been that simple. He downed his drink, stood up and left.

Gillian went to her bedroom, but she doubted she would be able to sleep. Her mind was racing. She kept going over the few conversations she'd had with her sister in the months, weeks and days before all this.

What had Rebecca been thinking? Why hadn't she taken the incriminating evidence to the police? Had she really thought Marc would just agree to a divorce?

No, she thought. That's why Rebecca had hidden not only the ledger, but also her son.

As she pulled on a nightgown and climbed into bed, she was reminded that she wasn't alone in the house. That should have given her more comfort than it did. She was very…aware of Austin Cardwell. It surprised her that she could feel anything, as exhausted and distraught as she was. Mostly, she felt…off balance.

She closed her eyes, praying for the oblivion of sleep.

"I might need your help."

Gillian's eyes came open as she recalled something her sister had said. The conversation came back to her slowly.

"You know I will do anything for you."

"I don't like involving you, but if things go wrong..."

"Becky, what's going on?"

"I keep thinking about when we were kids."

"You're scaring me."

"I'm sorry. I was just being sentimental."

"Is everything okay, Becky?"

"Yes," her sister said, laughing. *"I was just remembering how much fun it was growing up. I love you, Gillian. Always remember that."*

Oh, Becky, she thought now as tears filled her eyes. Things had gone very wrong. Unfortunately, Gillian had no idea what to do about it and now she had a Texas cowboy in her spare bedroom.

She wasn't going to get a wink of sleep tonight.

Marc scratched the back of his neck and glanced in the rearview mirror. He caught sight of a large gray SUV two cars behind him. Without slowing, he drove from Victor's toward downtown Helena. At the very last minute, he swung off the interstate and glanced back in time to see the gray SUV cross two lanes to make the exit.

He sped up, wanting to lose the tail. That damned Victor. He'd put a man on him. Marc shouldn't have been surprised. Had he been Victor, he wouldn't have trusted him either. Victor had to know that with the ledger and his testimony, his "friend" Marc could walk away from this mess a free man while Victor rotted in prison.

Not that Victor would let him live long enough for that to happen.

Swearing, he slowed down and pulled into a gas station. He saw the gray SUV go past to stop a few doors down in front of a fast-food restaurant. Getting out, he filled his tank and considered what to do next.

His throat felt dry. He would kill for a beer. The problem was stopping at just one beer. It would be too easy to get falling-down drunk. Still, he headed for one of the bars he frequented. Behind him, the gray SUV followed.

Victor's going to have me killed.

Not until I find the ledger.

The thought turned Marc's blood to ice.

But it was quickly followed by another thought.

In the meantime, Victor couldn't chance that the ledger would turn up and fall into the wrong hands. *Checkmate,* he thought with relief until he had another thought.

Unless Victor decided he could do a better job of getting the whereabouts of the book from Rebecca.

That thought echoed in his head, making his heart thump harder against his chest. Marc felt the truth of those words racing through his bloodstream. What if Victor decided to take things into his own hands?

He thought of Rebecca lying in her hospital bed. If Victor paid her one of his famous visits...

Marc reminded himself that Victor never got his own hands dirty even if he could find a way to get near Rebecca in the hospital.

What if Rebecca really had mailed the ledger to the FBI? His pulse jumped, heart hammering like a sledge in his chest. He wouldn't let himself go there. No, she'd hidden the book thinking she was smarter than he was, thinking she could force him into the divorce and take Andy from him. Stupid woman.

He tried to concentrate on what to do now. Because if she hadn't sent the book to the FBI, he had to assume she didn't know what she had in her possession. That was the good news, right?

The bad news was that no matter the outcome, he and Victor were finished. Even if he found the book and turned it over, Victor would never trust him again. Not that he could blame him. The information in that book could bring them all down. Victor would have him killed.

If he didn't find the ledger and the cops did, he was going to prison for a good part of the rest of his life. Of course that life wouldn't be long since Victor and his buddies would be in prison with him.

He still couldn't believe the mess he was in. He realized there was only one way out of this. He had to get to Rebecca before Victor did. Once she understood the consequences if she didn't turn over the ledger…he'd give her the divorce and custody. She would hand over his ledger and then when she thought she was safe, he would kidnap his kid and skip the country.

Why hadn't he thought of that in the first place? Because the woman had made him so furious. Also, he'd thought she would tell him where the ledger was with only minor persuasion.

He parked beside the bar in a dark spot away from

the streetlamp and put in a call to the hospital. Rebecca was still unconscious. Swearing, he hung up.

The clock was ticking.

Inside the bar, Marc Stewart took a stool away from everyone else and ordered a beer. The bartender gave him a raised eyebrow at his bandaged face and the black eye that was almost swollen shut, but was smart enough not to comment.

The first beer went down easy. The second took a little longer. He was doing a lot of thinking. Mostly about Rebecca and how he'd underestimated her. He kept mentally kicking himself. He had to get over her betrayal and think about what to do.

"Another beer?" the bartender asked as he cleared away his second empty bottle.

Marc focused on an old moose head hanging on the wall behind the bartender that could have used a good dusting. It reminded him of something. "No, I'm good," he told the bartender. Something about the moose head still nagged at him, but his head hurt too badly to make sense of it.

He slid off the bar stool, picked up most of his change from the bar and pocketed it. But as he looked toward the door, he told himself he had to ditch the tail that he knew would be parked outside waiting.

Marc smiled to himself even though it hurt his face to do so and put in the call. It was time to take care of business.

Chapter 15

Gillian thought she would never be able to sleep again. At the very least she'd expected to have horrible nightmares.

She must have fallen into a deathlike sleep. She couldn't remember anything. Now, though, it all came back in a rush, including the Texas cowboy in her spare bedroom.

What did she really know about Austin Cardwell? Nothing. Nothing except he'd saved her life twice and made her feel… She wasn't even sure how to describe it other than she felt too aware of the man.

She caught the smell of bacon cooking. *Austin?* Grabbing her robe, she opened her door to find him standing in her kitchen with a pancake flipper in his hand. He was wearing one of her aprons, which actually made her smile.

"You didn't find bacon in my refrigerator," she said.

He turned to smile back at her. "Nope. Apparently you exist on wine."

"I haven't gotten to the store in a while."

"I noticed." He flipped over what she saw were pancakes sizzling on her griddle. "Hungry?"

She started to say she wasn't. Just as she'd thought she'd never be able to sleep again, she thought the same of eating. But her stomach growled loudly at the smell of bacon and pancakes.

Austin chuckled. "I'll take that as a yes." He motioned for her to have a seat at the breakfast bar.

"I should change," she said, pulling the collar of her robe tighter.

"No need. Eat them while they're hot." He slid a tall stack of three-inch pancakes onto her plate along with two slices of bacon. "This is my mother's recipe for corn cakes. It's the Texan in me. Wait until you taste the eggs. I hope you like hot peppers."

She felt her eyes widen in surprise. "You made eggs, as well? I really can't—"

"Insult me by not trying some?"

She couldn't help but smile at him in all his eagerness. "Are you trying to fatten me up?"

"You could use a little Texas cooking—not that you aren't beautiful just as you are."

"Good catch," she said, knowing it wasn't true. She hadn't been taking good care of herself because she'd been so worried about her sister. "Thank you."

"My pleasure." He joined her, loading his plate with pancakes, bacon and eggs before putting a spoonful of the eggs onto her plate. "Just try them. Some people aren't tough enough to handle my cooking."

It sounded like a dare—just as he'd meant it to. She studied him for a moment. What would she have done without him? Died night before last in the snowstorm beside the road and no doubt yesterday in Island Park.

Austin handed her the peach jam he'd bought. "Try some of this on your pancakes. Much better than maple syrup."

"Why not?" she said, doing as he said.

"Now take a bite of the pancake and one of the egg. Sweet and hot."

She did and felt her eyes widen in alarm for a moment at the heat. But he was right. The sweet cooled it right down. "Delicious."

"Now add a bite of bacon for saltiness and you've got an Austin Cardwell Texas breakfast." He laughed as he took a bite, chewed and, closing his eyes, moaned in obvious contentment.

Gillian was caught up in his enjoyment of breakfast and her own, as well. She couldn't remember the last time she'd eaten like this and was shocked when she realized that she'd cleaned her plate.

"Well?" he said, studying her openly. "Feeling better?"

She was. Earlier when she'd awakened, she'd felt lightheaded and sick to her stomach. Now she was ready to do whatever had to be done to save her nephew, and she was pretty sure that had been Austin's plan.

"Don't you dare tell me you lost him," Victor said when he saw who was calling that morning.

"Sorry, boss. He let me think he knew he was being tailed and had accepted it."

He swore, but quickly calmed back down. He hadn't

gotten where he was by losing control. True, Marc had already pushed him to the point of losing his temper. Marc Stewart had been a mistake. When he'd first met him, Marc had impressed him. He'd seemed like a man who had all his ducks in a row. That, added to the man's hunger for the finer things in life, and his charm and willingness to bend the rules, had made him a perfect associate.

Even when he'd realized the man had his flaws, he'd told himself that most men did. Unfortunately, the flaw Victor hadn't seen in Marc Stewart was about to bring them all down.

"Marc won't get far from home," Victor said. "John, I need you to watch his auto shop. Get Ray to keep an eye on the Friendly Bar over on the south side of town. It's Marc's go-to bar when things aren't going well. If either of you spot him again, stay on him. Trade off. Don't lose him again."

He hung up, hating that he hadn't put Jumbo on him. Jumbo wouldn't have lost him. Victor had realized last night after talking to Marc that he couldn't trust anyone with this, especially Marc. He'd already bungled things.

Changing into a clean sport shirt and a pair of jeans, Victor pulled on his lucky buffalo-skin boots and checked himself in the mirror. His unthreatening good looks had always served him well. He hoped they didn't let him down when he went to visit Rebecca Stewart at the hospital in Bozeman.

It was good to see some color in Gillian's face as they finished cleaning up the breakfast dishes together and she excused herself. Last night Austin had been worried he was going to have to take her back to the hospital. He was surprised she'd even been on her feet after the car wreck, the concussion and yesterday's events, not to mention Marc knocking her around before that. Her strength and endurance surprised him and filled him with admiration. If he had almost lost one of his brothers…

The thought was a punch to the gut and a wake-up call. He realized that he'd taken his four brothers for granted, assuming they would always be there.

He pulled out his cell phone and dialed his cousin Dana. He didn't want to have a long discussion with any one of his brothers. He knew it was cowardice on his part, but at the same time, he wanted to let them know he was all right and that he would try to make Christmas and the grand opening.

Actually, he didn't want to have to explain himself to anyone, even his cousin Dana. He'd hoped he would get her answering machine and he groaned inwardly when she answered on the third ring.

"Hey, Dana. It's Austin, your cousin?"

"The elusive Austin Cardwell? Hud said he met you, but I haven't had that opportunity yet."

"Sorry, but I'm afraid it could be a while yet."

She chuckled. "Hud said not to expect you for dinner until I saw the whites of your eyes."

"Your husband is one smart man."

"Yes, he is. I suppose you're calling me with a message for your brothers."

"Hud's wife is pretty sharp, as well."

She laughed. "What would you like me to tell them?"

Austin thought about that for a moment. "I'll try to make Christmas, but if I don't…"

"They're determined you will be at the grand opening. They're going to put it off until you're here. Don't see any way out for you."

"I guess it's too much to hope they'll go ahead without me if I don't show."

"Yep. Should I tell them you'll be getting back to them?"

"Tell them… I'll see them as soon as I can. You, too. If I can make Christmas, I will be there with bells on."

"Your cabin will be ready."

"Everything all right?" Gillian asked as she saw him pocket his cell phone.

"Fine. I talked to my cousin. She'll let my brothers know that I've been…detained."

She hated that he already had problems with his brothers and now she was making it worse. He followed her into the living room, the two of them sitting as they had the night before. "Are your parents still alive?"

He nodded. "Divorced. I was born in Montana, but my mother took all five of us boys to Texas when we were very young. My father stayed in Montana. Now my mother has remarried, and she and her new husband just bought a place near here where three of my brothers are living." He shrugged.

"You're lucky to have such a large family. After we lost our parents, it was just Becky and me. With her…" She fought the stark emotion that had her praying one moment and wanting to just sit down and bawl the next.

"I'm sure you already called the hospital. How is she doing?"

"There's been no change, but the doctor did say she is stable and he is hopeful. Have you ever lost anyone close to you?"

"A friend and fellow deputy." Austin hadn't gone a day in years without thinking about Mitch. "He was like a brother." He'd been even closer to Mitch than he was to his brothers. "He was killed in the line of duty. I wasn't there that day." And he'd never forgiven himself for it. He'd been away on barbecue company business.

"I'm sure it gets better," she said hopefully.

He nodded. "It does and it doesn't. You can never fill that hole in your life. Or your heart. But you put one foot in front of the other and you go on. Your sister, though, is going to come back."

"I hope you're right." She cleared her throat. "Right now I can't imagine how to go on. I'd hoped Becky had left me a letter, some kind of message...." Her voice broke.

"Tell me what you remember she said in what time you did have with her yesterday. It might help."

Shaking her head, she got up and walked to the opening into the living room. The December day glistened with fresh snow and sunshine. The bright sunlight poured through the leaded glass windows. Prisms of color sparkled in almost blinding light. She'd always loved this room because of the morning sunlight, but not even the sun's rays could warm her right now.

"Becky talked about our childhood."

"Where did you grow up?"

"In Helena. But we spent our summers at our grandfather's cabin. My sister mentioned the time the wind blew down an old pine tree in a thunderstorm. Becky and I loved thunderstorms and used to huddle together on Grandpa's porch and watch the lightning and the waves crashing on the shore." A lump formed in her throat. She couldn't lose her sister.

"Where is your grandfather's cabin?"

"Outside of Townsend on Canyon Ferry Lake."

"You think your nephew is at your grandfather's cabin?"

She shook her head. "The cabin's been boarded up for years. That's why what she said doesn't make any sense."

"Maybe she left you a message there," Austin suggested. "The only place she mentioned was the cabin, right?"

Gillian nodded.

"If your sister was in her right mind enough to hide her son and try to get Marc Stewart out of his life, then anything she said might have value. Can we get to the cabin this time of year?"

"The road should be open. They get a lot less snow up there than we do down here."

"What is the chance Marc knows about the cabin and will go there?" Austin asked.

She felt a start. "If he remembers it... I think Becky took him there once when they were dating. Since it was nothing like his family's place in Island Park, I don't think he was impressed."

"I suspect there is a reason your sister reminded you of the downed tree and your grandfather's cabin. How soon can you be ready to leave?"

Chapter 16

Marc watched his side mirror as he drove toward Townsend, Montana. His mind seemed sharper this morning. His face still hurt like hell, though. He'd changed the bandage himself, shocked at the damage his wife had done and all the more determined to kill her.

Last night, he'd managed to lose his tail and find a cheap motel at the edge of town, where he'd fallen asleep the instant his head hit the pillow.

It was this morning after a shower that he'd thought of that old moose head he'd seen at the bar and remembered his wife's family's cabin. Rebecca had taken him to see it when they were dating. As far as he knew, though, Rebecca and her sister still owned the place.

She'd been all weepy and sentimental because the cabin had belonged to her grandfather who'd died. Apparently she and her sister had spent summers there with the old man. He didn't get the weepy, emotional significance of the small old place in the pines. That was probably why he'd forgotten about it. That and the fact that they'd never returned to the place.

But he was good at getting back to a place he'd only been to once. He paid attention even when someone else was driving. Given how his wife felt about the old cabin, wasn't it possible she might return there when she had something to stash?

He drove toward the lake. The sleep had helped. He felt more confident that he could pull himself out of this mess. Ahead, he saw a sign that looked familiar and began to slow. If Rebecca had hidden the ledger at the cabin—which he was betting was a real possibility— then he would know soon enough.

Marc hoped his instincts were right as he turned off the main highway and headed down the dirt road back into the mountains along the lake. It had snowed so there was a fine dusting on the road, but nothing to worry about. This area never got as much snow as those closer to the mountains.

The road was the least of his worries anyway. He thought of Gillian and the cowboy deputy. Would Gillian think of the cabin?

Swearing under his breath, he realized that if he had, then she would, too. Maybe she was already there. Maybe she already had her hands on the ledger. The thought sent his pulse into overdrive.

But as he turned onto the narrow road that led up to the cabin, he saw that there were no other tracks in the new dusting of snow. His spirits buoyed. Maybe he would just wait around and see if Gillian showed up.

It was a great place to hide out, especially this time of year.

He knew her. If she thought the ledger might be hidden at the cabin, she wouldn't tell the police. She would come for it herself. This cabin meant too much to her to have the police tearing the place apart looking for the ledger and any other evidence they thought they might find.

Even if the Texas deputy was still with Gillian this morning, it would just be the two of them. Marc hoped he was right. He'd brought several guns, including a rifle. This cabin that meant so much to his wife would be the perfect place to dispose of Gillian and the cowboy.

The cabin was back in the mountains that overlooked Canyon Ferry Lake. Huge green ponderosa pines glistened in the midday sun among large rock formations. It had snowed the night before but had now melted in all but the shade of the pines.

"Turn here," Gillian said when the road became little more than a Jeep trail.

Austin noticed tracks where someone had been up the road. He figured Gillian had noticed them, too. It could have been anyone. But he was guessing it was Marc Stewart. As the structure came into view, he saw that the windows were shuttered. At first glance, it didn't appear anyone had been inside for a very long time.

But as he parked, Austin saw that the front door was open a few inches and there were fresh gouges in the wood where whoever had been here had broken in. The old cabin looked like the perfect place for a wounded fugitive to lie low for a while and heal. Even though there was no sign of a vehicle and the tracks indicated that whoever had been here had left, he wasn't taking any chances.

"Stay here," Austin said as he opened his door and pulled his weapon. Long dried pine needles covered the steps up to the worn wood of the small porch. There were footprints in the wet dirt, large, man-sized soles. Austin moved cautiously as he pushed open the door. It groaned open.

A stale, musty scent rushed out. Weapon ready, Austin stepped into the dim darkness. The cabin was small so it didn't take long to make sure it was empty. As he looked around the ransacked room, it was clear that Marc had been here. From the destruction, Austin was betting the man hadn't found what he was looking for, though.

In a small trash container in the bathroom, he found some bloody bandages. From the amount of blood, it appeared Marc had been wounded enough to warrant medical attention. But no doubt not by anyone at a hospital, where the gunshot wound would have had to be reported.

When he returned to the porch, he found Gillian sitting on the front step looking out at the lake in the distance.

"He was here, wasn't he?" she said. "Did he—"

"I don't think he found anything."

Gillian nodded.

"You don't use the cabin?" Austin asked as he looked at the amazing view.

"No. It stayed in the family, but after my grandfather died…well, it just wasn't the same."

He watched her take a deep breath of mountain air before letting it out slowly. "I haven't been here in nine years. I doubt my sister has either, but I continue to pay the taxes on it."

Austin didn't want to believe that Rebecca Stewart had just been babbling when she'd mentioned the cabin. She had to be passing on a message.

"Would you mind taking a look around and see if your sister might have left you anything inside that Marc missed? He made a mess."

She nodded and pushed to her feet. There were tears in her eyes as she entered the cabin and stopped just inside the door.

Austin gave her a moment. He tried to imagine what it must have been like to visit here when Gillian's grandfather was alive. He and his brothers would have loved this place. Even at his age, he loved the smell of the pine trees, the crunch of the dried needles beneath his boot heels, the feeling of being a boy again in a place where there were huge rocks and trees to climb, forts to build and fish to catch out of the small stream that ran beside the cabin.

At the sound of her footfalls deeper in the cabin, he went inside to find her standing in the small kitchen. "My grandfather liked to cook. He made us pancakes." She looked over at Austin. "You remind me of him."

He couldn't help being touched by that. "Thank you."

Dust motes danced in the sunlight that streamed in through the cracks of the shutters. The interior of the cabin looked as if it might have been decorated in the 1950s or early 1960s. While rustic, it was cozy from the worn quilts on the couch and chairs to the soot-covered fireplace.

"There's nothing here." She shook her head. "Becky hasn't been here. She would have left at least a glass or two in the sink and an unmade bed. Everything is just as it was the last time I was here—except for the mess Marc made searching the place."

Austin couldn't help his disappointment. He'd hoped Rebecca had mentioned the cabin for a reason. Maybe she *had* been out of her head. As much as he wanted to find this ledger that would nail Marc Stewart to the wall, his greatest fear was for the boy. With whom would a woman possibly not in her right mind have stashed her ten-month-old son?

Marc had waited after he'd searched the cabin looking for the ledger. It wasn't there. He'd looked everywhere. He'd thought that maybe if Gillian really hadn't known what her sister had done with it that she and the cowboy might show up at the cabin.

But he'd never been good at waiting. Still, even as he was leaving, he hadn't been able to shake the feeling that Rebecca *had* been there. Had she left some message that he hadn't recognized? Frankly, he'd never thought his wife as that clever. But then again, he'd been wrong about how strong she was.

Belatedly, he was realizing that he might not have really known his wife at all.

Raw with emotions, Gillian looked around the cabin for a moment longer before turning toward the front door to escape even more painful memories.

She stumbled down the porch steps, breathing hard. Even the pine-scented air seemed to hurt her lungs. It, too, filled her with bittersweet memories.

Behind her, she heard Austin locking up the cabin. She felt as if she was going to be sick and stumbled down to the fallen tree her sister had reminded her about. Why hadn't Becky left her a clue? She'd wanted Gillian to find the ledger, get Marc put away and take care of Andy. But how did she expect her to do that without some idea of where to start? What had Becky been thinking?

She prayed that her sister had left Andy somewhere safe until she could find him.

"Is this the tree that blew over?" Austin said behind her, startling her.

Gillian stood leaning against it. The pine was old and huge. It had fallen during a summer thunderstorm, landing on a large boulder instead of falling all the way to the ground. Because of that, it lay at a slight slant a good three to six feet off the ground. She and her sister used to walk the length of it, pretending they were high-wire artists. Gillian had a scar on her arm from a fall she'd taken.

She told Austin about the night the tree fell and how she and Becky had played on it, needing to share the memories, fearing they would vanish otherwise. "It made a tremendous sound when it crashed," she said, her voice breaking.

"I was thinking earlier how my brothers and I would have loved this place."

She watched Austin walk around the root end of the tree. Most of the dirt that had once clung to the roots had washed off over the years in other storms. But because of its size, when the tree had become uprooted, it had left a large hole in the earth that she and Becky used to hide in.

"Gillian."

Something in the way he said her name made her start. She looked at his expression and felt a jolt. He was staring down into the hole.

"I think you'd better see this." ·

Chapter 17

Austin stood back as Gillian hurried around the tree to the exposed roots and looked down into the deep cave of a hole. "What is that?"

She made a sound, half laugh, half sob. "That's Edgar."

"Edgar?" he repeated as she clambered down into the hole. She picked up what appeared to be a taxidermy-type stuffed crow on a small wooden stand and handed it up to him before he helped her out.

The bird had seen better days, but its dark eyes still glittered eerily. She took the mounted crow from him and began to cry as she held the bird to her as if it were a baby. "Edgar Allan Poe. Becky and I made friends with Edgar when he was young and orphaned. We fed him and kept him alive and he never left. He would fly in the moment we arrived at the cabin and caw at us from the porch railing. He followed us everywhere," she said excitedly and then sobered. "One time we came up and we didn't see him. We looked around for him…and found him dead. It was our grandfather's idea to have him mounted. Edgar had always looked out for us, Grandpa said. No reason he couldn't continue doing that."

Austin thought of the odd pets he and his brothers had accumulated and lost over the years and the attachment they'd had with them. "Your grandfather was a wise man."

She nodded through her tears. "Becky and I took Edgar to our tree house so he could keep an eye out for trespassers."

"Your tree house? Is that where you left him?"

Gillian met his gaze, hers widening. "Becky put Edgar here. That's what she was trying to tell me…" She pushed to her feet. "She *did* leave a message, since the last time I saw Edgar he was still in the tree house standing guard."

"Did Marc know about it?"

Gillian frowned. "I doubt it. He didn't like the outdoors much and his family's cabin was so much nicer on the lake in Idaho. Also I'm not sure how much of the tree house is even still there. It's been years."

Austin followed Gillian into the woods. They wound through the tall thick ponderosa pines. The December day was cold but clear. Sunlight slanted in through the trees but did little to warm them. The skiff of snow that had fallen overnight still hung to the pine boughs back here, making it feel even colder.

As they walked, he watched the ground for any sign

that Marc had come this way. It was hard to tell since the ground was covered with pine needles.

They had gone quite a ways when Gillian stopped abruptly. He looked past her and saw what was left of the tree house. It was now little more than a few boards tacked up between trees. The years hadn't been kind to it. What boards had remained were weathered, several hanging by a nail.

He could feel Gillian's disappointment as they moved closer, stepping over the boards that had blown down. A makeshift ladder had been tacked to a tree at the base of what was left of the tree house. Austin tested the bottom step.

"I don't think it's safe for you to go up there," Gillian said.

"Your sister must have climbed up there." But he knew Rebecca weighed a lot less than he did as he tried the second step. The board held so he began the ascent, hoping for the best. It had been years since he'd climbed a tree. He'd forgotten the exhilaration of being high above the ground.

When he reached what was left of the tree house, he poked his head through the opening and felt a start much like he had when he'd seen Edgar down in the roots of the fallen tree.

"Do you see anything?" Gillian called up.

A fabric doll with curly dark hair sat in the corner of the remaining tree house floor, its back against the tree. It had huge dark eyes much like Gillian's and it was looking right at him. As he reached for it, he felt the soft material of the doll's yellow dress and knew it hadn't been in this tree long.

Other than the doll, there was nothing else in what

had once been Gillian and Rebecca's tree house. He stuck the doll inside his coat and began the careful descent to the ground.

Gillian set Edgar down next to the base of a tree, thinking about her sister. Rebecca had always liked puzzles and scavenger hunts. This was definitely feeling like a combination of both.

As Austin pulled the doll from his coat, she stared at it in surprise for only a moment before taking it and crushing it to her chest in a hug.

"The doll looks like you," Austin said.

She nodded, afraid if she spoke she would burst into tears again. Her emotions were dangerously close to the surface as it was. Being here had brought back so many memories of the summers she and Becky had spent here with their grandfather.

After a moment, she held the doll at arm's length. The dolls had been a gift from their parents, she told Austin. "Mother had a woman make them so they resembled Becky and me. We never told her, but I found them to be a little creepy and used to turn mine against the wall when I slept. I half expected the doll to be turned around watching me when I woke up. But Becky loved hers so much she even took it when she went to college." That memory caused a hitch in her chest.

"The doll has to be a clue," Austin said.

"If it is, I have no idea what that clue might be." She studied the doll. Its dress was yellow, Gillian's favorite color, so she knew it was hers. The dress had tiny white rickrack around the collar and hem and puffy sleeves. She looked under the hem, thinking Becky might have left a note. Nothing. She felt all over the doll, praying for a scrap of paper, something sewn inside the stuffing, anything that would provide her with the information she desperately needed. Nothing.

When she looked at Austin, she felt her eyes tear up again. "I have no idea what this means, if anything."

"The doll wasn't in the tree long. Since it seems likely your sister left it there, it has to mean something."

She almost laughed. "If my sister was thinking clearly she wouldn't have climbed up into that tree to put my doll there without a note or some message…"

"Your sister was terrified that Marc would find not only the ledger but their son, right?" Austin asked.

She nodded.

"I know all this seems…illogical, but I think she knew she had to use clues that only you would understand, like Edgar."

"I hope you're right," she said, smiling at this man who'd been there for her since that first horrible night in the blizzard.

"Are you leaving Edgar here?" he asked.

Gillian nodded. "Becky always said this was his favorite spot. He used to fly around, landing on limbs near the tree house, watching over us as we played. I know it sounds silly—"

"No, it doesn't. I get it."

She saw that he did and felt her heart lift a little.

"So there were two dolls?" he asked. "Where is your sister's?"

Victor straightened the white clerical collar and checked himself in the mirror before picking up his Bible and exiting the car in the hospital parking lot.

He couldn't be sure how much security the cops had

on Rebecca Stewart. He suspected it would be minimal. Most police departments were stretched thin as it was. This was Montana. Security at the hospital was seldom needed. Victor was counting on the uniform outside her room being some mall-type security cop that the hospital had brought in.

The security guard would have been given Marc Stewart's description, so the man would be on the lookout for him—not a pastor. The guard would have been on the job long enough that he would be bored and sick of hospital food.

As he walked into the lower entrance to the hospital, he saw that his "assistant" was already here sitting in one of the chairs in the lobby thumbing through a magazine. He gave Candy only a cursory glance before he walked past the volunteer working at the desk.

While some hospitals were strict about visitors, this wasn't one of them. That's what he loved about small Montana communities. People felt safe.

He already knew the floor and room number and had asked about visiting hours, so he merely tipped his head at her and said, "Hope you're having a blessed day."

She smiled at him. "You, too, Reverend."

At the elevator, he punched in the floor number. A man and woman in lab coats hurried in. Victor gave them both a solemn nod and looked down at the Bible in his hands. Before the doors could close, a freshly manicured hand slipped between them. He caught the flash of bright red nail polish and the sweet scent of perfume.

As the doors were forced open, Candy stepped in, turning her back to the three of them.

He had told her to dress provocatively but not over the top. She'd chosen a conservative white blouse and slim navy skirt with a pair of strappy high heeled winter boots. The white blouse was unbuttoned enough that anyone looking got teasing glimpses of the tops of her full breasts. She smelled good, that, too, not overdone. Her blond hair was pulled up, a few strands curling around her pretty face.

Victor was pleased as the elevator stopped and the doors opened. They all stepped off, the man and woman in the lab coats scurrying down one hallway while he and Candy took the other. He let her get a few yards ahead before following. The way she moved reminded him of something from his childhood.

If I had a swing like that, I'd paint it red and put it in my backyard.

It was a silly thing to come to mind right now. He worried that he was nervous and that it would tip off even the worst of security guards. So much was riding on this. If he could just get into Marc's wife's room…

At the end of the hallway, he spotted the rent-a-cop sitting in a plastic chair outside Rebecca Stewart's room.

The security guard spotted Candy and got to his feet as she approached.

Chapter 18

Austin found himself watching his rearview mirror. If he was right, Rebecca Stewart had left a series of clues that only her sister could decipher. She'd used items from their past, the shared memories of sisters and things that even if she had mentioned to Marc, he wouldn't have recalled. It told Austin that she'd been terrified of her husband finding their son.

He could see that it was breaking Gillian's heart, these trips down memory lane with her sister. Had Rebecca worried that she could be dead by the time Gillian uncovered them? He figured she must have known her husband well enough that it had definitely been a consideration.

No wonder she hadn't told her sister a thing. Gillian would have done anything to save her sister and Marc would have known that. He must have realized Gillian didn't know the truth. Not that he hadn't planned to use her to try to get her sister to talk. There was no doubt in Austin's mind that, in an attempt to save her sister, Rebecca had pushed Marc and his rotten temper so he would lose control and kill her. If Gillian hadn't thrown herself at Marc when she had…

The drive north to Chinook took the rest of the day. They traveled from the Little Belt Mountains to the edge of the Rockies, before turning east across the wild prairie of Montana. It was dark by the time they reached the small Western town on what was known as the Hi-Line.

Chinook, like most of the towns along Highway 2, had sprung up with the introduction of the railroad. Both freight and passenger trains still blew their whistles as they passed through town.

A freight train rumbled past as Austin parked in front of a motor inn. Gillian had called ahead but had gotten no answer at the Baker house. Austin could tell that made her as nervous as it did him. Was it possible that as careful as Rebecca had been, Marc had been one step ahead of them?

"I can't believe Rebecca would have confided in anyone," Gillian said. "But if there is even a chance Nancy knows where Becky left Andy…"

Gillian had explained about her sister's doll on the drive north. Nancy Rexroth Baker and her sister had been roommates at college. Becky had been Nancy's maid of honor when she'd married Claude. While as far as Gillian knew the two hadn't stayed in touch when Nancy had a baby girl last year they'd named her Rebecca Jane. That's the name Nancy and Becky used to call her doll at college. Touched by this, her sister had mailed Nancy her doll.

"She told you this?" Austin had asked. "Wouldn't Marc have known?"

She shook her head. "Since my sister has apparently had this plot of hers in the works for some time, I wouldn't think so. But Marc is anything if not clever. He could have known a whole lot more than Becky suspected."

Gillian tried the Baker home number again. The line went to voice mail after four rings. "Maybe we should drive by the house."

Austin didn't think it would do much good, but he agreed. She gave him the address, which turned out to be in the older section of the town just four blocks from the motel. The houses were large with wide front porches, a lot of columns and arches.

The Baker house sat up on the side of a hill with a flight of stairs that ended at the wide white front porch. There were no lights on behind the large windows at the front, no Christmas decorations on the outside, and the drapes were drawn.

"Let's see if there is an alley," Austin said and drove around the corner. Just as he'd suspected, there was. He took it, driving down three houses before stopping in front of a garage. "I'll take a look." He hopped out to check the garage. As he peered in the window, he saw that it was empty.

It came as somewhat of a relief. As he climbed back into the SUV, he said, "It looks like they've gone somewhere for Christmas."

"Christmas." The way she said it made him think that she'd forgotten about it, just as he had, even with all the red and green lights strung around town.

He thought of his brothers all gathered in Big Sky

for the holidays, no doubt wondering where he was. He quickly pushed the thought away. They should be used to him by now. Anyway, his cousin Dana would have told them he was tied up. Her husband, Hud, the marshal, would have a pretty good idea why he was tied up since he would have heard about Marc Stewart's attempted murder of his wife, the kidnapping of his sister-in-law, Gillian, and the BOLO out on Marc.

As Austin drove them back to the motel, he said, "We need to get into that house because if I'm right, then this family has your nephew and he's safe. The doll brought us this far. There has to be another clue that we're missing."

"The key," Gillian said on an excited breath. "The one I found at the house after Rebecca and Andy left. Do you still have it?"

"I'm going to walk back and get into the house," Austin said after they returned to the motel. He'd gotten them adjoining rooms, no doubt so he could keep an eye on her, Gillian thought.

She was grateful for everything he'd done. But she was going with him. She came out of her room and stood in front of him, her hands on her hips. "You're not going alone."

He shook his head. "Maybe you don't understand the fine line between snooping and jail. Breaking and entering is—"

"I'm going with you."

He looked like he wanted to argue, but saw that she meant what she said. "Wear something dark and warm. It's cold out."

She was already one step ahead of him as she reached

for a black fleece jacket she'd grabbed as they were leaving her apartment. Donning a hat and gloves, she turned to look at him.

He was smiling at her as if amused.

"What?" she said, suddenly feeling uncomfortable under his scrutiny. She knew it was silly. He'd seen her at her absolute worst.

"You just look so…cute," he said. "Clearly breaking the law excites you."

She smiled in spite of herself. It had been a while since a man had complimented her. Actually, way too long. But it wasn't breaking the law that excited her, she thought and felt her face heat with the thought.

The night was clear and cold, the sky ablaze with stars. She breathed in the freezing air. It stung her lungs, but made her feel more alive than she had in years. Fear drove her steps along with hope. The bird, the doll, all of it had led them here. She couldn't be wrong about this. And yet at the back of her mind, she worried that none of this made any sense because Rebecca hadn't known what she was doing.

At the dark alley, Austin slowed. It was late enough that there were lights on in the houses. Most of the drapes were open. She saw women in the kitchen cooking and families moving around inside the warm-looking homes. The scenes pulled at her, making her wish she and her sister were those women.

A few doors down, a dog barked, a door slammed and she heard someone calling, "Zoey!" The dog barked a couple more times; then the door slammed again and the alley grew quiet.

"Come on," Austin said and they started to turn down the alley.

A vehicle came around the corner, moving slowly. Gillian felt the headlights wash over them and let out a worried sound as she froze in midstep. Her first thought was Marc. Her heart began to pound even though she knew Austin had his shoulder holster on and the gun inside it was loaded.

Her moment of panic didn't subside when she saw that it was a sheriff's department vehicle.

"Austin?" she whispered, not sure what to do.

He turned to her and pulled her into his arms. Her mouth opened in surprise and the next thing she knew, he was kissing her. His mouth was warm against hers. At first, she was too stunned to react. But after a moment, she put her arms around his neck and lost herself in the kiss.

As the headlights of the sheriff's car washed over them, the golden glow seemed to warm the night because she no longer felt cold. She let out a small helpless moan as Austin deepened the kiss, drawing her even closer.

As the sheriff's car went on past, she felt a pang of regret. Slowly, Austin drew back a little. His gaze locked with hers, and for a moment they stood like that, their quickened warm breaths coming out in white clouds.

"Sorry."

She shook her head. She wasn't sorry. She felt… light-headed, happy, as if helium filled. She thought she might drift off into the night if he let go of her.

"Are you okay?" he asked, looking worried.

She unconsciously touched the tip of her tongue to her lower lip, then bit down on it to stop herself. "Great. Never better."

That made him smile. For a moment, he stood merely

smiling at her, his gaze on hers, his dark eyes as warm as a crackling fire. Then he sighed. "Let's get this over with," he said and took her gloved hand as they started up the alley.

There was only an inch of snow on the ground, but it crunched under their feet. If anyone heard them and looked out their window, she doubted they would think anything of it. They would appear to be what they were, a thirtysomething couple out walking on an early December night.

She looked over at Austin. Light from one of the yards shone on his handsome face, catching her off guard. He wasn't just handsome. He was caring and kind and capable, as well. She warned herself not to let one kiss go to her head. Of course she felt something for this man who'd saved her life twice and probably would have to again before this was over.

But her pulse was still pounding hard from the kiss. It had been the best kiss she'd ever had. Not that it meant anything.

She reminded herself that this was what Austin Cardwell did for a living. Not kiss women he was trying to save, but definitely doing whatever it took to save those same women.

She'd bet there was a long line of women he'd saved and all of them had gone giddy if he'd kissed them like that. That was a sobering thought. He could have ended up kissing all of them. Or even something more intimate.

That thought settled her down. She was behaving like a teenager on a date with the adorable quarterback of the football team. She told herself it was only because she hadn't dated all that much, especially since she'd started her business. True, she hadn't met anyone she cared to date. But she wasn't the kind of woman who fell head over heels at the drop of a kiss. Even one amazing kiss on a cold winter night.

But any woman in her place would be feeling like this, she told herself. She'd never believed that knights on white horses really existed before Austin Cardwell. It was one reason she was still single. That and she liked her independence. But mostly, it was because she'd never met a man who had ever made her even consider marriage.

Becky's marriage to Marc certainly hadn't changed her mind about men in general. She'd known Marc was domineering. She just hadn't known what the man was capable of. She doubted Becky had either.

Just the thought of her sister brought tears to her eyes. She wiped at them with her free gloved hand, determined not to break down, especially now. Austin hadn't wanted to bring her along as it was.

She needed to be strong. She concentrated on finding Andy. Becky had hidden him somewhere safe. Gillian had to believe that. What better place than with someone she could trust, like her former college roommate, Nancy Baker?

Gillian hated that she'd let Marc keep her from her sister. But the few times she'd visited he'd made her so uncomfortable that she hadn't gone back. And Marc had put Becky on a leash that didn't allow her to come up to Big Sky to visit often. It wasn't that he forbade it, he just made sure Becky was too busy to go anywhere.

Rubbing a hand over her face, she tried to concentrate on what lay ahead rather than wallowing in regret. Becky was stable. Gillian couldn't count on her regain-

ing consciousness. It was why she had to find Andy—
and that damned ledger before Marc did.

Austin slowed as they reached the back of the Baker
house. She saw him look down the alley both ways before he drew her into the shadows along the side of the
garage. The yard stretched before them. Huge pines
grew along the sides against a tall wooden fence.

They walked toward the back of the house staying in
the deep cold shadows of the pines. At the back door,
Austin hesitated for a moment. She could tell he was
listening. She heard voices but in the distance. Someone was calling a child into the house for dinner. Closer,
that same dog barked.

Austin headed up the steps to the back door. She
followed trying to be as quiet as possible. The houses
weren't particularly close, but this was a small town.
Neighbors kept an eye on each other's homes, especially
when they knew a family was away for Christmas.

That was where the Bakers had gone, wasn't it?

Gillian took a deep breath as she saw Austin pull out
the key. It was such a long shot, she realized now, that
she felt silly even mentioning it. But it didn't matter if
the key worked or not. She knew Austin would get them
into the house. She was praying once they got in the
house that they wouldn't find evidence of Marc having
been there—and especially not of any kind of struggle.

She held her breath as he tried the key. It slipped right
in. Austin shot her a look, then turned the key. She felt
her eyes widen as the door opened.

"Rebecca left the key," she said more to herself than
to Austin. She knew she sounded as disbelieving as he
must have felt. Her heart lifted with the first feeling of

real hope she'd felt since Marc had abducted her. "It has to mean that Nancy has my nephew, that Andy is safe."

As Candy approached, the security guard ran a hand down the front of his uniform as if to get out any wrinkles and remind himself to suck in his stomach. He stood a little straighter as well, puffing up a bit, without even realizing he was doing it, Victor thought, amused.

"May I help you?" the guard asked her.

Candy gave him one of her disarming smiles.

Victor saw that it was working like a charm. He looked into one of the rooms, before moving down the hall to Rebecca's. He could hear Candy asking for directions, explaining that her best friend had just had her third baby.

"Ten pounds, eleven ounces! I can't even imagine."

Victor smiled and gave a somber nod to the guard as he pushed open the door to Rebecca's room. He was so close, he could almost taste it.

"Just a minute," the guard said, stopping him.

"I told the family I would look in on Mrs. Stewart," Victor said.

"Did you say first floor like down by the cafeteria?" Candy asked the guard, then dropped her purse. It fell open. Coins tinkled on the floor. A lipstick rolled to the guard's feet.

The guard began to stoop down to help pick it up, but shot Victor another look before waving him in.

"I'm so sorry," Candy was saying as the door closed behind Victor. "I'm so clumsy. How did you say I get to my friend's room? I would have sworn she said it was on this floor."

Victor approached the bed. He'd met Marc's wife

only once and that had been by accident. He liked to keep his business and personal lives entirely separate. But there'd been a foul-up in a shipment so he'd stopped by Marc's auto shop one night after hours. Marc had told him he would be there so he hadn't been surprised to see a light burning in the rear office.

As he'd pushed open the side door, though, he'd come face-to-face with a very pregnant and pretty dark-haired woman. She'd had a scowl on her face and he could see that she'd been crying. It hadn't taken much of a leap to know she must be Marc's wife. Or mistress.

"Sorry," she'd said, sounding breathless.

He'd realized that he'd startled her. *"I'm the one who's sorry."*

"Are you here to see Marc?"

"I left my car earlier," Victor had ad-libbed. *"The owner said he might have it finished later tonight. I saw the light on...."*

She'd nodded, clearly no longer interested. *"He's in his office,"* she'd said and he'd moved aside to let her leave.

As the door closed behind her, Marc had come out of his office looking sheepish. *"I didn't know she was stopping by."* He'd shrugged. *"My wife. She's pregnant and impossible. I'll be so glad when this baby is finally born. Maybe she will get off my ass."*

Victor hadn't cared about Marc's marital problems. He'd never guessed that night that Rebecca Stewart might someday try to take them all down in one fell swoop.

As he stepped to the side of the bed and looked down at the woman lying there, he could see the brutality Marc had unleashed on her. His hands balled into fists at his side. He'd known this kind of violence firsthand and had spent a lifetime trying to overcome it in himself.

"Rebecca?"

Not even the flicker of an eyelid.

"Rebecca?" he said, leaning closer. "How are you doing today?"

Still nothing. Glancing toward the door, he could hear Candy just outside the room, still monopolizing the guard's attention.

Victor pulled the syringe from his pocket. He couldn't let this woman wake up and tell the police where they could find the ledger. He uncapped the syringe and reached for the IV tube.

Rebecca's eyes flew open before he could administer the drug. She let out a sound just a moment before the alarm on the machine next to her went off.

Chapter 19

Marc could feel time slipping through his fingers like water. He tried to remain calm, to think. With a start, he realized something. If Gillian knew where the ledger and Andy were, then she would go to both. Once she had the ledger in her hot little hands, she would turn it over to the cops. Victor would be on his private jet, winging his way out of the country—after he had Marc killed.

Which meant Gillian really didn't know where either item was. It was the only thing that made any sense because otherwise, by now, the ledger would be in the hands of the police.

But she would be looking for it. Was she stumbling around in the dark like he was? Or had her sister given her a hint where it was? Unlike her, he had cops after him. He felt as if he was waiting for the other shoe to drop. Once that ledger surfaced... He didn't want to think about how much worse things could get for him.

For a moment, he almost wished that Rebecca had cut his throat and he'd died right there at her feet—after he'd pulled the trigger and put the both of them out of their misery.

Marc shook himself out of those dark thoughts. If he was right and Gillian didn't have a clue where the ledger was any more than he did...well, then there was still hope. He dug out his cell phone.

When the hospital answered, he asked about Rebecca's condition.

"I'm sorry," the nurse said. "I can't give out that information."

"There must be someone I can talk to. I'm her brother. I can't fly out until later in the week. I'm afraid it will be too late."

"Let me connect you to her floor."

He waited. A male nurse came on the line. He could hear noise in the background. Something was happening. Was it Rebecca?

When he asked about his "sister's" condition, the nurse started to say he couldn't give out that information over the phone. "How about her doctor? Surely I can talk to someone there." He gave him his hard-luck pitch about not being able to get there right away.

"Perhaps you'd like to talk to the pastor who just went into her room," the nurse said.

Pastor? Marc stifled a curse. *Victor.* That son of a...

"I'm sorry, I don't see him," the nurse said. "Why don't I have the doctor call you?"

Marc slammed down the phone and let out a string of oaths. How dare Victor. Marc had told him he'd handle this. Not only that, he wanted to be the person who killed her—after he found out where she'd hidden the ledger and his son.

So was Rebecca dead? The last person Victor had paid a visit to while dressed as a pastor...well, needless to say, that person had taken a turn for the worst.

Once the door of the Baker house closed behind them, Austin snapped on his small penlight and handed a second one to Gillian. The silence inside the house gave him the impression that no one had been home for some time.

They were standing in the kitchen. He swung the light over the counter. Empty. Everything was immaculate. No dishes in the sink. Stepping to the refrigerator, he opened it. There was nothing but condiments. No leftovers that would spoil while the family was gone. As he closed the door, he noticed the photographs tacked to it and the children's artwork. There was no photo of Gillian's sister.

"They're gone, aren't they?" Gillian said from the doorway to the living room. "But they must have Andy. My sister wouldn't have left me the key unless..." She stopped to look at him in the dim light.

He agreed, but he knew they both wanted proof. "Let's check the kid's room upstairs." It made sense that if this family had Andy they might have left something behind to assure Gillian that her nephew was fine, or, better yet, another clue as to where Gillian could find the ledger and put Marc away for a long time.

As they moved through the living room, Gillian whispered, "No Christmas tree. No presents. They aren't coming back until after Christmas."

Or until they hear that it's safe, he thought. Had Rebecca told them she would call them when it was safe? But what if she couldn't call?

They climbed the stairs to the bedrooms. It didn't take long to find the child's room. It was bright colored with stuffed animals piled on the bed. Gillian stepped to the bed. He knew she must be looking for her sister's doll. It wasn't there.

"Do you see anything of Andy's?" he asked.

She sighed and shook her head. "His favorite toy is a plush owl, but it's not here. Then again, it wouldn't be. He'd want it with him, especially if he wasn't with his mother." Her voice broke.

They checked the other rooms but found nothing. Going back downstairs, Austin looked more closely in the living room. Rebecca had been scared of her husband. But her clues for Gillian did make him wonder about the state of her mind. He reminded himself that she'd been terrified of Marc. The clues had to be vague, things only Gillian would understand.

They searched the house, but found nothing that would indicate that Andy Stewart had been here. Like Gillian, he kept telling himself that Rebecca had left them a key to this house. Didn't that mean that the Bakers had Andy and all were safe since there was no sign of a struggle in the house?

He'd stopped to go through a desk in the study when he heard Gillian go into the kitchen. She had looked as despondent as he felt. He'd been so sure they would find—

Gillian let out a cry. Austin rushed into the kitchen to find her standing in front of the refrigerator. Her hand was covering her mouth and her eyes were full of tears as her penlight glared off the refrigerator door.

He'd checked the kitchen first thing and hadn't seen anything. As he moved closer, she pointed at what he'd assumed had been artwork done by the daughter. What he hadn't seen was a note of any kind.

"What?" he asked, looking from Gillian to the front of the refrigerator in confusion.

She carefully plucked one of the pieces of artwork from the door. "Andy."

He looked down at the sheet of paper in her hand. It was a drawing of an owl with huge round eyes. Someone had taken a crayon to it. The owl was almost indistinguishable under the purple scribbles.

"Andy?" he repeated confused.

"I told you. He loves owls."

That seemed a leap even to him.

Gillian began to laugh. "Rebecca drew this at my house when she and Andy came up to visit. Andy's favorite color is purple."

"You're sure this is the same drawing?" he asked. He couldn't help being skeptical.

"Positive. Look at this." She pointed to a spot on the owl. The artist had drawn in feathers before they had been scribbled over. In the feathers he saw what appeared to be numbers. "It's a phone number. I'm betting it is Nancy Baker's cell phone number."

Victor pocketed the syringe as he stepped back from the hospital bed. Rebecca Stewart's eyes were open. She was staring right at him, a wild, frightened look in her dark eyes.

As a doctor and two nurses rushed in, the security guard at their heels, Victor clutched his Bible and moved aside.

"What happened?" the doctor demanded.

"Nothing," he said. "That is, I was saying a prayer over her when she suddenly opened her eyes and that alarm went off."

The doctor began barking orders to the nurses. "If you don't mind stepping out, Pastor."

"I have other patients I promised to see, but I will check back before I leave," Victor said, but the doctor was busy and didn't seem to care.

On the overhead intercom, a nurse was calling a code blue as he walked toward the door. He felt the security guard's gaze on him as he stepped aside to let a crash cart be wheeled into the room. Without looking at the man, Victor started down the hallway away from all the noise and commotion in Rebecca's hospital room.

He half expected the security guard to call after him, but when he glanced back as he ducked into the first restroom he came to he saw that the guard was more interested in what was going on in Rebecca's room.

Reaching into his pocket he put on the latex gloves, then carefully removed the syringe from his other pocket and stuffed it down into the trash. Removing the gloves, he discarded them, as well. After washing his hands, he left.

The security guard didn't look his way as Victor turned and walked down the hallway, stopping at one of the empty rooms for a moment as if visiting a patient.

The guard hadn't asked his name. No one had. As he left the empty room, he saw a nurse coming out of Rebecca's room with the crash cart. He couldn't tell by the woman's face what the outcome had been for the patient.

Nor did he dare wait to find out. Turning, he walked out of the hospital.

Chapter 20

Marc felt sick to his stomach. His fingers shook as he dialed the hospital. Again, he pretended to be her brother.

"I have to know her condition. I can't get a flight out because of the weather right now. Tell me I'm not going to get there too late."

"Just a moment. Let me check," the nurse finally said, relenting.

He waited, his heart pounding. As long as Rebecca was alive, he stood a chance of fixing this mess. He would do anything she wanted. He would convince her to give up the ledger to save not just her own life but his and their son's. She had no idea the kind of people who would be after her and Andy.

But if Victor had killed her... *Hell,* he thought. The

cops would think he'd done it! Or paid someone to do it. What had Victor been thinking?

The answer came to him like another blow, this one more painful than the crystal tumbler. Victor planned to kill everyone who knew about the ledger and what was in it. He would take his chances that wherever Rebecca had hidden it, the incriminating book wouldn't turn up. Or if it did, the finder wouldn't have a clue what it was and wouldn't take it to the authorities. Or…it was this third option that made his pulse jump. Or… Victor was tying up loose ends before he skipped the country.

The nurse came back on the line. Marc held his breath.

"Good news. Your sister's condition has been upgraded. She had an episode earlier, but the doctor is cautiously optimistic about her complete recovery."

He tried to breathe. Victor had failed? His relief was real. "Can I talk to her?"

"I'm afraid not. The doctor wants her to rest. She is drifting in and out of consciousness. Perhaps by tomorrow…"

Gillian couldn't bear to wait until they returned to the motel to make the call, but Austin was anxious to get out of the house. She tried the number she'd found on Rebecca and Andy's artwork on the walk back to the motel.

The phone was answered on the second ring. "Gillian?"

"Nancy." She began to cry.

"Is everything all right?" Nancy asked, sounding as anxious as Gillian felt.

"I'm sorry, I'm just so relieved. Tell me you have Andy."

Several heartbeats of unbearable silence before Nancy said, "He's safe."

"Thank God."

"He keeps asking about his mother, though. Rebecca said she would join us before Christmas."

Gillian didn't know how to tell her. "Rebecca's in the hospital. The last I heard, she's unconscious."

"Oh, no. And Marc?"

"He's on the loose. Tell me you have Andy somewhere Marc wouldn't dream of looking."

"We do."

"A deputy sheriff from Texas is helping me try to find a ledger that will send Marc to prison. Do you know anything about it?"

"No. Rebecca only told me that Marc was dangerous and she needed Andy to be safe until she could come get him. She doesn't even know where we are. I was to tell her only when she called."

"Good. I don't need to know either. I can't tell you how relieved I am that Andy is with you and safe. But did Rebecca give you a message to pass on to me if I called?"

"She did mention that it was possible you would call."

So her sister had feared she wouldn't be able to call herself. Gillian felt sick.

"Becky said that if you called to tell you she forgives you for the birthday present you gave her when she turned fourteen and that she is overcoming her fears, just as you suggested. Does that make any sense to you?"

Gillian tried hard not to burst into uncontrollable sobs. "Yes, it does," she managed to say. "That's all?"

"That's it. Whatever is going on, it reminded me of how much your sister always loved puzzles."

"Yes. I'm just grateful that Andy is with you and safe. Give him my love."

She disconnected, still fighting tears. "Andy's safe."

"I heard. Your sister left you another clue?" he asked.

Before she could answer, she saw that she had a message. "The hospital called." She hurriedly returned the call, praying that it would be good news. *Please let Becky be all right. Please.*

"Yes," the floor nurse said when he finally came on the line. "We called you to let you know that your sister is doing much better. She has regained consciousness."

"Can I talk to her?"

"I'm sorry. The doctor gave her something for the pain. She's asleep. Maybe in the morning."

Gillian smiled through fresh tears as she disconnected. "Rebecca is better." She gulped the cold night air. "And I think I know where she hid the ledger."

Marc hung up from his call to the hospital, still shocked that Victor had failed. Rebecca was alive. Didn't that mean he had a chance to reason with her? He knew it was a long shot that he could persuade Rebecca of anything at this point. But if she realized the magnitude of what she'd done, given the criminal nature of his associates, maybe she would do it for Andy's sake...

He wished he'd explained things in the first place instead of losing his temper. He thought of Victor, Mr. Cool, and began to laugh. Victor must be beside himself. He was a man who didn't like to fail.

Would he try to kill Rebecca again? Marc didn't think so. It would be too dangerous. He was surprised that Victor had decided to do the job himself. That, he realized, showed how concerned the man was about cleaning up this mess—and how little confidence Victor had in him.

I'm toast.

If he'd had any doubt that Victor wouldn't let him survive, he no longer did. Now he had only one choice. Save himself. To do that, it meant going to the feds. But without the ledger…he couldn't remember names and numbers. He'd been told he was dyslexic. But he knew that wasn't right because he'd heard dyslexics had trouble writing words and numbers correctly. He thought it had more to do with not being able to remember. He could write just fine. That's what had him in this trouble.

When Victor had asked him why he'd done something so stupid as to write everything down, Marc hadn't wanted to admit that there was anything wrong with him. He'd hired someone else to handle the details at his auto shop.

But he couldn't very well do that with the criminal side of his work, could he? He told himself it was too late to second-guess that decision. He had to get his hands on the ledger. He realized there was a second option besides turning it over to the feds. He could skip the country with it. The ledger would be his insurance against Victor dusting him.

Without the ledger, though, he had no bargaining power.

Sure he knew some things about Victor's operation, but not enough without the ledger. It contained the names and dates, names he knew the feds would love to get their hands on.

Rebecca! What did you do with that damned book?

It wasn't as if he hadn't been suspicious that she was up to something in the weeks before. He'd actually thought she might be having an affair. But he'd realized that was crazy. What would she have done with Andy? It wasn't like she had a friend to watch their son. No, he'd known it had to be something else.

He wondered if she'd taken up gambling. He didn't give her much money, but she had a way of stretching what he did… No, he'd ruled out gambling. Unless she won all the time, that didn't explain her disappearances.

He had started making a habit of calling home at different hours to check on her. She was never there. Oh, sure, she made excuses.

Andy and I were outside in the yard. I didn't hear the phone. Or she didn't have her cell phone on her. Other times she was at the park or the mall. She would say it must have been too noisy to hear her phone. He told her to put it on vibrate and stick the thing in her pocket.

"Was there something you wanted?" she'd asked.

He hadn't liked the tone of her voice. She'd seemed pretty uppity. Like a woman who knew something he didn't. He'd said, "I was just making sure you and Andy were all right. That's what husbands do."

"Really." She'd actually scoffed at that.

Not only had he resented her attitude, he'd also hated that she acted as if she was smarter than him. Or worse, that she thought for a moment that she could outwit him.

That's why he'd started writing down the mileage on her car.

He had checked it each night after that since he usually got in after she and the kid were asleep, and then he would compare it the next night. It had been a head-scratcher, though. She had never gone far, so while he'd continued to write it down, he hadn't paid any attention lately.

He fished out the scrap of paper he'd been writing it down on from his wallet and did a little math. At first he thought he'd read it wrong. She'd gone over a hundred miles four days ago. The day before she'd drugged him with his own drugs, stolen his ledger and hidden his son, she'd driven more than fifty miles that morning alone.

What the hell? Marc realized that he hadn't seen his son that day. Had she already hidden him away somewhere the day before? He tried to remember. He'd gotten home late that night. He glanced into his son's room. He hadn't actually seen the boy in his bed. It could have been the kid's pillow under the covers.

He let out a string of curses. Where had she gone? Not to her family cabin, he'd already checked it. Then where? He refused to let her outsmart him. He pulled a map of Montana from the glove box. It was old, but it would do. Suddenly excited, he drew a circle encompassing twenty to twenty-five miles out from Helena. Rebecca thought she was so smart. He'd show her.

Chapter 21

"What do you want to do?" Laramie asked his brothers. They were all sitting around the large kitchen table at their cousin Dana Savage's house on Cardwell Ranch. They'd just finished a breakfast of flapjacks, ham, fried potatoes and eggs. Hud had motioned his wife to stay where she was as he got up to refill all of their mugs with coffee.

"I hate to put off the grand opening of the restaurant," Tag said.

"Can't it wait until Austin can be here?" Dana asked.

Jackson got up to check on the kids, who were eating at a small table in the dining room. "We might never have a grand opening if we do that."

"Jackson's right," his brother Hayes said. "We know how Austin is and now apparently he's gotten involved with some woman who's in trouble." He looked toward Hud for confirmation.

The marshal finished filling their cups and said, "He got involved in a situation where he was needed. That's all I can tell you."

"A dangerous situation?" Dana asked.

Hud didn't answer. He didn't have to. His brothers knew Austin, and Dana was married to a marshal. She knew how dangerous his line of work could be.

"This is the woman he met in the middle of the highway, right?" Laramie shook his head. "This is his M.O. He'd much rather be working than be with his family."

"I don't think that's true," Dana said in her cousin's defense. "I talked to him. He can't just abandon this woman. You should be proud that he's so dedicated. And as I recall, there are several of you who are into saving women in need." She grinned. "I believe it is why some of you are now married and others are involved in wedding planning."

There were some chuckles around the table.

Laramie sighed. "Some of us are still interested in the business that keeps us all fed, though. Fortunately," he added. "Let's go ahead with the January first grand opening. I, for one, will be glad to get back to Texas. I am freezing up here."

His brothers laughed, but agreed.

"Maybe Austin will surprise you," Dana said.

Laramie saw a look pass between Dana and her marshal husband. He was worried about Austin. Last July, Austin had been shot and had almost died trying to get some woman out of a bad situation. He just hoped this wouldn't prove to be as dangerous.

* * *

Marc went to an out-of-the-way bar. He hadn't seen a tail, but that didn't mean there wasn't one again. In a quiet corner of the bar, he studied the map and tried to remember any places Rebecca might have mentioned. He had a habit of tuning her out. Now he wished he'd paid more attention.

They'd gone to a few places while they were dating, but he doubted she would be sentimental about any of them, the way things had turned out. He had never understood women, though, so maybe she would hide the ledger in one of those places because she thought it was a place he would never look.

Just trying to think like her gave him a headache. He wanted to choke the life out of the woman for putting him through this. He realized he hadn't heard from Victor demanding an update. Which he figured meant he was right about one of Victor's men tailing him again.

He'd lost the tail the first time, but maybe Victor had put someone like Jumbo on him. Jumbo was a more refined criminal, not all muscle and no brains, which made him very dangerous.

Marc folded the map and put it away. He couldn't do anything until daylight. Between songs on the jukebox, he put in another call to the hospital with his brother story. He knew he was whistling in the dark. He'd be lucky if he even got to talk to Rebecca, let alone convince her he was sorry. But it was a small hospital and he doubted the cops had done more than put security outside her room, if that, since Victor had circumvented whatever safety guards they'd taken.

Still to his amazement, he was put through to Rebecca's room.

"Hello?" she sounded weak but alive. "Hello?"

"Becky, listen," he said once he got past his initial shock. "Don't hang up. I have to tell you something."

Silence.

"Are you still there?" He hated that his voice broke and even more that she'd heard it.

"What could you possibly want, Marc?"

Humor. He bit back a nasty retort. "That book you took, it doesn't just implicate me. The people I work for... Rebecca they won't let you live if I don't get that book back."

"Don't you mean they won't let you live?"

"Not just me. They'll go after your sister, too." He could hear her breathing. "And Andy." His voice broke at the thought.

"You bastard, what have you gotten us all into?"

"Hey, if you had left well enough alone—"

"What is it? Drugs?"

"It doesn't matter what it is. I was only trying to make some money for Andy. I wanted him to have a better life than I had."

"Money for Andy? You are such a liar, Marc." She laughed. It was a weak laugh, but still it made his teeth hurt. "You hid that money for yourself."

And now she had a large portion of it. She'd hidden that, too, he reminded himself. He felt his blood pressure go through the roof. He still couldn't believe she'd done this to him. If he could have gotten his hands on her... He took a breath, trying to regain control, as he reminded himself that he needed her help.

"Rebecca, honey, you just didn't realize what you were getting in to. But we can fix this. I can save you and your sister and our son. These people...sweetie, I need to know what you did with the ledger. Did you mail it to the police?" Her hesitation gave him hope. "I know I reacted...badly. But, honey, I knew what would happen if that ledger got into the wrong hands. These people aren't going to stop. They will kill you. I suspect one of them has already tried. You didn't happen to see a man dressed as a pastor, did you?"

Her quick intake of breath told him she had. "A blond guy, good-looking. He was there to kill you."

She started to say something, but began coughing. He could hear how weak and sick she was.

"He isn't going to give up. The only way out of this is the ledger. I can save us both. Honey, I'm begging you."

"Begging me?" She sounded like she was crying. "You mean like I begged you for a divorce?"

"I'm sorry. I'll give you a divorce. I'll even give you custody of Andy. I'll give you whatever you want. Just tell me where the ledger is so I can make this right."

"I don't think so," she said, her voice stronger. "It's over, Marc. I never want to see you again. Once the police arrest you..."

He swore under his breath. "I'll get out of jail at some point, Rebecca."

"Not if I have my way." The line went dead. As dead as they were both going to be, because if he went, she was going with him one way or another.

"So she told you where we could find the ledger?" Austin asked as he and Gillian walked back to the motel. She'd grown quiet after the call. He wondered if this last clue was one she didn't want to share. Was she worried she couldn't trust him?

When she said nothing, he asked, "Is something wrong?"

She looked over at him, her dark eyes bright. "I'm glad you're here with me."

Her words touched him more than they should have. There was something about this woman… He smiled, his heart beating a little faster. "So am I," he said, taking her gloved hand.

As if the touch of her had done it, snow began to fall in thick, lacy flakes that instantly clung to their clothing.

Gillian laughed. It was a wonderful sound in the snowy night. "Andy is safe, my sister is going to be all right and Marc Stewart is going to get what's coming to him." She moved closer to him as they walked. "How do you feel about caves?"

"Caves?" he said, looking over at her in surprise.

"Assuming my sister was in her right mind, she hid the ledger in a cave." She repeated the so-called clue Nancy Baker had given her.

"And from that you've decided the ledger is in some cave?"

"Not just some cave. One up Miners Gulch near Canyon Ferry Lake. Rebecca is terrified of close places, especially caves. It's a boy's fault we ended up in one on her fourteenth birthday. I had this horrible crush on a boy named Luke Snider. He was a roughneck, wild and unruly, and adorable. I was sixteen and dreamed of the two of us on outrageous adventures. I thought I would see the world with him, live in exotic places, eat strange food and make love under a different moon every night."

They had almost reached the motel. He hated to go

inside. The night had taken on a magical quality. Or maybe it was just sharing it with Gillian that made him feel that way.

"You were quite the romantic at sixteen."

She laughed. "I was, wasn't I? It didn't last any longer than my crush. Luke graduated from high school, went to work at his father's tire shop. He still works there. I bought a tire from him once." She smiled at that. "I definitely dodged a bullet with Luke."

He laughed as he let go of her hand and reached for the room key.

Gillian turned her face out toward the snow. He watched her breathe in the freezing air and let it out in a sigh. "If I'm right about this clue then my sister is getting even with me for being such a brat on her birthday that year." She seemed as reluctant as he did to leave the snow and the night behind, but stepped inside.

"I suspect caves have something to do with Luke and your sister's birthday," he said.

Gillian shook snowflakes from her coat. As she slipped out of it, he took it and hung her coat, along with his own, up to dry when she made no move to go into her adjoining room.

"I overheard Luke and his friends say they were going to these caves in the gulch. I knew they wouldn't let me go along, but if I just happened to run into them in the caves… I didn't want to go alone to look for them, and my friends could not imagine what I saw in Luke and his friends. You know how it is when you're sixteen. Just seeing him, saying hi in the hall, could make my day. I wanted him to really notice me. I figured if he saw how adventurous I was in the caves… So I told my sister I had a surprise birthday present for her."

He shook his head, smiling, remembering being sixteen and impulsive. He'd also had his share of teenage crushes. He hated to think of some of the things he'd done to impress a girl. He offered her the motel chair, anxious to hear her story, but she motioned it away and sat down on the end of his bed.

"Rebecca is claustrophobic so the last place she wanted to go was into a cave. I told her she needed to overcome her fears. Her message she left with Nancy was that she was now overcoming her fears."

"She mentioned this birthday present, so you think she put the ledger somewhere in these caves?"

"If I'm right, I know the exact spot." Gillian gave him a sad smile. "The spot where Rebecca totally freaked that day." Tears filled her eyes.

Austin reached across to take her hand. "Ah, childhood memories. I can't even begin to tell you about all the terrible things my brothers and I did to each other. It's just what siblings do."

She shook her head. "I hate that I did that to her."

"And yet, when the chips were down, she went back into those caves with you."

She smiled. "If I'm right."

His voice softened. "You've been right so far about everything."

Gillian felt a lump form in her throat. Her pulse buzzed at the look in his eyes. If he kissed her again… "I should—"

"Yes," he said, letting go of her. "We should get some sleep. Sounds like we have a big day ahead of us tomorrow." He rose and stepped back, looking uncertain as if he didn't seem to know what to do with his hands.

She thought of being in his arms and how easy it would be to find herself in his bed. She told herself she was feeling like this about him because he'd saved her life, but a part of her knew it was more than that. It was...chemistry? She almost laughed at the thought. It sounded so...high school.

But she couldn't deny how powerful it had felt when he'd kissed her. Or now, the way he'd looked at her with those dark eyes. She marveled at the feeling since it was something she hadn't felt in a long time. Nor had she ever experienced anything this intense. The air around them seemed to buzz with it.

He'd felt it, too. She'd seen it in his expression. What made her laugh was that she could tell he was even more afraid of whatever was happening between them than she was.

"Something funny?" he asked.

Gillian shook her head and took a step back in the direction of her room. She realized she loved feeling like this. It didn't matter that it couldn't last. "Thank you again for *everything*."

He smiled at that and almost looked bashful.

"Everything," she repeated and stepped through the doorway, closing the adjoining door to lean against it. Her heart was pounding, her skin tingling and there was an ache inside her that made her feel silly and happy at the unexpected longing.

Chapter 22

Marc spent the night in a crummy old motel. He couldn't go home. Not only were the cops looking for him but also he had Victor's enforcers on his tail. Victor had failed yesterday at the hospital. That meant he'd be in an even fouler mood. Marc hoped he wouldn't have to see him for a while. Never would be even better.

He'd fallen asleep after staring at the map for hours. His face hurt like hell, not to mention his shoulder. He'd drunk a pint of whiskey he'd picked up at the bar. It hadn't helped. He thought about changing the bandage, but wasn't up to looking at the damage this morning in the mirror.

Picking up the map, he stared again at the circle he'd drawn around Helena. Maybe he should expand it. That one day, she'd driven a hundred miles. He made another circle, this one fifty miles out around the city.

Where the hell did she go? He had no idea since he couldn't conceive of a place she might think to hide the ledger. She knew him and he'd thought he'd known her. She would have had to up her game to beat him, and she would have known that.

He thought back to the days before he'd awakened still half drugged and found her note telling him how things were going to be now.

Marc started to shake his head in frustration when he recalled coming home early one day to find Andy crying and Rebecca looking…looking guilty, he thought now. She'd been standing in the kitchen.

He'd told her to shut the kid up, which she had. Then she'd disappeared into the bedroom to change her clothes. He frowned now. Why had she needed to change her clothes? At the time, he couldn't have cared less. They hardly ever had sex except when he forced the issue. He hadn't been in the mood that day or he might have followed her into the bedroom and taken advantage of the situation.

What had she been wearing that she'd had to change? His pulse jumped and he sat up straighter as he imagined her standing *before* him—before she'd changed her clothing. She was wearing the pair of canvas pants he'd bought her for hunting. She'd only worn them once when she'd tagged along. It had been early in their marriage. He'd made the trip as miserable as he could since he had been hoping she wouldn't ask to come along again.

Why would she have been wearing such heavy-duty pants? He recalled that their knees had been soiled. And Rebecca's hair had been a mess. She'd looked as if she'd been working out in the yard. But there'd been snow on the ground. Where had she been that she'd gotten what had looked like mud on the pant knees?

He realized with a start that it must have been the same day she'd put so many miles on her car.

He looked at the map again.

The no trespassing sign was large, the letters crude, but the meaning clear enough. Austin looked from it to Gillian.

The climb up the steep mountain reminded him of the difference in altitude between Montana and Texas. Add to that a sleepless night in the motel knowing Gillian was just yards away and he found himself out of breath from the climb.

They'd wound up a trail of sorts from the creek bottom through boulders and brush to reach this dark hole in the cliff. It looked like rattlesnake country to him. He was glad it was winter and cold even though there were only patches of snow in the shade—just as there had been near her family's cabin.

It amazed him how different the weather could be within the state. "It's the mountains," Gillian had said when he'd mentioned it. "Always more snow near the higher mountains."

"This isn't a mountain?" he'd asked with a laugh as he looked out into the distance. He could see the lake, the frozen surface glinting in the winter sunlight.

"Have these caves always been posted like this?" he asked as he looked again at the sign.

"It's always been closed to the public," she said with a shrug.

Great, he thought. They would probably end up in

jail. But if they found the ledger, they would at least have a bargaining chip to get out.

"Would your sister really come up here alone?" he asked. He couldn't help being skeptical. Rebecca was desperate, and desperate people often did extraordinary things. Still… "What about her son? She couldn't have brought him."

"It definitely isn't like Becky, I'll admit. She must have trusted someone with Andy, someone none of us knew about. The more I'm learning about my sister, the more secrets I realize she kept from me."

They were wasting time, but he wasn't that anxious about going into the caves. He didn't think Gillian was either, now that they were here. The adorable young Luke Snider wasn't in there with his friends to entice her.

They'd stopped at an outdoor shop on the way and bought rope and headlamps, along with a first aid kit, hiking boots and a backpack. He'd brought water and a few energy bars. He hoped they wouldn't need anything else.

"I'm assuming you remember the way?" he asked.

Gillian nodded but not with as much enthusiasm as he would have liked. "It's been a while."

"Your sister remembered," he reminded her.

"Yes, that's assuming I'm right about her message. Also, this was probably the most traumatic thing that happened to my sister until she married Marc Stewart."

"You're not reassuring me," Austin said as he stepped into the cool shade of the overhanging rock. The cave opening was large. They climbed over several large boulders at the entrance before the cave narrowed and grew dark. They turned on their lamps. A few candy wrappers, water bottles and soda cans were littered on the path back into the cave. Apparently he and Gillian weren't the only ones who'd ignored the no trespassing sign.

They hadn't gone far before the cave narrowed even more. Gillian sat down on a rock that had been worn smooth and slithered through the hole feetfirst. He followed to find the cave opened up a little more once they were inside.

Austin could feel them going deeper into the mountain. They hadn't gone far when they came to a room of sorts. Water dripped from the rocks over their heads. The air suddenly felt much colder.

"You doing all right?" he asked, his voice echoing a little.

"It was easier when I was sixteen," she said, but gave him a smile.

"That was because you were in love and chasing some cute boy."

Their gazes met for a moment and he felt as he had last night after he'd kissed her. He tamped down the feeling, not about to explore it right now. Probably never. "We should keep moving."

She nodded and led the way through a slit in the rocks that curved back into a tunnel of sorts. They climbed deeper and deeper into the mountain.

Marc Stewart had shared one shameful secret with his wife. He was claustrophobic. He hated being in tight spaces. When he was a kid, a neighbor boy had locked him in a large trunk. He'd thought his heart was going to beat its way out of his chest before the idiot kid let him out.

As he parked next to the white SUV below the mountain, he'd told himself if he hadn't already been in a foul mood, this would have definitely put him in one. Even when he'd seen the gulch on the map, he hadn't wanted to believe it.

But at the back of his mind, he remembered bits and pieces of stories he'd overheard between his wife and her sister. Being trapped in some cave had been one of the worst experiences of Rebecca's life. Somehow her sister Gillian was to blame.

That he knew about the caves was no mystery. He'd grown up in Helena. Every kid knew about them. Most kids had explored them. Marc Stewart was the exception.

The last thing he didn't want to believe was that his wife had gone back into the cave where she'd experienced the "then" worst thing in her life. He could imagine she'd experienced worse things since then, him being one of them.

The moment he'd seen the rig the deputy had been driving parked next to the creek below the caves, he'd sworn, hating that his hunch had been right. As he cut the engine on the old pickup, he told himself that he didn't have to go *in* the caves. He could just sit right here and wait for them to come out with the ledger.

That made him feel a little better before he realized that once they saw another vehicle, even a strange one, parked down here, they might hide the ledger. Add to that, the cowboy was a sheriff's deputy. He would probably be armed.

No, Marc realized he was going to have to go up

there. He wouldn't have to go inside, though. He could wait and ambush them when they came out.

Getting out, he locked the pickup and looked around. He didn't think he'd been followed, but he couldn't be sure. Not that it mattered. He should have the ledger in his possession within the hour.

Then what?

Turn it over to Victor? Make a deal with the feds? Or make a run with it?

He didn't kid himself. He would be damned lucky to get out of this alive.

He thought of Rebecca and felt his stomach churn as he climbed the mountain. The steepness of the slope forced him to stop a half dozen times on the way up. He was trying to hurry, but he couldn't seem to catch his breath. If he didn't get to the top before they came out…

What difference would it make if some Texas deputy shot him? Really, in the grand scheme of things, wouldn't that be better than what Victor probably had planned for him? he thought as he stopped to rest a dozen yards from the cave opening. Maybe that would be the kindest ending to all of this.

The thought spurred him on. He reached the opening and slipped behind a rock to wait. The winter sun was bright but not warm. He'd never been good at waiting. His mind mulled over his predicament until his head ached.

He glanced toward the opening. Still no sound. He couldn't wait any longer. He was going to have to go in. Why hadn't he realized the cave was the perfect place to dispose of the bodies? The last thing he wanted to do was kill them outside the cave where the deed would be discovered much quicker. But if he killed them in the cave, hell, maybe he could make it look like an accident. Drop some rocks on them or something.

Warmed by that idea, he pulled his gun and headed into the cave.

Deep in the cave, Gillian stopped to get her bearings. Her headlamp flashed across the cold, dark rock. "It's just a little farther," she said. "I remember it being… easier, though, at sixteen."

"Everything is easier when you're sixteen and think you're in love."

She smiled at that. "Was there a girl when you were sixteen?"

"Nope. I was still into snakes, frogs and fishin'. It took me another year or two before I would give up a day fishing to chase a girl."

Gillian chuckled as they moved on, climbing and slipping over rocks, as they went deeper and deeper into the mountain. She thought of Becky and how she'd forced her to come along that day—on her birthday. A wave of guilt nearly swamped her when she thought of how scared Becky had been.

Then she was reminded that if she was right, Becky had come in here alone. Gillian smiled to herself, proud of her sister. She'd always felt that she needed to protect her. She realized that she'd never thought of Becky as being strong. As it turned out, Becky was a lot tougher than any of them had thought.

She saw the opening around the next bend. Rebecca hadn't been stuck exactly at this point in the cave. The opening was plenty wide. It was just that the trail dropped a good four feet as you slipped through the hole. Unable to see where she was going to land, Rebecca had frozen.

Gillian remembered a high shelf in the rocks. She scrambled up the side of the cave wall to run her hand over it, positive that would be where her sister had hidden the ledger. Nothing.

No, don't tell me all of this has been for nothing.

As she started to climb down, she saw it. A worn, thick notebook with a faded leather cover, the edges of the pages as discolored and weathered as the jacket. She grabbed it and almost lost her balance.

As usual, Austin was there to keep her from falling. He caught her, lifting her down. She clutched the ledger to her chest, tears of relief brimming in her eyes. Finally, they could stop Marc.

"Are you sure that's it?" he asked.

She held it out to him. He glanced at the contents for a moment from the light of his headlamp before handing it back.

"No, you hang on to it," she said.

He smiled and stuck it inside his jacket.

She started to move past him on the trail they'd just come down when he grabbed her arm. "Shh," he whispered next to her ear.

Gillian froze as she heard someone coming.

Austin heard what sounded like a boot sole scraping across a rock as the person stumbled. He motioned for her to turn off her headlamp as he did the same.

It pitched them both into total darkness. "You don't think…?" Gillian whispered.

That Marc had followed them? He wasn't about to underestimate the man. A whole lot was riding on this ledger. Marc had already proven how far he would go to get his hands on it. Austin hoped it was only kids coming into the cave, but he wasn't taking any chances.

He touched Gillian's hand. She flinched in surprise before he took her hand and led her back a few yards in the cave. He remembered a recessed area they'd passed. If they could wedge themselves into it... Otherwise, if they stayed where they were, they would be sitting ducks.

He found the opening by brushing his free hand along the rocks. Stopping, he drew her closer and whispered, "There's a gap in the rocks where we can hide. Can you slip in there?" He led her to it, still holding her hand. As she slipped in, he moved back into the crevice with her, trying to make as little noise as possible. From there, with luck, they would be able to see who passed without being noticed—if they stayed quiet. If it was Marc, then he would have recognized Austin's rental SUV. If it was kids...or cops...

The footfalls on the rocks grew louder. Austin pulled his weapon, but kept it at his side, hidden, in case it was the authorities or kids.

It didn't sound like kids, though. It sounded like a single individual moving stealthily toward them.

A beam of light flickered off the walls of the cave. Austin pressed himself against Gillian as the light splashed over the rock next to him.

Marc felt the cave walls closing in on him. He swung his flashlight, the beam flickering off the close confines of the walls as he moved deeper into the cavern. He was having trouble breathing.

His chest hurt, his breathing a wheeze. He stumbled again and almost fell. When he caught himself on the rock wall, he lost his grip on the flashlight. It hit, rolled, smacked a rock and went out. For a few terrifying moments, he was plunged into blackness before it flickered back on.

He lurched to the flashlight, the beam dimmer than before. Picking it up, he stood, listening. Earlier when he'd entered the cave, he'd thought he heard noises. Now he heard nothing. Was it possible he'd taken the wrong turn? The thought made his heart pound so hard it hurt. He tried to settle down. There hadn't been a fork or even a tunnel through the rocks other than the one he was on large enough to move through. He couldn't have taken a wrong turn.

More to the point, Gillian and the cowboy were in here. He'd recognized the SUV. If only he could be patient enough to find them. What if they had heard him coming? What if it was a trap and the cowboy was waiting for him around the next corner of the cave?

He shone the light into the dark hole ahead of him. His breath came out in rasps. Suddenly, there didn't seem to be enough air. If he didn't get out of here now…

He spun around, banged his head on a low-hanging ledge of rock and almost blacked out as he tried not to run back the way he'd come. To hell with the ledger. To hell with Gillian and her cowboy. To hell with all of it. He was getting out of here.

Chapter 23

Victor believed in playing the odds. He'd always known the day could come when this life he'd built might come falling down around him. He would have been a fool not to have made arrangements for that possibility. He was no fool. He had a jet at the airport and money put away in numerous accounts around the world, as well as passports in various names.

So what was he waiting for?

He looked around his mountain home. He'd grown fond of this house and Montana. He didn't want to leave. But there was a world out there and really little keeping him here.

So why wasn't he already gone? He didn't really believe that Marc was going to save the day, did he? Isn't that why he'd gone to Rebecca Stewart's hospital room himself? It had been foolish, but he'd hoped to get the information from her and then take care of the problem. That's what he did, take care of problems. He'd especially wanted to take care of her.

He hated that he'd made this personal. He'd always said it was just business. But a few times it had felt personal enough that he'd taken things into his own hands. Killing came easy to him when it was someone he felt had wronged him. In those instances, he'd liked to do it himself.

But he'd failed and he was stupid enough to try to kill her again.

Victor glanced at the clock on the wall. Was he going to wait until the FBI SWAT team arrived? Or was he going to get out while he could?

He pulled out his phone. "Take care of Marc."

Jumbo made a sound as if he'd been eagerly awaiting this particular order. "One thing you probably want to know, though—he's gone into a cave apparently looking for his missing ledger."

"A cave?"

"He's not alone. There's a white SUV here." He read off the plate number. It was the same one Victor's informant had given him.

"The Texas deputy and Marc's sister-in-law." Victor swore. "Where is this cave?"

Jumbo described the isolated gulch.

"Make sure none of them come out of the cave."

"What about the ledger?"

Victor considered. "If he has it on him, get it. Otherwise…"

Austin held his breath. The footfalls had been close. He'd almost taken advantage of the few moments when the person had dropped his flashlight. But he hadn't wanted to chance it, not with Gillian deep in this cave with him.

What surprised him was when the footfalls suddenly retreated. The person sounded as if he were trying to run. What the—

"What happened?" Gillian whispered.

"I don't know." He kept listening, telling himself it could be a trick. Why would the person turn back like that? The only occasional sound he heard was some distance away and growing dimmer by the minute.

"I think he left," he whispered. "Stay here and let me take a look."

He eased out of the crevice a little, his weapon ready. In the blackness of the cave, he felt weightless. That kind of darkness got to a person quickly. He listened, thought he heard retreating footfalls, and turned on his light for a split second. He'd half expected to hear the explosion of a gunshot, but to his surprise, he heard nothing. He turned his light back on and shone it the way they'd come. Whoever it had been had turned around and gone back.

The cave, as far as he could see, was empty.

He had no idea who it might have been.

Austin felt Gillian squeeze his arm a moment before she whispered, "Are they gone?"

"It appears so, but stay behind me," he whispered.

She turned on her headlamp and they headed back the way they'd come.

"You think someone will be able to make sense of this?" Gillian asked as she watched Austin thumb through the ledger. They'd stopped to catch their breaths and make sure they were still alone.

"Yeah, I do." He looked up at her. "This is big, much bigger than some guy who owns an auto shop."

She heard the worry in his voice. "If you're going to tell me that there are people who would kill to keep this book from surfacing—"

He smiled at her attempt at humor, but quickly sobered. "I'm afraid the people your brother-in-law associated with would make him look like a choirboy."

"So we need to get this to the authorities as quickly as possible," she said and looked down toward the way out of the cave. "You think that was Marc earlier?"

"Maybe. Or one of his associates."

"Why did he turn around and go back?" she asked with new concern.

"Good question." He tucked the ledger back into his jacket. "When we get to the opening, if anything happens, you hightail it back into the cave and hide."

"You think he's waiting for us outside?"

"That's what I would do," Austin said.

"That day with my sister? I never did see Luke. I saw him go into the cave, but I never saw them come out. There must be another way out of the caves. But I have no idea where."

Austin seemed to take in the information. "Let's hope we don't need it."

Gillian followed him as they wound their way back the route they had come. The cave seemed colder now and definitely darker. She turned off her headlamp at Austin's suggestion to save on the battery, should they need it. She could see well enough with him ahead of her lighting the way.

But just the fact that he thought they might need that extra headlamp made it clear that he didn't think they would get out of here without trouble.

As Marc stumbled headlong out of the cave, he gulped air frantically. His whole body was shaking and instantly chilled as the December air swept across his sweat-soaked skin. He bent over, hands on his thighs, and tried to catch his breath. So intent on catching his breath, he didn't even notice Jumbo at first.

When Jumbo cleared his voice, he looked up with a start to see the big man resting against a large boulder just outside the cave.

"Where is the ledger?" Jumbo asked.

"Inside the cave."

Jumbo lifted a heavy brow. "Why don't you have it? You were just in there."

Marc shook his head as he straightened. His gun bit into his back where he'd stuffed it in the waistband of his jeans. "My wife's sister has it." Jumbo's expression didn't change. "If you are so anxious to have it, then go into the cave and get it yourself."

Jumbo acted as if he was considering that. At the same time the thought dawned on Marc, Jumbo voiced it. "If I go in for the ledger, then what do I need you for?"

Marc's mind spun in circles. Why hadn't Jumbo just come into the cave? Something told him the big man didn't like caves any better than he did. "Good point. I guess I'd better go get it."

Jumbo smiled and stood. "Or I can simply wait until she comes out of the cave and take it from her."

Marc shook his head. "You don't want to kill her and

the deputy out here where their bodies will be found too soon. Anyway, the cowboy's armed and expecting trouble. Give me a minute and I'll go back in so I can take care of them."

Jumbo's smile broadened. "You're smarter than Victor thinks you are."

He wasn't sure that was a compliment, but he didn't take the time to consider the big man's meaning. He drew his gun and fired.

Austin heard the gunfire outside the cave. It sounded like fireworks in the distance, but he knew it wasn't that.

"Stay here," he said to Gillian. "I'll come back for you."

She grabbed his jacket sleeve. He turned toward her, pushing back his headlamp so as not to blind her. In the ambient light, her face was etched in worry.

He drew her to him. She was trembling. "You'll be all right. I'll make sure of that."

"I'm not worried about me."

He leaned back a little to meet her eyes. "Trust me?"

She nodded. "With my life."

"I will be back." He kissed her, holding her as if he never wanted to let her go. Then he quickly broke it off. "Here." He leaned down and pulled a small pistol from his ankle holster. "All you have to do is point and shoot. Just make sure it isn't me you're shooting at."

She smiled at that. "I've shot a gun before."

"Good." He didn't want to leave her, but he hadn't heard any more shots. He had to get to the cave entrance now. "Gillian—"

"I know. Just come back."

He turned and rushed as fast as he could through the

corkscrew tunnel of the cave until he could see daylight ahead. Slowing, he listened for any sound outside and heard nothing but his own breathing and the scrape of his footfalls inside the cave.

Finally, when he was almost to the cave entrance, he stopped. No sound came from outside. A trap? It was definitely a possibility. He eased his way toward the growing daylight of the world outside as he heard the roar of a vehicle engine.

He rushed forward, almost tripping over a body. The man was large. Austin didn't recognize him. It appeared he'd been shot numerous times.

Below him on the mountain, an old pickup took off in a cloud of dust and gravel. He spun around at a sound behind him to find Gillian standing in the mouth of the cave. She had the gun he'd given her in her hand.

"I thought you might need me," she said as she lowered the gun.

"Marc's not done," Gillian said as she watched Austin try to get cell phone coverage to call the police. She realized she still had the gun he'd given her. She slipped it into her pocket without thinking. Her mind was on Marc and what he would do now. "He gave up too easily. Why didn't he wait to kill us, as well?"

"He's wounded," Austin said and swore under his breath. "There is no cell phone coverage up here."

"How do you know that?"

Austin pointed to several large drops of blood a few yards from the dead man. "Right now he's headed to a doctor. Hopefully at a hospital. This is almost over."

Gillian shook her head. "I hope you're right."

He stopped trying to get bars on his phone and looked at her. "Then where is it you think he's gone?"

"If he is headed for a hospital it's my sister's. If he thinks we have the ledger and it's over... I have to get to the hospital. Now!" She could tell that Austin thought she was overreacting. "Please. I just have this bad feeling...."

"Okay. As soon as we can get cell service I'll call the hospital and make sure there is still a guard outside your sister's room and that she is safe, and then I'll call the police."

"Thank you." She couldn't tell him how relieved she was as they hurried down the mountain. Austin seemed to think that the reason Marc had left was because of his wound. The one thing she knew for sure was that Marc wasn't done.

If he'd given up on getting the ledger, then he had something else in mind. She feared that meant her sister was in danger.

Victor exited his car and started across the tarmac to his plane. A bright winter sun hung on the edge of the horizon, but to him it was more like a dark cloud. Jumbo hadn't gotten back to him to tell him that all his problems had been handled up the gulch. He'd been right in not waiting to see how it all sorted itself out.

He squinted and slowed his steps as he saw a figure standing next to his plane. Jumbo?

Marc Stewart stepped out of the shadow of the plane. He had his hands in the pockets of his oversize coat. "Going somewhere?"

Victor smiled, accepting that Marc wouldn't be here if Jumbo was alive. "Taking a short trip."

Marc nodded and returned his smile. "I told you I would take care of everything."

He cocked his head. "I assume you have, then."

Anger radiated off him like heat waves. "I thought you had more faith in me. Sending Jumbo to kill me? That hurts my feelings."

Victor didn't bother to answer. He'd noticed that Marc seemed to be favoring his right side. Was it possible Jumbo had wounded him?

"I can't let you get on that plane," Marc said, his hands still in his pockets. "Not without me."

"I doubt you want to go where I'm going. Nor do I suspect you're in good enough shape to travel. I'm guessing that you're wounded and that if you don't seek medical attention—"

Marc swore. "Give me the briefcase."

Victor had almost forgotten he was carrying it. He glanced down at the metal case in his right hand. "There's nothing in there but documents. You've forced me to buy myself the same kind of protection you would have had if you'd been able to get your ledger back."

"Jumbo said I'm smarter than you think I am. Actually, that was the last thing he said. Now give me the briefcase. I know it's full of money."

Before Victor could say, "Over my dead body," Marc pulled the gun from his pocket.

He glanced toward the cockpit but saw no one. Nor was there any chance of anyone appearing to turn things around. Realizing it *would* be over his dead body, Victor relented. Marc might have killed his pilot, but Victor was more than capable of flying his own plane. A flight plan had already been filed.

All he had to do was settle up with Marc. It was just

money and as they say, he couldn't take it with him if Marc pulled that trigger.

Stepping toward him, Victor said, "It's all yours. A couple million in large untraceable bills." He started to hold the case out to him. At the last minute, as if his arm had a mind of its own, he swung the heavy metal case. It was just money, true enough, but it was *his* money.

He'd never thought Marc particularly fast on his feet. Nor had he thought Marc had the killer instinct. But circumstances could change a man. In retrospect he should have considered that somehow Marc had bested Jumbo. He should have considered a lot of things.

The first bullet tore through his left shoulder just above his heart. The impact made him flinch and stagger. As the second bullet punctured his chest at heart level, Marc wrenched the briefcase out of his hand.

Victor dropped to his knees and looked up at the man as his life's blood spilled out on the small airstrip's tarmac.

"I made you," he said. "You were nothing before I took you under my wing."

"Yes, you made me into the man I am now." Marc Stewart stepped to him, placed the barrel of the gun against his forehead. "You shouldn't have told Jumbo to kill me." He pulled the trigger.

Chapter 24

Marc stood over the dead man. He wiped sweat out of his eyes, chilled to the skin and at the same time sweating profusely from the pain and the adrenaline rush.

It made him angry that Victor had put him in this position. None of this should have happened. If Rebecca hadn't— He stopped himself before he let his thoughts take him down that old road again.

What was done was done. Jumbo was dead and so was Victor. He stared down into that boy-next-door face. Victor looked good, even dead. The man's words still hung in the air. Yes, Victor had made him. He'd turned him into a killer.

Marc had been happy enough running his own body shop. Hell, he'd been proud of himself. He'd made a decent living. He hadn't needed Victor coming into his life.

But there was no going back now. *That* Marc Stewart was dead. He was now a man *he* didn't even recognize. But he felt stronger, more confident, more in control than he ever had before. Rebecca hadn't understood his frustration, his feelings of inadequacy. He'd struck out because he hadn't felt in control.

But now…he knew who he was and what he was capable of doing. He hefted the briefcase as he walked to his pickup filled with a sense of freedom. He had more money than he could spend in a lifetime. He could just take off like Victor was planning to do. He wouldn't be flying off in a jet, but he could disappear if he wanted to.

Without his son.

That thought dug in like the bullet from Jumbo's weapon that had torn through his side.

Or he could finish what he started. He thought of Rebecca. It galled him that she might win. He thought of his son. *My son,* he said under his breath with a growl.

Then there was Gillian and the cowboy deputy. He tucked the gun back into his jacket pocket as he climbed into his truck and started the engine. Once he got bandaged up… Well, the people who had tried to bring him down had no idea who they were dealing with now.

Austin put in the call as soon as they neared Townsend and he was able to get cell phone coverage. As he hung up, he looked over at Gillian. "The guard is outside your sister's room. Rebecca is fine. I told the doctor we are on our way."

She nodded, but he could tell she was no less worried.

He called the police, knowing there would be hell to

pay for leaving the scene. Right now his main concern was Gillian, though. He'd always followed his instincts so how could he deny hers?

The drive to Bozeman took just over an hour since he was pushing it. Gillian said little on the trip. He could see how worried she was.

When his cell phone rang, he saw it was Marshal Hud Savage, his cousin-in-law. Had Hud already heard about what had happened back up the gulch?

"I was worried about you," Hud said.

With good reason, Austin thought. "I'm fine. Gillian Cooper is with me. We have Marc Stewart's ledger. We're pulling into the hospital now so Gillian can see her sister. Rebecca has regained consciousness, the doctor said. Gillian's worried that Marc is also headed there and not for medical attention. He's wounded after killing a man neither of us recognized. I spoke with the nurse earlier and all was fine, but—"

"I'll meet you there," Hud said and hung up.

The first thing Gillian saw as they started down the hallway toward Rebecca's room was the empty chair outside her door where the guard should have been. Austin had seen it first. He took off at a sprint. She wasn't far behind him, running down the hallway toward her sister's room.

Out of the corner of her eye, she saw that there was no nurse at the nurses' station. In fact, she didn't see anyone in the hallway.

The hospital felt too quiet. Her heart dropped at the thought that they'd arrived too late.

Austin crashed through the door into the room, weapon drawn, yelling, "Call security!" to her. But it was too late for that. She'd been right behind him and was now standing next to him in the center of Rebecca's room. Even if she had called security, it would have been too late.

"I wouldn't do that if I were you," Marc Stewart said. He stood shielded by Rebecca, his gun to her temple. The security guard who'd been posted at the door lay on the floor next to a nurse. Neither was moving. "Drop your gun or I will kill her and everyone else I can in this hospital."

Austin didn't hesitate, telling Gillian that he'd realized the same thing she had. Marc Stewart was no longer just an abusive bastard. He'd become a killer.

"Now kick it to me." After Austin did as he was told, Marc turned his attention to her. "Now, you. Lock the door."

Gillian stepped to the door and locked it before turning back to the scene unfolding before her. Rebecca was conscious, her condition obviously improved, but she still looked weak. What she didn't look was scared.

"You found the ledger in the cave, didn't you?" Marc said, although he didn't sound all that interested anymore.

"I have it right here," Austin said and started to reach inside his coat.

"I wouldn't do that if I were you," Marc warned.

She could hear voices on the other side of the door. But if she turned to unlock the door, she feared Marc would shoot her sister.

"You can have it," Austin said and took a step toward Marc. "You can make a deal with it."

Marc shook his head and motioned for him to stay back. "Too late for that. Could have saved a lot of bloodshed if I had gotten the ledger back when I asked for it." Her sister made a pained sound as Marc tightened his hold on her for emphasis. "Now a lot of people are going to die because of it. Starting with you, cowboy!" He turned the gun an instant before the shot boomed.

Gillian screamed as Austin went down. She dropped to the floor next to him. She felt something heavy in her jacket pocket thud against her side. The gun. She'd forgotten about it. She reached for Austin. He'd fallen on his side. She'd expected to find him in a pool of blood, but as she knelt next to him she saw none. She could hear him gasping for breath.

"Any last words for your sister, Rebecca?" Marc demanded over the sudden pounding on the hospital room door.

Rebecca was crying. She'd dropped to the floor at Marc's feet when he'd let go of her to fire on Austin.

"Come on, don't you want to tell her how sorry you are for what you did?" Marc demanded. "I'd like to hear it. But make it quick. We don't have much time left."

Seeing that Marc's attention was on his wife, Gillian started to stick her hand in her pocket for the gun. In that instant, she saw Marc's thick leather ledger lying next to Austin, a bullet lodged somewhere in the pages. Austin's hand snaked up and took the gun from her.

"Stand up, Gillian," Marc ordered. "Rebecca, I want you to see this." He reached down to take a handful of his wife's hair and pulled her to her feet. As he did, Rebecca grabbed Austin's weapon up from the floor where he'd kicked it. She pressed the barrel into Marc's belly.

Suddenly aware of the mistake he'd made, Marc swung to hit his wife. The gunshots seemed to go off simultaneously in what sounded like cannon fire in the hospital room.

Gillian saw Marc's reaction when both Austin and Rebecca fired. He took both bullets, seeming surprised and at the same time almost relieved, she thought. Before he hit the floor, she thought she saw him smile. But he could have been grimacing with pain. It was something she didn't intend to think about as Austin got to his feet and she rushed to her sister.

In that instant, the door to the hospital room banged open as it was broken down. Marshal Hud Savage burst into the room, gun drawn. Within minutes the room was filled with uniformed officers of the law.

Chapter 25

Christmas lights twinkled to the sound of holiday music and voices. Suddenly, a hush fell over the Cardwell Ranch living room. The only sound was the crackle of the fire. Dana saw the children all look toward the door. She had heard it, as well.

"Are those sleigh bells?" she asked in a surprised whisper.

The Cardwell brothers all exchanged a look.

Dana glanced over at Hud. "Did you—?"

"Not my doing," he said, but Dana was suspicious. She knew her husband was keeping something from all of them.

She felt a shiver of concern as she heard the sound of heavy boots on the wooden porch. A moment later, the front door flew open, bringing with it a gust of icy air and the smell of winter pine.

A man she'd never seen before stomped his boots just outside the doorway before stepping in. Because he looked so much like his brothers, though, she knew he had to be Austin Cardwell.

He carried a huge sack that appeared to be filled with presents. The children began to scream, all running to him.

"I told you Austin would be here for Christmas," she said as she got to her feet with more relief than she wanted to admit. "I'm your cousin Dana," she said. "Come on in."

It was then that she saw the woman with Austin. She was dark haired and pretty. Dana thought she recognized her as the jeweler who lived up the road, although they'd never officially met.

She knew at once, though, that this was the woman Austin had met in the middle of the highway and the reason he'd been missing the past few days.

"This is Gillian Cooper," Austin said as he set down the large bag and put an arm around the woman.

Dana knew love when she saw it. There was intimacy between the two as well as something electric. She smiled to herself. "Come on in where it's warm. We have plenty of hot apple cider."

She ushered them into the large old farmhouse and then stood hugging herself as she looked around the room at her wonderful extended family. Having lost her family for a while years ago, she couldn't bear not having them around her now.

Her sister Stacy took their coats as Austin's brothers pulled up more chairs for them to sit in.

The children were huddled around the large bag with the presents spilling out of it.

Mugs of hot cider were poured, Christmas cookies eaten. An excited bunch of children was ushered to bed though Dana doubted any of them would be able to sleep.

"They think you're Santa Claus," she told Austin.

"Not hardly," he said.

"I'm amazed that you remembered it was Christmas," Tag teased him. "At least you didn't miss the grand opening."

"Wouldn't have missed it for the world," Austin said and they all laughed.

"Gillian," Laramie said. "Please stay safe until after New Year's. We want all five brothers together."

Austin looked over at Gillian. They'd just busted a huge drug ring. Arrests were still being made from the names in Marc's book. Rebecca and her son were finally safe. It was over, and yet something else was just beginning.

"We'll be there."

Snow had begun to fall as Gillian left the ranch house later that Christmas Eve night with Austin. They walked through the falling snow a short way up to a cabin on the mountainside. Austin had talked her into staying, saying it was late and Dana had a big early breakfast planned.

"It should just be you and your family," Gillian had protested.

But Dana had refused to hear it. "Do you have other plans?" Before Gillian could answer, Austin's cousin had said, "I didn't think so. Great. Austin is staying in a cabin on the hill. There is one right next to it you can stay in."

Gillian had looked into the woman's eyes and known

she was playing matchmaker and this wasn't the first time. Three of Austin's brothers had come to Montana and were now either married or headed that way. She suspected Dana Cardwell Savage had had a hand in it.

Gillian was touched by Dana's matchmaking, not that it was needed. Fate had thrown her and Austin together. In a few days, they had lived what felt like a lifetime together. But they lived in different worlds, and while maybe Austin's other brothers could leave their beloved Texas, Austin was a true Texan with a job that was his life.

"Did you have fun?" Austin asked, interrupting her thoughts as they walked toward the cabins up on the mountainside.

"I can't remember the last time I had that much fun," Gillian answered honestly.

He smiled over at her as he took her hand. "I'm glad you like my family."

"They're amazing. I don't know what makes you think you're the black sheep. Clearly, they all adore you. I think several of them are jealous of your exciting life."

Austin laughed. "They were just being polite in front of you. That's why I begged you to come with me. They couldn't be mad at me on Christmas Eve—not with you there."

"Is that why you wanted me here?"

He put his arm around her. "You know why I wanted you with me. Making my brothers behave in front of you was just icing on the cake. You're okay staying here?"

"Your cousin does know I won't be staying in that cabin by myself, doesn't she?"

"Of course. I saw the look in her eyes. She knows how I feel about you."

"She does, does she?" Gillian felt her heart beat a little faster.

Austin stopped walking. Snow fell around them in a cold white curtain. "I'm crazy about you."

"You're crazy, that much I know."

He pulled off his gloves and cupped her face in his hands. His gaze locked with hers. "I love you, Gillian."

"We have only known each other—"

He kissed her, cutting off the rest of her words. When the kiss ended, he drew back to look at her. "Tell me you don't know me."

She knew him, probably better than he knew himself. "I know you," she whispered and he pulled her close as they climbed the rest of the way to his cabin. To neither of their surprise, a fire had been lit in the stone fireplace. There was a bottle of wine and some more Christmas cookies on the hearth nearby.

"It looks as if your cousin has thought of everything," Gillian said, feeling an ache at heart level. She was falling in love with his family. She'd already fallen for Austin. Both, she knew, would end up breaking her heart when Austin returned to Texas.

She should never have let him talk her into coming here tonight. Hadn't she known it would only make things harder when the two of them went their separate ways?

She looked around the wonderfully cozy cabin, before settling her gaze on Austin. It was Christmas Eve. She couldn't spoil this night for either of them. He'd promised to stay until the grand opening of the restaurant. In the meantime, she would enjoy this. She would pretend that Austin was her Christmas present, one she could keep forever. Not one that would have to be returned once the magic of the season was over.

Because naked in Austin's arms in front of the roaring fire, it *was* pure magic. In his touch, his gaze, his softly spoken words, she felt the depth of his love and returned it with both body and heart.

The night of the grand opening, Austin was surprised by the sense of pride he felt as Laramie turned on the sign in front of the first Texas Boys Barbecue restaurant in Montana.

He felt a lump form in his throat as the doors were opened and people began to stream in. The welcoming crowd was huge. A lot of that he knew was Dana's doing. She was a one-woman promotion team.

"This barbecue is amazing," Gillian said as Austin joined her and her sister and nephew. He ruffled the boy's thick dark hair and met Gillian's gaze across the table. Andy had made it through the holidays unscathed.

As soon as Rebecca was strong enough, the Bakers had brought him down to Big Sky, where the two were staying with Gillian. Rebecca had healed. Just being around her son and sister had made her get well faster, he thought. Marc was dead and gone. That had to give her a sense of peace—maybe more so because she'd had a hand in seeing that he never hurt anyone again. She was one strong woman—not unlike her sister.

"Everything is delicious," Rebecca agreed. "And what a great turnout."

Austin looked around the room, but his gaze quickly came back to Gillian. He felt her sister watching him and was sure Rebecca knew how he felt. He was in love. It still bowled him over since he'd never felt like this before. It made him want to laugh, probably because he'd given his brothers Hayes, Jackson and Tag such a hard time for going to Montana and falling in love with not only a woman but the state. He had wondered what had happened to those Texas boys.

Now he knew.

Dana threw a New Year's party at the ranch for family and friends. Austin got to meet them all, including his cousin Jordan and his wife, Liza, Stacy's daughter, Ella, as well as cousin Clay, who'd flown up from California. The house was filled with kids and their laughter. His nephew Ford was in seventh heaven and had become quite the horseman, along with his new sister, Natalie.

As Austin looked at all of them, he felt a warmth inside him that had nothing to do with the holidays. He'd spent way too many holidays away from his family, he realized. What had changed?

He looked over to where Gillian was visiting with Stacy. Love had changed him—something he would never admit to his brothers. He would never be able to live it down if he did.

Suddenly, Dana announced that it was almost midnight. Everyone began the countdown. Ten. Nine. Eight. Austin worked his way to Gillian. Seven. Six. Five. She smiled up at him as he pulled her close. Four. Three. Two. One.

Glitter shot into the air as noisemakers shrieked. Wrapping his arms around her, he looked at the woman he was about to promise his heart to. Just the thought should have made his boots head for the door.

Instead, he kissed her. "Marry me," he whispered against her lips.

Gillian drew back, tears filled her eyes.

"I'm in love with you."

She shook her head. "I've heard all the stories your brothers tell about you. *All Austin needs is a woman in distress and it's the last we see of him.* Austin, you've spent your life rescuing people, especially women. I'm just one in a long list. I bet you fell in love with all of them."

"You're wrong about that," he said as he cupped her face in his hands. "And don't listen to my brothers," he said with a laugh. "You can't believe anything they tell you, especially about me."

"I suspect your brothers are just as bad as you. After listening to how they met their wives, I'd say saving damsels in distress runs in this family."

He grinned. "You're the one who saved me."

Her eyes filled with tears.

"Remember our first kiss?" he asked.

"Of course I do."

"I knew right then you were the one. Come on, you felt it, didn't you?"

Gillian hated to admit it. "I felt…*something.*"

He laughed as he drew her closer and dropped his mouth to hers for another slow, tantalizing kiss. It would have been so easy to lose herself in his kiss.

She pushed him back. True, the holidays had been wonderful beyond imagination. She'd fallen more deeply in love with Austin. But her life was here in Big Sky, especially since she couldn't leave her sister and Andy. Not now.

She said as much to him, adding, "You love being a sheriff's deputy and you know it."

He dragged off his Stetson and raked a hand through his thick dark hair. Those dark eyes grew black with emotion. "I did love it. It was my life. Then I fell in love with you."

She shook her head. "What about the next woman in distress? You'll jump on your white horse and—"

"Laramie needs someone to keep an eye on the restaurant up here. I've volunteered."

She stared at him in shock. "You wouldn't last a week. You'd miss being where the action is. I can't let you—"

"I've been where the action is. For so long, it was all I've had. Then I met you. I'm through with risking my life. I have something more important to do now." He dropped to one knee. "Marry me and have my children."

"*Our* children," she said.

"I'm thinking four, but if you want more…"

She looked into his handsome face. "You're serious?"

"Dead serious. You may not know this, but I was the driving force originally behind my brothers and I opening the first barbecue joint. I can oversee the restaurant—and take care of you and kids and maybe a small ranch with horses and pigs and chickens—"

Just then, they both realized that the huge room had grown deathly quiet. As they turned, they saw that everyone was watching.

Austin shook his head at his brothers not even caring about the ribbing he would get. He turned his attention back to Gillian. "Say you'll marry me or my brothers will never let me live this down," he joked, then turned serious. "I don't want to spend another day without you. Even if it isn't your life's dream to become a Cardwell—"

"I can't wait to be a Cardwell," she said and pulled him to his feet. "Yes!" she cried, throwing herself into his arms. He kissed her as the crowd burst into applause.

From in the crowd, Dana Cardwell Savage looked to where her cousin Laramie was standing. "One more cousin to go," she said under her breath and then smiled to herself.

* * * * *

HARLEQUIN
PLUS

Try the best multimedia
subscription service for romance
readers like you!

Read, Watch and Play.

Experience the easiest way to get
the romance content you crave.

Start your **FREE TRIAL** at
<u>www.harlequinplus.com/freetrial</u>.